The
TEA
CHEST

JOSEPHINE MOON

ALLEN&UNWIN

First published in Great Britain in 2014 by Allen & Unwin

First published in Australia in 2014 by Allen & Unwin

Allen & Unwin
c/o Atlantic Books
Ormond House
26–27 Boswell Street
London WC1N 3JZ
Phone: 020 7269 1610
Fax: 020 7430 0916
Email: UK@allenandunwin.com
Web: www.allenandunwin.co.uk

A CIP catalogue record for this book is available from the British Library.

ISBN 978 1 76011 056 7

Set in Minion Regular by Post Pre-press Group, Australia
Printed in Italy by Grafica Veneta S.p.A.

10 9 8 7 6 5 4 3 2 1

For Alwyn, who believes in dreams.

Judy, I realise it will come as a shock that I have decided to leave my share of The Tea Chest to Kate and not you. But I know you, Judy. And I know you won't allow The Tea Chest to continue to grow. I know you never wanted to be involved. And I wish to thank you, sincerely, for helping me realise my dream. I do acknowledge that The Tea Chest wouldn't exist today if you hadn't stepped in when you did.

Family and business is never an easy mix. And ours certainly wasn't.

Kate, I've never been more proud. You have been the model employee and a dear and trusted friend. Equally, The Tea Chest wouldn't be what it is today without your vision, talent, commitment and passion. I know from the bottom of my heart that you will take it to new heights. This is a big responsibility. I know that.

Other people will tell you that you can't do it, but you can.

Trust yourself.

Simone

1

Kate Fullerton's second home for the past six years had been The Tea Chest. It sat in leafy Ascot and was the original store, opened long before the Sydney one. It was nestled between a boutique Brisbane fashion label, specialising in hats and fascinators for the nearby racecourse, and a fine-dining restaurant with crisp white linen and spotless glassware. An enormous, gnarled jacaranda tree, planted on the footpath decades earlier, sheltered the entrance to the store and laid a soft, purple carpet at its feet every October.

Kate turned the key and opened the white French doors, letting the river breezes enter the shop, pick up the scents of bergamot, Indian spices, lemons, rose and caramel and swirl them towards her in a morning greeting she would never tire of.

Susan wasn't far behind. She clicked her way across the polished wooden floor to put her things down behind the counter and clipped on her Manager badge.

'Morning,' she said.

'Good morning to you too,' Kate said, and gave her a hearty smile. Susan had been a bit tetchy of late, understandably. Simone was gone; Kate had been propelled from the role of tea designer to equal owner of the company; and the future of The Tea Chest was in doubt. She could appreciate why Susan was nervous but it wasn't helping Kate to find her own feet in this new world in which she'd landed.

The prospect of going to London and opening a new store from scratch was alarming. Possibly crazy. And undoubtedly life-changing.

It didn't help that no one had confidence in Kate's ability to pull it off, including Kate.

'I had such a great weekend,' Susan said now, going to the storeroom to switch on the urn and get the teapots and teacups ready for tastings.

'Tell all,' Kate said, turning on the fairy lights that were strung around the room.

'I met someone,' Susan said, poking her head out of the store-room and fastening her white frilly apron around her waist. 'At the pub, of all places.'

Kate let Susan talk on, half listening to the life of a fellow thirty-something and musing on how different her own life could be if she were still single with no children. The other half of her attention was busy working on a solution for her current problem—how to save The Tea Chest, her career, the employees in both Sydney and Brisbane, and Simone's legacy.

She loved it here—not just her job, but the actual store itself. The Tea Chest was a wonderland. Circular walls gave the impression of being inside a giant teapot. Fairy lights twinkled from the ceiling. Concentric circles of products filled the belly of the room. White porcelain bowls contained tea for customers to shake and smell. Rows of teapots and Turkish tea glasses were laid out for taste tests. Toasted coconut marshmallows, chocolates, gingerbread men, Turkish delight, chocolate-coated raspberries, crystallised ginger and truffles all sat in tall glass jars. Melting moments were piled high on cake stands under glass domes with gold handles.

There were teapots, silver spoons, giant cups and saucers, diffusers, strainers, napkins, lace tablecloths, sugar cubes and books about tea. The teas themselves were stacked from floor to ceiling. They were in glass jars for display, as well as in boxes of pale pink, yellow, rose red, powder blue, white and gold to take home. Each was tied with a bow, the ribbon stamped in silver with the logo of an open antique tea chest.

The walkways had the effect of directing customers in dreamlike wandering. Patrons paid for their goods at an enormous clunky old-fashioned cash register and left with their parcels hand-wrapped in gold paper and rich ribbon.

It was simply too special to lose.

The bell above the door tinkled and in walked Priscilla, a regular at The Tea Chest.

'Good morning,' Kate greeted her.

'Kate,' Priscilla said, breathless in her designer jogging outfit. A slight sheen of sweat sat atop her makeup. 'I'm so glad you're here today. I'm hosting a baby shower this weekend and I want you to design an individual blend for each of my guests.'

Since she'd started offering individually designed blends, her fame had spread quickly through the city. The *Brisbane News* had featured a full-page colour photo of her, dressed in the white shirt and apron she wore to The Tea Chest each day, surrounded by porcelain bowls of tea ingredients.

The service had been a hugely successful addition to the business and it wasn't just Brisbane that had embraced it. She even took Skype, phone and email consultations to come up with special blends. And customers were happy to pay handsomely for them too. Handing over the beautifully wrapped boxes and special labels filled Kate with pride for days and reaffirmed to her, and hopefully to Judy, why Simone had hired her to be the company's lead designer all those years ago.

Then again, Judy seemed to get that loud and clear, if today's voicemail was anything to go by.

Kate, really, we need to wrap this up. Every day that passes loses us money. You've said it yourself—you're a designer, not a business owner.

'How many guests?' Kate said, reaching for her notebook.

'Twenty-two,' Priscilla said. 'Will that be okay? I know it's a lot and it's short notice.'

'No problem at all. It's my absolute pleasure. This is what I do best.'

It was true. She could say with pride that she was a talented artist and she loved her career with all her heart. But she'd never thought of herself as a business person. She'd always dismissed 'that side' of things as something other people did, declaring she had no talent for numbers, spreadsheets, projections or management.

Was she really cut out to take on Simone's vision for The Tea Chest and launch a new store in London followed by more in other countries?

Both Judy and Mark kept asking her that same question but for different reasons. Judy wanted out. Mark was worried for their family and his own career.

But the real question, she was coming to see, was whether she had allowed a lack of confidence to limit herself to a smaller life than she might have had. And was she brave enough to take a chance on herself now to find out?

e

Leila stared at the semicolon.

It was wrong.

Wrong. Wrong. Wrong.

Just like it had been the first three times this document had passed through her in-tray. Just like another dozen errors she'd already corrected but were still on the pages in front of her.

She took a deep breath, letting it out in a controlled fashion, trying to release the fury that was twisting like a python around its prey. She could simply take her red pen and mark this page again. She could put it back in the folder, enter her remarks in the database for this project and shuffle it off her desk and back to the writer for the eighth time since her team had taken it on.

She could also stick needles in her eyes and set herself on fire.

While she debated her options, the voice of the writer himself floated to her from three cubicles away.

'I know, George, I know. But it's these editors. What can I do?'

Leila's heart rammed against her chest. Her skin flared hot. Her head swam.

Our fault? How is this possibly our fault?

'I'm up against a rock and a hard place, Georgie Boy. I know it's past the due date but I can't release it until these girls sign off on it. Quality assurance process and all that.' He sighed. 'I don't know what's up with them. It's a no-brainer.'

Leila could imagine Carter leaning back in his chair, the look of an innocent child on his face, nodding in agreement with the long-suffering customer.

You incompetent, sexist, geriatric fool. YOU are the idiot standing in the way of this document being finished.

She tapped her pen furiously against the desk, her breathing sharp and painful.

'I'll take it to my manager, Georgie Boy, and see what we can do about them.'

No you don't.

Leila threw the pen down with a clatter against her keyboard, picked up the document and marched to Carter's desk. Towering over him, she pursed her lips, tilted her head to the side and glared at him, hoping steam was shooting from her nose.

'George, I'll have to call you back.' He chuckled nervously and hung up the phone.

Leila threw the pages onto Carter's desk, knocking over the last of his coffee.

'Listen, cutie,' he said, jumping out of his seat and pushing his glasses up his nose.

'Don't *cutie* me. I've had enough of you. How dare you blame this crap on us?'

Frustratingly, she felt her throat tighten and her eyes sting. She was half a second away from bursting into hysterical sobs. Dimly, she was aware of people gathering behind her, heard Lucas's voice ask if everything was okay. Her ears filled with noise. Black spots appeared in her vision. She registered Carter's sneering smile and watched his eyes travel to her breasts for the hundredth time.

Something cracked.

It was a loud popping sound and it might actually have come from inside her.

She shoved him, pushing the heel of her hand hard against his chest to get his lecherous self away from her body. He fell backwards into his chair and rolled away from her.

'Leila.' Lucas was behind her.

Normally, his voice would have made her warm and tingly.

But she was lost. Lost to rage and frustration and deep unhappiness. She grabbed Carter's stone paperweight and threw it. She threw it as hard as she could, feeling power roar through her while regretting she couldn't throw it even harder and straighter.

But it was hard enough. The paperweight smashed into the floor-to-ceiling window of the ninth floor and it cracked in a lightning bolt from top to bottom. There were gasps and exclamations from people in nearby cubicles.

'What the hell are you doing?' Carter bellowed.

Leila's knees went weak as the adrenaline flooded through her. Her arms began to shake and her breath rattled as she wheezed and gasped. She felt sick.

One thing she knew for sure: she was fired.

So if she was going to lose her job, then she might as well finish off this knob standing in front of her.

She lunged for Carter. He shrieked like a little girl and covered his face with his hands.

'Leila.' It was Lucas again. He grabbed her around the waist to pry her off the cowering Carter. Then he took her by the elbow and led her away.

She laughed hysterically.

'Get a grip,' Lucas hissed.

If Elizabeth had known today was the day she would appear on Brisbane's nightly news dressed only in her lingerie, she might not have got out of bed. As it was, when she awoke, she chose to shower and put on a brand-new cream chemise, brush her teeth and climb back into bed beside her sleeping husband. She laid her long body against his back, reaching around him with her left hand to stroke the hair on his chest, and nuzzled his ear.

It was not that she was overcome by a surge of passion for his body, limp as it was with sleep and odorous with morning breath; her enthusiasm was thanks to the results of the test she'd just taken. Today, she was ovulating.

Twelve hours later, she checked into the Stamford Plaza, still wearing nothing but her chemise and wrap, handed over her husband's credit card, silently thanked the reception staff, who asked no questions, and retired to her own king-sized bed, with a minibar and a range of pillows to choose from.

She lay in a bubble bath, drank vodka, cried, pummelled pillows and roared like a bear, slept a little, then spent the rest of the night in a chair by the window, watching the lights in the street below.

If only she had known this morning what she knew now.

She might have at least put on jeans.

2

At home in the chilly late autumn morning, Kate cut a rose from the bush and inhaled the delicate aroma. This courtyard had been the selling point of their first foray into home ownership. It was her experimental tea farm. She grew oranges, lemons and limes in pots along the wooden fence. The raised herb garden overflowed with parsley, coriander, basil, thyme, peppermint, lemongrass, spearmint and sage. Bright red chillies gleamed next to terracotta figurines of cherubs and fairies. Wind chimes tinkled. She grew chamomile, calendula and *Camellia sinensis*, the most common tea plant in the world.

The courtyard, with its stone water feature in the centre, had often been the source of inspiration for new blends. She could pull leaves straight from the lemon myrtle tree and put them in the teapot. She could scratch the bark of the cinnamon tree and inhale the spicy warmth for solace after a hard day at The Tea Chest. The lavender went straight into the teapot and so did the rose petals.

Today was Sunday, a day she and Mark tried to reserve for family time. At least one day of the week saw all four of them in the one place at the one time. Today was the first sunny day in weeks and the boys were itching to get outside. But all she really wanted to do was sit in the autumn sun and relax with a cup of rose tea.

'Are you ready to go?' Mark popped his head out through the stained-glass doors. His face fell when he saw her with secateurs and roses in hand.

'You making tea?'

The sound of the boys fighting in their upstairs bedroom floated down through the annexe window. Both she and Mark raised their eyes upwards. There was a loud thump. Then a wail of frustration. A shout. A slamming door.

'What do you think I should do?' Kate said.

'Get dressed for a start.'

'I mean about the business.'

Mark stepped out onto the warm sandstone pavers and closed the doors behind him. 'We probably don't have time to get into this now.'

'I know. But when's it ever a good time? One of us is always rushing somewhere and we need to make a decision soon.'

He sat down on the carved wooden bench next to the pink geraniums. He looked at her without speaking and her heart quickened.

'Just tell me,' she said.

'I'm worried about the boys,' he said.

'So am I.'

'Taking on this level of commitment would be a huge upheaval.'

'I know.'

'We've only just got things the way we want them.'

She flinched. She knew him well enough to know this wasn't as much about the boys as it was about him. Mark had a thriving acupuncture clinic now, but its success had been delayed when she'd first started at The Tea Chest. They'd decided to put their young children's needs first and Mark had restricted the growth of his business to care for them. Now the boys were older and he had the clinic he'd always wanted, one that was expanding each month. He was fulfilled in his career for the first time.

'I wouldn't ask you to give up your work,' she said.

'But how else would we manage? You'll be overseas for weeks, maybe even months, at a time, probably every year.'

She shivered as a cloud passed across the sun, casting them into shadow.

'Do you want me to sign Judy's papers to wind up the company?'

'I miss you,' he said, taking her hand. 'I want to see more of you. I'm sorry if that's selfish, but it's true.'

'I want to see more of you too,' she said, giving him a wry smile. 'Isn't it great we still want each other so much?' She squeezed his wrist.

He ran his hand over his shaved head. 'I guess as far as marriage problems go, it's a good one to have.'

But she knew more was bothering him. Things he didn't really want to say.

'Let's talk about money,' she said, getting straight to the point. 'If we wind up the company now, everything will be sold off and we'll get a good—a *very* good—payout. That's undeniable. Is that what you want?'

'Think about what we could do with that money. We could travel. Together. All four of us. It could set us up comfortably for years to come. You'd have the freedom to stay home and I could finally put the hours into my clinic.'

'I . . .' She paused, searching for the right words. 'I don't know that I want to stay home. The Tea Chest is more than a job for me.'

Mark stood and began to pace.

'Mark, love, think what might happen if I do go to London. This is an amazing opportunity to take the company to a whole new level. The financial rewards in five years time could be beyond our wildest dreams. Think about the doors that would be open to us then. It could set us up for the rest of our lives.'

'Or,' he said calmly, 'this London shop that is currently draining money from the company every day while it sits waiting for someone to move it forward could be a huge bust, and when the company is wound up at a later date the payout for us would be much less.'

Kate took a deep breath. Of course she'd considered that.

'I think we should take what we've got now, thank our lucky stars, and move on. Judy wants out now and she won't wait for a buyer,' Mark said.

Judy. The thorn in her side. 'Why is she so stubborn? Why won't she wait for a buyer for her share?'

He shrugged. The cloud shifted again and he squinted against the sun.

'It's not just about money for me,' Kate said. 'It's about me having the chance to do something I never thought I would do, to make something bigger for me, us and our children. The Tea Chest could be *their* legacy one day. It's about me following and honouring my passions—something I know you believe in.'

That got him. He straightened. And for a second she was thrown back a decade to their days as newlyweds when they lay on a blanket under a gum tree and talked of their dreams and values. The days when taking risks and doing what made you happy were far more important than financial security.

She asked the question she needed him to answer. 'Don't you think I can do it?'

He rubbed his forehead, thinking. 'I think we have different skill sets and your strengths lie as an artist, a visionary, a dreamer and designer. And . . .' He held up a hand to silence her protest. 'And you've said that yourself.'

That got *her*. It was true. Hadn't she declared over and over that business wasn't her thing? Hadn't that been why she'd jumped at the chance to work at The Tea Chest? All she had to do was be her creative, gifted self and someone else could worry about the finances.

The door opened and James's tear-streaked face appeared. 'Can we go now?'

Mark cleared his throat. 'What's wrong, buddy?' He reached out a hand towards his five-year-old son.

'Keats stood on my head.'

'I did not,' shouted Keats from inside. 'It was an accident. I was climbing down from my bed.'

'And he called me a toe.' James went on, indignation set in his freckled face.

'No I didn't,' Keats called from the kitchen, his voice laden with eight-year-old big-brother superiority. 'I called you a *toad*.'

Mark rubbed James's back and kissed him on the top of his head. 'You need some shoes before we can go,' he said. Kate tried to smile at him reassuringly. James nodded and disappeared inside.

Nothing could pull on her heartstrings like the little men in her life. They were her world. Of course they were. You couldn't create a life, nurture it, watch it grow and develop its potential without this being so. And that was exactly where she was with The Tea Chest. She was arguably just as much a part of that company as Simone had been. They'd come together and created new life. She may not have had the skills to be a mother when she became pregnant, but she'd learned. She'd educated herself, lost many hours sleep and gave it everything she had. Surely she could do it again.

'We used to say we valued doing what we loved above all else,' she said.

'True. But maybe there are different types of happiness and you just need to choose one version and stick to it.'

There was possibly some truth in that. But which version should she choose: one with a known guarantee or one with unlimited potential?

e

Leila wore her best navy suit. It was a surprisingly hot day for May and she would rather have taken off the jacket. But this was no time to be distracted by trivial things like comfort. She was heading to the human resources department of Strahan Engineering. And she was about to lose her job.

People she passed in the corridor moved away from her like she was bad luck.

Yesterday seemed a lifetime ago. A lifetime since she'd lost her mind. A lifetime since Lucas had ushered her into the elevator and down to the ground floor and out to the courtyard of the common room. A lifetime since he'd told her to go home and that he'd phone her later. An age since she'd received first his phone call and then the call from Maryanne, requesting a formal meeting at eleven o'clock the next day to discuss The Incident.

Now, she ignored the sweat pouring from her armpits, ignored Eric the Humping Dog as he sneered in satisfaction at her from beneath his carefully groomed goatee, ignored the acrobatics in her belly in honour of her impending sacking, and knocked on Maryanne's door. There was a pause in the murmur of voices from behind the wooden facade, then a voice called, 'Come in.'

Three of them sat at a round table.

There was Maryanne, the human resources manager of the whole company. There was Carol, the human resources manager of Leila's division. Carol and Leila were certainly well acquainted, if not particularly friendly. Leila had put in enough complaints in the past for Carol to grimace when she saw Leila coming towards her office. And there was Ernie, her manager. He smiled but she wasn't sure why.

'Thank you for coming, Leila,' Maryanne said. She mispronounced Leila's name as *Leela* and jolly little Ernie helpfully corrected it to *Layla*, which Maryanne ignored. 'Take a seat.' She shuffled papers on the desk and clicked her pen twice.

'How are you?' she said, and Leila was sure the question was only driven by a professional duty of care rather than her actual desire to know, an impression reinforced by the fact that Maryanne looked away as soon as she'd asked the question and made a mark on the paper in front of her.

Ask the employee how they feel: tick.

'Fine,' Leila said, eyeing Ernie carefully. If anyone was going to fight for Leila's job it would be him. He liked her. He believed in her. He gave her glowing annual performance reviews. He listened to her complaints and empathised whole-heartedly. Bought her vodka after work.

But he never did anything to solve the problems.

She ground her teeth, looking at his sticky-out ears and neatly brushed hair.

She knew that beneath his easygoing, approachable, everybody's-friend demeanour, he was simply weak. He was a salesman—saying whatever he needed to in order to leave a meeting looking like the good guy. He could talk anyone into anything. He knew the jargon and twisted it around and around to say the same thing ten different ways until he wore the person down. And he was a master at taking credit for other people's work. Including hers.

Ernie's gift of the gab could be useful. But that all depended on whose side he was on today and who he needed to impress to get another bonus.

'Why don't you start by telling us about yesterday,' Maryanne said. 'I'm just going to take some notes while you talk.'

I'll bet you are.

In a company like this, documentation ruled. Everyone focused on documenting so they never actually had to go ahead and make changes.

Where should she start? She was sick of having men look at her tits. She was sick of wanker men being promoted just because they could yell louder. She was bored to tears with reading engineering data. She was sick of the dirty splotches on the wall next to her cubicle. She was sick of seeing Eric the Humping Dog climbing everything that moved, including the photocopier. She was sick to death of eating lunch at her desk and rarely feeling sunshine on her body.

What could she possibly say that hadn't already been said and documented before? But even with all of that she knew she could never justify physically attacking someone.

'What can I say?'

The three exchanged glances.

She turned to face Carol, vaguely hoping for some support. After all, Carol had heard it all before. But Carol turned her pointy features away and looked down at her notes. She wasn't on Leila's side.

Ernie was her only chance now.

'I cracked. Lost it. Temporary insanity.' Her heart rate accelerated to full speed. Her palms sprang leaks. Her chest tightened.

These days, all she had to do was imagine Carter's pushed-up face, whining voice and thinning hair and she snapped. She was permanently angry. Constantly ready to attack or be attacked. Blind rage was her response to everything.

No paper in the copy machine. Printers jamming. Idiot men. Too much work. Not enough work. Rage. Rage. Rage. All the same. She'd turned into a version of herself she would never have thought possible.

Now, this meeting was pushing her over the edge. She could feel her body twitching, ready to run.

'Could you please hurry up and fire me?'

Eric spoke then, using his appeasing voice. 'Leila, you know I think the world of your work ethic and abilities.'

Don't cry, don't cry.

'But it's obvious to everyone here—' he pointed to the thick folder full of Leila's complaints sitting in front of Carol '—that you've been unhappy for some time. Would you agree?'

She looked to the ceiling, not blinking, biting her lip.

'We'd rather not terminate your position,' Maryanne said plainly, tapping her pen.

Of course they wouldn't. That would open up a whole world of paperwork hurt.

'But you will if I don't resign?'

19

'We want what's best for you,' Eric said—the smiling assassin.

'I see.'

'You can take some time to consider your position and your options,' Maryanne said.

She could take time but, regrettably, the outcome would be the same. She'd sealed her fate the second the heel of her hand had connected with Carter's pasty body. Her life here at Strahan was over. At least she could choose to leave on her own terms.

'Don't bother. I quit.' And Leila Morton, senior editor, team leader and woman-with-a-future, walked out the door and out of the building into the great unknown.

e

Wincing, Elizabeth fought her way free of a tangled mess of sheets and picked up the hotel room's phone. She had a killer hangover.

'Greetings from miserable London.'

Obviously, Victoria had spoken to John.

'So you've heard,' Elizabeth said. 'News travels fast to the other side of the world.'

'Yes. The episode on the bridge freaked us all out a bit. I was nervous about calling. I didn't know what state you'd be in.'

Elizabeth sat upright, then instantly regretted it as the room spun violently.

She remembered the choppers and television crews flying overhead. She remembered the flashing lights as the traffic stopped on the Story Bridge. The sound of the police as they shouted at her through the megaphone.

Step away from the edge.

'How do you know about that?' she asked shakily.

'John called us. And the clip's on YouTube.'

'Marvellous.' She heard the click of the lighter as Victoria lit a cigarette. 'Are you at home? Do Mum and Dad let you smoke in the house?'

'Yes. And no. I'm outside. I said I'd call you. Mum was all flappy about it and Dad was all throat-cleary. What the hell were you doing on the bridge anyway?' she said. 'I don't believe for a second you were going to jump.'

Elizabeth pulled herself from the bed, crossed the floor, and closed the door to the bathroom. She sat down gingerly on the edge of the cool bath. Something about the solid whiteness helped ease the spinning.

'What do you think I was doing on the bridge?'

There was a pause. 'Honestly, I'm not sure. I spoke to John, you know.'

Elizabeth waited to feel something in response to her husband's name. But there was nothing.

'He said he's been calling you.'

'I threw my phone out the window of the taxi last night. How'd you find me anyway?'

'You used his credit card to check into the hotel. Apparently, the staff were a little unnerved by your appearance and had your home contact details. Rather than calling the police they called John.'

'Oh.' Elizabeth caught sight of herself in the bathroom mirror. She looked frightful. Swollen eyes and puffy face. Long, frizzy brown hair. And that bloody cream chemise. She wanted to rip it off.

And right there was another problem: she had no clothes.

'You might as well tell me what the knob had to say,' she sighed.

'That it was all his fault you wanted to kill yourself. That he was a cheating dog. That he had a whole other family in Japan.'

'I wasn't going to kill myself.'

'Then what were you doing?'

'Just thinking.' Elizabeth ran a hand through her hair, working out knots with her fingers and gradually smoothing it down. 'I must have lost track of time. The next thing I knew I was surrounded and people were shrieking and pointing. Apparently you can't stand on the edge of a bridge in your nightwear without people taking it the wrong way.'

'It's exciting, though, isn't it? Your husband is this whole other person and you didn't even know. It's like Jamie Lee Curtis and Arnold Schwarzenegger in that film.'

'*True Lies.*'

'Yes. Just like that.'

'Except not funny. Not funny at all. And not sexy, no. No seduction scene in a hotel room. No ballroom dancing. No international travel. No adventure and mystique. Just a complete tosser who left me for a second wife and two kids and a career as a karaoke king.'

'Are you serious?'

'Apparently he's a popular white-man personality. Something equivalent to being the winner of one of our reality television shows . . . like *The Biggest Loser* or something.' She stood up to pace the room, stepping carefully so as not to set off the spinning again. 'You know what? Japanese tourists used to stop us and ask for photos. I just thought they were being, you know, *Japanese*, with their cameras. But now I realise it's because they knew him.'

'Oh, Lizzie, all this time you were married to a famous person.'

'He didn't tell you the rest, did he?' Elizabeth said.

'There's more?' Victoria had never liked John. And at this moment Elizabeth wasn't sure if that made her angry or grateful.

'He had a vasectomy.'

'Shut *up*.'

'Years ago. He said once he'd had the kids in Japan he knew that was it for him. Besides, he couldn't afford any more.' She laughed, the way people laughed at inappropriate moments, like at funerals, or after accidentally handing your husband a glass of apple cider vinegar instead of apple juice, which she'd quite like to do now.

'Isn't that a hoot? I thought he was making business trips back and forth to Japan to develop property and invest money in complexes and he was really taking his sons to the zoo and to football games.' She screwed up her face. 'If they even do that sort of thing there.

'He watched me go through all that pain. Month after month and all the while he's shooting blanks.' She grabbed a neatly folded plush white towel, ripped it off the rack and threw it against the wall.

'So is this it for me now?' Elizabeth's voice twisted. 'I'm thirty-one. Why can't I have the husband *and* the baby? It doesn't seem so unreasonable. Quite normal, really.' Her legs shook and she reached for the edge of the basin.

Victoria was speaking, saying things that were supposed to be calming, interspersed with fierce denunciations of the dickhead husband, and a few scathing remarks about Australia too. Elizabeth found it hard to follow.

'What should I do?' she interrupted. 'I can't go home. I thought he loved me.'

'Tell me, what's one thing, just one thing, I can do to help right now?'

What *could* she do? Her sister was on the other side of the world and was a bit hopeless, really.

But right at this moment Victoria was all she had.

She clawed at the chemise that slithered around her body. 'I've got no clothes,' she whimpered. 'I've got no clothes and I can't go home.'

The next few hours rolled on and around Elizabeth like some horrid dream she was sure would end any moment. But it didn't.

Victoria had gone and done the one sensible thing she could have done from her post in London. She'd called her workmate, Annie—solid, reliable, friendly, calm Annie. Like a Shire horse.

Elizabeth fell into her strong arms at the door of the hotel and wept on her shoulder.

'This is such terrible news for you,' Annie said.

She led Elizabeth gently back to the bed and presented her with a bag of clothes, freshly bought from Myer and smelling of clean, air-conditioned new beginnings.

'Shouldn't you be at work?' Elizabeth sniffed.

'I'm at a client meeting,' Annie grinned. 'You're my client. How am I doing?'

'Great, thank you. You're just the person I need.' She felt her face crumple. 'You must think I'm such a fool.'

'No. Absolutely not. The only fool in this story is that tosspot husband of yours who couldn't see what he had in you. Wanker.'

They sat in silence for some time while Elizabeth cried. Annie passed her tissues and fetched her a glass of water, tidied up her bed, hung up her bath towels and tipped the empty minibar bottles into the bin.

Then she stood in front of Elizabeth, her hands on her hips. 'Now, this is the plan.'

Thank God. There was a plan. She didn't have to try to figure out this horrible mess herself. She just had to follow the plan.

'I've told work you're not coming in for a few days. Your sister has organised for John to be out of the house for the next two hours. We're going to your place and we're packing three suitcases of your things. Then you're coming back to my house for two days, and I will feed you cups of tea, chocolate, ice cream and vodka on constant rotation as the mood necessitates. You can resign from your job when you feel ready. Then you're getting on a plane.'

'A plane?'

'Your parents have organised a ticket home to London.'

Elizabeth stared at Annie. She was going home to London? To live with her parents?

'Surely . . . isn't this a bit premature? It's only just happened.'

Annie arched a bushy brow. 'Well,' she said calmly, 'do you intend to go back to him?'

Go back? She turned this option over in her mind. Played the idea like it was a movie: arriving home, John saying he was sorry, going about business as normal.

But there was no normal anymore. He had another wife. They couldn't exactly all live together.

Her hand flew to her mouth. John would have to choose one of them.

Would he divorce Elizabeth?

He would, of course. He had no choice. He had children with the other woman.

It was so unfair. So shameful and sordid. So *humiliating*.

'It's really over, isn't it?'

Annie took Elizabeth's hand in her own warm one.

'I think I'm going to be sick,' Elizabeth said, and Annie helped her to the bathroom just in time.

Twenty minutes later, Annie led Elizabeth by the hand to the underground car park and they were on their way.

And two days, a kilo of chocolate, a litre of vodka and two tubs of ice cream later, Elizabeth was on a plane to London.

3

Six years earlier

'I've been following your tea for a while now,' the woman said. Her voice carried the last vestiges of an English accent. She sniffed a bowl of Kate's Christmas Stocking blend. Manicured fingers shook the white porcelain gently, releasing the scent of cinnamon. She inhaled, closing her eyes.

'Really? Thanks.' Kate smiled, adjusting Keats to sit his small frame on her left hip. He sucked his thumb and swung his tiny shoes against her leg. Kate hardly noticed it anymore. She swayed slowly, rocking him, grateful for his patience and tolerance. Not many people would brave taking a two-year-old to work with them at the markets each week. But Keats was a pro.

The Riverside markets were frantic leading up to Christmas and it was shockingly hot, even though it wasn't yet mid-morning. The roof of their pop-up stall provided shade, but the humidity clung to her skin. Beside her, Mark was in consultation with a bare-chested man wearing fisherman pants, who wanted acupuncture for his knee. He was half out in the sun and she was momentarily concerned his shaved head might be getting sunburned as he tapped needles into the man's thighs.

'Can I help you choose something?' she prompted, simultaneously eyeing two teenage girls who had a box of spearmint and mandarin Afternoon Tea in their hands and were discussing the value of it as a gift for their mother.

The woman screwed up her nose as she sniffed Mark's Chinese tea blend that was part of a liver detoxification program. She hastily replaced it on the table.

'Do you have anything new?' she said. 'I've tried everything here already.'

'Everything?'

'Yes.'

The woman's charm bracelet jangled as she picked through the boxes of tea. She pushed a strand of smooth dark hair back into the clip at her nape and waited for Kate to respond.

Kate reached her own hand up to the shabby orange scarf covering her unwashed hair. A shift in air pressure brushed against her bare back, exposed in the cotton top she'd picked up for ten dollars.

This apparently rich and sophisticated woman had tried not just one but all of the tea blends Kate mixed on the wooden table in her courtyard at the back of her falling-down rented home in West End.

The woman sidestepped a twin pram and two sweating parents as they pushed through the walkway.

'Have you even tried the Christmas Stocking tea?' Kate said, suddenly anxious. 'I only brought it out last week.'

'Yes, I know, I picked it up at your other stall on the south side.'

Kate was simultaneously flattered that this woman appeared to be some kind of tea groupie and mortified she hadn't noticed her before now.

The back of her neck tingled. She extended her hand.

'I'm Kate.'

'Lovely to meet you,' the woman said, taking Kate's hand. 'I'm Simone.'

On the day of their first meeting, Kate checked the back of Simone's heavy gold business card, which carried the scent of the same Chanel perfume Simone had been wearing at the markets.

The Emporium. Tuesday 11 am. Cocktail lounge.

She'd heard of the newly opened Emporium, but she'd never been there. She'd left the side of town she was more familiar with—where dried ducks hung upside down in Chinatown windows, a young guitarist busked outside the Night Owl, and men with more facial piercings than face stood against graffiti-covered walls near the Hare Krishna café. Now she was on the other side of the Valley, where men in impossibly tailored suits and crisp pale-pink business shirts stood with lattes and mobile phones, watching women strut international fashion labels from behind thousand-dollar sunglasses, and where shopping for a Mercedes-Benz was something people did on their lunch breaks.

Her nerves were taut from the intense traffic and multi-lane one-way streets. And now, standing in front of the entrance to the Emporium, her hands began to quiver.

The tall double doors, with their gold-leaf pattern, loomed before her. They opened with a gentle *pft* of air.

The Emporium was red and black and glass and gold. A doorman in a suit and cap watched Kate enter the building. Soft lighting bounced off shiny surfaces. Even the air felt cushiony and welcoming, neither noticeably cool nor too warm.

'Wear something nice,' Simone had said at the markets. Kate had baulked, but now she was grateful. She was wearing her organic cotton black pants, beautifully tailored, and a red Asian-inspired sleeveless cowl-neck top from a Brisbane label she admired but could rarely afford.

Inside, Simone was already seated in a plush, high-backed red armchair. Her glasses were perched on the bridge of her nose, her mobile phone was jammed to her ear and her laptop and papers lay strewn across the glass table top at her knees. Above her, a chandelier sparkled. A sleek, black baby grand piano sat idly by and Kate wished someone would start to tinkle its keys, if only to complete this scene that looked straight out of a Hollywood movie.

Simone caught her eye and waved her over.

'I've got to go, Judy. Kate's just arrived.'

She snapped her phone shut and stood, clutched Kate's biceps with her gold-polished fingernails and kissed her on the cheek.

'I'm so glad you could make it. Take a seat. You look stunning, by the way.'

Kate arranged herself neatly on the armchair next to Simone, careful not to bump knees with her. She had read books on body language and knew that if she sat directly opposite Simone she was setting up an air of confrontation, and she already felt awkward enough.

Simone signalled the barman. He appeared a millisecond later carrying cocktail menus with an elaborate gold typeface. He was as shiny and sparkly and squeaky clean as the bar behind him.

'Let's celebrate,' Simone said, smiling.

Kate smiled too. Part of her wanted to challenge Simone (*I haven't accepted anything yet*) and part of her purred under Simone's infectious enthusiasm. Kate's ego was deeply thrilled. It wasn't every day she was offered a job by a complete stranger.

'She must want you,' Mark had said. 'She's not the type to haul you over for a meeting just to chat. The job's yours.'

'If I want it,' Kate had said, kissing him as he ran his hands up under her shirt.

Simone ordered without looking at the menu. 'Long Island iced tea,' she said. She squinted her eyes at Kate in a wincing gesture. 'I know it's rather retro but I do love them.'

Kate fingered the menu, her mouth watering at the descriptions of chocolate decadence, summer fruit-inspired bouquets and exotic numbers she would never have dreamed of. It would be a toss-up between at least five of them, if she drank alcohol.

'I'll have a lemon, lime and bitters,' she said. Beside her, Simone sat up straighter, just enough to alert Kate to the possibility that she'd offended her. According to body-language rules, she should be mirroring Simone and in this case that meant ordering a cocktail.

'I'm pregnant,' Kate explained, going with the easier option. People were always so suspicious when you said you didn't drink.

'Oh.' Simone's eyes dropped automatically to Kate's navel, her expression unreadable. Kate thought it best to get the conversation over with as quickly as possible.

'That's not a problem, is it?' she said lightly, trying to keep her voice even.

'Not at all.' Simone recovered. 'Congratulations. When are you due?'

'May twenty-first, give or take a few days. It's our second. Obviously. You met Keats the other day.'

Simone seemed to register all of this as mildly as if Kate had given her the weather forecast for the next few days.

'Right, let's get down to business,' she said. She handed Kate a manila folder that was stuffed with pamphlets and A4 papers. 'Here, you can read these in your own time. They'll give you lots of information on The Tea Chest, its history, its products and so on.'

'Yes, I've looked up your website,' Kate said. 'You've got a lovely range.'

Simone nodded. 'It's served us well up till now, but we need a fresh new line to keep our customers interested. A line that will run alongside the old favourites while keeping new ones coming all the time to hold interest. That's where you come in. We'll be culling half our current lines at least. Women have entered a new era—one of self-determination, autonomy and celebration. I need someone with flair and creativity to lead us into the future, keep us ahead of the game. I'm offering good money with all the perks, including—' she again cast an eye south to Kate's navel, '—twelve weeks paid maternity leave.'

Kate nodded, breathing to quieten her beating heart. It was a dream.

'You can have flexible hours and you can even work from home half the time, so you can achieve that whole working-mother, super mum, work–life balance thing.'

The drinks arrived and Simone murmured with delight at her first sip.

'This is very generous,' Kate said, humbled. 'I don't know what to say.'

'I'm a businesswoman, Kate. The Tea Chest is *my* baby. I have birthed it, watched it grow and mature into a profitable business. Now, it's ready to expand, with a second store in Sydney in the first phase of development, then one in London and another one overseas—I've yet to decide exactly where—in the second phase.

'Our customers are smart, loyal women, an interesting mix of stay-at-home mums and fully corporate working women. They work hard and know how to treat themselves, know good tea, value luxury and beauty and modern lifestyles but also retain old-fashioned values at their core. They're nostalgic, maintain strong relationships with their family—even if they don't have children. Do you see?'

She paused and Kate stared at her in admiration.

'We know our customers down to their weekly incomes, their star signs, shoe sizes and menstrual cycles.'

'Really?'

'No. That was a joke.' Simone leaned forward. 'We don't know their shoe sizes.' She winked at Kate and laughed. 'So what do you say, Kate? Would you like to come and work for The Tea Chest as the lead designer and pull us all into the Age of Aquarius?'

Kate didn't hesitate. 'Yes. I would like that very much.' She raised her glass and clinked it to Simone's.

'That's my girl. Now, when can you start?'

'We'll have to arrange childcare for Keats. Maybe in a week's time?' She felt a sudden pull in her heart as the reality of leaving Keats behind for at least half the week sank in. She had to fight back sudden tears. Her excitement about this job was intense but the cold winds of guilt and a good dash of pregnancy hormones threatened to undo her.

Simone finished her drink. 'Call me as soon as you can. I'll have to organise a time for you to meet Judy Masters, by the way.'

'Who's Judy?'

Simone's face closed and her foot began to tap on the chocolate-brown carpet at her feet. 'Jude's my financial investor. I started The Tea Chest but I needed some capital to get it to where it is now. She's not really supposed to have anything to do with the day-to-day running of the business but her involvement has grown more than I'd like, frankly.' She signalled to the waiter to bring her another drink.

Kate decided to ask nothing more about Judy Masters until she'd met her herself.

When Elizabeth was a normal person who lived in Brisbane, she had a life. A job, a husband, friends, a garden and plans for a baby. Of a workday evening, she left her office cubicle and swapped her silk and heels for lycra and running shoes and jogged home.

The Beautification office, where she was a content (if not terribly excited) dispatch manager for organic beauty products, overlooked the Brisbane River. But Elizabeth's path home weaved through the suited pedestrians on Park Road, passed the school where her future children would be educated, and climbed the hills to Rosalie.

The first thing she saw when she reached her house was the immaculately tended garden, in which she'd spent time on the weekend nurturing her ferns and hedges and her carefully hand-mown four square metres of lush green lawn.

Breathing hard from the last segment of her run, she'd turn her key in the lock of their perfectly renovated colonial cottage, pausing first under the bullnose verandah to sit on the white-washed bench and remove her running shoes.

Inside, she was greeted by stained timber floors, whitewashed walls, an open-plan space that seemed far too large for such a tiny home, and a romantic, curving internal staircase that led to the master bedroom.

Each day, she worked hard to ensure the master bedroom was neat, clean and inviting, that the doors to both sets of walk-in wardrobes were closed properly (John was distracted by a door being even slightly ajar), and that the modern white bathroom had fresh towels and bath oils ready to go.

The baby-making business was hard work.

If John was late coming home, or if he was on one of his overseas trips, Elizabeth delighted in sitting on the bedroom's balcony with a cup of herbal tea, enjoying the expansive views of the city and thinking positive thoughts about her upcoming pregnancy.

Sometimes, she allowed herself to imagine what her life with John and this child might be like. Saturday mornings wandering Rosalie's gourmet market and selecting imported cheeses, breads, dips and marinated baby octopus. Weekday afternoons waiting under the huge leafy trees on the perimeter of the school for Jessica (if it was a girl) or Geoffrey (if it was a boy) to come running out, backpack swinging and bursting with excitement over the day. Or perhaps they would take a drive up to the bookstore and sit in the children's corner and read aloud together.

Perhaps the boy would look like John and the girl would look like her. Or maybe it would be the other way around. That was if they were lucky enough to have more than one. Maybe both Jessica *and* Geoffrey.

But at the rate they were going, she'd be lucky to get even one.

Apparently, that was a premonition she should have heeded.

Now she found herself back in her family home on Hemberton Road, Clapham, childless, husbandless, jobless and humourless. And right at this moment lacking in sobriety.

'Elizabeth, dear, you look dreadful,' Margaret Plimsworth said, clutching her daughter to her chest and rocking her roughly from side to side in a manner Elizabeth supposed was meant to be nurturing. 'What an awful, wicked man.'

Elizabeth was touched by her mother's stern sympathy and relaxed into her wiry arms.

'The shame of it,' Margaret went on. 'How will you ever be able to hold your head up high again?'

Elizabeth pushed herself out of her mother's arms. 'Thanks a lot.'

Margaret studied her face. 'Is there no chance it could all work out?'

'You just called him wicked.'

'Of course, yes. It's just that he was always so thoughtful at Christmas time. He did have some good qualities, didn't he? I mean, he didn't smoke, never drank too much, opened the car door for you, did some housework and was always pleasant on the phone.'

Oh great. Perfect. She was trapped here now and had no strength to contest her mother's absurd list of qualities necessary in a marriage. Like, say, fidelity.

Victoria closed the door behind them. She'd met Elizabeth at the airport, having plenty of time to fill. From what Victoria had told her on the ride home, her finest accomplishment of late was completion of a one-week at-home course to become a nail technician. Her nails were currently zebra-striped with diamanté details and tiny gold bells that jingled when she waved her hands. Which was a lot, given she tended to leave sentences incomplete and insert vague gestures in the spaces.

Elizabeth dragged herself down the narrow entranceway. It had been five years since she'd last visited but the house looked almost the same as she remembered. There was still the forest-green carpet from an era that pre-dated the Mesozoic, the frosted-glass windows, the smell of years of frying bacon, and her father in front of the blaring television in his reclining chair.

'Hello, Dad!' she shouted.

'Kitten, I didn't hear you come in.' Her father rose from his armchair, his huge grin revealing his missing lower tooth. Elizabeth noted that in this room the carpets had been cleaned, the walls painted white, and a new red recliner now sat waiting to cradle her father's buttocks. At least they'd made a start somewhere on improving the dated home. But she grimaced in anguish, remembering the lovely floating white curtains in her bedroom in Brisbane and the double sink ensuite with glittering lights around the mirror. Her parents' single pedestal basin in the bathroom with grout falling from between the tiles was really not going to offer her the same tranquillity or privacy.

'How was your flight?' Bill kissed her on the cheek. Her father still looked the same, really, just a bit greyer and a little softer in the face. That was one thing she was glad hadn't changed much.

'Don't ask.'

'She found a new boyfriend,' Victoria said.

'What?' Margaret gasped. 'You haven't been doing any of that seven-mile-high thing, have you?'

'She sat next to the loveliest guy on the plane,' Victoria went on. 'He had to help her off, actually, as she was so trolleyed.'

'I was no such thing.'

'We had a fine chat while you were in the toilet,' she said. 'He asked me lots of questions about you. Anything you hadn't already talked about on the plane. Apparently you had quite a lot to say in between the dozens of vodkas.'

Elizabeth opened her mouth to tell her sister to bugger off but then stopped. She had hazy memories of talking to the man but she couldn't remember him saying much in return. She might have thought he had a nice smile, though. And she had woken up with her head on his shoulder at one point.

She shook away the memories.

'His name's Haruka.' Her sister was still talking. 'I've got his details if you want them.'

'Victoria, the last thing I need is a short Japanese man asking me out on a date.'

'She's a bit touchy,' Victoria whispered to their parents. 'Just because John has a wife in Japan she thinks all Japanese should be sent back to . . .' She waved a hand. 'And he's not short.'

Just the mention of her husband's name made Elizabeth tremble with anger. He'd made many attempts to contact her via Victoria's phone in the two hours she'd been in this country. He'd sent text messages begging her to please give him a chance to explain. But there was nothing to explain.

'Japanese?' Margaret brought a hand to her chest. 'Goodness.'

Elizabeth exited this conversation, escaping up the creaking stairs to her old bedroom. She stopped in the doorway. Her childhood room had been converted into a shrine to unicorns. A unicorn mobile hung from the ceiling. A unicorn bedspread covered the single bed against the wall. The books had been removed from the shelves and replaced with all manner of unicorn statuettes and figurines. Unicorn posters covered the wardrobe doors.

'Oh, this.' Her mother hovered behind her. 'It's your father's latest thing. But your bed's still there. It's still your room.'

Elizabeth turned to face her mother, beaten by the jet lag, alcohol and trauma. She wanted badly to ask about the unicorns, but she was sure she lacked the energy for whatever her mother's response would be.

'Why am I here?' she said instead.

'You needed help. We couldn't let you stay in that shameful marriage in Brisbane. You needed to come home.'

'Home?' she said, flinging her arm around the room, thinking this space was the size of her walk-in wardrobe at *home*. Her face twisted in pain.

She was totally discombobulated. Home. It seemed so strange now to think that the beautiful home she'd worked so hard on was no longer her home at all. That it had probably never really been a home. Not in the true sense of the word.

'What else were you going to do?' her mother said.

The truth in that question stabbed through Elizabeth. She was defeated.

There was a yell from the lounge room.

'Quick, Margaret, it's on.'

Elizabeth followed her mother back down to the lounge. Her father arranged himself in his red recliner, his mug of black coffee beside him (no, the mug hadn't been updated either) and his crocheted rug over his knees—something his own mother had knitted while she was still alive.

The television was so old and groaning it took half an hour to warm up. Rather than risk missing any of their favourite shows, her parents just left it on all day long. Sometimes, when guests came over, they turned down the sound out of respect.

'*The Coeliac Killer* is about to start,' he said. 'It's a new program. Come and watch, girls.'

Elizabeth furrowed her brow. *The Coeliac Killer*?

Her father loved his crime shows. He highlighted the television guide each week, read all the reviews, and had even joined an online chat group to dissect them afterwards. He thought he was quite the crack punter at working out whodunnit.

'It'll stop me getting Alzheimer's now I'm retired,' he'd said on the phone during one of their fortnightly calls.

'Dad, I think that's crosswords,' she'd replied, the phone jammed under her jaw as she applied polish remover to her toenails.

'All those poor coeliacs,' he muttered now. 'As if life isn't hard enough, not even being able to have a piece of toast, without a killer after them.'

Elizabeth stood at the back of the room as her mother and sister sat on the old brown couch and the theme music started.

It was a pity her father's hearing wasn't as sharp as his mind. It wasn't the *coeliac* killer at all. It was the *steely-eyed* killer.

'You were *fired*?'

'How do you know that? And I wasn't fired; I resigned.'

'I can't believe it. That was a perfectly good, well-paying, respectable job. This is just awful news and not how I raised you, Leila. *And* I had to hear about it from some man who picked up your desk phone.'

'Who?'

'Oh, I don't know. I couldn't hear him too well. It sounded like he was eating a sandwich or something. Something like Rafter.'

'Carter. And it would have been a beef and gravy roll with extra onions. The greasy smell would have got into the air conditioning and been ducted through the whole floor. He would have been sitting near my desk because he wanted to talk to Eric the Humping Dog about car racing. If I'd been there, I would have told him to shove off and take his disgusting food elsewhere because it was making me feel ill.'

41

Leila couldn't believe Carter could still ruin her day even when she no longer worked there.

Her mother was obviously on the road. She could hear the familiar sounds of cars passing, the tick-tock of the indicator and that tunnel sound you always got when someone was talking while driving.

'He said you were fired for assaulting him.'

'Again, I wasn't fired, I quit. And I didn't . . . okay, I did *technically* assault him.'

'Leila!'

'Can we change the topic? Are you on your way to an appointment?'

'Yes, a new specialist medical team on the south side. I've got a new anti-psychotic drug used for people with schizophrenia.' Her mother trailed off then and murmured a few thinking-related sounds.

'Mum.'

'Hmm?'

'I don't have schizophrenia.'

'I didn't say that. Anyway, no we can't change the topic. How could you let this happen?'

'He had it coming, Mum. You've no idea how awful and sexist and—'

'I don't care how unpleasant he was. That was a perfectly good job and good jobs don't just grow on trees. Haven't I taught you anything? You can't rely on anyone but yourself, Leila. You should know full well the way life works, and that means you can't have a good job and a good man at the same time. And you had a good job and no man, and now you have no job and no man. You're a single woman with no security, no backup plan, no income and not even any references for a new job.'

Leila took a deep breath. Then another. She counted to five. She closed her eyes. Breathing. Breathing.

'Hello, are you listening to me?'

'Unfortunately.'

'What?'

'Look, Mum, I wasn't ready to talk to you about this. I think we should continue this conversation another time. I'm going to have to go now.'

'Off to an agency, I hope. You know they're always looking for admin temps. It could tide you over and at least pay your rent. You can't be out of work for long. The longer you're off, the harder it will be.'

'Bye, Mum.'

Leila was eating chocolate for breakfast. Muffins for lunch. Frozen food and red wine for dinner.

Lucas came to see her every other night to bring commiseratory takeaway.

'How's Looney Leila today?' he said, squinting in the bright fluorescent light in the hall outside her unit.

'Shut up. Did you bring won tons?' Leila reached out her hand for the bags of Chinese.

'And chocolate.'

She grunted, pulling out two plates.

'How's work?' *Without me.*

Lucas was working as part of a proposal team. She'd been working in the same team with him for months, bidding to win a job to design and construct a new prison. Lord knew what the writers were doing to her carefully designed templates. Screwing them up, no doubt.

'It's fine. Alex is giving me the runs but I just need to find a way to use his expertise without letting him bulldoze over the rest of the procurement group.'

They sat on the couch with their beef and black-bean sauce, fried rice and lemon chicken.

'What exactly do you *do*?' she said. It was a running joke. Lucas's job title seemed to change every few months. He was a good manager without a team to manage, and was moved around from project to project, and sent overseas and interstate for conferences and training seminars. Apparently he was some kind of systems manager. Whatever that meant.

'I'm between jobs right now,' he joked.

'No, I think I win that title.'

'Ouch. Sorry.'

She put her plate down on the coffee table and went to open a bottle of wine. 'White or red?'

'White.'

'Really? Don't you think this is a red wine kind of meal?'

'Red then. I don't care.'

'Then again, we've got both chicken and beef. What does one do in this situation?'

'Beer?'

She opened the white.

'I really must do some kind of wine appreciation course,' she said, handing him a glass. 'Be nice to know what I'm talking about. I've got time up my sleeve now.'

'If it tastes good, drink it down.'

She clinked her glass to his. 'Sounds reasonable to me.'

He leaned across her to reach for the lemon chicken and a whiff of his Polo scent made her lose her train of thought, her skin receptors suddenly primed for his touch.

Her desire was as strong today as it had been a year ago,

when she'd first met him.

Her first day at work had, unexpectedly, coincided with her division's annual team-building day. She'd had to swap her brand-new charcoal suit for army greens, as the overwhelming number of men in her new place of employment had voted for an afternoon of paintball. She, Lucas and three others had found themselves in the blue team and were running for their lives from the green team, whose goal was to annihilate the blues using their combined knowledge, skills and workmanship. It didn't sound very touchy-feely to Leila, but she'd been used to working with women before this job, and their idea of team building involved lashings of cake, chardonnay and gossip. To say Leila felt out of her comfort zone was a huge understatement.

Lucas had caught her eye as she'd struggled to pull down her safety goggles, feeling a wave of anxiety as the blue team's captain barked out orders to spread out and hide in unexpected places to launch an unforgiving counterattack. Lucas had grinned at her, an almost-dimple in his left cheek, his teeth white against the black and green camouflage paint he'd smeared across his face.

'Stick with me,' he'd said. 'I've got your back.'

She gave him a grateful smile.

They rushed off into the bush, Leila thudding along behind Lucas's broad back, wondering where he was taking her in the assembly of walls, towers, pillars, staircases, netting, gullies, trees and bushland. She carried her marker—a fake gun that shot bright orange paint—awkwardly down near her hips and it swung from side to side as she loped along.

Out in the field, Lucas appeared every bit the team leader his current job title said he was. The other men naturally looked to him for direction and he obliged with hand signals and encouraging nods, which they followed without question. She caught up to his side, breathing heavily while he whispered instructions into a comrade's ear. Then, when the comrade took off to hide inside a cement tunnel at the base of three huge eucalypt trees, Lucas grabbed Leila by the elbow, his touch sending a bolt right to her spine, and led her into a wooden maze.

They crept along a wall, now able to hear the smashing branches and bushes as the green team galloped towards them. Apparently, stealth wasn't going to be one of their tactics.

Leila was genuinely nervous. She was being hunted by large men in a surprisingly dim forest. Her breathing was much louder than she would have liked. Lucas turned to wink at her and motioned with his hand for her to crouch lower, even though the walls of the maze were several feet higher than their heads. And so they kept creeping, every now and then passing a peephole, which Lucas peered through to see what might be coming.

Leila fiddled with the trigger on her marker gun and wondered if she'd be able to shoot someone before they shot her.

Just then, there was a sudden burst of fire on the other side of the wall, and yelling and more breaking of branches. The green and blue teams were in full combat. She and Lucas froze. An almighty crash against the wall right next to Leila shook the wood and made her squeal and jump. Lucas grabbed her, one muscly arm braced across her chest, narrowly missing her breasts, the other hand clamped over her mouth. She gasped as best she could while breathing through her nose. His hand smelled of ink and peppermint and she had an unprecedented desire to poke out her tongue and lick it.

She could feel his heart banging through his chest against her back.

He held her steady while the engagement continued only feet

from them. And then the noise disappeared and the silence of the bush returned, leaving her and Lucas alone.

He gently released his hand from her mouth and let his arm drop from her chest. She turned slowly to face him. His eyes met hers and held them for a moment. Then he suddenly checked himself and took half a step back, raising a hand to run it over the back of his hair.

'Well. We appear to be the only ones still alive,' he said.

'Right. Yes,' Leila said, lost for words. She wanted him to put that strong arm back where it had been and pull her to him.

'Must be time for a beer then,' he grinned.

'I'll say.' And Leila followed him back through the bush, her heart now racing not from fear but with unsatisfied lust.

'What are you going to do with all this free time?' he said, licking lemon sauce from his finger and leaving a shine on his lower lip. She supressed a strong urge to kiss it off.

She shrugged. 'I'm not sure. Maybe play tennis.'

'Tennis?' He laughed. 'Didn't I see you trip over your own shoes last week?'

She poked him with a chopstick.

'Besides, the way you throw paperweights, I think we should be looking at something like softball.'

'Yes,' she agreed. 'I haven't played a team sport since high school. It could be fun. How about a mixed team? You could come too.'

'Assuming I could find the time,' he said. He held her gaze, his amber eyes lingering on her own for longer than was comfortable.

She looked away first and reached for her wine. She took a deep breath, gathered her courage and said, 'Maybe I'd meet someone. Or you'd meet someone?'

She was on shaky ground, deliberately testing what had

remained unspoken between them since the night on the boat all those months ago.

Lucas was her work husband—someone she confided in, had coffee with daily, laughed with and went to for advice. They joked about it often and around the office she was known as 'the little woman' in Lucas's life.

But more than once she'd caught herself wondering what it would be like to be his real wife.

Unfortunately, Lucas had his reasons for keeping Leila at arm's length, though they frustrated her no end. She knew she should give up hoping for anything more, but she still longed for him to take this opportunity to say he wasn't interested in anyone else, that it was only her he wanted. He could reach out a hand to touch her face, lean in slowly, silently asking permission, and kiss her, right now.

She wanted it so much it hurt.

But he didn't move. He didn't speak.

Her nerves frayed and she jumped to her feet. 'I need some water.'

e

Early in her new job, Simone warned Kate about the dreaded Judy.

'She's a witch,' she said. 'No talent, judgemental and with a profile like a Scottish terrier—and yes, her eyebrows do stick out just as much. She hates everyone. Couldn't see the funny side of a clown's arse.'

Kate wasn't sure if she was supposed to laugh or not.

'Would you like some tea?' she offered. She'd recently made a fun afternoon blend of lavender, mint and orange peel in a base of hibiscus—something reviving for the team.

'Hell no,' Simone said. 'Awful stuff.'

Kate couldn't keep the shock off her face.

'Don't look at me like that, Kate. I've drunk so much tea since I opened The Tea Chest the mere sight of it sends me to the bottle.' She paused. 'Of course, I'm sure it's lovely. It certainly smells lovely. Discuss what sort of packaging you'd like with the graphic designers. Then *go home*. You've been here far too long.' Simone looked at her gold watch. 'Blimey, look at the time. No wonder tea's turning my insides. It's positively cocktail hour. On second thoughts, go straight home to your man. You can chat to the designers in the morning.'

Kate had fallen quickly into a work routine at The Tea Chest, whose sumptuous surrounds greeted her each morning like a theme song to her life.

'We're selling more than just tea here,' Simone had said. 'We're selling a dream. You can't just drink the tea, you must experience it.' Simone encouraged Kate to take the time to build a relationship with every tea in stock.

And when Kate wasn't drinking tea, she was talking to customers and recommending products and gathering data about their preferences and values. She played with the dried leaves and fruits and spices from the huge glass containers of sample stocks in the storeroom, blending and experimenting. She offered tests to customers, recording their responses and making adjustments. She spoke to the staff members at length, taking on board their thoughts and ideas about the future of the business and deliberately fostering good relations, especially with Susan, the manager, who'd seemed to prickle when Kate was first introduced.

In the first week especially, she missed Mark's company. Whenever she came home from work, bursting with things to talk about, he was rushing out the door to see clients. With no one to talk to, she found it hard to wind down. It was better on the days she worked at home. She could talk to Mark as he entertained Keats while she made teas.

'Maybe you should ask for an electricity allowance,' he said, watching her boil yet another jug of water in the tiny chipboard kitchen. She laughed and continued to ramble on about her days at work and the people, while inhaling the smell of frying onion and meat from the Lebanese takeaway nearby.

'Susan's clearly threatened. But I'm not there to take her job. I couldn't care less about managing the place. I just want to make tea. I made her laugh today, though, so I'm sure I'll win her over eventually.'

She went on. 'And Simone only comes in once a day. She likes to keep the time of her visit a secret so she can surprise everyone. You should see them all duck for cover when she marches in the door.'

'Bit of a dragon, is she?' Mark asked, cajoling Keats into a nappy change.

'Da-gon?' Keats repeated.

'I don't think so. I think she's funny. And an amazingly cluey businesswoman.'

Since Simone had mentioned her customers' star signs during their first meeting at the Emporium, Kate had been thinking. Maybe she could design a range of zodiac teas. She could research all the profiles and match tea characteristics to personalities. More conservative signs, like Virgos and Taureans, would probably like teas with rose and lavender and black teas at their base. More adventurous signs, like Aquarians and Leos, would be more willing to take a risk on spices and herbs and offbeat fusions. Maybe after that she could move on to Chinese birth year blends, like Year of the Ox and so on. But what sort of tea would an ox enjoy?

Or a rabbit? A dragon? Perhaps she should pitch the zodiac tea first and see how that went.

She carried a notebook with her everywhere and brimmed with ideas. She often woke in the night and switched on the light to scribble down her thoughts.

Mark would groan and twist the pillow over his eyes.

'Sorry. Just one more minute.'

'You're obsessed,' he'd say. But then he would roll over and grab her around the waist and bury his head in her breasts. 'But since you're awake . . .'

It was their midnight ritual.

Simone's in-depth knowledge of her customers' profiles taught Kate to think critically about her markets and taught her more about business than she could have learned from any book. Though, at the end of the day, she was glad to leave the technicalities behind and just *feel* a new tea blend emerging.

She drank litres of tea from The Tea Chest range, trying every blend every way possible—with sugar, honey, lemon, milk, no milk, soy, black, iced and hot. One night, Mark came home after his appointments to find her rolling on the couch like something bloated and beached.

'I'll be peeing for months,' she said. 'It's bad enough peeing for two but now I'm peeing for all of England.'

Mark pinched her arms lightly, as though testing her hydration levels.

'It's official,' he said. 'You've blown ninety-eight on the tea-alyser. Please step away from the tea, ma'am. You'll have to come along with me.'

'I don't think there's a tea on the market I haven't tried,' she groaned.

'Have you checked the web for teas overseas?' he said, flopping into the sagging brown chair near the television.

'No. I hadn't even thought of that.'

He shrugged. 'Might be worth a look since Simone's plans are for overseas development.'

'Yes. Thanks.'

'I'm here to help,' he said.

When Kate finally met Judy, it was without warning.

She was at The Tea Chest, handing out glasses of a tea she called Asian Delight. It was late in the afternoon and she'd just been hit with a nap attack, all the long hours and pregnancy taking their toll on her energy. She squinted against the afternoon light as it breezed through the doorway and thought the shadowed figure moving towards her must be a customer. As she got closer, Kate took in her fawn suit, pearl necklace and matronly shoes. The woman stopped in front of her.

'Kate?'

'Yes?'

'Judy Masters.'

Judy Masters' mouth was set in a straight line and she had the same English accent as Simone. She offered no smile, and directed her gaze up and down Kate's body as though assessing a horse for sale and finding it not worth the price being asked. Kate returned the assessment and concluded that Judy was in her early fifties, a handful of years older than Simone. And Simone was right; she did look like a Scottish terrier.

'Simone couldn't make it today,' Judy said.

'Oh.' Kate tried and failed to keep the disappointment out of her voice. 'Nothing serious, I hope.'

'Flu. She'll be off all week.'

Kate got the impression Judy didn't tolerate sickness.

'I hear you have a proposal for a new tea line. Something to do with star signs. Tell me about it.'

Kate stammered, surprised by such a direct line of questioning and the way Judy punctuated the words 'star signs' with a raise of her left eyebrow. Once for each word. She fidgeted with her tray of mostly empty glasses.

'Well, they're teas. You know. Based on astrology. Zodiac tea.' She also punctuated her words with exaggeratedly enthusiastic facial gestures, but even as she did so she could feel the blood trickle down through her limbs like water through leaky pipes.

Judy's eyes went to the ceiling.

Kate reined in her fleeing courage, got angry with it and tapped her foot to direct the blood back to her face. Anger was better. This woman had no right to come in and judge her. She'd never even set eyes on her before.

'Perhaps you'd like to sample the teas so far?' Kate began. 'We could talk about the ideas behind them. I'm in again tomorrow . . .'

Judy glanced at her silver watch. 'Meet me in the restaurant next door in fifteen minutes,' she said, already turning her back.

The sales team was fully engaged in service, tidying and dusting, all eyes downcast, their bodies visibly shrinking away from Judy as she marched around the shop, running her finger across shelves, like a drill sergeant inspecting the barracks with a white glove.

Kate ran the flat of her sweaty hand down the side of her skirt. She forced her feet to move and take her to the alcove that functioned as the storeroom. She gathered her proposal materials and scooped samples of the teas from the first four signs of the zodiac—Aries to Cancer—into gift bags. She squared her shoulders and marched out the door. Her plan was to get to the restaurant first, choose the best location, place her order and be waiting for Judy when she arrived. She needed to get the upper hand and reclaim some power in this situation. She returned to basic body language rules—to be confident, she had to act confident.

It was a good plan.

Unfortunately, Judy wasn't playing the game by Kate's rules. She kept Kate waiting for forty minutes beyond their scheduled meeting time, during which Kate had drunk two coffees and was trembling with the caffeine, feeling jittery and anxious and hoping she hadn't just sent her baby into a disco state.

'I've only got a few minutes,' Judy said when she at last arrived. She sat down.

Kate signalled the waiter, wanting to appear generous and mindful of Judy's need to be served quickly. But when the waiter appeared, Judy shook her head.

'No time,' she said.

Kate gave him a small, apologetic smile, to which the waiter tipped his head politely.

'What's your rationale for this star tea?' Judy said.

'Rationale?'

'Reason. Logic. Why star tea?'

'Zodiac tea,' Kate corrected. 'I felt it was a good idea.'

Too late, the words had left her lips.

Wrong, Kate. Wrong.

Judy leaned back in her chair, pushing Kate's printed report across the table. 'Where's your research?'

Research? Kate's face went cold as she realised she hadn't done any of the sort of research Judy was requesting. Kate's research had involved reading a couple of books on star signs and coming up with a character profile she could match to the characteristics of ingredients. That's what she did, after all.

She was the lead designer. That's why Simone had hired her. But she hadn't done any research into why people might actually *buy* the tea. Judy was a financial partner. All she cared about were the figures and analysis, the sales record and her share of the profits.

'Everybody has a star sign,' Kate said weakly. 'Star signs are very popular. Every woman's magazine includes them. Everybody reads them.'

'I don't. And don't those star sign pieces predict the future? Will your tea predict the future? Are we reading tea leaves now?' Judy cackled.

'Actually, I hadn't thought about that.' For a fleeting moment, Kate was excited, considering this aspect of the teas. But when she attempted to engage Judy in the idea it became clear the other woman had been mocking her.

'I believe—Simone and I believe—that this range has real market potential,' Kate said.

'Well, I need more marketing research than a high school girl's belief that something is a good idea. This—' she picked up Kate's report by the corner and dangled it like a dirty dishcloth '—is not a marketing plan. This is a good attempt to convince yourself of your own worth.'

Kate couldn't have been more shocked if Judy had stood on the table and taken off all her clothes. She opened her mouth to correct her on her age (she was twenty-nine, after all) but closed it again in stunned realisation. This woman was nasty. Simple as that. And she was supposed to be a silent partner. Simone ran the business and made the decisions. Simone had hired her. Who was this woman to think she could speak to her this way?

'Simone liked it,' she at last managed to say, her heart booming with more than the caffeine.

'Indeed. But if Simone was as smart as all that, then she would never have needed a financial investor to bail her out of trouble.'

Trouble?

Judy stood. 'Simone won't be in for the rest of the week. Do this report again but with solid data to back up your *belief*.'

Kate had never been so glad to see someone leave. She sat at the table for quite a while longer, wiping away her tears of embarrassment and anger. She felt assaulted. And shaky. And cold. It was shock, she realised. That's what it was.

At home that night, she put Keats to bed with three books and a song, and sat at the kitchen table with a plate of falafel and salad that Mark had left for her. She opened her laptop, trying to make lists of all the places she could go in order to research her proposal. To her left, a bunch of roses sat in a blue vase. They were browning and floppy, cream petals scattered across the yellow table top. She realised with a start that she had no idea how long those flowers had been there. Mark had obviously picked them for her and arranged them and she hadn't even noticed them until now. She slammed the lid of her laptop shut and howled. Mark was out again and wouldn't be home before ten o'clock. She missed him dreadfully and the fear that they were drifting apart made her cry even harder, her sobs echoing in the wooden house.

It wasn't worth it—this job, the stress on her relationship, the stress that Judy must have caused her unborn child today, the tiredness, the hours and days she was missing from Keats's life. It just wasn't worth it.

5

The bell chimed above the doorway. Kate looked up from the computer printouts of lists and stocktaking figures she and Susan had been going through. She didn't normally have to invest so much brainpower in this end of the business as the financial year ended. Normally, she was concerned with launching a new tea blend to sit alongside the products with end-of-year discounts, to take advantage of sale-happy customers.

Normally, Simone did this.

She paused mid-conversation with Susan to smile at the new customer. Except it wasn't a new customer at all. It was Judy.

Judy strode through the door with her heels clunking on the floor, her face set like stone.

Even today, the day when Judy was going to get everything she wanted, the woman still couldn't crack a smile.

Kate continued to point out figures on the sheet and circle profit margins with a yellow highlighter, willing Judy to go away.

'Ahem,' Judy said. 'I think we have some paperwork to discuss.'

'I'll be with you in a moment.'

Judy paused for an irritated second before heading out the back to the storeroom.

'Is this really it?' Susan whispered, her huge doll-like eyes filled with disbelief and sadness. 'Is it really over?'

Kate and Mark had agreed that she would sign the papers and wind up the business, take the financial payout and start again. She'd nodded reluctantly, pulled herself from under the purple mohair rug draped over her lap, and carried her plate to the kitchen bench. It still had half her snapper and vegetables on it, untouched.

He'd followed her, placing his empty plate beside hers, and put his hands on her shoulders from behind. They both stared out through the wooden louvres to the street, the view expanding over the Paddington hills towards the bright lights of the city. This home had been acquired in large part because of Kate's successful career so far and the choices they'd made as a family to get here. It was not just finances they were risking.

'This is what I want,' he'd said. 'This is what I think is best. But I want you to know I do trust you. And I do believe you can do anything. If winding up really isn't what you want . . . if you *really* feel it's not the best thing to do for our family . . . I will support whatever you decide.'

'It's the best thing to do,' she'd said, talking herself around to his point of view. They'd been over and over the different options, weighed up the pros and cons, and agreed to take the safer route.

There was no risk involved in winding up the company now, so why would she even consider jeopardising that in favour of the risky option of London?

That was the logic, anyway. Still, her heart hurt.

Now, she took a deep breath and squeezed Susan's arm. 'I'm sorry,' she said. 'But I want you to know we'll look after you. You'll be okay.'

Susan turned back to the spreadsheet in front of her.

In the storeroom, it was clear Judy was forgoing any niceties. She leaned against the small kitchen sink with her arms crossed and the papers clutched in one hand.

'What?' Kate said. 'No going-away parties, no speeches, no champagne?'

'Let's just get this over and done with,' Judy replied. 'Then we can both get on with our lives.' She flicked open the pages and held them towards Kate. 'You need to sign here, here and here.'

Kate nodded. Her hands moistened. Her heart trotted.

'Judy, there's something I just still don't understand.'

Judy's eyes narrowed.

'Tell me again, why exactly are you so keen to dissolve this business? Why not look for a buyer?'

Judy tapped her foot in a mini tantrum. 'I'm ready to retire, Kate. I never wanted to be a part of this company anyway. We've been over this. It would take too long to find a buyer and every day we hesitate drains more money from the company. That empty shop Simone leased in London is sucking us dry. We should cut our losses and get out now while we've still got profits to share. That's the sensible thing to do.'

'So you keep saying. But don't you think we should at least try? Don't you think we owe it to Simone?'

Judy snarled, 'I want this to be over, Kate. Don't you see that? I've spent more years than I'd like to count propping up this business for Simone while she drank herself to death. There wouldn't even be a business here without me. I think we owe it to *me* to finish this chapter of my life so I can move on.'

Kate looked away. Simone's alcoholism was something she still hadn't come to terms with, something her mentor had managed to keep hidden from her almost until her death. Simone had given her so much—including half a company. She'd been her friend and it seemed disloyal to focus on her failures.

Simone drank to obliterate the pain of losing her mother at just ten years of age, followed by her father's marriage to Elaine. When her father died a year after that, Simone had been left with Elaine and Elaine's daughter Judy, and not long after they'd relocated to Australia so Elaine could marry again, this time to a businessman with mining interests.

A couple of times Simone had drunk too much wine and she'd shared with Kate snippets of her Cinderella-like life with Elaine, Judy and her stepfather, Dennis. How Elaine had split her time between their magnificent home on the river at Yeronga during the hot months, and their home in Mount Isa in the middle of Queensland during the colder months. The girls had been sent to boarding school. Simone had been taken away from everything she knew and loved.

But Simone was a survivor. And this shop in London was her chance to finally go home.

'If Simone was so useless, then why did you ever agree to be a financial partner in the first place?' Kate asked now.

Judy glared at her. 'Look, Kate. You don't like me and it's no secret I'm not your biggest fan. So let's just sign these papers and we'll never have to see each other again.' She thrust the papers and a silver pen at Kate.

Kate took the pen and the papers and lay them on the kitchen sink. She hesitated as a memory suddenly opened.

It was the day after Judy had first criticised Kate's zodiac tea idea. She'd gone to Simone's house to see her, only to find that

Simone wasn't down with the flu but had crashed her car and had whiplash. The accident had occurred after a drinking binge, but that was something Kate only found out years later. After this, her opinion of Judy had improved slightly, due to her loyalty and protection of Simone's privacy. It also went some way towards explaining Judy's bad attitude the day they'd discussed the zodiac tea.

Kate had sat on Simone's plush eggshell couch, looked at the Brisbane River and poured out the story of her meeting with Judy. Tears flowed down her face.

'So I've decided to resign,' she finished.

Simone snorted, sitting stiffly with her neck in a brace while wrapped in an elegant crimson satin gown, a glass of brandy ('for the pain') beside her.

'Nonsense. Judy hasn't the first idea about what makes a business successful. You're a talented artist, Kate. I don't care if you don't have the profit projections and statistics and the boring-as-bat-doo-doo *evidence* to back it up. You have instinct. You have intuition. And you, my dear, are going to be a star.'

She'd smiled at Kate and handed her a box of tissues. 'You just need to trust yourself.'

Now, Kate stood up in the storeroom to face Judy. Simone had been right. Her instincts were good. The zodiac tea had been the most profitable line in years. She didn't need stuffy suit-types telling her what would be successful. She just knew.

Just as she knew that signing these papers was wrong.

I will support whatever you decide. Mark might not like it, but he'd given her his blessing. There must have been some small part of him that believed it was possible.

She dropped the pen on the sink with a clatter.

'I won't be signing these papers today,' Kate said, turning back into the shop. A customer in the sweets section collected fudge and coconut ice.

Judy stomped after her. 'What do you mean you're not signing?' Her voice, normally so deep and raspy, was high-pitched with outrage.

'I own half this business, Judy. And it's time I started acting like it. I'm not selling. I'm not dissolving it. I'm going to England and I'm going to make this work.'

Out of the corner of her eye, Kate saw Susan's expression change from surprise to delight.

Judy's face twisted and turned and puffed and grimaced, finally settling on an ugly sneer. 'And what about your family?'

Kate had to hand it to her; Judy knew exactly where her vulnerabilities lay.

'We'll be fine, thank you. Mark can look after the boys.'

Judy lashed out. 'You think you can run an international business? You think you can go to England and build a new store from scratch before the money drain sinks the entire company? You think you can *sell tea to the English*? You think you can keep a family and marriage together and you have the balls to deal with people in the cold, hard world of business? *And* you think can do all of this by yourself? Well, you're in for a shock. You've no idea what it takes to run a company. You're a *tea designer*, Kate.'

It was true. She wasn't ready for this. She wasn't a business mogul. She'd never even been out of the country. She was a foolish little girl.

But then Simone's words cut through the jangle in her mind.

Trust yourself. She'd said it that day in her apartment and she'd said it again in the note the solicitor read out. Sometimes, someone else could see something in you that you couldn't see yourself. Maybe, even if Kate didn't quite trust herself, she should trust Simone.

'Who do you think is going to deal with the hard side of the business, Kate? Because it certainly won't be you.'

Kate took a deep breath, smoothed down her shirt and straightened herself. She spoke quietly, forcing Judy to concentrate on her words.

'Yes, I will need help if I'm going to be doing what I do best.'

'So who is this person going to be then?'

'It's all sorted, Judy,' she lied. 'You'll find out about it when they start next week.'

Judy stormed past her and ripped open the door, sending the bell into crazy action and shattering any peace left in the shop.

'Do you know what I've realised?' Mark said.

He came bouncing in the door, startling Kate as she packed the dishwasher. He was sweating profusely, with a dark V-shaped patch on his shirt and pools beneath his armpits. He'd obviously run up a lot of the steep hills that surrounded their home to get his emotions and thoughts in order.

That had been his response to her news that she'd decided to go to London. After a few exclamations of shock, tinged with anger and even a touch of betrayal, he'd screwed up his face and declared he needed to run. Kate had been silently pleased. At least he'd be calmer when he said what he needed to say.

Now she braced herself, a plate held limply in her hand halfway to the rack, and waited for his declaration, whatever it might be. That she was selfish. That he didn't want to be in this marriage anymore. That she was a total fool and he was an idiot for trusting her to make the right choice.

'I've turned into my father,' he said.

That was unexpected. 'What?'

He paced in circles. 'I've become grumpy. Conservative. And worse yet, last election I actually voted Labor instead of Green.'

'Well, that *is* alarming. You didn't tell me that. We always vote Green.'

'I know. And do you know why I voted Labor? Because I've turned into my father. I'm channelling him, obviously. He's somehow possessed me.'

'All the way from Melbourne?'

'Exactly.'

'Thank goodness you got on top of it now,' she said, smothering a laugh. Really, it was difficult to take him seriously at this moment.

She put down the plate and passed Mark a handful of paper towels, motioning to the sweat dripping from his forehead.

'Money was never my priority,' he said. 'You know that. I was the one who told you not to take the job at The Tea Chest for money but only for love. Only for passion. That's what we believe. That's what we want our kids to believe. And here I am trying to convince you not to follow your passion but to play it safe. What the hell's wrong with me?'

Kate shrugged. 'We had kids. Got a mortgage. A bigger car. Health insurance.'

'Don't get me started on the rort of health insurance.' He looked stricken. 'See—I'm my father.' He pretended to strangle himself. 'And another thing; I used to be funny.'

'It's called growing up, I guess,' she said.

'I used to have hair.'

'You still have hair,' she said, 'it's just not on your head.'

He grabbed her by the arms, his strong fingers holding her so she could feel his energy coursing into her body. 'We're not those people, Kate. And I think you know that. Somewhere inside, you managed to keep that optimism and strength.'

'I did?'

'Yes. But me?' He let her go and flung himself down on the couch.

She wrinkled her nose and refrained from telling him not to get sweat all over the fabric.

'I turned into a grumpy old man. I've been focusing on the wrong things. I've been so busy building up my practice, thinking I'd finally got my chance to reap the financial rewards of all the hard work I've put into it.' He shook his head sadly. 'And I'm sorry.'

'What for?'

'Because part of me has been jealous of you and your success. I'm still a man in a western capitalist culture and even after all these years it's still hard for me not to be the biggest breadwinner. And honestly, I hate myself for that.'

He looked utterly stricken. She wanted to rush to him to soothe his fears but his stiff shoulders told her he just needed to accept and deal with them on his own.

'It's okay,' she said. 'It's okay to feel like that.'

'It is. But it's not okay if I let that feeling dictate my decisions. So, thank you.'

'What for?'

'For reminding me what my priorities are. And I promise you that grumpy old Mark is gone.' He swept his hand from left to right, drawing a line in the air. '*Finito*. You won't see him again. Not unless the guy from the 7-Eleven looks at my belly pityingly again when he next hands me my block of chocolate.'

'Perhaps, if you're going to go back to voting for the Greens, you should get a new supplier. Maybe an organic food store with fair trade chocolate? Gosh, Mark, I didn't realise you'd become such a consumer. Voting Labor and buying secret stashes of chocolate. Should I be worried?'

'No. But I should. This is exactly what I'm talking about. I've become so mainstream.'

'Are you saying you think I did the right thing?' she said, getting back to the discussion at hand.

Mark jumped up, his shoulders a couple of inches above hers, his breath caressing her face. He let his eyes wander lovingly over her lips. 'Yes.' He smiled, his previous angst vanished. She'd always admired how quickly he could do that—come to a conclusion about himself he didn't like, accept it, decide to change it, and move on. It took her days to wade through the complexities of those sorts of emotions. But he could do it in minutes. It was quite a skill.

'Unequivocally, you did the right thing,' he said. 'In a totally surprising event, you were right and I was wrong.'

A delicious quiver as her skin came alive under his gaze.

'Then we should celebrate,' she said.

'Indeed.'

'Let's get you into the shower.'

After their shower, Kate and Mark lay in bed together, their limbs entwined, their breathing in sync with each other's. She felt pleasantly heavy, a deep sense of peace melting her skin into the sheets and into her husband's body so she wasn't sure where hers ended and his began.

Mark played with her fingers, stroking them lightly and twisting them through his.

'Why don't we all come with you?' he said. 'To London. We could visit Madame Tussauds and walk the trails of Jack the Ripper.'

'That's not exactly what we want our boys to be doing,' she murmured sleepily.

'Then we'll ride the London Eye and wave to the Queen. I've been meaning to visit her for a while, actually. She's been on my to-do list. It was my New Year's resolution to invest more time in my relationships. I'll start with her.'

'The boys could try and make those freakishly stiff guards laugh, the ones at Buckingham Palace with the fluffy hats who act like they're statues who'll topple over if you poke them.'

'And we could eat spotted dick and bread and butter pudding.'

'What *is* spotted dick?'

'I don't know.' His voice drifted off, his eyes closed, and his breathing slowed. Kate waited for him to continue, to come to the conclusion that it wasn't realistic. But Mark was floating away to dreamland.

She sat up quickly, and his eyes jerked open.

'You're not serious, are you?'

His chest rose beneath her hand as he took a deep breath to regain consciousness. He shrugged. 'Maybe.'

'But what about your business?'

'Ah. Yes, that. I guess that's complicated. This working for yourself thing is a bit of a drag when it comes to wanting time off. No holiday pay or sick pay or conjugal-visits-to-your-wife-in-London pay.'

'And we need your income right now to keep everything going here in Australia. You know, bills and other such annoyances. Until this current crisis is sorted out in some way.' Guilt needled her. 'See, you're an important hunter and gatherer too.'

His fingers moved to her hair, playing with the long gentle curls.

'And it would be really disruptive to take the boys out of school,' he said.

'Yes. But then again, they're only small. What does it matter if they lose a few months of Australian school time? Wouldn't the experience and worldly adventure be a trade-off?' she said, momentum gathering for the plan.

'True. But we'd be in your way. And it's expensive. We'd have to spend so much more on flights, and accommodation, and living expenses.'

'Money we can't really afford right now with the risk we're taking.' She could almost see Mark's dream cloud above his head disintegrating into wisps of smoke and floating away. Tinges of disappointment hung in the air instead. 'But you wouldn't be in the way,' she said. 'You're never in the way. Though it's true I wouldn't have much time to spare. And it could be rather stressful. I'd hate to be cranky with you all the time.'

'You're *never* cranky. Only ever slightly less happy.'

'And it would be awful if I failed,' she said, not meeting his eyes. 'It could all be over and done with in three weeks and we'd have to come home with our tails between our legs.' It was a truly terrifying thought having the boys watch her attempt such a huge task only to have it fall over.

'Impossible,' Mark said. 'You're already the most talented and inspirational person in this family. The boys adore you. Nothing could change that.'

'It would be nice if that were true,' she said.

'So I think we've agreed the boys and I should stay here. Do you need to write a list of pros and cons?'

She groaned and rubbed at her eyes, a huge yawn expanding from somewhere deep in her chest, suddenly weary beneath this weight of responsibility and adulthood.

'No. I think we know for sure.'

He nodded. 'Yep. No warm beer in stuffy pubs for me.'

From nowhere, her eyes filled. 'But how will you cope on your own?'

'Probably badly,' he said.

'You're supposed to be making me feel better.'

'It'll be fun. We'll be bachelors. A frat house. The Fullerton Frat House. We'll sleep in tents and make fires by rubbing sticks together and learn how to bring down the crazy postman by throwing boomerangs at his head. And we'll eat pizza every night. Vegetarian, to make sure the boys are getting their daily quota.'

'Maybe we should rethink this plan after all.' She moved to roll away from him and turn on the light, mentally composing her pros-and-cons list for the notepad beside the bed. Instead, Mark grabbed her around the waist and pulled her to him, making her laugh under his roving hands.

'We'll be fine,' he said with authority. 'You should go and have a wonderful time making your dreams come true. Now perhaps you could come here and show me how very grateful you are.'

Leila's rate of chocolate consumption and wine (she'd downgraded to buying it by the cask, on account of being unemployed) increased in accordance with how far and wide the news of her fall from grace spread.

Her younger brother called from the barracks in Darwin and offered to put her in touch with an army recruitment officer.

Andrea from her Zumba class had taken her for cocktails and sushi in New Farm and enthusiastically maintained that she'd done absolutely the right thing and Carter had it coming and she was far too good for that place and she didn't need them anyway, she was perfectly capable of something much bigger and better so she should drink up and enjoy her impromptu holiday while she could.

Gemma, an executive assistant at Strahan Engineering, had emailed her sympathies and support with a lot of exclamation marks and promises of catching up for coffee, which Leila knew would happen once and never again.

And on it went. Phone calls and emails from people excited by the flush of fantastic gossip and scandal but who wouldn't be there in a week's time when Leila was pacing the apartment in the middle of the night and eating discarded chocolate cake from the kitchen bin.

Which she was doing now.

She'd thrown away the rest of the cake that afternoon in a flash of motivation to pick herself up and get over it. She'd also cleaned the kitchen and vacuumed the lounge room and bought the paper for the jobs section liftout. Finding nothing appropriate there, she'd turned to the online job ads and shortlisted and highlighted and uploaded her résumé to a few places, but had ended the day wholly disheartened. Editing jobs were few and far between, especially ones that paid as much as Strahan did, as her mother was so fond of reminding her.

She'd gone to bed anxious and restless and got up again around midnight, itching for something comforting to eat. Sadly, the fridge only contained pots of jam and jars of nuts, a bag of slimy lettuce, some suspicious-smelling milk and bottled sauces. If only she hadn't thrown away the cake.

Perhaps if she just checked the bin. Perhaps it was still wrapped in plastic and hadn't touched anything else.

She carefully lifted an empty can of soup, damp paper towels from her kitchen cleaning, an apple core and some tissues to find the cake was buried there and at least half of it hadn't been touched or soiled by anything else. She pulled it out and cut off the bits that were still okay and ignored the voice in her head telling her it was rather disgusting and she must have hit rock bottom.

She tucked in, squeezing all the crumbs together, inhaling the smell of cocoa, and licking the icing from her fingers.

She washed her hands and face and went back to the laptop. Maybe she should be looking for something other than a straight editing job. She had a diverse set of skills that someone would want, surely. So she searched in business categories and came across an interesting ad. Better yet, the job was based in London. What a fabulous way to escape the depressing confines of her current life.

Position Vacant:

Assistant Business Planner and Developer for expanding gourmet tea business.

Short-term appointment (3 months, with possible extension)

Based in London. Immediate start. Click here for full description.

She didn't really have all the experience the ad required, but she had to be in it to win it. It wouldn't hurt to apply.

Seven months earlier

Lucas first told Leila about Achara on the boat.

'She's eleven years old now,' he said, passing her a laminated photo that he kept in his wallet. Leila simultaneously reeled from the shock of the unexpected news and hummed with affection for a man who would keep a photo of his child in his wallet. It was so retro. And so sweet.

The photo showed a small girl with shoulder-length dark hair, dark skin and dark eyes, and with a bright open smile that was both typical of the good nature of the Thai people and strikingly familiar.

'She's got your smile,' she said.

'Poor girl.'

Leila slapped him lightly on the arm. 'Stop it. She'd be lucky to have any of your good looks.' She shot Lucas a sly sideways glance, but his eyes had taken on a faraway expression as he gazed at the other party boats forging white V shapes through the water of the river.

In the dim lighting on deck, Leila studied the photo once more, taking in the sand plastered up Achara's lower legs as she squatted on the beach, a stick in her hand scribbling in the wet grains, the skinny dog in the top right corner, and her bright yellow dress, a couple of sizes too big for her slight frame.

'She's pretty,' Leila said, her voice affected by some sort of emotion, though she wasn't sure which one exactly.

Lucas replaced the photo into his wallet. 'Her name means pretty angel.'

'And you've still not met her?'

He shook his head and threw back the last of his drink.

'I didn't even know about her until this year. It was an

accident, obviously. I was in Thailand at the full moon festival at Ko Pha Ngan, on the beach. It's quite famous. Happens every month and tens of thousands of tourist go there for a huge rave. She—Achara's mother, Nootsara—was working the bar. I was young and so was she, and ridiculously pretty.'

Leila winced.

A trio of workmates came shrieking and yelling across the deck, arms linked, Christmas tinsel wound around their shoulders like boas. Leila gave a smile and a small wave, wishing them away.

'So what now?' she asked Lucas, once the cackling group had moved on.

Lucas rolled the now-empty glass between his hands, the coloured light bulbs strung above them reflecting in the cut edges. He took a few moments to answer her.

'I want to meet her, of course,' he said, his face set in concentration in the familiar way he had when assessing a logistics problem at work. 'She's in a village with her mum, grandparents, aunties and cousins. The whole village family thing. I think she's quite okay, from what Nootsara has said in her emails. She's not on the streets or anything. But—and I don't want to sound all white imperialist or anything—I think I could make her life better.'

He turned to Leila for understanding. 'I mean, she goes to school, but I don't think it's anything like what we have here.'

'You want to bring her to Australia?'

'No. I don't think so. All I know is that I need to work hard, because if I can't be there, on the ground, doing the things a dad should be doing, then I can at least do what I'm good at here. Make money. Focus on my career. Take every opportunity that comes my way to get as much as I can. Because one day she'll need it. I'm sure of it.' He raised his eyebrows, thinking. 'And one day it will be her inheritance,' he said, as if only just fully realising it.

He stroked his chin thoughtfully. 'Maybe one day she'll want to come to Australia and start a new life. Or maybe it will buy her a new life in Thailand. Who knows? Whatever happens, all I know is that the more money I earn, the more options she'll have in life. And that's pretty fantastic.'

She reached over and took his hand in hers. 'You're a good man, Charlie Brown. Achara's lucky to have you.'

She longed for Lucas to give that kind of devotion to her. He stared at her, looked down at their entwined hands, squeezed hers and raised it to his chest.

Leila's heart thundered as her hand felt his warmth, the firmness of his chest.

He lifted her hand to his lips and held it there, warming her fingers.

The water slapped at the sides of the boat and they rocked from side to side. The coloured lights twinkled. It was the perfect moment for him to kiss her fingertips.

But then he gently passed her hand back to her and the cool air whipped around her skin.

'Leila?'

'Yes?'

'I can't get distracted,' he said carefully.

She blanched and shifted backwards in her seat. 'What do you mean?'

'I don't want to risk my career right now for something that may not work and that might hold me back from my commitments.'

Her face burned. Her lips tightened.

'I need to focus one hundred per cent on my career now, so that I can take some time off next year and spend it with Achara and get to know her.'

'Of course you do,' Leila said, crossing her legs and wrapping her hands over her knees, pulling against them till her knuckles went white.

'And who knows,' he ploughed on, seemingly oblivious to her discomfort, 'if I set it up right, maybe I could take a few months off. Be a dad. For the first time.' He smiled, the thought of being with his daughter lighting up his eyes. 'I need to keep things simple. Not complicated. I can't make ties that might get in the way.'

'Absolutely,' she said, ignoring the pulling around her heart. She plastered on a brave smile. 'You've got to do what's right for you and your child.'

6

'Strahan Engineering, Lucas Harris speaking.'

'Hi, Lucas, my name is Kate Fullerton. I'm phoning because Leila Morton has applied for a job as the assistant business planner and developer for The Tea Chest and she's listed you as a referee. I'm wondering if you have time to talk?'

'Certainly. I was hoping to hear from you,' he said warmly.

'Great.' Kate paused, taking a moment to look down at her notes. This was the first time she'd hired anyone and her nerves were twanging like a plucked string. Leila had been impressive in the interview. Kate had no doubt about her confidence or her management ability. Her only questions lay around her business dealings and experience.

'So, I'm wondering mostly about how much involvement Leila has had with the business dealings of the company. Could you tell me a little about that?'

'I've worked with Leila on a number of proposal teams,'

Lucas said, his tone encouraging. 'She always had to work with the writers to guide them and manage them through the schedule of putting together tenders and coming up with better systems. We have multiple writers who work on different parts of the tenders and Leila had to find a way to pull all those disparate pieces together, usually at the last minute. She had to coordinate everything with writers based in other cities, on other floors, and with a huge variety of backgrounds.'

'Did she ever come up with new business ideas or forecast cash flow?'

Lucas hesitated. 'She wouldn't have had much opportunity in that role; however, in editing those tenders and other business documents, she frequently saw problems, spotted errors and raised valid points about risk management and personnel management. She had quite a lot of input into how the proposals were structured, identifying our strengths as a company and playing to those.'

Kate nodded silently. Lucas was confirming her own impressions: that Leila's management ability and all-round talent were valuable assets, though her dealings with the nitty-gritty numbers and spreadsheets was limited.

But she'd been the best candidate overall. She had a wonderfully positive approach to her work and was clearly a creative problem solver. At the end of the day, it was Kate's responsibility to deal with the nitty-gritty. What she needed was a Jill-of-all-trades to keep things moving. The position was for an assistant, after all. Besides, she needed to get on a plane next week. She didn't have time to wait any longer.

'So would you recommend her?'

'Without hesitation,' he said.

Kate relaxed. 'Thank you so much for your time.'

'Not a problem.' He waited half a beat and then added, 'She's a great . . .'

Kate waited, expecting from the tone of his voice for him to finish with 'girl'. But he pulled himself up in time.

' . . . employee.'

'What's this?'

'It's a present,' Leila said. 'To say thank you for giving me a good reference. I would be dead in the water if I didn't have you to help. I don't think people who assault co-workers normally get favourable references.'

Lucas put down his pappadum to open the envelope and Leila handed over the six-pack of Crown Lagers to the waiter.

'Awesome!' Lucas said, reading the voucher. 'I've always wanted to go up in a hot-air balloon. Thank you.'

'I know.'

'And it's for two, so you'll have to come with me,' he said, putting the voucher back in the envelope and coming to her side of the table to hug her tightly. She leaned into him, relishing the feel of his arms around her.

'You don't have to take me,' she said, though of course that was the idea. 'It's yours to enjoy with whoever you want.'

'Nonsense. We'll do it when you get back from London.'

The waiter arrived with two opened beers. 'Are you ready to order?'

'Actually, I haven't even looked at the menu,' she apologised. 'Another minute?'

'I'm really happy for you,' Lucas said. 'This is an amazing opportunity.'

'It is.' She gritted her teeth. 'The stakes are high, though. After my colossal disaster at Strahan, and my mother's fervent shame at my disgrace, I feel like I've got a lot to prove.' She played with her napkin. It was difficult to admit failings, especially to someone who meant so much to her. 'It's actually quite scary.' She gave him a nervous smile.

He thought about this for a moment and took a sip of beer. 'Kate sounded really nice and as though she really liked you.'

'She must be desperate.'

'Yeah, I think she is, actually,' he laughed. 'But that doesn't mean you're not the right person for her.'

'I feel like this is my last chance.'

'No. It's just a deviation in the road you thought you were on. I'm not saying what happened was good. It wasn't. But it's not the end. You're still young, not even thirty, you've got plenty more opportunities to muck things up.'

'That's inspiring.'

'And you've got plenty more opportunities to make them right again. Same for me. I have a chance to make things right with Achara and Nootsara and that's what I'm going to do. No point dwelling on what I did wrong.'

And there's no point wishing for a man I can't have.

He raised his beer and she followed suit, the bottle necks crossing above the fake flame on the table. 'Here's to your outrageous success in London,' he said.

'I can't believe I'm actually going.'

'You'll do great.'

'I'd better. Or my mother will disown me.'

Leila's smiling face beamed back at Kate from the front seat of the taxi. Even from where Kate stood at the picket fence, it was easy to see just how liberated and excited she felt. Her skin shone as though it had been scrubbed squeaky clean.

Mark called for the boys to come and say goodbye.

The boys thundered down the stairs and out into the weak sunshine. Keats had his school uniform on the top half and his Cheeky Devil pyjamas on the bottom. He hadn't brushed his hair yet and she smoothed it down with her hand. She kissed the crown of his head and held his face in her hands until he squirmed away.

'Be a good boy for Dad,' she said, her throat tight.

He nodded and ran his hand through his hair to mess it up again.

'Will you see Prince Harry?'

She smiled. 'Maybe.'

'Cool.'

She knelt down and held out her arms for James. He sidled into them and leaned against her as she wrapped him into a hug. His hands, still so small, reached up to grab on to her. She breathed in the scent of porridge and squeezed him that little bit tighter, closing her eyes and feeling his imprint on her soul.

'I'll be back before you know it,' she said. 'I'm just a phone call away.'

He nodded and the taxi beeped again.

Reluctantly, she let go and stood. James looked up at her and she was shocked to realise just how much like her he was. 'You're getting so big.'

That made him smile. 'Measure me,' he said. He delighted in seeing the line move up the growth chart on the back of the kitchen door, racing towards his brother's marks.

'Sorry, little man, but we don't have time right now,' she said, the first real quivers of emotion threatening to unstick her.

'We'll do it after Mum goes,' Mark said, putting his hand on James's shoulder. Then he picked up Kate's bags and carried them across the footpath to the taxi's boot. She followed, holding a hand of each of her boys in her own.

With all the bags stowed, there was nothing left to do but hug them goodbye again. Then she stood to face Mark, her nostrils flaring with emotion, a sure sign she was about to burst into tears.

Mark smiled with affection at the tell-tale sign and put his hand behind her neck. 'We knew this would be hard,' he said, with more bravery than she knew he felt. 'We just have to keep the big picture in mind. Far bigger opportunities for the whole family than we ever thought possible.'

She nodded, willing her throat to lock the wave of waterworks firmly below.

'And more importantly, we follow our dreams in this family,' Mark said. 'That's an incredibly important lesson to teach our boys.'

She sniffed and wiped at the tears that had started to fall. 'Absolutely.' She held him close. He bent his head to rest his chin in the crook of her neck.

'Text me when you get there,' he said.

'Look after my little men,' she said, her voice wavering.

'With my life.'

'And text me every single day. About anything. Everything counts. Peanut-paste fights. Lost socks. Anything at all. I don't want to miss a thing.'

'I promise you'll get a daily Fullerton Frat House Report.'

She opened the yellow cab door to get in.

'And Kate,' Mark said, 'I love you.'

She bit her lip and blinked hard, her chest tight. 'I love you too.'

'And Kate?'

'Yes?'

'You're going to be a star.'

7

Kate dragged her luggage out of the black cab and she and Leila stood on the footpath of Kings Road, Chelsea. The cab pulled away, leaving them to lean on their suitcases and gaze at the shop in front of them.

This was it. This was the address.

'It's gorgeous,' Kate squealed. 'I knew it. Simone was a genius. This place is perfect.'

To the left was a fashion store, with its tall glass windows displaying a range of mini dresses, and to the right was a glass and black-walled beauty salon. The Chelsea Classic Cinema sat at the end of the block. The position was perfectly chosen to attract just the sort of customers they wanted—wealthy, concerned for their health and harmony, and nostalgic.

It was only eight o'clock in the morning. Looking up and down the street, most of the shops were still shut but they watched one or two shopkeepers emerge to place signs on the footpath.

They turned back to the shop in front of them.

'Do you have a key?' Leila said.

'No, we have to pick it up from the agent.' Kate grinned. 'I just couldn't wait to see it.' She stepped carefully towards the big darkened window. There was a silver logo of a teapot and teacup embossed onto the glass. It was sweet. Still, it was odd Simone hadn't used The Tea Chest's original logo. She must have decided to change it for the English market for some reason.

Kate held her hands on either side of her face and pressed her nose to the glass. Leila did the same beside her and together they breathed steam marks onto the pane. It was dark inside, but they could make out high-backed wooden booths and round filigree tables and chairs. The floor was tiled in an ornate rosebud pattern.

Roses—her favourite.

She stepped back from the glass to take it all in. Rectangular flower boxes lined the windows. Purple, pink and white blooms tumbled out, waving in the breeze.

'I can't believe how much work's been done already,' she said. 'It looks so real, so official and so complete. A bit too much like a tearoom, rather than a shop. I thought there was still heaps of work to do, but we could open tomorrow.'

Leila jigged up and down with excitement. 'Maybe we can. Maybe it'll be easy.'

They grabbed each other at the elbows and skipped on the spot with joy.

Just then, the door of the store jangled open. Both Leila and Kate turned to face a thin woman, her grey hair in a bun, wearing a long woollen skirt and white cashmere twin set with pearls.

'Can I help you?' she said, eyeing their luggage and jeans.

'Who are you?' Kate said, with more accusation in her voice than she'd intended.

The woman peered at her with a raised brow. 'The back-packer hostel is a few miles that way,' she said, pointing down the road.

'Are you the caretaker or something?'

'My name is Lady Heavensfield and this is my establishment.' She pointed above her head to a tasteful sign announcing Heavensfield House. 'We will open in another hour if you care to come back then.' She proceeded to back away and pull the door shut.

'Wait,' Leila said, grabbing the doorframe. 'Let's start again. This is Kate Fullerton and I'm Leila Morton. We've come to arrange the opening of The Tea Chest. Kate's the owner.'

'What has this to do with me?'

Kate was indignant now. 'This is my store.'

'It most certainly is not.'

'It most certainly is too. I have the paperwork here.' Kate rifled through her handbag. She extracted her passport, purse, boarding pass, comb, an old packet of Gummy Bears and tissues before dragging out the battered lease agreement. She turned to the page that listed the shop's address and thrust it at Lady Heavensfield.

'See?'

Lady Heavensfield cast a reluctant eye over the page. 'I think you'll find that number is a six, not a five, and your *tea shop* is over there.'

Kate and Leila spun their heads to gaze across the road to where Lady Heavensfield's knobbly finger pointed and saw a boarded-up shop front with graffiti, a broken window above the paint-peeled door.

'If you'll excuse me.' Lady Heavensfield pulled the door shut behind her, leaving Kate and Leila alone on the footpath to consider the decaying metal over the window frame of their new shop, orange flakes of rust falling to the ground before their eyes.

The lettings agent resided in a tiny one-room office at the top of a long stairwell in a converted warehouse in West London. He wore red braces and dabbed at his forehead with a handkerchief in his overly warm room.

Kate and Leila were breathing hard when they reached the top of the building, not only because of the many flights of stairs but because they were still dragging their luggage. Mr Clive Evans stroked his braces.

'Good flight?' he said, edging back behind his stainless-steel desk. A dinosaur computer whirred uncomfortably on the edge, its lights reflecting in the shiny steel.

Apparently, the rich people who owned the shop in Kings Road liked to save their money when it came to agent fees.

'What's happened to the tea shop?' Kate demanded, pressing her hand to her flushed face. 'It's a wreck. A disaster. Where are the contractors?'

'I'm afraid I have no idea,' he said. 'Simone signed the lease with an agreement to accept the shop as it was—subject to a building inspection, of course, which it must have passed because she went ahead.' He adopted a meaningful expression. 'The rent was reduced on account of its need of repair.'

'Repair? It looks like it should be condemned. And the rent we're paying for that shop could feed a third world nation.'

'It's Kings Road,' Clive said, his neck wobbling like a turkey's. 'What do you expect?'

Kate flopped down in an overstuffed faux-leather armchair. She was woozy. She wasn't sure what day it was, not really, not if she was thinking Australian time, and she hadn't slept for more than an hour or so during the long flight. Judy was right. Mark's first instinct had been right. It was a disaster.

Leila gave her a sympathetic grimace then turned to Clive. 'Mr Evans, do you by any chance know who Simone contracted to do the refurbishments on the tea shop?'

'Hmm.' He looked off into the distance and intertwined his fingers on top of his belly. 'Now, she may have mentioned it. I'll have to think.'

'Please try to remember,' Leila prompted, smiling. 'It would mean a great deal. We're a little lost, you see, with Simone's unexpected passing.' She placed emotional gravity on the phrase.

'Yes, quite,' he said. 'I am sorry for your loss, by the way.' He looked at Kate.

'Thank you.'

Leila waited a beat and then pressed on. 'Would she have left you any paperwork, or would the contractors themselves not have come to you for a key?'

He shook his head. 'No, can't say they did.' He flicked through some piles of paper on his desk. 'Never turned up for the key.'

Kate groaned. They'd never find another contractor at this late notice.

'Would there be an email?' Leila said.

Clive stopped and looked at the ceiling. 'An email. Now that's a possibility.' He turned to face his groaning computer and tapped single-fingered at the keyboard. Leila and Kate waited in silence, exchanging looks.

For goodness' sake, one of my boys could do it faster.

Eventually, he spoke.

'Ah, now, there is an email from Simone.' He looked up briefly to smile at them.

Kate leaned forward in the armchair and Leila rested her hands on the desktop, craning to see the screen.

'What does it say?' Leila asked.

Clive read in silence, tapping the arrow on the keyboard to scroll down the page.

'Golly, look at the time,' he said suddenly. 'I've a meeting to get to. I'll tell you what, I'll print out this email for you and you can take it with you.'

'Fine,' Kate said. 'And we'd like the keys while you're at it.' She shocked herself with the forcefulness of her voice. Within seconds she'd swung from feeling like she was twenty feet under and a complete failure, to feeling huge and bossy and wanting this man to do exactly as she asked.

Clive's printer whirred and he fished through a huge filing cabinet for a set of keys.

'Here you are,' he said, handing over a normal small silver door key with a standard plastic key ring. 'And here's your email.'

Kate took them both and shoved them into her handbag. 'Thank you.' She made moves to leave, but Leila put a hand on her arm.

'Just one other thing,' Leila said. 'In respect to our circumstances, we're wondering if there might be a clause in the contract allowing for compassionate grounds for breaking the lease without penalty.' She smiled sweetly at Clive.

Kate was startled. She hadn't even considered that. In the wake of Simone's passing and all the pressure Judy had put on her to dissolve the company, and Mark's reluctance for her to go ahead with the business, she hadn't even thought there might be an escape clause in the contract. Her emotions rapidly ran from being grateful and excited there might be a way out of this, to irritated and betrayed Leila could suggest such a thing. Even

Leila. Was there no one who thought she could do this? Then her anger dissolved and she acknowledged the enormity of the situation of a five-year lease with a huge price tag and disappearing contractors leaving them even further behind. She turned her eyes to Clive hopefully.

He shook his head. 'I'm sorry.'

Kate deflated.

'I'm no lawyer,' Leila said, still smiling, 'but surely the lessor has some power to grant an exit without penalty. That just seems like common sense to me.'

Clive shuffled. 'Only the owner could grant such an exemption.'

'Could you ask them?' Kate said, sliding down an imaginary rabbit hole.

Clive began packing up the papers on his desk and then reached for his coat, slipping it on over his broad shoulders. 'Certainly. I'll phone you as soon as I get a response.' He picked up a battered brown briefcase. 'It's been a pleasure to meet you but you'll have to excuse me, I have an appointment to make.'

He walked to the door and opened it, smiling at them with the same false warmth Leila had been using on him.

Kate and Leila looked at each other and then popped up the handles on their suitcases to wheel them to the door.

'Good day,' Clive said as they exited to the landing. Then, realising they all had to go down the stairs together, he pushed past them with a forced chuckle and scooted ahead. Kate and Leila followed slowly, their luggage thumping down each step behind them.

For the third time that day, they hopped into a black cab and directed the driver to take them to their hotel. They dropped their bags with relief inside the calming earth tones of the twin room, flicked on the television, raided the minibar for peanuts and crackers, flopped onto a bed each and promptly fell asleep.

When they woke, it was nearing six o'clock in the evening and their ravenous stomachs protested loudly.

'Come on,' Leila encouraged, pulling Kate to her feet. 'What we need is some stodge. A really traditional English pub meal with a pint or two of beer.'

'Beer?' Kate grimaced.

'Or lager or vodka. Something to wash down your bangers and mash.'

'Bangers and mash?'

Kate rolled the words around her mouth. At home, Mark normally cooked Asian stir-fry and she cooked soups and vegetarian quiches and pies. They tried to eat healthily and set a good example for the boys. (Well, *she* did. Mark's recent chocolate confession was something else.) They would never eat bangers and mash. But suddenly, tired and hungry and in a different country, it seemed like the most natural thing in the world. More than that, it actually sounded healing, as though it would soothe her depleted soul.

ᐟᐟ

Elizabeth and her sister found themselves in The Victoria, not far from Hyde Park Gardens.

'We *have* to go there,' Victoria had said. 'You've been away forever. I wasn't even legal drinking age last time you were here. The pub's named after me. And that's, you know, fate or something.'

Elizabeth had spent the better part of two weeks hiding in the unicorn room, living in her pyjamas, sleeping most of the day and crying most of the night. Occasionally she watched crime shows in silence with her father. She didn't allow herself to think of anything, feel anything. The world might as well have stopped while she hovered in a bubble of nothing.

Finally, Bill had come and sat on the edge of her bed and said, 'Well done, kitten.'

'What for?' she said.

'You didn't die. Good job. Now it's time to start again.'

So she'd had a long soak in the peach-coloured bathtub. She shampooed her hair and put a colour rinse through it that Victoria had picked up for her. Shaved her legs. Put on a face peel. Allowed her sister to do her nails with a simple French polish.

The place was packed wall to wall with after-work drinkers and the jovial ambience was familiar and homey. Elizabeth suddenly realised how much she'd missed the tradition and architecture of English pubs.

She wanted to get drunk. Fast. She fished in her purse for pounds. It was so strange to be searching for English pounds rather than Australian dollars. Her insides swirled, as if they'd been affected by the magnetic pull of the earth and were spinning the opposite way, just like water down a drain in the northern hemisphere.

'Are you alright?' Victoria said. 'Looked like you were about to keel over and you haven't even started yet.'

'Mind my purse. I'll go for drinks,' Elizabeth shouted above the din.

She was three-deep from the bar and being jostled from behind. She smiled amicably as a man who'd just left the bar with three pints slopped a little on her boots.

'Sorry,' he said, winking.

'No worries,' she replied—a phrase she'd picked up since being in Australia.

She took a moment to bask under his open stare and assessment of her body. She was wearing a black velvet skirt that came to just above her knees, revealing black tights and the latest knee-high boots with silver buckles. Well, they were fashionable in Australia at any rate. Her outfit was probably a season behind here in Europe. A figure-hugging wrap top made the most of her silhouette.

She was confident she looked good, but made a mental note to hit the shops and update her wardrobe to European standards, courtesy of John's credit card. Then realised, with deep shock, that she'd have to go and find another job in London. She gazed at the harassed bar staff, wondering if she could get a job here. She'd have to start all over again.

Or would she? Didn't the wronged woman in these situations get a good divorce settlement?

Divorce. *Divorce?* The word spun her further off balance.

She stepped forward in the queue, inching her way to the bar. She squeezed in next to a pretty young woman with a gold and diamante 'L' around her neck. Elizabeth smiled as their bodies were pressed together in the heaving crowd and rolled her eyes good-naturedly.

'Sorry,' she said.

The woman smiled back. 'No worries.'

'You Australian?'

The woman nodded. 'From Brisbane.'

'Me too. What part?'

'New Farm.'

'Oh.' A small shudder snaked its way up Elizabeth's spine as she remembered the humiliation of the news story about her on the bridge.

'You?' The woman moved closer to be heard above the noise.

'Rosalie.'

'Huh.'

'What?' Elizabeth asked, her heart trotting.

'It's just that you look familiar.' She squinted at her, clearly trying to remember where she'd seen her.

Elizabeth forced a laugh. 'People say that all the time. I must just have one of those faces.'

They reached the bar and Elizabeth leaned against the damp edge of the polished wood.

'I'm Leila,' the woman said.

'Elizabeth.' She held out her hand and they shook. 'Are you here alone?'

'No. My boss is over there.' Leila turned and pointed to Kate, who was craning her neck around the pub looking for a seat.

'We were hoping for a feed but it doesn't look like we'll get a table,' Leila said.

'We've got a table,' Elizabeth said. 'You're welcome to join us.'

'Really? Great.'

They sorted their drinks, collected Kate, and navigated their way back to the table where Victoria was busily tapping the screen on her phone. She looked up at their new friends and waved. 'Hiya.'

Elizabeth made the introductions and got everyone seated, then they ordered food, Kate choosing bangers and mash and Leila a pie with extra chips to share.

'Bugger the food,' Victoria said. 'Bring on the drinks.'

Victoria set the rules for the night. Each round of drinks was to be a surprise, all four drinks were to be the same, and they had to drink whatever was put in front of them. Victoria kicked off the first round and brought back four pints of Kilkenny.

'You're mad,' Elizabeth said. 'That stuff will knock us over for the night. We won't even make it to the next round.'

But maybe this was the perfect way to finally forget that she'd lost everything, including her beautiful modern home in a warm, sunny city she'd grown to love, and now lived in a damp, musty, aged terrace house, in her childhood bedroom with her father's unicorns.

Yes, on second thought, a pint of Kilkenny was exactly what she needed to send her past packing.

8

Kate boiled the little kettle in the hotel kitchenette and took deep breaths. What had got into her? Here she was, halfway around the world, trying to lead a company into a new phase of growth, and instead of behaving like a leader, she'd played follow-the-leader and downed drink after drink.

The kettle clicked off and she poured the water over a diffuser of Glowing Skin tea, one of the teas from her Rejuvenate line. It was full of calendula flowers, mostly, and was a mild detoxifier.

Across the room, Leila stretched across the starched sheets and groaned and rubbed her eyes. 'What time is it?'

'Eight fifteen. You want some tea?'

'Mmm. Thanks.'

Leila sat up in bed nursing her mug while Kate sat in the chair at the polished executive desk.

'Is it just me, or did we sing a bad version of ABBA's "I Have a Dream"? Or was that, by any chance, a dream?'

'Sadly, no. You also led a chorus of "Gimme! Gimme! Gimme! (A Man After Midnight)" and had several solid offers of a ride home.'

Leila groaned again. Then giggled. 'I haven't had a night like that in a *long* time.'

'I've never had a night like that,' Kate said.

'Really? Not even when you were young-*er*?'

Kate shook her head. 'I was never really into alcohol. Never liked the way it made me feel. Now I know why. I won't be doing that again. My kind of night out was going to the beach with Mark to walk in the moonlight, listening to the waves. I really must call him,' she said suddenly. 'He'll be wondering what's happened to me.'

Elizabeth had ignored her mother's early knock on the door calling her to breakfast and shoved her head further under the pillow. But now the thirst was so bad she couldn't ignore it any longer. She sat up on the side of the bed and waited for her head to stop throbbing before she risked standing. The smell of bacon still wafted under the door, which had a huge unicorn poster taped to it.

She reached out to steady herself on the bedside table, knocked over a white and gold porcelain unicorn, breaking it in two, and just managed to reach the metal bin under the desk. The retching roused her mother's batlike hearing.

'Elizabeth,' she said, knocking loudly on the door. The knob turned and she entered, her hair in rollers. She screamed when she saw Elizabeth hunched over the bin.

'It's alright,' Elizabeth managed. 'I'm just a bit hung-over, that's all.'

But her mother rushed past her to the night table where the unicorn lay in two. 'This was your father's favourite piece,' she said. 'He'll be heartbroken.'

She carried the pieces in her hand as though they were that of an injured animal, and disappeared out the door again.

'Tsk, tsk,' Victoria said, now standing in the doorway and chomping on some toast. 'You're going to have to toughen up, old girl. Last night was just the beginning. I'm not near finished with you.'

Elizabeth stared at Victoria and flashes of the night reeled by. Dancing on a chair because there was nowhere else to go. Singing 'I've Never Been to Me'. And—oh no—flirting with the man from the bar who had slopped beer on her boots. She shuddered.

'Come on,' Victoria said. 'I've made coffee.'

Leila chomped down on her ham and cheese croissant and flicked through last night's *Evening Standard*. Muggings, global warming, British PM losing face with the public, Harry up to no good again. Much like reading the paper at home, really.

She heard Kate swipe the card in the door and push it open.

'How's Mark?' she asked.

Kate shrugged. 'I decided just to text instead.'

'Oh.' She watched Kate's face. There was a deep line on her forehead from frowning and she looked pale. And not just hungover pale, but worried pale. 'Is everything okay?'

'It's just that I don't really know what to tell him,' she said. 'I mean, we haven't achieved anything yet.'

She was right. 'Sorry if I led you astray last night,' Leila said. 'I think it was the shock of it all. New country, new city, new job, the sight of the shop.'

'No, it's okay. We needed a chance to catch our breath and find our feet.'

'We found our dancing feet at any rate.'

Kate held her hands out, palms upwards. 'What am I going to say to Mark? The tea shop is a rat-infested hovel, we've no idea where the contractors are, and he was right in the first place: I'm no good at this.'

To fill the hours on the flight, Leila had completed a risk assessment for The Tea Chest's success. She'd come up with three key areas of concern: the alarmingly short timeframe of six weeks to get a whole shop up and running; the tight financial situation, compounded each day by the rent they were paying on the empty shop; and the lack of following and brand-name recognition to get the money rolling in quickly once the shop did open. She had ideas for how to manage those three areas.

But now she saw clearly that there was one more area of risk she hadn't considered: Kate. She was nervous and lacked confidence in herself. She was clearly a wonderful artist but was intimidated by the size of this task.

'Come on,' she said, jumping up and clapping her hands to motivate Kate. 'Let me pull myself together and we'll get on to it. Then you'll have something to report to Mark and the delightful Judy.'

Forty-four years earlier

Judy strode down the mahogany hallway of Brisbane Anglican Ladies' College, smoothing her messy hair and hastily thrown-on uniform. She blinked through sleepy eyes and the dim night lighting as she passed the door to each dorm room. She'd only been asleep for a few hours when the deputy headmistress woke her, summoning her to Headmistress Kenny's office.

Judy's Latin test—not her strongest subject—was tomorrow. History and bookkeeping were her strengths and she was on track to win the annual prize for them again this year. Not so for Latin.

She paused outside the heavy wooden door of the head-mistress's office and took a breath to quieten the racing of her heart. Whatever Simone had done now was obviously serious enough to warrant Judy's removal from her bed in the middle of the night.

She rapped on the door.

'Enter,' the headmistress called.

It was a wood-panelled room, lined floor to ceiling on three sides with bookcases bulging with books. The fourth side of the room displayed a white and green flag—the school colours—bearing their motto.

Ferreus opus semino prosperitas: hard work breeds success.

There were bronze rowing trophies. And there were framed black-and-white photographs of past pupils who'd become successful, including one who was now the headmistress of her own college, a scientist and an opera singer.

'Take a seat, Miss Knight,' Headmistress Kenny said, pointing to the leather-backed chair across from her neat desk. Judy sat stiffly, back straight, knees together and hands clasped at her thighs. To her left sat her stepsister, slumped, rumpled, her cinnamon hair hanging loose, her eyes directed to the ceiling and her lips pursed. Judy shot her a glare but Simone's eyes remained focused elsewhere.

'Let me get straight to the point,' the headmistress said, leaning back in her chair and looking down her nose at Judy in order to see over the thick bifocal lenses.

'Tonight, your stepsister was caught drinking liquor in the gardens, along with Mary Montgomery, from a bottle they'd stolen from the private quarters of one of our teachers.' Headmistress Kenny squirmed with irritation.

Judy's chest tightened.

Simone snickered. But at the headmistress's sudden glower, her head dropped down, teeth set on her bottom lip to control her laughter.

Judy fixed her eyes on the headmistress.

'I'm sure I don't need to tell you that, as the college captain, your behaviour, and the behaviour of your relatives, is on display at all times and is judged accordingly.'

The headmistress tightened the belt of her thick grey wool cardigan against the winter chill that seeped through the towering glass windows at her back.

'Normally, in a situation as serious as this, we would call in the parents. But as your mother and stepfather are currently in Mount Isa, and—' here she paused, tilted her head and considered the pale-faced captain in front of her '—and as your parents are generous benefactors of this college, the last thing we want to do is to suggest to them that we are in any way ungrateful.'

Judy's fingers reached for the captain's badge on the collar of her uniform and twisted it back and forth.

The headmistress's eyes flicked to the movement and Judy pulled herself up again, returning her hands to her thighs.

'This incident is the third of its type this semester,' she said. She indicated a piece of paper on the desk in front of her on which notes were jotted in shorthand. Judy couldn't read them from where she sat, but she was sure they were about Simone.

Beside her, Simone had begun to tap her foot.

It was all Judy could do to restrain herself from reaching over and pinching her stepsister's skinny arm. Didn't she realise how serious this was? Didn't she care about Judy at all? Everything Simone did in this school affected Judy. Why couldn't she control herself? She was such an ungrateful wretch.

'We would prefer to keep this incident quiet,' the headmistress went on. 'Once a faculty member is involved it can become quite a sensitive issue. Do you understand?'

'Yes.'

'Good.'

Headmistress Kenny rose, towering over Judy and casting a shadow across both her and Simone.

'So I am releasing Simone into your care, Miss Knight. Do you understand? We are washing our hands of her for the remainder of this year and we won't be accepting her back after she's finished Junior. Until then, we expect to see behaviour worthy of her sister's highly regarded position in this school. And we're certain you will ensure it is so, or risk losing that position.'

Judy longed to protest. Simone wasn't even related to her, not really. It was only by bad fortune that Judy was now stuck with her. It simply wasn't fair to place this sort of responsibility on her when she was working so hard to finish Senior and maintain her duties as college captain and captain of the rowing team. It wasn't her fault her mother had sent them both to this place while she travelled around to be with Dennis, a man Judy didn't even like, Simone hated, and even her mother seemed barely able to tolerate.

At least that was one thing they had in common. Simone had dubbed him Desperate Dennis and it did give Judy a small boost every time she saw him having to look up to her mother's face as she glided effortlessly around him. Every now and then,

Simone would catch Judy's eye and snicker and Judy would smile inwardly, knowing she wasn't alone.

She could complain to her mother, but she knew it wouldn't get her anywhere. Elaine was busy with the Country Women's Association in Mount Isa and her tennis club in Brisbane and already thought Judy should have left school after Junior. What was the point in a Senior education when she would only marry and have children? Judy had had to work hard to convince her mother to let her stay on. The last thing she needed was to give her an excuse to pull Judy out of school when she was this close to finishing.

So she remained silent and simply nodded her understanding. Like it or not, she was stuck with Simone and her stepsister was her responsibility now.

Fullerton Frat House report: Beds made. Green(ish) vegetables consumed. Fingernails clean. Hair brushed. All is well. xx

'Oh. My. God.' Kate punctuated each word with increasingly panicked facial expressions.

Leila's heart skipped a beat but she managed to control her gasp of horror. The shop was worse, much worse, than either of them had anticipated.

'It's not that bad,' Leila lied. 'Look. There're marvellous red bricks behind that . . . that . . . whatever that is.' She reached a hand to snap away a section of tattered wall covering. 'What *is* that?'

'I don't know,' Kate said, wheezing through the dust. 'I don't even have any building language to describe this. I've no idea what to even call this mess.'

Leila wiped her hands. 'Some sort of plaster, I imagine.' She picked her way over piles of dirt and rubble and skipped out of the way of a drip from the ceiling. She looked up. 'And look, there's wonderful big beams up there.' She didn't know what sort of wood it was but it looked solid, old and sturdy. 'That's something.' She trailed off, noting the large spreading of damp that had pooled over a smoke-damaged section.

'It smells like there's been a fire in here,' Kate said. She'd released her hands from her face and was trying to inspect the shop, ducking out of the way of cords and electrical wires dangling from above. Light filtered in from the corner of a dirty window.

There were no obvious signs of any form of tradesman having been in the place. No ladders or scaffolding, no wheelbarrows or hammers, no bags of cement or stacks of tiles. Kate's lip trembled and her eyes shone.

Leila was used to working under pressure. She was used to four-hundred-page tenders—completely untouched by an editor—landing on her desk with a day to go before printing. She was used to wading through absolute crap and finding the solid structure underneath in order to work with it, to straighten, tidy, delete, add impressive flourishes, use the right words to call out to an investor, and make it shine.

This was no different.

She felt the thrill of the challenge charge through her veins. She was an editor and a bloody good one at that. No document had ever got the better of her, no matter how bad.

She pulled Kate outside to the street.

'Look,' she said. 'The placement couldn't be better.'

The shop was cradled between Elegance fine china on the right and Roulette imported gourmet produce on the left.

Spinning around to the other side of the street, they could see Lady Heavensfield's tearoom opposite their own shop. Indulge beauty salon sat to her right. On the other side of Heavensfield House was Kylie's of London, selling high-end fashion. And Bartlett's handmade chocolates, imported coffee and fine teas was two doors down.

'This is all brilliant,' Leila affirmed. 'There's nothing better than being placed with similar stores that attract a similar clientele.'

Kate nodded, agreeing, though doubt still flickered in her eyes.

Leila took her back inside and walked around the store. 'But it's wonderful really,' she said kindly, trying to coax Kate into trusting her. She gestured to the overhead beams, the brickwork behind the walls, and the uneven but charming stone floor beneath their feet.

'The structure is sound,' she said. 'Really solid. All we need to do is to release its beauty.'

'You think?'

'Absolutely. Kate, you're a *designer*. You see beauty and opportunity in the world where there wasn't any before. You take ideas and make them into reality. You've done it for years. This is the same, just a bit different.'

'I appreciate your enthusiasm.'

'We can do this, Kate. I know it. Underneath all this chaos is your new creation just waiting to be released. We need to give it wings. That's all. You can't turn away from her now; she's ready to be born.'

'She?'

Leila shrugged and placed her hand to the wall. '*She* just *feels* right.' She was speaking Kate's language. Kate was intuitive and sensitive and believed in the life-force energy of the world. If she could just use the right words to tap into that, to show Kate that she was in sync with her vision, she might be able to convince her they could make a go of this. And Leila needed her to make a go of this.

Kate took a long, controlled breath and closed her eyes. When she opened them, her face had changed. There was a spark in her eye that had replaced the doubt.

'It's the new era,' Kate said quietly. 'It's what Simone said to me when she offered me a job. She said we'd entered a new era and she needed me to lead the way.'

Now *that* was the kind of language Leila liked to hear.

'I think you're right,' Kate said. 'This shop does have feminine energy.' Now Kate was moving around the space, peeling off paint flakes and rubbing them between her fingers. 'And she's been neglected for far too long.'

Leila smiled. 'Shall we rescue her then? Get her to the day spa for some pampering? Help her remember who she is?'

Kate held her hands out to the side and spun slowly in a circle, as though delighting in winter sunshine or summer rain. 'Absolutely.'

They sat down to tea made in a fine china pot, detailed with hand-painted roses and gold-leaf trimming, and a three-tiered cake stand of goodies. Leila pulled her notebook and her favourite pen from her leather satchel.

'I love this part,' she said. She wobbled the pen in between her index and middle finger, balancing its weight. She revelled in fresh stationery. And as nutty as it sounded, only her favourite pen could really pull the good ideas from her mind.

Kate chomped down on tiny sandwiches, moaning with joy. 'Real high tea.'

Leila murmured in agreement. 'You know, I was all prepared to hate London, but there is something so utterly charming about a tearoom with a real fireplace and real silver teaspoons with pictures of the royal family on them.'

'The tea tastes better too,' Kate said. 'English breakfast tea really does belong in England.'

'Right, let's get this sorted. We'll start with a list of things to be done.'

Just then, Kate's phone chirped to life. She hastily replaced her cup on its saucer and answered.

'Oh, Mr Evans, thanks so much for . . .' Kate's face fell and she nodded silently. 'Yes, I understand. Thanks so much for calling.'

She returned the phone to her bag and took a deep breath. 'Well, that was Clive, confirming there would be no compassionate release other than the full payment of the five-year term.'

Leila sucked in air between her teeth. 'Well, that's that then, isn't it?'

Kate took a moment to think about it. 'Yes, I guess it is. Onwards and upwards. We can't turn back now.'

'Congratulations,' Leila said. 'You just became the proud owner of a shop.'

'Yes, I suppose you're right. First things first—we have to find the contractors.'

'The email,' Leila mumbled, pushing the last of a butterfly cake into her mouth and wiping at the crumbs on her lips. 'We completely forgot about it.'

Kate dived back into her handbag to dig it out.

She spread it out in front of her while Leila reached for a rose-water cupcake with tiny pink and white sugar roses on top.

Dear Mr Evans,

RE: Kings Road Lease

Thank you for the contract for the shop space on Kings Road as discussed. You will find a scanned copy of the signed lease attached to this email and the original copy is in the mail.

Please note that I have contracted the Holy Trinity to begin work on the shop immediately.

Kind regards,

Simone Taylor

'Who's the Holy Trinity?' Leila asked through a mouthful of cake. She pushed some crumbs into her mouth with her thumb. 'Are they religious types? Was Simone religious?'

Kate shook her head. 'No. She had a great distaste for religion after boarding school.'

'Well then . . .' Leila dusted her palms together and drained the last of her tea. 'Let's go.'

'Where?'

'To find the Holy Trinity.'

A quick scan through the White Pages UK revealed many Holy Trinity businesses—primary schools, churches, parishes and hospitals. And one building contractor business.

Leila punched the numbers into the phone inside the ageing red phone box and held the mouthpiece away from her for fear of inhaling germs. She deliberately avoided looking at the paper cup on the floor filled with something suspiciously like urine in colour, or the blobs of green and white chewing gum on the glass next to her shoulder. Kate stood outside, waiting.

'Holy Trinity, how may I serve you?'

It was an Indian accent.

'Is this the number for the Holy Trinity building contractors?'

'How may I serve you?' the man repeated.

'I want to speak to the person in charge of the contracting job for The Tea Shop on Kings Road.'

There was a startled squawk, a short pause, and then the voice was back. 'I'm sorry but we cannot help you. Have a nice day.'

The phone clicked off.

'What happened?' Kate said, wedging open the door with her shoulder.

'They hung up.'

'What? Why? Try again.'

Leila dialled the number again but this time it went to an answering service. She hung up without leaving a message.

She looked again at the listing in the White Pages. 'No address listed. Just the mobile number.'

She tried to call once more but this time the phone rang out without even going to a message service.

'Crap.' Kate's jaw muscles clenched and unclenched as she took deep breaths.

Leila exited the grimy phone box. 'Let's go back to the hotel and try to find them online. Then let's get a UK sim card for our mobiles asap so I never have to set foot inside a phone box again.'

9

One of the good things about being back in London was the shopping. It was almost seven o'clock and Elizabeth and her sister were still at it. Elizabeth swung her five bags of loot from the shops in Covent Garden, Regent Street and Oxford Street and wished she had a driver to hand them over to while she kept going.

'While you're splashing cash, how about shouting me a new wardrobe too,' Victoria said, walking and texting at the same time.

Elizabeth was just about to protest, thinking of the rates bill that was coming next month, the plumber's bill that still hadn't been paid, and the protein powder she'd promised to order John. But then she realised none of it mattered because none of it existed in her life anymore. It was John's problem now.

And this credit card wouldn't last forever either. So she might as well get what she could. After all, didn't she deserve it after what he'd put her through?

'Sure.'

Victoria's thumb paused and she looked up at Elizabeth with wide eyes. They were so filled with excitement that Elizabeth had a flashback to her sister's face on Christmas Day when she was small and Elizabeth a teenager.

She was suddenly deeply grateful Victoria had organised Annie to rescue her, brush her hair and hold her hand as she wept her way through the airport. Grateful Victoria had met her at Heathrow. Grateful that she didn't ask a lot of questions and had just got on with quietly adding to her life with gifts of hair dye and coffee. It was just possible that her annoying little sister wasn't quite as annoying as she used to be.

She put an arm around Victoria's shoulders, still swinging a large John Lewis bag containing her new strappy dress for the English summer, and pulled her sister close.

'You deserve it,' she said, 'as thanks for organising to get me out of Brisbane. You've actually been helpful and even a bit of fun.'

They'd just made their way into Crabtree & Evelyn, looking for perfume, when Victoria's phone rocked out a phrase of a Lady Gaga song to signal a text message.

'It's from those two larks the other night,' she said.

'Which two larks?' Elizabeth said, her insides seizing as she immediately thought of her behaviour with the beer man.

'You know. The two Aussies. Leila and Kate.'

Elizabeth frowned. She couldn't remember them exchanging phone numbers. But then there were quite a few blank moments from that night. Sadly, giving the beer man coy smiles wasn't one of them. Nor was her divulgence of the sordid details of the many sexual positions she'd tried in her efforts to conceive.

'They want to catch up tomorrow for coffee.' Victoria began tapping out a reply.

'What are you saying?'

'I'm telling them to meet us at Bar Italia at eleven o'clock.'

'And what if I don't want to?' Elizabeth snapped, childish sibling defences kicking in, her new affection for her sister vanishing as fast as it had arrived.

'Tough,' Victoria said. 'Besides, what else are you going to do? Stay home and watch the telly with Mum and Dad?'

Elizabeth quickly racked her brain for something else she could do the next day, just to spite Victoria. But the problem was it would mean she'd be doing it on her own. And Victoria's endless chatter was a fantastic distraction from the thoughts that circled her mind like sharks.

'Fine. But make it midday.'

Bar Italia was a long, narrow shop jammed with people and equally jammed with deli goods, cakes and gelato, strings of garlic hanging from the ceiling and a fusion of smells. The wall mirrors along the length did a good job of giving the impression the room was bigger than it was but the noise, physical closeness and jostling at the counter did not.

The four seated themselves outside on the footpath under the greyness of threatening clouds and a chill wind.

'Thanks so much for coming.' Kate smiled at them. She was wrapped in a huge oyster woollen shawl that should have made her look granny-ish, but teamed with a bright turquoise bracelet and earrings, it just made her look arty. 'It's really nice to see you again.'

Elizabeth sipped a cappuccino with a love heart in the froth. She had to admit she was pleased to be here. In the past few days she'd begun to feel a little homesick for her friends back in Brisbane. Especially Annie. More than once, Annie's lunch-time sushi wisdom had helped Elizabeth to see the light ahead when sadness and desperation had darkened her cubicle at work.

They'd been emailing and texting, but it just wasn't the same. And it was all so humiliating that talking to Annie just seemed to poke at the painful spots. Yet somehow she'd managed to blurt it all out to Kate and Leila. Having it out in the open was both dis-appointing—she didn't want potential new friends to see her as the scorned, broken woman—and a relief she didn't have to keep dodging questions or concerns.

'Leila and I have done some recon,' Kate went on, nodding at Leila.

Elizabeth looked over Leila's chocolate-coloured pantsuit and smoothed-back hair. The 'L' necklace was really quite pretty. It sat on her smooth brown cleavage between the lapels of her jacket and added a feminine touch to the ensemble. Actually, looking a little closer, she could see the marks of a well-tailored suit. It clung to her in all the right places and moved beautifully with her. Leila was clearly a person who lived in these suits and knew how to make the most of them.

'And we've made some decisions. First, we need help and fast. We're on a tight deadline and the tea shop is in much worse shape than we'd like, frankly. We've got issues with the contractors and we need someone with local London knowledge to help us mud-dle through.'

Victoria leaned back in her metal chair and lit a cigarette, watching Kate with mild interest. Elizabeth glared at her.

Kate paused for a moment and looked at Elizabeth and Victoria. 'I'd like to offer you each a job,' she said.

'Really?' Elizabeth was shocked.

'Yes, really. We don't have time to advertise and interview people. We need to start work as soon as possible.'

'Today,' Leila chimed in, tapping a French-polished nail on the side of her cup. Victoria's gaze drifted to the nail and she tilted her head to one side, studying it.

'So I'm just going to call our meeting at the pub the other night an interview and jump straight to hiring you, if you're interested,' Kate finished.

Elizabeth knew The Tea Chest's products well, always having at least one blend in her own tea chest at any given time. She and Annie had often shared a pot of Inspire tea in the afternoon. And she'd been working in sales already—with beauty products, granted, but it was all about feeling good wasn't it? And she needed a new job, thanks to her louse of a husband. It was perfect.

'Yes,' she said, giving Kate a big grin as excitement surged through her. 'Absolutely.'

'Great,' Kate beamed. She turned to face Victoria. 'What do you think, Victoria? You interested?'

Victoria squinted and exhaled a long plume of smoke.

Elizabeth waited, unsure of what her sister would say. As far as she could tell, her sister had successfully avoided any form of work at all for the past two years. Even if she said yes, Elizabeth had no idea if she could actually hold down a job successfully. Maybe she was just too irresponsible.

'I'm interested, but I don't know much about tea,' Victoria said. She sounded vulnerable and Elizabeth wanted to reach and out and squeeze her arm.

'Would you like to learn?'

'Yes.'

'Then that's all you need. We'll teach you as you go.'

Victoria hesitated for a moment before stubbing out her ciga-rette. 'Okay, I'm in.'

'Wonderful. Just no smoking during work hours, okay?'

'No problem.' Victoria sat up straighter in her chair, her eyes fixed on Kate's face as though waiting for an instruction so she could get going straight away.

Kate held out her hand. 'Welcome to The Tea Chest.'

The Hindu man in a bright ochre turban, the Buddhist with red prayer beads around his neck and the Muslim with a knitted white head-covering shrank within the Holy Trinity office when Kate announced who they were.

She and Elizabeth were there alone, having left Leila and Victoria to go and buy industrial-level cleaning products so they could get started on The Tea Chest.

Elizabeth took in the recycled government-looking furniture and grey walls of the one-room office, noting the only colour on the walls was provided by religious images depicting their three denominations.

The Hindu man closed the book on the front counter and held up both hands in surrender.

'Sorry, Madamz, but we cannot help you,' he said, shaking his head.

'But we have a contract,' Kate insisted. 'It was signed with Simone Taylor and the commencement date is long past. We have a shop in urgent need of repair and there's no way we can find another contractor at such short notice.'

Elizabeth could hear the strain in Kate's voice.

The Buddhist fiddled with the prayer beads at his chest. 'So sorry, ma'am. Things change.'

'Can you tell us what exactly has changed?' Elizabeth asked.

The three men turned to each other and spoke in a mixture of English and other languages Elizabeth couldn't identify. There was much gesticulating and fluctuating of tone.

At last they broke away and the Buddhist gave a tiny bow to Kate and Elizabeth before walking calmly out of the office.

The Hindu man straightened his tall and wiry body, resolute. 'No contract,' he said, and passed his hands over each other in a gesture of no more.

Kate turned to Elizabeth, her gaze rigid with controlled panic.

'Can you tell me,' Elizabeth said, intrigued now, 'have you actually been out to the shop? You must have seen it to offer Simone a quote?'

He stiffened and dropped his eyes to the counter, stroking his beard with his thumb and forefinger.

There was a long silence.

Then he nodded once.

Elizabeth looked at Kate and raised an eyebrow. 'And did something happen while you were there?'

There was something rumbling in the back of Elizabeth's mind. Something she'd read in the newspaper not long after arriving in England.

'Like vot?'

Yes. She had it now. It was a news article on the British government's attempt to crack down on illegal immigrant workers.

'Oh, I don't know. Did anyone *say* anything to you?' she prompted.

Kate was looking confused now and the Muslim was pacing back and forth.

Elizabeth waited patiently, her eyes fixed on the Hindu man in a staring contest, which one of them had to win. Her eyes were watering by the time he looked away, prompted by the Muslim's tugs at his shirt.

More words in broken English passed between them and she only caught one or two, but one word seemed to mean something to Kate because she suddenly jerked towards them across the counter, with her hand gripping the metal edge.

'Did you say *Heavensfield*?' she said.

The men returned to vibrant word exchanges and gestures.

'What's Heavensfield?' Elizabeth said.

'Lady Heavensfield. She's the woman who owns the tearoom across the road from us. We met her on the first day.' Here, she blushed. 'We were confused, actually, and thought her place was ours. It's beautiful. But then she came out and sent us packing in no uncertain terms. She clearly didn't like us.'

'Huh. Do you think she might see you as competition?'

Kate shrugged. 'It's possible. She was pretty down on the state of the shop and not helpful in any way.'

Elizabeth smiled. 'I think I might know what's happened.'

e

Leila and Kate now shared a room in Hemberton Road, Clapham, boarding with Elizabeth and her family. It was one of the first tasks Kate had given Elizabeth—to help Kate and Leila find some accommodation for the next three months or so.

'Done,' Elizabeth had said immediately. 'Mum and Dad were thinking of renting out one of their rooms to make a few pounds. It's on the ground floor. It's nothing special, but it would be cheap and comfy and help keep your costs down. If you can stand my parents, that is.'

Kate had waved her hand casually. 'We'll be working so hard we'll hardly ever be there.'

So they'd moved in. The room had beige walls and heavy brocade duvets. It was once the sewing room and was located behind the television room, where Bill's crime shows played at all hours.

It was over scrambled eggs at the kitchen table one morning that Leila first mentioned Lucas.

'Lucas pours honey on his eggs. Don't you think that's weird?'

Kate had frowned, chewing. 'Lucas? The same Lucas I spoke to after your interview?'

Leila's hand had paused with the fork in the air. 'Ah, yes.'

'So you two know each other well then?'

Leila relaxed her shoulders. 'We're mates, yes.'

'Oh.'

'Is something wrong?'

'No. I guess not.' And Kate continued to eat her eggs in silence.

10

*Fullerton Frat House report: Minor incident with boys on a choco-
late bender. Coaxed them out of gutter with Hair of the Hotdog. All
is still well. I promise. xx*

Kate studied Leila's hand-drawn chart of a risk assessment for
The Tea Chest, including the schedule, budget and marketing.

'Growing a business organically can take many years of
slow development,' Leila said, her eyes bright. She and Kate
were in their pyjamas, sitting on their beds in their room at the
Plimsworths' place.

'Competition will surface all around us and we need to be
ahead of the pack so we're not swallowed whole by businesses that
have more capital behind them. It's sad, but it won't matter how
wonderful The Tea Chest is, how much you love it and believe
in it—the business models that have the capital will outstrip us.'

Leila's words sounded familiar, a lot like Judy's criticism of Kate's zodiac tea all those years before. It didn't matter how much she felt it was right. Good business relied on more than that. It relied on figures, numbers, statistics and projections.

All the things Kate had tried to avoid. Until now.

This was what she had fought for the right to do. This was what she'd risked her finances and her family life for. To prove that she could step up and be more than just a designer and could take this business to a new level; give herself the chance to do *more*.

'The window of opportunity is small,' Leila said, opening a pot of night cream and rubbing it into her face and décolletage. 'Both Richard Branson and Sam Walton advocated that whenever there was a cash flow crisis the answer was not to contract but to expand. We need to act in a timely fashion and take advantage of our market position. Strike while the teapot is hot,' she finished.

'So what do you propose?'

'Capital. Investors. Big marketing campaign—television, radio, magazines, bus shelters. Expensive and thorough market research. Bling. Red carpets.'

Although the sound of this made Kate squirm, she also knew she had to embrace bold ideas. She was a leader now.

'Where would we get money like that?' she said, pointing to the red square marked *Budget* on Leila's chart. 'We'd never get another loan. Venture capitalists? Is that what they're called?'

Leila shook her head. 'From what I know, venture capitalists wouldn't like us. We're too small and the wrong type of industry for a start. They normally go for high-tech industries, like IT and biotechnology. We want an angel investor. I've done some research and found a website where we can post a proposal.'

Kate thought it was only polite to keep her co-owner informed of such a big financial decision, given that The Tea Chest would likely have sunk years ago if Judy hadn't been there to cover Simone's transgressions. Whether she liked it or not, Kate wouldn't be the owner of this company today if it hadn't been for Judy's input.

But Judy laughed heartily at the idea of an angel investor when Kate told her.

'An *angel* investor? Oh, Kate. Maybe you can find a fairy god-mother while you're at it.'

Kate had a moment of excitement, just as she had when Judy asked if the zodiac tea would mean they'd be reading tea leaves. Another avenue sprang to mind. The fairy godmother idea wasn't as silly as it sounded. She'd read about a fairy godmother in Tasmania who helped people achieve their dreams and made life better. Maybe they *could* approach her.

'Good luck with that, Kate,' Judy continued, her voice drip-ping with sarcasm. 'Only divine intervention can save you now.'

Fullerton Frat House report: Have decided to teach Keats how to wash clothes. Fullerton boys are thriving. (But not so much we can do without you.) xxx

'I know this will sound like a strange idea,' Kate said, addressing her crew, 'but I think we should make tea.'

The Holy Trinity contractors were due to begin work tomorrow, so Kate had called a team meeting. They were perched in a circle on top of crates, stools or chairs, their hair pulled back from their faces and their most unattractive, yet practical, cleaning clothes on.

She had enlisted their help that morning to make the shop prettier. They'd scrubbed, swept, mopped, dusted and de-cobwebbed and finally felt the place was ready for the contractors to begin their makeover.

'There's no reason we should have to look at ugly bits while we're progressing,' Kate had said, handing out packages. Inside were strings of paper lanterns lit from within with LED lights, strings of pale-pink cloth flowers with small lights at their centres, and some posters with motivational quotes to tack to the bare walls.

Now, they found themselves smiling, their spirits lifted by the small touches of beauty amid the chaos.

'Tea?' Elizabeth said.

'Yes.' Kate began to distribute teacups and glass teapots from a large box. 'Actually, not tea—chai. We're going to have a chai tasting.'

Elizabeth clapped her hands. 'I love chai.'

'I've never had it,' Victoria said, her face conveying apprehension.

'That's precisely why we're doing this,' Kate told her. 'We're about to enter an intense period of work and what I want us to remember is this: first and foremost, we are all about the tea. And chai comprises a huge portion of our total sales. It's worth really getting to know chai because unlike something simple, like peppermint, English breakfast or chamomile tea, chai is different everywhere you go. The word *chai* is actually a generic term for *tea blend*, so a chai can be made up of almost anything. It can be confusing for customers, particularly if they are new to the tea world. But it's also a wonderful way to bring back connoisseurs again and again because the variations are limitless.'

Each woman now had her own teapot and cup, so Kate began to pull out boxes and packets of tea from a blue paper bag.

'I've been shopping,' she said, and as she began to hand around the packs to the circle she could feel the fatigue of the workload lift under the new wave of enthusiasm for what she loved best.

'So here's four different chai brands I picked up today on my way to work. Our own stocks haven't arrived yet, but for the purpose of tea tasting we can play with anything.'

'Masala Magic,' Leila said, popping open her tin and shaking the contents to release the smell.

'Masala chai refers to the traditional Indian chai,' Kate said. '*Masala* means *spiced*. My personal favourite. For me, nothing else comes close. Having said that, there are some huge differences between masala chais too, depending on who's blended them.'

'I've got strawberry chai,' Victoria said.

'Oooh, that sounds great,' Elizabeth said. 'I've got a green tea chai.'

'And I've got a rooibos chai,' Kate finished.

'So what do we do?' Victoria asked, clutching her red cardboard box.

Kate handed out paper and pens and walked them through the tea-tasting process. First, they each opened their tea packets or tins and inhaled the aromas, making notes as they went. They poured some out into their hands and vigorously rubbed it between their palms, then cupped them to their noses to smell it again.

'You'll probably notice the big notes first,' Kate said, 'then more subtle notes.'

'The first thing I noticed was the black tea itself,' Leila said, 'then the cardamom.'

'Good. Keep going. What else can you smell?'

Leila waved her hand under her nose in a circle. 'Nutmeg, I think.'

Kate nodded encouragingly. There weren't any right or wrong answers. 'Victoria, what did you notice?'

She smiled. 'Strawberry. Yum.'

'Okay. If the strawberry scent is that strong, it's probably because flavour scents have been added into it. Read the ingredients. How far down the list is the strawberry?'

Victoria squinted at the packaging and twisted her lips to the side in concentration. 'A fair way down. Second last, actually.'

Elizabeth jumped in. 'Well, I don't know what it is exactly that I can smell, but it's strong. Almost unpleasant?' Her forehead was wrinkled as though she was worried she'd got it wrong.

'That's probably the green tea itself,' Kate said. 'It can have a really strong smell, depending on the age and how it's been processed. It can be overpowering.'

Kate inhaled the contents she had between her own hands. 'Mmm. I love the smell of rooibos. It's so warm and sweet. I can smell a good deal of honey in this blend.'

'Honey?' Leila said.

'Yes. It's not common to see honey in tea blends, but it does happen. And it's traditional to sweeten chai, so this company's done the job of adding the honey for you. It complements rooibos perfectly.'

Next they steeped their teas in their teapots, watching the colour of the water change over time. They made notes on the colours: honey-brown for Leila's masala chai; brown-green for

Elizabeth's green tea chai; a lovely caramel for Kate's rooibos; and red-brown for Victoria's strawberry chai.

'Aha,' Victoria declared triumphantly. 'They must have colouring in it too.'

'Exactly,' Kate grinned.

'Blimey, I feel a bit cheated now,' Victoria said, swirling her teapot critically.

They carried on for a good hour, tasting their teas next with all sorts of additions of milks or sugar or honey. It took on the mood of a fun school project, with each of them presenting a summary of 'Today I'm drinking . . .' to their peers. Kate mentally patted herself on the back, enjoying listening to their voices growing in confidence. Her idea had been a success both in terms of adding to their knowledge levels and to the camaraderie between them.

As the light above them began to flicker—thankfully, an electrician was booked to do the wiring in a few days time—and the yawns began to come faster, she called their team meeting to an end, congratulating them all on their insights so far.

'Now, there's one more thing,' Kate said. 'I'm giving you homework.' She grinned at their anxious faces. 'I'm giving you an assignment to complete over the next couple of months. To research chai and to come up with your own new blend.'

'It's not a pass or fail situation. You can't get it wrong. Think of it as a creative experiment. An art project. And as you read about chai, and see what other people are selling, and work with the teas here in store, you might find you start to catch the creative vibe and imagine new blends. Go with it. And you never know—we might even produce your new tea under our label.'

11

Two weeks to go.

That was all the time they had before the grand opening. Kate sat in the shop behind the mahogany carved counter, which was a lucky find from one of her neighbours' antiques store and was a real centrepiece. It featured exquisite winding vines and wildflowers, like something out of an enchanted garden. It curved in an arch and looked rich, warm and proudly Celtic. As soon as she'd seen it, she knew she would build the store around it.

She shuffled through papers and sipped on liquorice tea. She was still waiting for phone and internet connection and in the meantime, Susan in Brisbane and Bryony, the Sydney store manager, were both emailing through reports and updates to her personal email account, which she printed off each day at the house and carried with her in her bag, ready for any moment she could spare to look them over. It was frustrating having to divide her attention but she needed to keep in touch with what was going on back home. Fortunately, they were both competent managers and so far all seemed to be going smoothly, which was just as well because she really needed to concentrate fully on getting this store together.

Simone's vision for each new Tea Chest store was focused on uniqueness. Each one had to reflect the beauty and distinctive culture of its location. Simone had detested the term 'chain' store—the McDonaldisation of tea. She preferred to think of the collection of locations as a charm bracelet—everything connected but each piece an individual with a story.

The Brisbane store had the magic teapot feel, drawing on the Enid Blyton books that Simone had so loved when she was young. The Sydney Tea Chest was cutting-edge contemporary— an expensive design that meant frequent upgrades—built on a theme of wealth, fashion and ambition, yet with just enough warmth and nurturing touches to embrace the old-world values Simone had believed critical to The Tea Chest's success. As for this store? She hadn't left any instructions or notes on it. Whatever Simone had in mind was out of Kate's reach.

Kate ran her hand along the polished bench top. This store had to be truly exceptional. It was Simone's legacy but it was also Kate's future.

The vision she'd come up with filled her with equal parts excitement and sheer terror. It was a theme that called for multiple professionals, foresight, and the investment of a significant amount of capital from their already overstretched finances. It was a risk, but Kate believed in her heart it was one worth taking.

You think you can sell tea to the English?

Judy's warning crashed through Kate's reverie. Her legs weakened.

Looking around the room before her, the final vision for this store was nowhere to be seen. Instead, her eyes fell on gutted walls, exposed beams and piles of rubble that seemed to grow faster than they could be taken to the footpath where they awaited collection. One of the Trinity's illegal workers, a young man from Afghanistan, chipped at old tiles and they clinked to his feet, leaving shards scattered across the wooden floor.

But anytime she began to feel overwhelmed, she reminded herself to look up.

Even though Kate had no idea what Simone's vision for this store had been, she felt a magical bond align them because of one architectural feature that would allow Kate's vision to come to life. Almost every store on Kings Road sat at ground level with multiple floors of flats or office space directly above it. But every so often, the floors above were partially set back from the footpath, leaving a space above the store below. By some miracle, The Tea Chest had such a design. The front half of the shop had nothing above the roof. It was the key to Kate's design. She looked up to the ceiling beams now and sent a silent prayer of thanks to Simone for getting it right.

The sound of the electrician's drill brought her back to the present and she watched him thread wires. The lighting for this store had to be as good as any West End theatre production.

'So far so good,' Elizabeth said, placing a bucket of soapy, grimy water on the counter top and wiping her hands down her overalls. 'No raids or arrests.'

'Quick: touch wood,' Kate said, tapping on the bench top.

Elizabeth knocked it too.

'What did you say to them, anyway?' Kate said, nodding at the Trinity and their workers. 'They haven't said a word all day.'

Elizabeth tilted her head to the side. 'Well, first that if they didn't honour their contract with us then we'd sue them and dob them in to Immigration anyway. Then, to get them to move their feet, I said I'd read in the paper this morning that Immigration will be conducting spot checks on businesses in this part of London in a couple of weeks time so if they wanted to avoid any trouble they'd better be finished by then.'

'I can't help but feel sorry for them,' Kate said.

Elizabeth shrugged. 'They nearly ruined your store, remember that. Anyway, how's the internet drama going?' She nodded at the laptop perched on the edge of the counter.

'Slowly. Dealing with these things in Australia's bad enough. I'm certain Telstra is the devil incarnate sent to tempt everyone with thoughts of murder and violence.'

At those last words, the Hindu man, whose name was Kamal, looked up from his wheelbarrow of plaster and adjusted his turban nervously.

'But BT's just as bad. It's a global evil conspiracy.' She clicked uselessly at her mouse. 'I need Leila here to yell at them for me. I've run out of energy.'

'She's still out looking for an angel?'

'Yes.'

'I'll do it instead,' Elizabeth said, bouncing in her pink plimsolls.

Kate arched a brow. 'Channelling your anger for good?'

'Well, I can't yell at John. Everything I feel towards him is so large it's not possible to put into words. I was sure it was over, but now? I don't know.' She screwed up her nose. 'But I need to yell at someone so you might as well take advantage of it.'

At that moment, two Eastern European workers dropped a large metal ladder and it crashed to the floor, making everyone jump. It knocked a huge tray of nails and screws and other unidentifiable bits and they sprayed across the room with a tremendous clatter.

Several of the workmen began gesturing and arguing in foreign languages—several different ones by the sound of it—until Kamal whistled for time out and shooed them all back to their jobs. Each worker was just slinking back to his corner when a man in a suit, carrying a clipboard, crunched across the store's threshold. He paused for a moment to wipe grit off his shoe.

'I'm looking for Katelyn Fullerton,' he said. He slid his eyes across the motley crew of workers, who ducked their heads and turned their backs to him.

Kate cleared her throat. 'That's me.'

The man handed her a business card. 'I'm Robert Drizzle from the council.'

'Right. How can I help?'

'We've received a complaint from a business in this road.'

Kate immediately looked past Robert Drizzle to the door of Heavensfield House, catching sight of Lady Heavensfield's pointy features peeking through the window. 'Of course you have.'

'What sort of complaint?' Elizabeth demanded, hands on hips. She was almost shouting.

'The rubbish piling up on the footpath is against safety regulations. And your fellow shopkeepers feel it's turning customers away.'

'For goodness' sake,' Elizabeth sighed. 'The waste bins were supposed to be here yesterday but were held up due to some rubbish convention, or something. They'll be here this afternoon.'

'Even so,' Drizzle said, 'you'll need to have it removed immediately.'

'Of course,' Kate soothed, placing a hand on Elizabeth's arm. 'We'll do it right now.'

'One more thing,' Drizzle said, twisting his mouth into what was obviously a thinking gesture. He tapped his pen against his board. 'The complainant also alleges there are illegal workers here.'

Kate felt every person in the room collectively hold his or her breath. The young Afghani man dropped his metal spatula to the floor, where it twanged against the floorboards.

Beside her, Elizabeth burst into hysterical laughter.

'Oh—oh, how funny,' she gasped, her hand at her throat. 'Do you really think we'd be so silly, opening a new store, risking everything, knowing we're being watched by a spiteful neighbour like Lady Heavensfield?'

Drizzle shuffled. Clearly, the complaint was supposed to be anonymous.

'Mr Drizzle, I assure you there's nothing going on here except for a woman being jealous of a new competitor. I'm so sorry she's wasted your time.'

Elizabeth now spoke so sweetly and charmingly that Kate couldn't believe it was the same person who'd practically yelled at this man minutes before.

'Of course we'll clean up the rubbish immediately,' she continued. 'We might even bake Lady Heavensfield a tea cake to say how sorry we are and keep the peace. We can't have you dragged over here on useless missions like this. I'm sure you're very busy and have much more important things to do with your time.'

Drizzle studied her, and then to Kate's astonishment he relaxed his face.

'Yes, well, it's not the first time a neighbour in this street has tried to cause trouble for a new business,' he said carefully.

'Of course,' Elizabeth agreed. 'We totally understand. Here,' she said, reaching into the brass antique teapot that held the business cards. 'Please come back and visit us at our grand opening and we'll be pleased to give you some free samples for yourself and the lady in your life.' She subtly eased him towards the door.

'Thank you,' Kate called politely to his retreating back. The room maintained its frozen state until Elizabeth returned, smiling, dusting off her hands to signal that everything was taken care of.

'Well, you heard the man,' she said to the room at large. And the workers returned to their silent, industrious pace.

Thirty-five years earlier

Judy's mother was in the kitchen, skewering cabanossi, white and green cocktail onions, and chunks of cheese with toothpicks and arranging them on the brown and orange plate. Judy wanted to take this moment, before the guests for the end-of-summer party began arriving, to voice her concerns.

She picked up a frosted-glass platter and began to move mini quiches from the baking tray.

'Mother, I want to talk to you about Simone.'

Elaine reached for her glass of Californian Almaden champagne and took a large mouthful. 'Mmm?'

'I don't think it's good for her to be spending so much time with Beverley Parnell.'

Elaine said nothing, but reached for the brown fondue stand.

'They're out dancing almost every night,' Judy went on. She glanced at the drink in her mother's hand. 'And I think they drink quite a lot.'

'She's young,' Elaine shrugged.

'Only two years younger than me and I had a job and was going steady with Graham at that age.' She paused to consider the diamond on her engagement finger. 'What's she doing with her life?'

Her mother popped a sliced strawberry into her champagne and adjusted the silk scarf at her neck. 'It's really too hot for silk,' she said absently.

Judy waited, hoping her mother would see how serious this was. Simone might be an adult now, but they were still all the family she had. Didn't her mother worry that she rarely heard from her anymore? Didn't she care about what Simone was doing with the money Elaine had distributed to her out of her father's inheritance when she'd turned twenty-one?

Simone was far from Judy's favourite person, but surely someone should be keeping an eye on her. Elaine's legal responsibilities towards her stepdaughter might have ended but surely she still had some sense of moral concern for her.

'I was thinking maybe we should have her over for a Sunday roast,' Judy tried again. 'Just to see how she's going.'

'I don't know,' Elaine said, pouring the rest of the Almaden into the punch bowl and scooping up a glassful to taste. 'Everyone's so busy these days. And you know how Dennis feels about her. It might be more awkward than helpful.'

Judy thought of how Dennis always sniffed through one nostril whenever anyone mentioned Simone, as though he'd unexpectedly come across a pile of rotting rubbish.

'Yes, I'm sure you're right. It was silly of me.' She picked up the platter of quiches and left the room.

e

Five months earlier

Leila and Lucas were working late. The sky was dark outside the windows of the ninth floor and the city's office buildings glowed with fluorescent lights. At street level, an occasional car horn could be heard as the peak-hour traffic extended past seven o'clock.

Leila was helping Lucas with a training manual for a new computer system that was being delivered to a customer next week. It predicted water flows and modelled stormwater movements.

'Shouldn't the IT guys be doing this?' she said, her hunger audible now. Down the corridor, a vacuum started up as the cleaner began her nightly routine in the Strahan building.

'The IT guys deal with numbers and dots and dashes. They can't string a sentence together. That's why we're here,' Lucas said.

Leila was tired. It had been a hugely stressful week so far and it was only Wednesday. She rubbed an eye. Her tights were sliding down her legs beneath her lined suit and the crotch had fallen to between her thighs and was irritating her. She'd long ago eaten the last muesli bar from the box she kept in her desk drawer and all she wanted was a curry, a cup of tea and a hot shower. But at the same time, she'd never turn down an opportunity to be with Lucas.

He grinned at her. 'You look like you need a coffee.'

'How can you be so cheerful?' she grumbled. 'And I need food.' She groaned and leaned sideways, resting her head on his shoulder, whimpering like a child.

He patted her thigh, and his hand rested there, the warmth seeping through the material of her skirt.

Her heart accelerated, always waiting for The Moment to arrive. She wished he'd slide his hand further down towards her knee and then run it back up under that skirt.

She hastily sat upright and reached for the printout of the manual. 'I guess we should get started.' She chastised herself for letting her mind daydream. Lucas had made it clear he wasn't interested in a relationship. She cast a quick glance at the framed photo of Achara next to his laptop. She was his motivation to keep going, accumulating more, working harder. She knew it was his daughter's face and the emails from her mother that spurred him on when he was feeling down or tired. He was single-minded about what he had to do.

No complications, that's what he'd said.

Leila was pretty sure he engaged in casual relations. There was a vibe sometimes that came off him. A mixture of distractedness, happiness and a pinch of guilt. An unexplained good mood. A failure to meet her eye and a vagueness when she asked what he'd got up to on the weekend.

Her insides burned with jealousy and resentment and she often got snappy with him and passed up that day's coffee outing.

She had to force herself to stop thinking about it. It drove her crazy to imagine him with anyone else. Why wouldn't he be seeing women on the side every now and then? He was a charming, good-looking, successful guy. He probably had legions of women ready to satisfy him whenever he needed.

Stop it, Leila.

'So, which bits do you want me to look at?' she said, focusing her exhausted eyes on the words in front of her. She stretched her neck, squeezed her eyes shut, looked off into the distance. There were only so many hours of staring at words she could manage before her accuracy began a rapid descent.

Lucas furrowed his brow. 'How about I go get a real coffee from downstairs and a bite to eat? Then we can start on this refreshed.'

Leila rubbed her eyes again. 'I think that's a good idea. I might head to the bathroom and splash water on my face and slap myself around a bit to try and wake up.'

'Okay.' He rose, shoving his wallet into his pocket. She stood at the same time and they faced each other, the space between their bodies a little too close for professional distance. She took half a step backwards.

Lucas went to leave, then stopped and turned back. 'Oh, I've just realised that the version you've got there—' he pointed to the manual on the desk '—isn't the latest. Mick Gee emailed me the latest just before he went home. Could you get it from my inbox and print it out while I'm gone?'

'Sure,' she said.

'Thanks.' He smiled at her, the kind of smile that said she was more than just a workmate; she was someone special. 'Don't know what I'd do without you.' He strode off.

Leila inhaled a deep, energising breath. She took a few steps towards the bathroom, then decided she might as well set the manual to print to save time while she was gone. She plonked herself down in Lucas's chair and clicked the icon for his inbox. It popped open and a dozen or so new, unopened emails sat waiting. She skimmed down the list, looking for the one from Mick Gee.

Lucas had his email preferences set to include a viewing pane down the bottom half of the screen so he could read a portion of an email without actually having to open it. She highlighted Mick's email and began to read in the viewing pane: *hey mate 3.2 latest version* blah blah. Leila quashed her irritation at the lack of capitals, punctuation or correct grammar.

She opened the email properly, double-clicked the attachment, and sent it to the printer down the hall.

She was just about to get up when another email caught her eye. It was from Nootsara. Achara's mother.

Leila hesitated, feeling the skin on the back of her neck prickle. This was Lucas's other world. The world that kept him from her. What did Nootsara have to say?

She pushed aside any thoughts of ethics and instead highlighted the email so she could read it in the viewing pane below.

Sawasdee krup Lucas. I ponder long time whether tell you but feel it right to do so. I know you want come visit end year but Achara not want. She like my new boyfriend told you of and say want him for her Phor not you. Very sorry. Know this hurt. Maybe Achara change mind by end year. Thought you want know. I keep send updates because I think important to keep touch. Photo joined. La Gon, Nootsara.

Leila read and reread the email in horror. The air conditioning suddenly felt several degrees too cold. Lucas had mentioned a while back that Nootsara had been seeing someone new. He didn't know much about him but had seemed pleased for her.

Leila scrolled uselessly up and down the viewing pane. This would absolutely destroy Lucas. She couldn't begin to imagine the pain it would bring to him, to any parent, to hear those words. Even though Lucas had never met his daughter, she knew he lived for the occasional emails and photos and his parental responsibilities had become the driving purpose in his life.

It was also the thing that was keeping them apart.

Her fatigued brain, now jolted with a generous amount of adrenaline, raced through potential scenarios. If she deleted the email, Achara might change her mind down the track and Lucas would be spared the pain of knowing his daughter had rejected him. Then again, Nootsara might mention it again in a later email and Lucas would be confused and ultimately hurt anyway, both by the news of Achara and by Leila's betrayal. If she left the email there for Lucas to read, his heart would be torn open, he would know the truth, she wouldn't compromise her ethics, and he would then be free to begin a proper relationship with her, the way it should be. Anyone could see that.

She sat immobilised.

Then she heard the ding of the elevator, a creak in the heavy glass door to the foyer and a rustle of takeaway bags, Lucas was back. Leila had no more time to think.

She hit the trashcan icon and the email was gone.

e

Fullerton Frat House report: Washing training update. Sticking to my conviction that it's character-building for boys to wear pink jocks and odd socks in face of Keats's protest. xx

12

Quentin Ripp was the first angel investor to respond to Leila's ad on the investor website. He asked her to meet him in a restaurant called Jim's American Pizza. It seemed an odd location for a business meeting, particularly at eight o'clock in the evening, but Leila packed up her prospectus information and smoothed her hair, fastening it with a snap of a snakeskin clip, and made her way there by bus, nerves making her twitchy.

Inside the pizzeria, she found Quentin at a red booth, hunched over papers strewn out across the wooden table, pen in hand. The place was warm, noisy, filled to capacity by the look of it, with lots of loud American voices, bright lights and USA memorabilia. On the walls were photos of Marilyn Monroe, Elvis Presley, JFK, pick-up trucks, baseball games, New York skyscrapers, Texan cowboys and Southern belles. The smell of pepperoni, onion and frying cheese was thick in the air.

Quentin wore a schmick dark suit and a crisp white shirt open at the top two buttons, allowing her a glimpse of his tanned chest.

He rose, smiled broadly, and held out his hand. 'Leila?' His accent was also American, though she couldn't pinpoint where he came from. He wasn't southern, though.

'Hi, nice to meet you,' she said. She gestured to his paperwork. 'Thanks for taking the time to meet me. It looks like you've got a lot on.'

'Nothing out of the ordinary,' he said, nonchalant.

They sat and Leila reached into her messenger bag to retrieve the prospectus, printed in colour and neatly bound at an office supply store. She'd had such fun perusing the aisles of notebooks and diaries and coloured pens while she'd waited for it to be finished. And when they'd handed her the final product she had the thrill she always got when a bunch of messy notes, abstract ideas, late nights, intense meetings and drafts of plans all came together in one beautifully organised crisp and, hopefully, flawless product.

She passed it across the table to him, savouring the moment. There was nothing she loved more than the completion of a task, and this one was a big deal, more significant than anything she'd ever done before. At Strahan she worked in large teams, but here she was a key person in a small team's survival.

'Thanks,' he said, and opened it immediately, turning the pages, nodding thoughtfully and murmuring in the right places at key sales targets and pie charts, investment return projections and the five-year timeline.

'I've also brought along tea samples,' she said, passing over a large box tied with ribbon. Inside were a dozen smaller, individually wrapped blends, hand-chosen by Kate.

To her delight, he held the box to his nose and inhaled. He nodded again. 'Thanks,' he said again. 'I'm more of a coffee person but I will try each one.' He flashed her two rows of white teeth.

'Do you have any questions for me?'

'Yes,' he said, leaning back against the vinyl booth seat. 'Tell me about you.'

The unexpected request made her baulk. She was instantly drawn back to The Incident at Strahan. It was like she couldn't escape it, even on the other side of the world.

'What do you want to know?' she said, maintaining her calm and her smile.

'I've already done my research. The Tea Chest has a strong, inspiring record in Australia and it's set to be a strong leader here too. I've got all the data here on the latest business trends in London.' He tapped the paper on the table. 'What I want to know is more about the women behind the scenes.'

'That's reasonable,' she said, though hesitantly. She wasn't sure if he was intimating that he planned to invest or whether he was still waiting to make up his mind and now they had to pass his talking test. This wasn't proceeding as expected. But then, she supposed, investors could likely act as eccentrically as they wanted.

'Well, you must make a time to meet Kate,' she said. 'Let me know what works for you and I can set something up.'

'Sure. Will do.' Then he leaned across the table and his eyes took on a suggestive glint. 'But let's start with you. I want you to show me what you've got.'

Leila sat immobile, an involuntary smile starting to spread across her lips. Who did this guy think he was? But somehow his flirting didn't turn her off as much as it intrigued her. She caught a faint whiff of the starch in his shirt.

'Okay,' she said, but then no more words came.

Quentin turned and looked over his shoulder towards the archway carved out of the back wall leading into the kitchen, where several chefs were in the throes of making pizza. Dough spun upwards into the air and landed on expert fists as someone else dolloped ladles of rich tomato sauce onto rounds of pale dough, smoothing it over with the underside of the ladle.

'Come on,' Quentin said, rising. 'Let's go.'

He led the way to the back of the pizzeria and shouts of recognition came from the black-aproned chefs behind the counter. Leila followed, wondering where they were going. Then, without warning, Quentin led them through the kitchen door and into the workings of the restaurant.

'Howdy, brother,' one of the men greeted, holding out a floured fist to shake.

'Hi, Glen, this is Leila,' he said. Glen nodded to Leila. 'We're here to make pizza,' Quentin said.

Leila stared at Quentin. *Make pizza?*

'Help yerselves,' Glen said. 'You know how it works.'

Quentin led Leila to a vat of flour and handed her a scoop.

'What's going on?' she said, taking the scoop and turning it upside down as if the answer would be on the bottom.

'This is one of my investments,' Quentin said, pride in this voice. 'This place. I've helped build it from the inside and that means I get to make all the pepperoni and clam pizza I like.' He passed her a long black apron that fell to her knees.

'Clam pizza?' That didn't sound appealing. Leila wasn't even sure she knew exactly what clams were. Something like mussels, perhaps.

Quentin tied the apron strings around his waist then, to Leila's shock, reached his arms around her waist and tied hers as well, crossing them over her back then bringing them to the front to tie in a knot above her belly button. It was unexpectedly exciting.

'I figure the best way to get to know you is to throw you into something you don't know anything about and see how we get on,' he said gleefully. 'You can recite all the info you like about your business. I'd expect nothing less. But I want to know there are brains, humour and a little bit of brawn behind the numbers too.' He put his hands on her hips, spun her around to face a stainless-steel bench top with pans and tools hanging from the ceiling above, and guided her to its edge.

'So let's get started,' he said. He dipped his hand into the container of flour, grabbed a fistful and sprinkled it across the bench, slowly running the flat of his hand around in it to cover the surface. He put her hands into the flour alongside his and they dusted the bench together.

'Okay,' she said. 'But after this we get to talk numbers. Deal?'

'Deal.'

The next day, Kate texted a reply to Leila.

'Was that Leila?' Elizabeth said, puffing with exertion.

They'd located a handyman with a battered truck, which was now parked illegally outside the store. They were hauling cement chips and plasterboard into the tray, regularly apologising to shoppers and shopkeepers who growled at them for the mess and the smashing sounds as the detritus hit the metal tray. Not Randolph and Manu, though, bless their Streisand-loving hearts. The couple from the deli next door were wildly supportive of The Tea Chest and sent the girls and the tradesman pink lemonade to keep them going. As for the rest of the shopkeepers, Kate made a mental note to send them all apology tea baskets.

'Yes. She got back late last night but I was so exhausted from all this pretending to be a brickie's labourer that I'd fallen asleep, and then I left before her this morning, so she's just updating me now.'

'I hope the olds aren't driving her mad,' Elizabeth said randomly, pushing damp strands of hair from her forehead. 'It'll be good once the internet's done and she can work from here instead of at home.'

'The olds have been a bit funny lately,' Victoria chimed in, tightening the blue scarf around her hair. 'Mum's been really jumpy. Like I keep springing her doing something wrong.'

Kate registered Victoria's comment about her parents but she didn't really have anything of value to add, since she didn't know them that well. She let the comment lie. Instead, she ruminated on Leila's activities.

It had taken her a few moments to reply to Leila's news that she'd met the first potential investor and that she had a good feeling about him. An investor was good news, except that it was a huge leap into the unknown and her phone call to Mark yesterday to discuss it hadn't gone as planned.

His phone had rung for a long time. And when it was answered, Mark wasn't talking to her, he was talking to someone else.

'Hello? Mark?' she'd repeated, raising her voice. She was pretty sure the phone was in the pocket of his pants because there was a swishing sound like material rubbing across it as he walked. And she knew he was at home because she could hear the neighbour's corgi doing the plaintive howling thing she did when they left her at home alone.

The other voice was a woman's.

Kate froze, straining to hear beyond human limitations. Mark had a woman in the house in the middle of the day.

She kept listening, pushing the phone hard against her ear until it hurt. The woman's voice was snappy and salesy and Kate definitely heard the words 'property' and 'market value'.

With a jolt, she comprehended that the woman was a real estate agent and was there to value the house.

She hung up quickly, not wanting Mark to discover her spying. Guilt nipped her. By taking on this venture, she'd put them in such a desperate financial situation that he was doing what *she* should have been doing and thinking a step ahead, preparing contingency actions for the possible failure of The Tea Chest.

It was a huge, sobering reality check.

'It'll be great when we've got an investor sorted,' Elizabeth said now, shoving a cardboard box out of the way.

'An investor can give us a kick start and a big ride forward— like a rocket,' Kate said, as much for her own benefit as anyone else's.

She'd learned the language. She'd read all the info Leila had given her. And she'd agreed with Leila. They were faced with a unique opportunity right now and they could choose to contract in the face of unexpected obstacles or they could choose to take a leap and play in a bigger arena.

But now, standing outside the gutted Tea Chest, Kate was wishing she'd had the chance to talk to Mark about it first, and that she hadn't heard the depressing conversation about house values.

'I'm putting the kettle on,' Elizabeth said, pulling off thick work gloves.

Kate checked her watch, calculating the time difference between London and Brisbane. She just had time to catch the boys before they went to bed.

Keats recounted his six and eight times tables to Kate, only stumbling over *eight sevens are fifty-six.*

'That's really good. I'm so proud of you,' Kate said.

'Dad put my maths test on the fridge. I got nineteen out of twenty and Dad said we could have fish and chips on Friday.'

'Make sure you leave it on the fridge till I get home. I can't wait to give you a hug.'

'Yeah.'

He passed the phone to James.

'Mummy, my feet feel mesmerised,' her youngest son said with great importance.

'Mesmerised? What have your feet been doing?'

'They're dreaming of fish.'

'Oh.'

He passed the phone back to Mark.

'Hi again.'

'What's with James's feet?'

'*Mesmerised* is his latest word. Last week it was *perplexed*, though he got the meaning confused with Perspex and kept asking me if our windows were perplexed.'

'I imagine they were. Where is he getting these words?'

They discussed the boys for a while until Mark finally said, 'So what's up, Katie?'

'That obvious?'

'Only to me.'

Kate took a deep breath and told him all about the investment plans. 'I don't know if I'm doing the right thing. I'd really like to know what you think.' She weighted her sentence, hoping he would realise it was okay for him to tell her he'd valued the house because he was worried.

He thought for a moment. 'Well,' he said, carefully, 'it's one of those things that has huge potential and possibly huge pitfalls.'

'So what're you saying? You think it's a bad idea?'

'I'm saying I think it's good to keep your options open. What about the contracts? What's the pound of flesh they'll want in return? And do you have to sign a personal guarantee? You hear stories all time about people who've signed a guarantee for someone's house loan and then they lose everything. We've taken a risk to be where we are now. You're in London, which is a hub of financial business, but you just need to be cautious about which wagon you hitch your ride to.'

'How very Western of you,' she laughed, wanting to add lightness to the gravity of the conversation. 'So what should I do?'

'Be careful. Do your research.'

She waited for him to tell her more about what he'd been doing, about his fears and his plans.

'I believe in you,' he said gently.

'Really?' *Then why are you valuing the house?*

'Yes, really.'

'Love, is there anything else you want to talk to me about? Anything going on at home you think we should discuss? I'm here, you know. We can still talk about anything you want. It doesn't always have to be about the boys and The Tea Chest.'

He paused and she heard him turn on the kitchen tap and start rinsing off some plates.

'No, I don't think so. Everything's under control.'

Leila briefed Kate on the investor progress so far. One went no further than an enquiry email, one had been a phone call and an emailed prospectus, another had met with her for five minutes on his way to Madrid but she'd heard nothing from him since. And then there was Quentin. He was the only one still in the running.

'Let's hope he's the one for us,' Kate said, rushing out the door to the shop, leaving Leila to meet up with Quentin again.

They met in the lounge of the hotel he was staying in, her new notebook and pen ready to capture what he wanted to see in the details of the contract. Wearing Armani, he filled most of a large chair, an empty coffee cup on the table in front of him. He rose when he saw her coming and held out his hand.

'Hi again,' she said, taking his hand in hers, though it seemed a little formal after spending the night making pizza with him. After working in a kitchen together he seemed more like a mate from school rather than someone she was trying to impress in a business sense.

While they'd kneaded dough together, he'd told her he came from a large family in California; missed the family dog, named Kermit, when he travelled; failed his driving test twice; and if he could have three people to dinner this weekend he'd have Matt Damon, Nelson Mandela and Ellen DeGeneres.

She'd told him she had just her mother and brother; no pets allowed; got her driving test first go; and if she could have three people to dinner this weekend she'd have Amelia Earhart, Angelina Jolie and Hugh Jackman.

'Why Amelia Earhart?'

'Everyone loves a good mystery. I want to know what happened.'

'Can I get you a coffee?' he said now.

'Mocha, please,' she said, settling herself on the chair next to him. She didn't take up nearly as much room in it as he did in his. A tall potted plant nearby extended its leaves towards her.

The air conditioning was strong and she shivered.

Quentin returned and noticed her rubbing her arms. 'Would you like my coat?'

'No, it's fine. I'll warm up in a moment when the coffee's arrived.'

Too late. He'd shrugged off his Armani coat and placed it around her shoulders. He sat down again and leaned forward with his elbows on his knees, gazing into her eyes.

Leila was instantly warm, and not just from the coat.

'Thanks. That's very kind of you,' she said.

'I'm trying out this new thing of acting like a gentleman,' he said, smiling. 'How do you think I'm going?'

She had to look at the carpet beneath her feet. 'I think you're doing well.'

'Excellent.'

Their coffees arrived, giving Leila the chance to look at the woman from the bar and fiddle with the glass mug instead of looking at Quentin.

When there was nothing left to fiddle with, she picked up her notebook again. 'Have you had a chance to read through everything I gave you? Tried any of the teas?'

He nodded, his face suddenly losing its friendly high-school jock charm. 'Yes.'

'Would you like to talk about where we can go from here?' she said, disappointed at the change in him.

And as fast as the disappointment came it was followed by a flaring of anger with herself. She was here to do a job. She was in love with Lucas. It was absurd to be feeling anything other than gratitude to this man for helping her and Kate achieve their dreams.

'This investment is pretty straightforward,' he began, leaning back in his chair, his voice serious now. 'It's similar to one I did in California last year for an independent dog food manufacturer.'

'Dog food?'

'Well, obviously tea and dog food are different. But the structure is similar and they had difficulty breaking into an already saturated market, just like you. But we overcame that.'

'How?'

He gave a tight smile. 'The same way we're going to deal with it for The Tea Chest. It worked for them and it will work for you too. You might want to write this down.'

'I'm ready.'

Elizabeth was exhausted—the kind of good exhaustion that leaves you feeling better than you did before. Though this time tomorrow her upper arms might not feel so good about all that work at The Tea Chest. She kicked off her shoes, slumped back in the red recliner in the lounge room, and muted the sound on the television. She closed her eyes, thinking she might actually get some sleep tonight rather than fretting and dreaming of disturbing things as she had each night since she walked out on John.

She'd just flicked up the footrest on the recliner to stretch her legs when her father walked in.

'Hello, kitten,' he said.

'Hi. Where's Mum?'

'Out.' He extended an envelope with a blue and white airmail sticker and several Australian stamps on the front. He hovered for a moment, scraping his grey hair to the side, smoothing it from its part. 'This came for you today.'

Elizabeth's mouth went dry.

'And he phoned again too,' Bill said. Then he left the room.

She stared at John's writing on the envelope. It had always bothered her, with its strange mixture of capital and lowercase letters, cursive writing and printing, the changes appearing randomly between the words and sometimes within the words themselves. It was as though he couldn't decide which way to go. And now it seemed like a huge sign she'd missed right from the start. He couldn't commit to one thing.

She also noted with a sickening jolt that he had hedged his bets with her name. There was some movement and blotching of the ink, as though he didn't know what to write, finally settling on *Elizabeth Plimsworth Clancy*.

She sat dumbly, staring at it, not knowing how to comprehend this signal. Was he afraid she'd gone back to her maiden name and the letter wouldn't reach her? Was he trying to be (ridiculously) respectful of her independence? Maybe he was hinting that it was time for her to let go of their marriage and the Clancy name and strip him from her life. He was too weak to make the decision himself so he'd left it up to her.

The letter inside might have contained some answers to these questions, but she screwed it up into a tight ball and crushed it in her hands.

Bill returned.

'What did he say?' he said, watching her carefully.

She shook her head. 'It doesn't matter. I'm not reading it.'

'Don't you . . . ? Wouldn't you like to . . . ?'

She held up her hand to silence him. 'No. It really doesn't matter what it says.'

And it didn't. She wasn't being deliberately petulant or stubborn or melodramatic. She just honestly believed there was no point. It didn't change anything. He was married to someone else. Had kids with someone else. He'd betrayed her in the most awful way. And anything he had to say now was simply to make himself feel better.

The way he'd written her name on the envelope summed it all up. She had to choose who to be now because no one else would do it for her.

13

Fullerton Frat House report: James's latest words—erectile dys-function. *I'm sure I caught Miss Hopkins sniggering at school pick-up.*

e

Portobello Road on Saturday was filled with the kinds of sights, sounds and smells that made tourism brochures sing. Market tents and stalls, gazebos and tables lined the streets. Brass antique kettles and pots overflowed off wooden trellis tables. Short men in jackets and caps spruiked made-in-China socks and rivets. Pyramids of handmade moisturisers and body creams in the most edible colours of pale lime and strawberry tempted Elizabeth as she walked. The smell of donuts, sausages and freshly ground Brazilian coffee made her tummy rumble. Pink and red parasols spun gaily in the breeze. Fine English crockery wobbled nerv-ously on uneven ground.

Elizabeth carried two cups of hot coffee in a cardboard tray and swung a bag of fresh croissants and sticky chocolate buns in her other hand. She sashayed her way through the throngs of market-goers. When she reached The Tea Chest's stall she was delighted to see Kate smiling and selling the cutest pink fleur-de-lis glasses to a small group of women, whose Roman noses made them look like sisters. Kate had decided they should head to the market, getting the word out onto the street in preparation for the launch. She was an old hand at markets and knew the power of word-of-mouth.

'I thought you could use this,' Elizabeth said, handing Kate the coffee.

'It's appalling, isn't it? I'm a tea designer and I'm drinking coffee. But, yes, these long nights are starting to wear a bit thin, I'm afraid.' She brushed some stray hairs from her face and Elizabeth noticed her eyes did indeed look tired. 'Not as young as I used to be.' She gave a wan smile.

'You're doing wonderfully,' Elizabeth affirmed. 'Believe it or not, Kate, this is really coming together. You're doing it. It's getting done. And it's going to be fantastic.'

Kate smiled. 'Thanks. I really don't know how I'd be doing this without your help. Or Vicky's.'

Elizabeth smothered the urge to correct Kate's use of her sister's name. It was such an Australian thing, this need to shorten names. Instead, she smiled gratefully in return. She was feeling good for the first time since that disastrous morning two months ago when John had confessed his sins. Lightness had returned to her walk and her tone of voice. The Tea Chest had come along at the perfect moment. Keeping busy, working hard and flexing her creative muscles—and some physical ones too—had given her a sense of pride and usefulness she hadn't felt in ages.

'What's she up to this morning?' Kate said, sipping her coffee and rearranging the tins of roasted fruit-and-nut blends on the table to make them more accessible to pedestrians.

'Victoria? She's resting up today. I don't think she's ever worked so hard in her life,' Elizabeth said, familial pride rising. 'Honestly, I really didn't think she had it in her. I'm starting to think maybe she has matured a bit after all.'

'She's been great,' Kate said. 'Did you know she's been borrowing books from the library to research tea?'

'No, I didn't. Good for her,' Elizabeth said, genuinely impressed. 'Sounds like she's taken to this business like a duck to water.'

'She's a good swimmer,' Kate smiled.

Elizabeth poked at some tea tins. 'Roasted nuts in tea?'

'They don't add much flavour as such, more of a body or essence. It gives the tea a really hearty feel, if that makes sense.'

Elizabeth opened the bag of pastries. 'It would go well with one of these then.' She tore off a piece of sticky chocolate bun, popped it in her mouth and washed it down with Irish cream–flavoured coffee. Perhaps she could use a similar flavour for her own chai design.

She closed her eyes and moaned with delight. 'I can't tell you how liberating it is to stop being good all the time. Now that I'm not trying to get pregnant every minute of the day I can do whatever I want. I haven't been to the gym in weeks.' She poked a finger at the flesh under her arm. 'I'm drinking and eating whatever I want. I even had one of Victoria's cigarettes the other night, just because I could.'

Kate took a twenty-pound note from a customer and popped it into her vintage flowered metal tea tin with shabby-chic rust around the rim. She wrapped a bottle of rosewater and a packet of masala chai and instructed the woman on how to blend them for an exotic iced-tea sensation.

Then she smiled at Elizabeth. 'Well, enjoy it while you can because those baby-making and -raising years are definitely consuming. Your body's not your own for a long time.' Kate finished the parcel with a shiny gold and black ribbon and handed it to the young woman.

Elizabeth swallowed her bun. 'Believe me, I will.' Just then, a range of teapots at the other end of the stall caught her eye. She hadn't seen them when she'd helped set up at the crack of dawn this morning. Now, she had no idea how she could have missed them. They were all Japanese teapots, the hexagonal types with tall, arched wooden handles, and delicate patterns of snow-covered branches reaching for stark skies. The sight of them was an unexpected blow.

Japan. She was shocked to realise that she had no idea where her husband was. Perhaps in Japan. Perhaps in a kimono. Or in nothing at all. His letter had been posted from Australia, but that didn't guarantee he was still there. He could have left again.

Love was a funny thing. It could so quickly turn to hatred and just as sneakily swing back the other way. Her chest hurt. A deep cavern of longing threatened to open up a torrent of waterworks.

Instead of thinking what a lying, cheating arse John had been, Elizabeth found herself thinking of surprising things. Like the time when she had the flu and had been in bed for days and he cleaned the house and made her chicken soup and rented her *E.T.* and *Bridget Jones's Diary* to watch on her laptop in bed. Or the time he phoned her at work and told her to go straight home and get changed into her finest clothes because they were going for a romantic, candlelit dinner on the river, just because he fancied her. Or the time he bought them tickets to see *Swan Lake* for her birthday, even though he hated ballet, just because he knew she'd always wanted to go.

He could be so charming when he wanted to be. And she suddenly ached to smell his Acqua Di Gio, which always struck her with its citrus notes first before warming into the patchouli scents.

She wiped at a stray tear.

'I do carry Pu'er as a loose tea,' Kate was saying beside her, showing the man in the silk scarf a brochure. 'But if you come to the store when we're open, you'll see an authentic tea brick on display and I can cut you some to take away with you.'

'That's fantastic,' the man said, pushing his thick black-rimmed glasses up his nose. 'So few people have aged teas in their original form.'

Elizabeth shook herself and took a deep breath. She mentally pulled down the curtains on memories of John and plastered a cheerful expression on her face.

'Well, thank you,' Kate beamed. 'I'll also be conducting weekly tea tastings on a Wednesday evening, which you might be interested in.'

He pushed the brochure into his jeans pocket and assured her he would be there.

Elizabeth felt herself radiate even more pride, this time for being part of a team of brave, creative women who were really out there and getting something right.

Take that, John, you bastard.

She rummaged under the tables to find her sketchbook and pencils. She took a seat and flipped open the pages to her current designs.

'Did you get Leila's latest notes?' Kate said.

'Yes,' Elizabeth said. 'She sent through another long list in an email last night. I printed it out. I've got it here somewhere, if you want to see it?' She gave a cursory glance at her bag then looked at Kate questioningly. They both erupted into giggles.

'It's okay,' Kate said. 'You just keep working on your own ideas. I know Leila's a bit full on right now. She's taking this seriously, which is what we need. I couldn't be doing all this without her.'

Elizabeth thought about that for a moment. 'I don't think you're giving yourself enough credit,' she said. 'We're all doing our bit, but it's really all about *you*, Kate. This is your baby now. Simone left it to you for a reason.'

'Yes.' She turned back to Elizabeth and looked down at her book. 'Do you mind? Can I see?'

'Sure.' She passed the book to Kate with a small flurry of nerves. The four of them had had a long meeting about the themes and designs of The Tea Chest and all the marketing support material: flyers, advertisements, business cards and the website. It was a meeting they'd combined with painting the new walls of the store at night, with their iPods blaring and pizzas to keep them going. Kate had a strong vision for the store but it was a huge task and they agreed they needed a graphic designer and interior decorator on board. The difficulty was going to be keeping them to task so close to the opening of the store.

'You know what these artistic types are like,' Kate grinned. 'All about the dreaming but not a business bone in their body.'

They knew they'd have to do a lot of the grunt work themselves to make sure all the different elements came together.

Elizabeth had been appointed as the coordinator to keep the designers happy and working towards their timeline goals and to help them source whatever they might need. She'd started keeping the sketchbook as a journal of ideas as they developed and morphed into what would be the most beautiful project Elizabeth had ever had the chance to work on.

'Wow,' Kate said now, flipping through the pages. 'These are really great ideas. You've got real artistic flair.'

'It's always been a bit of a hobby of mine,' Elizabeth said. 'I thought for a while I might actually pursue a career in design. But then I got caught up in working in Brisbane, met John, and the rest is history. But even at my old job at Beautification I'd started to carve out a bit of a marketing niche for myself.'

'How's your wardrobe going?' Kate said. 'I'm hitting the shops again later this afternoon if you're keen to come. I still don't quite have a full set of clothes in our theme yet.'

'I found the most gorgeous piece at the Camden Stables Market the other day. A beautiful pale pink. It's been wonderful, actually, to be thrown into a whole new style of dressing. I'm creating a whole new me.'

A small boy let out a shriek as a labrador on a lead snatched his hot dog from his hand. They watched the scene play out for a few moments, with mothers and dog walker and crying child all gesturing and consoling.

Then Kate spoke again. 'I'm so excited. Really. I know this part is stressful. But it's going to be stunning.'

'How could it not be? You're a visionary, Kate. Your design is amazing.'

Just then, Victoria pushed her way to the front of the stall. She was wearing a faux-suede jacket over skinny jeans and sandals. Her face was screwed up in concern and she puffed as if she'd be running.

Elizabeth jumped up. 'Victoria! Whatever's the matter?'

'You need to come home,' her sister wheezed. 'Mum's gone insane.'

Twenty-seven years earlier

Simone was here again, standing at Judy's door, carrying a blue paper bag with more boiled lollies, Judy presumed. Simone smiled, and somewhere in Judy's foggy mind she knew she should force herself to smile back, but it was still all too hard.

'I like your hair,' Judy managed to say. It wasn't true. She didn't fancy the modern trend of tight poodle curls, but she knew she had to say something and it was easier to lie than to speak the truth.

'Thank you,' Simone said, her eyes alight with hope that today their conversation might be different. She pushed her sunglasses up on top of her springy hair.

They walked up the wooden stairs and headed to the couch— the green one with white palm trees that matched the curtains in the lounge room. They sat as usual, with Simone near the window and Judy facing the television, which currently flickered with an American daytime soap.

'I was just in the neighbourhood, on my way to see a new client, and thought I'd stop in,' Simone said, leaning forward and straightening magazines on the coffee tables, and casually pulling a tissue from her handbag and rubbing at a coffee stain on the wood.

'Oh,' Judy said, picking at a food scrap on her T-shirt and wondering how long it had been there.

'Convenience stores are just going crazy for this stuff,' Simone said, passing Judy the bag. When she didn't take it, Simone opened it and held it under Judy's nose so she could see and smell it. It wasn't boiled lollies this time. It was actually a bag full of packs of sherbet.

'I've got a great overseas supplier,' Simone said. 'It's shamefully cheap and I can't get it into the country as fast as I'm taking orders for it. My house is jammed floor to ceiling with crates of the stuff. I think it's the reason I can't find a housemate.' She grimaced.

Judy took the bag and placed it on the couch beside her. She studied her stepsister's open, carefree face, and wondered how the tables had turned so quickly. When had Simone become the competent, organised, motivated woman and she'd become the one whose life was a shambles?

Of course, she knew the answer. The first chips had fallen when her mother died last year. And then Erin. A daughter born too soon. Her tiny body lying lifeless in Judy's hands. A prolapsed uterus and a hysterectomy. All hopes for the future gone.

Graham had work to go to with new prospects on the horizon. She, on the other hand, had given up her job as the bookkeeper for a large milk-delivery business, had painted the house and sewn curtains, filled a nursery and prepared for motherhood, finally, after so much struggle.

And now there was nothing but the darkness of every day looming ahead. A future that didn't look anything like it was supposed to.

Her friends were busy with families of their own, small children who demanded their time and tuckshop duty at school. They were uncomfortable with her grief, and fidgeted nervously on the edge of the couch, waiting for a polite time to make their excuses to leave.

But not Simone. For some strange reason, she came every few days, bringing gifts and stories of the outside world, stories that had nothing to do with family life and provided relief from having to think about it.

They were both orphans now, she and Simone. By a twist of fate, they'd both lost their parents, their homeland in England and were childless. It was a strange bond that held them together. A bond of what they didn't have rather than what they did.

'Oh, I nearly forgot,' Simone said, reaching into her bag. 'I just dropped into the video store down the road and picked up a couple of new releases. I got *Romancing the Stone* and *Ghostbusters*. I know *Ghostbusters* probably isn't your thing, but I heard it was funny.'

'Thank you,' Judy said, reaching for them.

Simone checked her watch. 'Well, I'd better be off. But I'll be back in a couple of days so if you think of anything you need, just give me a call.'

Judy suddenly seared with envy. She'd give anything to be going with Simone right now. To get out of these dank clothes and stuffy house and into the sunshine and bustling traffic. To have somewhere to go. Something to do. She was just about to open her mouth to say so when Simone pushed herself off the couch to leave.

The moment had passed.

Judy nodded. 'Thanks. I appreciate it.'

Margaret Plimsworth stood in the kitchen. It looked as though her dress was made out of heavy plum-coloured curtain material that ran from her neck to her wrists and below her knees and had been recycled from the fifties. Or maybe last century. Her mouth was set into lines of determination and a bulging carpet bag sat near her court shoes. Elizabeth's heart jumped. Perhaps her mother truly had gone insane. She belonged somewhere in the past. Or, at best, in a V.C. Andrews novel.

She cast her eyes upwards, wondering if there was perhaps an attic above their house she never knew about and whether she had strange incestuous siblings who had been hidden there for years.

She shook herself.

'Mum, what's going on?'

'Elizabeth, dear, you shouldn't have bothered coming. It's too late.'

'What's too late?'

'I'm leaving.'

'Where? Why?'

Margaret straightened her white gloves and adjusted her pearl earrings before folding her hands calmly in front of her like a choir girl.

Beside Elizabeth, Victoria took in a sharp breath and slapped her hand to her mouth. Elizabeth followed her sister's gaze to the back of the wooden chair at the kitchen table. There were three bloody fingerprints on it.

Then Elizabeth realised something. Something awful. The television wasn't on. There wasn't a sound to be heard. The house felt completely empty. Her thoughts returned to the imagined attic.

'Where's Dad?'

Margaret shifted. 'Somewhere you don't need to worry about.'

Elizabeth looked down at the carpet bag at her mother's feet. 'Mum, what's in the bag?'

Her mother's eyes flickered. There was stiff, awkward silence.

Elizabeth lunged for the bag. Margaret blocked her. Elizabeth darted to the side. Margaret blocked her there too. Elizabeth's heart hammered. She felt completely out of her body, as though she'd stepped into a bad dream.

'Mother, let me see what's in the bag.'

Margaret drew herself up to her full height. 'It's private.'

Seconds ticked by while Elizabeth and Margaret held each other's gaze. Then Victoria leaped through a small gap and threw herself on top of the carpet bag like a rugby player landing on the ball. She hugged it tightly to her chest. Margaret wailed and began slapping at her youngest daughter's head.

'Get off it, get off it!'

Victoria shrieked under her blows and Elizabeth tugged at her mother's arm to pull her away.

Victoria began to push herself along the linoleum floor with her feet, scooting herself towards the pantry and the door that led to the lounge room. Margaret clambered after her and Elizabeth after both of them.

Margaret stumbled and fell heavily to the floor, letting out a yowl as her knee collided with the ground. Victoria took her moment to spring to her feet, dragging the heavy bag with her. She stood gasping for breath near the doorway, defending the bag against further attack.

'Go on then,' Margaret dared. 'Open it.'

Victoria cast wild eyes at Elizabeth.

'Go on,' Elizabeth said, her hands shaking from the adrenaline. 'Open it.'

Victoria squatted and fumbled with the zipper. Slowly, she tugged, slicing open the bag and tipping it so it could spill its horrible contents to the floor.

Margaret whimpered as she did so, clutching her knee and screwing her face up in agony.

Before them all, rolling across chequered white and brown squares, was her father's entire unicorn collection.

Margaret reluctantly accepted an ice pack for her knee. She sat in the kitchen with a steaming cup of tea in front of her, a slice of lemon floating on top. Elizabeth and Victoria also sat. Unicorns covered the table top and a few still lay scattered at their feet. They'd been sitting in stiff silence for some time, Margaret's gaze fixed at some point on the wall.

Elizabeth cleared her throat. 'Mum, do you want to tell us what's going on?'

Margaret snorted like a teenager.

'Where were you going?' Elizabeth tried again.

'And where's Dad?' Victoria demanded.

'Your father is out for a jar, I should imagine,' Margaret said.

The sisters exchanged a look.

'Does he know what's, um, what's going on with you?' Elizabeth said.

Margaret snapped her head around to stare directly at her eldest child so fast it made Elizabeth jump. 'Of course,' she hissed. 'That's why he's down at the pub.'

'Mum, look, you're really going to have to do a little better here,' Elizabeth said, suddenly irritated. 'What's going on?'

Margaret sniffed and adjusted the icepack on her knee. 'I'm leaving your father. Simple.'

'No, not simple. Why? And why do you have all of his unicorns?'

'Why?' Margaret said, as though having to explain trivial matters to a four-year-old. 'Because I don't love him anymore, that's why.'

Elizabeth blanched. 'Oh.'

'I'm in love with someone else, actually,' her mother said smugly.

'Who?'

'Angus Reiner. He's the group leader at the local Alcoholics Anonymous group. That's where I met him.'

If Elizabeth thought she was confused before, she was dumbstruck now. Her mother an alcoholic? But she'd never been a drinker really. Just an occasional sherry. But maybe that was how it started.

'Wait,' Victoria said, slapping the table. 'You're an old lush, is that what you're saying?'

'No, dear,' Margaret said, using her patient voice again. 'I'm a caterer.'

Elizabeth thought her head would explode, both with the absurdity of this conversation, the insanity-inducing slowness with which her mother was divulging information, and the crazy notion that she could cook anything other than sausages and beans or bacon and eggs.

Victoria burst out laughing. Hysterical laughter. The kind that turns to tears if you let it keep going. Elizabeth felt herself ripple too. She placed a hand on her sister's arm to try to settle them both. Now it was her turn to adopt a patient voice.

'Oh, well, that makes sense. And you met this Angus man at a catering job.'

'That's right,' Margaret said, appearing relieved that someone was finally understanding her. 'I take sandwiches and refreshments down to the hall each day for their meetings. Everyone's always so grateful. Nothing like sharing one's secrets with the world to make one ravenously hungry. Angus always said it was my cinnamon toast that really made the difference on a difficult day.' She began to preen at the thought of Angus.

Elizabeth tried not to gag.

'What about the blood?' Victoria said, pointing to the finger-prints on the back of the chair.

'I cut myself accidentally, chopping pumpkin last night. I must have forgotten to clean it off.'

'Okay, so you're leaving Dad for Angus. But what about the unicorns? Is that some sort of revenge?'

Here, Margaret turned a watermelon pink. 'No. They're not your father's. They never were. They're mine.' She bit her lip and looked over at the wall again.

'Then why'd you say they were Dad's?'

'And why are you collecting them in the first place?' Victoria said.

Margaret closed her eyes. When she spoke, her voice was small.

'I suppose I was embarrassed.' Her eyes welled. 'I was just looking for some magic to come back into my life.'

And Elizabeth was sure, right then, her own heart might break too.

14

Fullerton Frat House report: Have explained erectile dysfunction is engineering term for problems with buildings.
PS Happy to report no building problems here. Looking forward to you joining the construction team once more ;)

Leila sat alone on the bus on her way back to Clapham. She jumped when her phone rang and she pulled it from her messenger bag. It was Kate.

'How's it going?' Kate said, and Leila could hear the tension in her voice. The days were quickly rushing towards the grand opening.

'Good. Quentin's given me details. I just need to put all the paperwork together, meet up with him again to check it's what he wants, then I should have it all ready for you sign.'

She searched her mind and heart to see whether or not she should tell Kate about Quentin's one big condition. It was likely to throw Kate off balance and that wasn't in their best interests right now. The fourth red square of her risk-assessment chart was all about Kate and her tendency to get the wobbles. Leila believed Quentin's plan was reasonable. But she didn't have time to assess her conundrum further because Kate was moving on, her voice energised.

'Great. That's great.'

'How's the shop looking? I feel bad having to work away so much, at meetings and at home on the internet. Maybe I should stop networking and come and do some labour?'

'No, we need you out there. We can't exist without an infusion of money so your job right now is arguably more important than ours. We can get this place up and running but without more cash it will fall over before the first hurdle, I'm afraid.'

There was a lot riding on Quentin, especially since he was the only serious bite she'd had in the timeframe she had to work in. For some reason, he'd chosen The Tea Chest as his latest target and was committed to following through. It had to be a good sign, surely. He must be convinced of the value of the company.

'Would you like me to tee up a time for you to meet with Quentin?' Leila said.

'That's a good idea. I've no idea when we'll fit it in. Time is rushing by so fast. Let me get back to you on that one.'

'Okay.'

'By the way,' Kate went on, 'Elizabeth and I have put together some press releases. I've left them on the computer for you to look at with your editor's eye, if that's okay.'

'Of course. I should be back at the house soon and I'll print them out and make them all shiny.'

Kate paused. 'Look, things were a bit strained at home when I left this morning. Bill's not in good shape, obviously, so I think it's probably a good idea if we give him as much space as possible. Can't feel good to have your wife of more than thirty years leave you for another guy in front of an audience of young women.'

'Poor Bill.' Leila meant it. He'd always been so lovely to her. When he'd discovered how much she liked Vegemite he'd popped into Tesco to get some so she could have it on her toast for breakfast. He'd smiled and smoothed his thinning hair and had looked so pleased when she'd clapped her hands in response.

And he'd gone to find an extra oil heater for Kate and Leila's room. 'Our summer's probably like your winter,' he'd said, wheeling it into position. She and Kate had been perfectly cosy in the room but they smiled gratefully and his care had made them both feel even more welcome.

'I'll be as quick and quiet as I can,' she promised.

Leila was nearly home when her phone vibrated in her pocket.

Gr8 news. Booked flight to Thailand. Keeping it a surprise from them till I get there. Not long till i c my girl.

Her feet came to an abrupt halt and she stared at the screen. The phone felt as heavy as a brick.

She'd often thought about what she'd done when she'd interfered with Lucas's emails. She'd pondered the virtue of her actions in the middle of the night, unable to sleep, terrified Lucas would find out what she'd done and turn on her.

But she'd done it in his best interests, hadn't she? If she really wanted the outcome to be in her favour she'd have let him read it, let him see his single-minded determination to pursue work over a relationship was wasted. Let him see *her*, waiting for *him*.

That night at the office, she hadn't had long enough to weigh it all up thoughtfully before acting. She'd had to make a choice on the spot and, rightly or wrongly, she'd chosen to spare him the pain. Her late-night dissections of her action inevitably arrived at the conclusion that she'd overstepped the mark. Then she was thrown into endless wondering if she should confess before he found out.

Surely, if she was going to tell him the truth, now was the perfect moment.

She hit reply. She began to type. Then hit the backspace button over and over again. Then hit *cancel* and shoved the phone back in her bag with a groan. A sudden gusty breeze shot through her jacket and made her wrap her arms around herself. There was really too much else going on right now for her to be able to give her reply the consideration it deserved.

By the time she got back to the house, her worries had turned more towards Bill. She took a deep breath and turned the key in the front door, calling out his name loudly as she entered.

There was only silence in return. No television. No answering cheery call as usual. She wasn't sure if he was out or was simply hiding behind the closed door of his bedroom. The sight of his tartan cap sitting on the hook near the umbrella stand made her heart lurch. The poor bugger.

She moved quietly down the hall, feeling like an intruder. She'd just have a shower, change her clothes, print out what she needed and do a bit of work online and then she could leave Bill alone to his grieving.

Three hours later, everything was ready. She'd edited the press releases for Kate and had typed up all the paperwork for the investment deal, using a contract template from the investor website on which she'd found Quentin.

It all looked in good order to her. She'd edited enough contracts, tenders and agreements to know what they should look
like. Of course, she'd still have a solicitor look at it. And once
again, the tight timeframe demanded she make a quick decision.
Fortunately, Clive Evans, the leasing agent, was an occasional
solicitor who'd agreed to look at it for a good price so she uploaded
it to her email message and sent it off.

Then she chewed a nail to shorten it, rather than finding a
pair of scissors, and sent the contract to the printer to get a clean
copy.

There was just that one point in the paperwork that would
send Kate into a meltdown.

Quentin had the investment money and was all ready to
go—on one condition. He accurately pinpointed one of their
weakest links, just as Leila had in her risk assessment: the fact
they were unknown in England and brought no loyal customers
or even word-of-mouth lead-in.

'You have a great business,' he'd said. 'But if you're to succeed
in the fiercely competitive London scene then you have to satu-
rate the market, fast. You need citywide exposure. I want to see
you on bus shelters, hear you in radio ads, and see you in magazines. You need to convince everyone that you've always been
here and your supremacy is unchallengeable.

'You need to trust me, Leila. This is what I do for a living. It's
in my interests to make sure this venture is a success. I need to
work just as hard as you. Failure is not an option.'

Leila chewed another nail. Kate would be more than a little
reluctant. But the grand opening was happening in two days.
She really had no choice. It was sink or swim. Kate wanted to
swim and Quentin was handing out flotation devices. They'd be
crazy to turn him down. Her job was to hold Kate's hand until

she could cross the deep waters. That's why Kate had hired her. For now, she'd just make that decision for her. Kate would thank her in the end.

She grinned then, suddenly filled with visions of the incredible success of The Tea Chest and the pivotal role she'd played in making it happen. Her career had taken the most wonderful, surprising, challenging and ultimately rewarding turn. Strahan Engineering was fast becoming a horrible dream she'd never have to think about again. Her mother would be proud. Lucas would be impressed. Perhaps Kate might even extend her role and this would be a whole new beginning for her.

Twenty years earlier

The night of Simone's fortieth-birthday dinner loomed heavy with clouds and rain that made all the guests wet and puffed when they arrived at the new Eagle Street Pier restaurant. Judy shook off her umbrella at the door and slid it into the stand, already bulging with others dripping water on the floor.

Simone was in place at the head of the long table, surrounded by friends, and looking fantastic in a kohl-coloured chiffon wrap blouse that showed off her trim figure. The ruched satin trousers did the same. Her hair was parted on the side and pulled back loosely behind her ears, the picture of casual elegance.

Judy ran her hand down her own black stirrup pants, brushing off raindrops and feeling much more than just two years older than her stepsister.

Simone's shriek of laughter cut through the music, chatter, kitchen noise and clinking glassware and signalled she'd already had at least two Long Island iced teas. She suddenly looked towards the door at Judy and Graham and waved excitedly, beckoning them to the table.

They sat a few seats down from Simone. Graham held out his hand to the friends already there, introducing himself and his wife, always so much more at ease with strangers than Judy. She didn't recognise any of these people, or even their names, come to think of it, and marvelled at how quickly Simone's friends seemed to come and go from her life. They were all young and fresh-faced, some singles, some couples, none who looked like they had children, some even wearing deliberately ripped jeans with their high heels, something Judy considered showed an appalling lack of taste in a fine restaurant such as this. She sat rigid, wondering if she and Graham were there because Simone had genuine affection for them or because Judy was a financial partner in Simone's latest business.

Joining in Simone's business ventures had been an easy thing to do in that time following the death of baby Erin and the dark, endless days that followed. Having inherited from both her mother and stepfather, Judy had cash to play with, time to fill, and bookkeeping skills to share. Simone needed start-up finance for each enterprise and Judy had to admit she had a flair for picking good opportunities. In the past seven years, Simone had moved on from lollies to handbags and then to coffee. She had a skill for picking niche growth opportunities, envisioning their future but never picking a 'star business' that followed a trend for a brief period and then burned out. Simone wasn't into building businesses around fads; she picked unique opportunities to supply new takes on classic favourites. And so far, they'd made good returns on each one.

But Simone seemed to get bored. She changed her business sights as many times as she seemed to change the home she was renting and the company she kept, something Judy found irritating, but for reasons she couldn't quite identify. After all, there'd been no major financial issues. So what did it matter?

Judy scanned the restaurant's menu. The sand crab lasagne sounded too good to ignore. The waiter flicked open her white starched napkin and laid it across her lap.

Beside her, Graham laughed heartily with the woman next to him over something she'd said, the lines around his eyes just that bit deeper now he'd passed forty-five. She loved those lines, envied them, actually. Envied that he'd managed to keep them after the loss of their daughter, whereas she'd simply developed new ones—long ones that ran down from the corners of her mouth where her face had been set with sadness and anger for so long. She resisted the urge now to reach out her finger and trace Graham's beautiful smile lines. Some days, his smile had been all there was to brighten her day and calm her racing mind, pushing away the endless questions and guilt.

Had she done something wrong? Was it her fault? Why would God send a child and then take her away before she'd even been in the world?

She took a deep breath now and sat up straighter, focusing her eyes on the people around her, and tried to pick up a thread of conversation to join.

At least she had her marriage to hold on to, and her successful business investments with Simone. Fair Trade was a new concept that was gaining momentum and Simone had combined this with the public's love of chocolate to import a select range of fine products from Guatemala. The business was booming. And it wasn't a totally unpleasant consequence to have quite a few samples in the house either.

Just then, a man in a suit jacket—Marco, if memory served—tapped his knife to his wine glass and held it high.

'To Simone,' he said, causing Simone to blush noticeably.

'To Simone,' everyone agreed. And Judy caught Simone's eye and gave her a warm smile. Simone was always so grounded at the beginning of a new business venture. Judy enjoyed seeing her thrive and each time she hoped it would last a little bit longer than the last.

15

Neil Diamond's music was playing in the café when Leila arrived with the paperwork. Quentin was singing along while reading the newspaper, dressed in jeans and a pale pink T-shirt.

'Neil Diamond's a bit daggy, isn't he?' she said, standing at his table.

'Hey there,' he said, pulling out a chair for her. 'Neil's timeless.'

'He will be soon. He's practically dead.'

Quentin flinched and covered his heart with his hand. 'Ouch.'

She took her seat and he closed his newspaper, the muscles in his forearms flexing in the process and she had to look away. She shouldn't be noticing anyone's forearms other than Lucas's.

Then again, why shouldn't she? Her mother always said a woman couldn't have a good job and a good man at the same time so you had to pick one and be happy with that. She had a good job now. By her mother's reasoning, men were off the table. Lucas certainly was and wasn't showing any signs of changing. Yet here was Quentin.

She looked back and this time gave him a long, appreciative stare.

He caught her glance and returned it with an outright flirty smile. She failed to suppress an embarrassed snort.

'Did you just snort?' he said.

'No.'

'Yes you did.'

'No I didn't.'

'Yes you did.'

'Should we look at the paperwork?' she said.

He leaned back, appraising her. 'Yes we should. But then we should have dinner. Somewhere nice.'

'It's only two o'clock.'

'Then we'll have a late lunch. And if we still like each other after that we'll just keep eating through the night.'

'Is that appropriate?'

'Eating? You're right. That much food is probably irresponsible. Children are starving in third world nations. Moreover, people are hungry on the streets of London. Maybe we should go find them and invite them to join us.' He stood up as if to go looking in the streets.

She laughed. 'Not the food—the date.'

He gave her that flirtatious glint again and her insides squirmed. 'Is it a date?'

'It sounds like a date.'

'Perhaps it is. It's probably not appropriate.'

She deflated.

'But I think it's necessary,' he said.

And she expanded with happiness once more.

Two days to go.

The tile grouting on the wall was almost sponged clean but Elizabeth kept rubbing anyway, just to make sure. She sat back on her haunches, her biceps aching from the repetitive motion. The Tea Chest looked good. Kind of. If you could ignore the unpainted window frames, the ladders, spilled plaster, unhung curtains, empty shelving, and cupboards waiting to be sanded, painted and have their handles attached. Not to mention all the stock to be displayed and all the fine touches.

Okay, on second look it was worse than they'd hoped it would be at this late stage.

All the tradespeople had left. To their credit, they'd all finished on time. It was just the four of them now to finish up. But what had looked like something they might knock over in a day was taking a shockingly long time.

Even so, Kate was proudly walking around the space with her laptop in hand, giving Mark and her sons a guided tour via Skype. Her eyes were lit up with joy to have them see the progress that had been made.

'It looks amazing,' she heard Mark say.

'What's that?' one of the boys said.

Kate was standing by a wooden barrel.

'It's a wine barrel.'

'Why?' That must have been James. He sounded young.

'Because it's pretty.' Kate smiled.

Over on the other side of the shop, Leila was struggling to measure up spots for wall hangings, to get them exactly evenly spaced and level. Considerable cursing was coming from that corner of the room. And Victoria was high on a ladder, taking her blessed time about applying a stencilled gold leaf pattern to parts of the ceiling.

'You better go and get ready for school,' Kate said now, wandering towards Elizabeth and hugging the laptop close.

'Bye,' the boys sang in unison and Kate blew them kisses and waved frantically at the screen.

'I'd better go too,' Mark said.

Kate spun the laptop around again so he could see Elizabeth. She smiled and waved. 'Bye, Mark. Have a good day.'

'Bye,' Leila sang through a pencil wedged sideways between her teeth.

'See ya,' Victoria said, spinning around on her ladder.

'Bye, ladies.' Mark grinned. 'You're doing the most amazing job. It's going to be sensational.'

Kate spun him back to her for a final goodbye. 'You're doing such a great job with the boys. I'm really proud of you guys. We do make great children.' She paused. 'As opposed to all those other kids we made that weren't any good.'

'It's the kids we reject that make our kids the best.'

Kate laughed and Elizabeth heard herself release an involuntary sigh in the back of her throat. What an incredible gift to have such a close relationship with your husband.

When Kate had finally signed off, Elizabeth smiled at her. 'You two are so cute together.'

'Yeah.'

'Where did you meet?'

'At a rally in the city. We were protesting against the logging of old-growth forests.'

'And did you know straight away that you were meant to be?'

Kate tilted her head to the side to think. 'Well, I wouldn't say I knew in those first few minutes of jostling together with placards, but I think by the time we'd finished our Vietnamese noodles later that afternoon I had a pretty good idea he was special.'

'You've gone all rosy and glowy,' Elizabeth laughed.

'What about you? Where did you meet John?'

'Nothing as exotic as that. I was cleaning his house, actually. It was less than a week after I'd arrived in Australia, on a holiday with my best friend Gail—former best friend after she dumped me for the first guy who shouted her a beer at the pub. I was doing anything to make some cash to get started on my great backpacking adventure. But I never got further than Brisbane because John swept me off my feet.'

'What did he do?' Kate said, joining Elizabeth on the floor and drinking from a bottle of water. She looked tired, unsurprisingly. None of them was built to be a labourer and these long hours were pushing them to their limits. They kept themselves going by joking about how svelte they'd look at the end.

'He offered to show me around Brisbane and he hired bicycles in the city and we rode together through the botanical gardens and along the riverbank. It was really lovely. And then he literally knocked me over. He ran into me by accident and I fell off the bike and injured my knee. He felt so awful and I couldn't work for a few days so he put me up in his spare bedroom and nursed me and that was it. I never left.'

Leila joined them, sitting down and leaning back on her hands, her legs stretched out in front and her ankles crossed. 'I met Lucas in army greens,' she said. 'He was my team's paintball captain. It's what the guys at Strahan do for team bonding. We had fake guns and war paint.'

'Couldn't they just oil themselves up and wrestle it out like they do at medieval festivals?' Victoria said, flopping down to join the circle. She had paint under her nails and proceeded to use the edge of a metal spatula to scrape it out.

'I thought you and Lucas were just mates?' Kate said.

'Hmm. We are, technically. But I guess we're a bit more than that too,' Leila said.

Elizabeth slid her eyes to Kate's face but couldn't read it. Kate was maintaining a steady gaze.

Leila changed the focus. 'What about you?' she asked Victoria. 'Any men in your life?'

Elizabeth caught herself holding her breath. It was fascinating getting to know her kid sister as a fully fledged adult.

Victoria shrugged. 'Nothing that's ever been serious.'

'That seems impossible,' Kate said. 'You're sweet, attractive and easy to get on with. And you have fantastic attention to detail too,' she said, gesturing to the stencil pattern on the ceiling.

It did look great. Elizabeth felt a pang of disappointment in herself. *She* should have said all those things about Victoria. She should be nicer to her.

Her sister waved a hand in the air, dismissing Kate's praise.

'It's true,' Elizabeth said. 'You have a lot to offer someone.'

Victoria's eyes locked onto hers and Elizabeth realised just how much Victoria still wanted her big sister's approval. She might not be pestering her to borrow her makeup or to tag along to Elizabeth's friends' houses, but inside, she was still the little girl who looked up to her. Elizabeth made a mental note to remember that.

One day to go.

Kate faced Leila, absorbing the news Leila had just tentatively delivered while handing her the final contract to sign.

Quentin was asking for a commitment of a quarter of a million pounds towards an advertising campaign. It was a sign of faith, of them meeting Quentin halfway while he put money into plant materials—blending machines, barrels, stills, supplies: anything that could be sold off later if he needed to get his money back. He was putting the weight of the risk largely onto them while still giving them a leg up.

It was fair, really, but it was almost more than Kate's exhausted mind and body could take. The Tea Chest was opening tomorrow.

She wiped her plaster-splashed hand across her face and turned to face the corner of the tiled wall she'd been working on, taking deep breaths. Leila huddled in close and continued speaking in hushed tones while the rest of the room went quiet, until Elizabeth started an inane conversation with Victoria about the latest song she'd heard. Then she turned up the radio to give Kate some sense of privacy and they began noisily moving plants around.

'Kate,' Leila said soothingly, 'I understand, truly.'

'Do you? Is it your finances, reputation and family on the line? Is it your company?'

Leila winced. 'No.'

'Because this is it for me. My last chance. If this all turns to poo, I . . . I don't know what I'll do.' She wiped at her dirty face. 'How could this happen so close to the opening? I've got no room to move now.'

'Well, to be fair, you said you'd get back to me about meeting Quentin but you didn't.'

Kate looked away. It was true. She'd got so caught up in the design that she'd pushed it to the back of her mind.

'It's just how it's unfolded,' Leila said. 'I did my best, Kate, but this juggernaut started back in Brisbane when you took control of a company in crisis.' She finished her lecture sternly, though her bottom lip quivered slightly.

Kate had never felt more homesick than she did in that moment. She would have traded the whole store, the whole company, for one hour in Mark's arms and some little-man time with her boys.

She needed to pull herself together or she wouldn't make it through the next day.

As much as she wanted to yell at Leila, this was what it meant to lead a company. This was what she'd signed up for. And this was why she'd hired Leila: to help make bold choices and see business weaknesses and advantages. She'd hired her on instinct. She had to trust that intuition.

But she'd made a mistake in not meeting Quentin. She wouldn't make a mistake like that again.

Fullerton Frat House report: We love you. You'll be the newest celebrities of London!!!!! xxxxx
PS James says you're cleverer than Bob the Builder.

Kate was more nervous than she'd been before the birth of either of her children. With them, it had been overwhelming and somewhat scary, but she'd also held a deep belief that she could do it. That some primal force of nature would make it happen. But with this there was no such force guaranteeing a result.

It had been all hands on deck until three-thirty in the morning to pull off this ambitious task in time for the grand opening, followed by express manicures from Victoria to tidy up their labourers' hands.

And, of course, there was Leila's bombshell to contend with.

Now, Kate had had about an hour's sleep.

She'd washed her hair and taken time to dress. She needed to look the part. All of their 'uniforms' had to fit the theme of the shop.

She'd bought herself a vintage cream princess dress. It had fine amber ribbons for shoulder straps that tied in delicate bows at the top of the bodice. The dress was embroidered all over. It had a full layered tulle skirt and a finely boned bodice to support her where she needed it. It was glamorous and very 'English garden tea party'. She'd matched it with cream Mary Jane pumps with a dangerously high heel and bows across the ankles. Her hair was scooped back with a floral hairband.

'You look amazing,' Leila had said as they left the house.

'You too.'

Leila was in a vintage 1950s pink cocktail dress—a young style Kate knew she was well past being able to pull off. It was strapless, showing off Leila's gym-toned shoulders, and had a lace-covered bodice and a layered pleated mesh and lace skirt.

'That colour really suits you,' Kate said. 'You've got a real glow about you that's totally unfair given how little sleep you've had.'

Leila's cheeks turned the colour of her dress.

Kate took the moment before the clock struck nine-thirty to apply some more deodorant. She was sweating with anxiety and didn't want to ruin her beautiful dress. Around the shop, Elizabeth and Victoria were also applying finishing touches, both also dressed in exquisite floral, lacy vintage pieces. Kate breathed deeply and mentally forced herself to drink in her surrounds—her vision come to life.

The shop had been designed as an exquisite English cottage garden. They had left bare as much of the stonework as possible and exposed beams, capturing the feel of an old English world. Structurally, the biggest renovation had been the installation of a row of skylights from one end of the shop to the other in the front half of the store—the structural feature that made Kate's whole creation possible. The skylights flooded the interior with natural light and they'd been able to create an indoor garden. Backup lighting that would illuminate the room on dark days had been designed and installed. Strategically placed UV lighting would assist the plants as necessary, particularly those towards the back of the store, where the shade-lovers grew. White fairy lights adorned the walls and ran around vertical wooden beams, to add to the sense of enchantment.

White picket-fence palings had been glued to the walls in among the flower beds and plants. A huge water feature dominated the centre of the room, with two white entwined doves topping the piece. A small wooden wheelbarrow with rusted metal wheels sat overflowing with bright purple, pink, white and yellow petunias. Scooped wooden gates with iron hinges acted as shelves and partitions. Two sets of wrought-iron round tables and chairs sat in corners for customers to rest on, as did a wrought-iron garden bench, all surrounded by pansies, snapdragons and irises. Climbing vines snaked their way along beams and shelves. Huge pots contained orange and lemon trees. The room glowed.

Nestled within the colour and greenery lay shelves, barrels and garden pieces that brimmed with the teas themselves.

But the *pièce de résistance* was the part that was closest to Kate's heart. It was a series of window boxes growing plants that served as an interactive tea-making centre. They could be seen through the windows from the footpath and would entice people in off the streets. Here, customers could pick their own ingredients, including mint, lavender, rose petals, dandelion petals and lemongrass, and The Tea Chest staff would make them their own tea design right there in the store, then they could sit in one of the welcoming spots to sip it. There were also vintage china pots with dried ingredients they could choose from. It was the *pot-pour-tea* section.

Looking around the room, Kate's chest swelled with satisfaction.

'It's time,' Elizabeth announced, taking Kate's hands. 'You ready?'

The media releases had done their work and people from several newspapers, an online news company and even a radio station turned up for the grand opening. The four gorgeous women were photographed in their frocks and some of the photos, shown to Kate on the viewing screen of their digital cameras, were so beautiful she couldn't believe it was her or her shop. They looked like they belonged in a glossy magazine. Many of the journalists picked up on the idea that the tea shop had embraced Kate Middleton's love of English gardens that was demonstrated when she brought the outdoors indoors to Westminster Abbey for her wedding and transformation to the Duchess of Cambridge.

The bell above the door didn't stop ringing all day with customers. Randolph and Manu came in from the Roulette deli next door and were effusive in their praise. Randolph stood with his thumbs hooked under the lapels of his purple velvet smoking jacket, which he wore to the store each day, and turned his face to the skylights, clucking with appreciation.

'Brilliance,' he gushed. 'Absolute brilliance. You've brought the outdoors inside. How very *Australian* of you.' He took a piece of icing-sugar-dusted crystallised ginger from a silver bowl and popped it into his mouth, closing his eyes and swooning in appreciation.

'Oh,' Kate said, looking up. 'I was going for the look of an English garden.'

'And you've got it, Princess,' Manu agreed. 'You'll be the talk of the town in no time.'

'You must come see us soon,' Randolph went on, sucking his cheeks as he finished his ginger. 'We have a new shipment of gourmet treats from Saudi Arabia arriving in the next week. Some would complement your store wonderfully.'

Kate promised she'd be over just as soon as she could.

Angelique from Elegance also came in. Her long carrot-orange hair was striking as it framed her lily-white face above her bright yellow dress. She made polite small talk and smiled congenially, but Kate could tell she turned up her nose at The Tea Chest's collection of teapots, ceramics and antiques. They were a far cry from her fine bone china wares.

It irritated Kate for a moment, this swift judgement of her store. After all, shouldn't Angelique be grateful for a neighbour who hosted *similar* products but not ones that were exactly the same?

'Would you like some tea?' Kate offered.

'Oh, thank you, but I can't stay. I have an appointment with a blue-ribbon customer in five minutes.' She checked her watch, which looked as though it was made entirely of diamonds. 'I just wanted to come in and wish you well,' she said, though Kate couldn't tell how much sincerity there was in the statement.

Angelique glided out the front door.

'Somehow, I don't think we'll be having her over for jelly shots after work,' Victoria giggled.

Lady Heavensfield did not make an appearance, though she did her best to make the most of the opening-day traffic as it came past her entrance, with enticing smells of food wafting out onto the footpath and neatly written chalkboards encouraging serious food lovers her way.

The old-fashioned cash register *ker-chinged* satisfyingly throughout the day with every purchase of tea, antique teapots, books and tea canisters. Kate was run off her high-heeled feet by midday, but she sent Victoria out for salad rolls and steak burgers from Picasso, on the other side of their neighbour, Roulette, and they just kept moving.

To her delight, Mark sent a huge bouquet of English roses from him and the boys to wish her well on her big day. *We're so proud of you*, the note said and for a moment tears threatened. Instead, Kate buried her nose in the red and white blooms and inhaled their beautiful aroma.

She expected some sort of message from Judy, some kind of token gesture wishing them well. After all, she still owned half the company—it was in her interest to hope for the best. But all was silent from her end.

Kate had little time to dwell on it, however, as the steady stream of customers kept her hopping. Even Robert Drizzle from the council came back to visit and did indeed bring his wife with him to collect her free samples. She was a small, mousey woman but exceptionally knowledgeable about tea and Kate spent a good twenty minutes indulging her passion.

'Green and white teas have the highest levels of antioxidants,' Kate told her. 'They've had little oxidation and are uncured as opposed to oolongs and blacks, which are oxidised before curing.'

'Are there any artificial flavourings?' Mrs Drizzle said, squinting at Kate in a manner that suggested she'd forgotten her glasses.

'Absolutely not. The flavours come from flowers, herbs, spices or smoking. Sometimes essential oils too. And they're mixed in metal drums or glass so they don't absorb any flavours they shouldn't. The trick is to get all the blends to taste the same as the last so that when you buy your favourite you know you're getting what you like.'

It was a valuable conversation that landed Kate a £150 sale.

Robert Drizzle smiled and waved as he shepherded his wife out the door and Kate knew she'd just made a lifelong customer.

Then she went to check on Elizabeth, who was weaving her way through the throng of people crowded in the shop. She'd been making tea for hours.

'I'm handing it out faster than I can make it,' she said.

'Here,' Kate said, taking a tray of freshly brewed Turkish delight tea in cups. 'Let me help.'

Over at the cash register, Leila was ringing up a sale for a well-dressed grey-haired gentleman (there was really no other word for him). He looked as though he'd started his Christmas shopping early. Leila was wrapping sets of colourful fleur-de-lis glasses and bottles for iced tea, packets of tea-infused truffles, embroidered vintage serviettes for elegant tea parties, DIY cotton drawstring bags for those inclined to make their own tea blends, pink heart-shaped sugar cubes, cotton bath bags for tea-infused bath times, as well as everyday products such as infusers and boxed teacups.

Kate rushed over to introduce herself and throw in some fudge and honeycomb drops to thank him and encourage him to come back. And into everyone's bag went a flyer advertising the upcoming tea tasting and tea workshops—Kate's personal passion.

At the end of the day, the four women closed the door and collapsed onto chairs and benches with groans and whimpers as their high heels came off and bruised toes were rubbed.

'I don't think I've ever been so tired,' Elizabeth groaned. Her hair had escaped its pins during the day and hung loosely around her shoulders.

Victoria snapped a photo of her on her phone.

'Are you mad?' Elizabeth grumbled.

'You look beautifully dishevelled,' Victoria said, and it was such a sentimental thing for her to say that no one said anything in response.

'Is there some kind of alcoholic tea?' Leila said eventually, stretching her arms above her head. 'We need to celebrate.'

'Peach tea and peach schnapps is a favourite of many of my clients back home,' Kate mused, staring at the floor, her eyes too heavy even to move.

'Forget that,' Elizabeth said. 'Champagne all the way, I say.'

And so they dragged their brutally punished bodies out the door, swinging their shoes in their hands, and made their way down the street towards the Chelsea Potter for champagne cocktails to celebrate their incredibly successful day.

16

Quentin came to visit the shop and meet Kate the day after the launch.

'Welcome, Quentin. Thank you so much for coming on such short notice. I'm sorry I haven't been able to meet you sooner, but I'm happy you're here now.'

'Pleasure to meet you,' he said, extending his hand and giving her a generous smile.

Kate looked up into his face and assessed it for information, some sign she was doing the right thing. His expression was open and calm. He was young, though. Probably not much younger than her, but younger than she'd expect an investor of his sort to be. She always imagined investors to be older, semi-retired or people whose experience had been gained from a lifetime of business acquisitions.

'The place looks fantastic,' he said, rubbing his chin and striding down the aisles, nodding and smiling, absorbing it in big, general notes rather than with any attention to fussy details.

'Thank you,' she said, settling into the feeling of pride that swept over her. The shop was busy again today, customers arriving the moment she'd opened the doors. The Tea Chest team had had no time to rest or regain their strength but just had to keep going.

Kate introduced him to Elizabeth, who was rearranging a display so it sat better in a walkway, and to Victoria, who was in the galley, ironing tablecloths.

'And Leila you know, of course,' Kate said, ending the meet-and-greet at the counter, where Leila was just finishing off wrapping a parcel for a customer.

'Hi again,' she said, flicking him a glance before returning to her raffia.

'Leila's been really helpful,' Quentin said. 'Her work's been impressive. I feel like I know The Tea Chest well.'

Two things happened to Kate at once. First, she felt a small bristle at his assumption that he could possibly know her company having only looked at it on paper and never before now experienced its spirit and tactile nature. And second, she sensed a vibe fizzing in the space between Quentin and Leila. She studied Leila but the other woman was intent on swiping the credit card through the machine.

'Well, that's wonderful,' she said, directing her eyes back to Quentin.

'Thank you, Kate, for giving me the opportunity to be part of such an exciting new company.'

'Thank you for your interest,' she said. 'Let's step next door to Roulette and go through the paperwork together before we send it off to the solicitor.'

'Fantastic idea,' he said congenially. Kate shot one more look at Leila but her eyes were fixed elsewhere.

The dinner Quentin and Leila shared had moved them into a different space. A not-strictly-business space. It was a bit too flirty. A bit too much laughter. A bit too much eye contact. A bit too much wine.

And she hadn't thought about Lucas once that night.

During the two weeks following the grand opening, any time Leila wasn't working in the shop, she was meeting Quentin. He took her for ice cream and to ride the London Eye. They walked the streets and fed ducks in the park. They ate constantly. And he refused to talk about business.

'Forget business,' he said. 'This is time in our other world, with just us. Anyway, there's nothing else to do. Once your solicitor sends back the contract we can sign it and Kate's getting the money organised—all we need to do now is get to know each other better.'

'What about the ads?' she said, biting into pink candy floss.

'They're under control and I'll bring them to you when they're ready. Now, how about a trip to Oxford and a punt on the river?'

'That sounds a bit romantic.'

'So let's be romantic. I'll punt and you can lie back with a glass of wine and watch my muscles ripple. And when we pass under a bridge at sunset I'll kiss you.'

And that's precisely how they shared their first kiss.

Elizabeth was in charge of the shop. It had been two weeks since the launch and the first week had been grand. So grand that Kate had said she felt it was the right time for her and Leila to take a short leave and go and explore new territories.

She had to begin addressing the company's long-term requirements. The business was going to need contacts with local growers and suppliers of additional ingredients so they could blend on site. It was essential that the tea sold in England tasted as though it belonged here. As much as possible the ingredients should come from local sources. It was their commitment to quality and community responsibility.

'We can't do much about the teas themselves,' Kate had explained. 'Almost all tea in the world comes from India and China and there's no point trying to beat that. But herbs, fruits and flowers taste different depending on the country or region in which they're grown. Lavender oil from France smells different and has different medicinal properties from lavender that comes from England or Bulgaria, for example.' If she was going to *sell tea to the English*, then the English had to believe it was worth buying. And selling local produce was a huge drawcard for the growing market of people who wanted to support ethical production of food.

As well as taking care of the food-chain supply, they were going to need to build a database of good and reliable people for transport, design work, sales and food production.

Leila had been sending through marketing plans and draft advertisements for her to look at and provide feedback on, but so far she'd had to do all of this outside of shop hours, as customers had been pouring through the door, babbling about the great review they'd read or even about the tea they'd tasted at their friend's place the other day.

Luckily, Elizabeth had Victoria to help and so far her sister was proving to be a valuable employee, something that both surprised and delighted her. Right now, Victoria was handing out tasting cups of iced rose, mint and vanilla tea, which had been made entirely of fresh ingredients. The teas made of fresh ingredients always tempted the customers to try to make their own blends from the garden or the dried supplies. Invariably, they ended up buying something pre-prepared from the shelf anyway, but it always inspired them and left them smiling.

Smiling was something Elizabeth now felt she could do more often. She deliberately saved her biggest smiles for the customers. Her face had started to feel heavy and set and she'd begun to fancy that her features were sliding south like a melting marshmallow. When her mother had moved out, the quasi homey feel of the house had gone with her. Her father's morose shuffling from one room to another was dispiriting in the extreme. She wanted to help him more, but she had enough on her plate with her own grief for herself and her marriage. The shop gave her an outlet to practise feelings of happiness and contentment.

John seemed to have given up trying to contact her, which was both a blessing and yet another barb of pain. She definitely didn't want to talk to him, but she still struggled to let go of the idea that he was going to fix all this and her old life might magically reappear.

Except, if she was honest, it hadn't been a happy life. Not really. So why couldn't she just move on?

She handed a gift box to a customer to fill with *pot-pour-tea*.

'Hey,' Victoria said, after she'd tied a gold ribbon around a parcel, *ker-chinged* the cash register and sent some customers out the door, 'what time are you free this evening?' She pulled out her phone to type yet another text message.

'I don't know—maybe around eight after I've looked at Leila's latest notes. Why?'

Victoria shrugged. 'Just wondering.' She moved off in her Roman sandals and flowing white baby-doll dress to greet more customers, her antique silver earrings swinging against her neck.

The phone rang beside her.

'Welcome to The Tea Chest, Elizabeth speaking, how may I help you?'

'Nice greeting. Makes me want to come and visit.'

'Kate, how are you going? Where are you?'

'The Cotswolds. It's amazing. Like something straight off a movie set. The buildings are mind-blowing, not to mention the farms. I'm in heaven. How's everything going in the shop?'

'Couldn't be better. Sales are great. I'm having a wonderful time. And Victoria's turning out to be quite the salesgirl,' she said proudly.

They chatted on for a bit about the shop and Elizabeth wrote down all of the jobs Kate had thought of for them to do while she was on the road, such as watering plants, calling the plant-servicing centre and sending thankyou notes to the Holy Trinity and the designers who'd worked so hard to get everything up and running in time for the opening.

'Also,' Kate said, 'Lady Heavensfield's been quiet lately. It's making me nervous. Do you think you could do up a gift basket of something for her?'

'No problem.'

'And while you're at it, let's send one to Randolph, Manu and Angelique to say thanks for coming to our opening.'

Elizabeth had worked her way through approximately half of Kate's list of jobs, humming happily, when the bell tinkled above the door. She turned around to greet the next customer.

Then jolted to a standstill.

It wasn't a customer at all. It was the Japanese man who'd sat next to her on the flight home.

'Hello.' He smiled. He was wearing a beige smart casual suit with a pale-green and white shirt underneath and casual loafers that should have been out of place, but somehow it all worked together.

'H-hello.'

He stepped into the shop and she made a concerted effort to adopt a more graceful pose.

Three things surprised her. First, he walked elegantly, seeming to glide nimbly across the floor, and she had the unexpected thought that he moved like a dancer. Also, he was taller than she remembered, with a small scar over his left eyebrow, just below his loosely swept fringe, that added considerable interest to his face. Last, he didn't have a Japanese accent at all.

She stood there dumbly until Victoria intervened.

'Haruka, hi.' Victoria took hold of his arms and kissed him on the cheek. The action shocked Elizabeth so much she actually did a cartoon double take. She stood in complete silence, looking from one to the other, both of them grinning at her like they expected her to do something.

'Er . . .' It was all she could manage. She took Victoria by the arm and dragged her to the other side of the shop, near a large potted orange tree, pulling her out of earshot of two grey-haired women peering at a box of matcha green tea powder through their reading glasses.

'Look,' one of them exclaimed. 'It says here you can cook with it too and make matcha tea cake.'

'It would be green,' the other said, wrinkling her nose.

'My niece would love this,' the first decided.

'What's going on?' Elizabeth whispered.

'It's Haruka, from the plane,' Victoria said, as though it was the most natural thing in the world for this complete stranger to enter their shop.

Then, shock. He *was* expected.

'*You* did this.'

Victoria shrugged, a wicked smile dancing on her lips.

'Why?' Elizabeth moaned.

'Look, he was really nice. And he really liked you. You might have been too drunk and delirious to realise it, but it was plain as day to me. You should have seen how carefully he adjusted your jacket and zipped up your carry-on bag when he handed you over to me at the arrivals hall. It was really sweet. We exchanged numbers and kept in touch. I was going to tell you but I've been waiting till you were in a better space.' She shrugged. 'I'm not sure if you are, but I still think you should go out with him.'

Elizabeth was outraged, both at her sister's Dr Phil psychology and at her gumption. 'You meddlesome fiend,' she cursed. 'You can't just make me go out with someone I don't know.' *Besides which, I'm married.* She wanted to pinch Victoria's arm in anger.

'Give him a chance. I think you'll find he's got a lot to offer. And,' she added, 'I prefer to think of it as helpful.'

'Meddlesome.'

'Helpful.'

'Meddlesome.'

'You say potato, I say vodka.'

'Ahem.' Haruka cleared his throat. 'Is everything okay?'

'Fine,' Elizabeth called over her shoulder. Then she hissed at Victoria, 'You'll pay for this.'

She returned to where Haruka was standing, looking a little less confident than he had a few moments ago. He put a tentative hand on the counter, then removed it again.

'I'm sorry if I'm not wanted here,' he said uncertainly.

Elizabeth realised now that his accent was actually English. Like hers. Her head spun. Among other things, she was wondering how she could have got this man so wrong in her mind. Her memories of him didn't account for this intriguing person standing here. Perhaps Victoria was right and she'd been so out of her mind she'd distorted him entirely.

'Your sister invited me to come and meet you. I'm sorry if I've offended you. I found you so charming when we were on the plane and I was quite affected when Victoria asked if we could keep in touch.'

Elizabeth burned with indignation, remembering all the texting Victoria had been doing since they arrived and trying to calculate how much of it might have been to Haruka. What on earth had she told him? Why did the people closest to her keep going around behind her back?

'I'll go,' he said, pointing to the door. 'I've only come from Hampstead.' He paused, gazing at her meaningfully. 'It's only two tubes. No big deal really.' He checked his watch. 'I've some business to attend to in Notting Hill, but I'd hoped we'd be able to meet up after work.'

His voice was hopeful, the tilt of his head inviting. And Elizabeth was, at her core, someone who didn't like to offend people or hurt their feelings and she was beginning to feel quite sorry for the man. What a pretty pickle her sister had created.

'I enjoy eating,' he said, a teasing smile playing on his lips.

When she still said nothing, he accepted her refusal and turned to go, his shoulders drooping in a way that made him look like a sad, rejected puppy. Just as his hand reached out for the doorknob, her heart squeezed back to life. She groaned.

'Wait,' she said.

He turned back towards her, his face hopeful.

'Please don't be offended. I was just taken by surprise.' She turned to glare at Victoria before continuing, 'I'll meet you at La Sophia in Notting Hill at eight o'clock.'

Fullerton Frat House report: Miraculous revelation—liquid soap dispensers don't actually refill themselves. I know, right? ;)
Can't believe how many things you do I never noticed before. Missing you xx
PS Also missing your hands. Could you take a picture of them and send it to me?

Kate held the bunch of lavender cuttings to her nose and inhaled. The smile across her face was instant. She rubbed the stems with her thumb and forefinger. There really was a good reason why lavender was so popular. It was the Swiss Army knife of plants. The essential oil held in those leaves and stems was beneficial for almost any condition of the body, mind or soul.

She sat down on the grass in between the long rows of bushes on this charming farm and watched the fat, furry yellow and black bumblebees doing their work among the flowers. She squinted into the sunshine and raised her face to the sky, taking a moment just to *be*.

They'd had such a hectic start to the day, navigating the hire car west from London along the M4 to reach a herb farm outside Reading. The owner of the farm, Grace Myrtle, was clearly buzzed to have Kate and Leila visit, and Kate liked her instantly. She proudly showed them through the greenhouses and they walked the hills of mature herb bushes. Like most farmers, Grace needed to make money from many avenues and had converted an old stone barn into a tea and gift shop. She was thrilled to supply The Tea Chest with her organic produce.

'I'm looking for the usual supplies of mint and chamomile,' Kate had explained to Grace's beaming round face, 'but I'm also interested in sourcing smaller quantities of less common herbs for tea, such as basil and calendula.'

Grace clasped her roughened hands together. 'No problem at all.' She'd pointed to a distant hill. 'We've actually just begun ploughing that section for new chamomile and I've a small section of basil closer to the lake.'

'Basil?' Leila said, screwing up her nose at Kate.

'Basil tea goes really well with tomato and cottage cheese on crackers. You'd be surprised,' Kate said.

'I'm sure I would,' Leila responded, sounding unconvinced.

'And basil has such wonderful health benefits for your heart, eyes, hair and skin.'

'Mmm. You wouldn't sell me on that,' Leila said.

'Okay, how about the fact that you can use the tea as a soup or broth and add your leftover meat and vegetables to it for dinner the next night?'

Leila shook her head. 'Nope. This isn't budget week for families, Kate. We're the haute couture of tea.'

Leila was right. She'd been married to Mark for too long and was confusing his passion, medicinal knowledge and healing business with her own. This was precisely what Mark and Judy had warned her about. She was an artist, with creative ideas and dreams, but sometimes lacking clear business direction.

Now, she lay down on the grass between the lavender rows at this farm in the Cotswolds, the visit to Grace at the Reading herb farm seeming an age ago, and closed her eyes to contemplate her expanding business some more. The droning of the bees around her, combined with the beautiful sunshine and heavenly aromas, lulled her into a meditative state.

It might not be fashionable, but she *was* passionate about the health benefits of tea. It was something she tried to put into every cup, even if it was hidden beneath generic statements about the tea being uplifting or soothing. She remembered Simone wrinkling her nose at 'medicinal' teas, but Simone had never understood that medicinal could be beautiful as well. All her tea had health benefits already; it was just that it was an aspect of tea sales they played down in favour of the enjoyment and ceremony of tea-drinking. Perhaps, down the track, she could launch a secondary label of teas—The Health Chest, perhaps—that produced high-end, pleasant-tasting remedy teas. Maybe it was even something she and Mark could do—a joint project that would see them working together rather than separated by time and space.

Right now, Mark was at home on his own and worrying about their finances. She wanted to ask him about it but since he hadn't raised it with her he'd obviously decided to be chivalrous and shoulder the burden for them both. It was reasonable he had doubts. But it still hurt.

The bees were soothing. She just needed to focus on the bees.

She jumped to attention when she heard her name and sat up, blinking into the light.

Leila was standing above her, grinning. 'Drift off, did we?'

'Huh?' Kate rubbed her eyes. 'Oh. I guess so. What time is it?'

'Three o'clock. I'm starving. We haven't even had lunch. You hungry?'

'Yes, actually.' Kate hauled herself off the soft grass with a granny groan that would put her actual granny to shame, if she were still alive.

They ambled to the limestone cottage that served as the tea and gift shop, similar to the one on Grace's farm. They ordered sandwiches and a pot of mint tea as well as coffees, and when they'd recovered their energy they set about purchasing gifts for their family and friends back home. Lavender soaps, wood polish, candles, boiled sweets and ice-cream syrup all made their way to the cash register.

'My mum will love this lavender wood polish,' Leila said, sniffing the solid white wax in the silver tin.

'I'd buy it with the best of intentions but I know I'd never get around to using it,' Kate said.

'Me neither. But Mum's one of those super-organised and tidy people. You know, the kind who say there's a place for everything and everything in its place.'

'That must have been fun to grow up with,' Kate said. She was trying to be light, but it clearly struck a nerve in Leila, who raised her eyebrows and twitched her nose.

'Sorry,' Kate said.

'It's fine,' Leila smiled, putting the polish away in her bag.

They hadn't met with the owners of the farm yet. They had an appointment booked for the next day, but Kate had explained she wanted to pop in like a normal visitor and get a feel for the place first. Her instincts would tell her if the plants here and the family who ran this farm were the right ones for her tea. If the plants were 'happy plants', treated with respect and love, then they'd make good tea. From what she'd seen so far, they were perfect.

La Sophia was as beautiful as Elizabeth had read it would be. A smart black metal fence with gold spikes on top greeted her at the footpath. Through the windows she could see wooden parquetry floors, warm hues on the walls and around the tables, a spiral staircase, soft chairs and soft lighting that illuminated the long dining rooms. Detailed mirrors, burnt oranges and greens and shiny curtains gave it a feeling of the Orient, or Middle Eastern caravans.

She crossed her arms, partly to keep warm against the slight chill and partly to stifle her nerves. She was still in the vintage dress she'd worn to the shop that day, though she'd changed her heels to shiny black ones and added a short-sleeved black top for extra warmth and to cover her bare arms. Cars whizzed up and down the street and couples strolled past, walking hand in hand.

What was she doing? What on earth had possessed her not only to agree to meet Haruka but to demand he take her to an expensive restaurant? It was cheeky and bold and very unlike her.

Then again, perhaps it was exactly like her. She'd been independent in another country only briefly when she and John started dating and she'd never looked back. She hadn't been asked out on a date in more years than she could count, so she couldn't possibly know if this was like her or not.

But she had no more time to consider this because Haruka was walking towards her. She was astonished at how her body reacted to the sight of him. Everything felt like a romantic old movie.

Oh no.

If she was the heroine of a romance, then this man, this *Japanese* man, was her hero. The big guy upstairs certainly had quite a sense of humour at times.

She braced herself as he reached her, smiling.

'I'm so glad you're here,' he said. 'I was afraid you wouldn't come.' His face fell and he looked away as if he'd just realised he shouldn't sound so needy and uncertain. 'Not that I . . . not that I think . . .' He laughed. 'You know.'

She heard herself laugh in response, noticed her hand reach to her hair to adjust it, and felt her skin burst with warmth and her heart quicken.

She'd turned all silly and girly.

This was terrible. How did people do this? She was right back in high school, desperately grateful for a two-minute conversation with Steven Jacobs, unable to take her eyes off him or stop giggling and feeling she might faint when his hand brushed her arm as he reached for the paintbrush in art class.

'Should we head on in?' Haruka said, tilting his head towards the door. 'Maybe start with a drink at the bar?'

Elizabeth nodded. *Great rivers of Egypt, yes.*

Haruka ordered a mojito and Elizabeth a vodka martini and it only took a sip and one brief pause for each of them before the conversation began to flow.

'I'm a ceramicist. Functional pieces only. I'm quite dreadful at figurines,' he said. 'My mother's English and my dad's Japanese. I was brought up here, mostly in boarding schools. My dad's an engineer on oil rigs and travels a lot, and my mother's a concert violinist, so she also travels.'

'Did you miss them while you were away at school?' Elizabeth asked, twirling the olive in her glass.

'Of course.'

Elizabeth popped the olive in her mouth and chewed thoughtfully. Her parents were right nutters but at least they'd been there. She couldn't imagine being thrown to the wolves and draughty halls of a cold boarding school at such a young age. Moreover, she couldn't imagine finally getting the baby she wanted so much only to ditch him a few short years later at a boarding school. It made her heart ache.

'Can you play the violin too?'

'A little.' He looked at his fingers. 'I think I play best when I'm drunk, actually.'

'Will you show me? Later on. We'll have to get you many more of these, though,' she said, signalling the barman.

'What about you?' Haruka said. 'What's your hidden talent?'

'Hmm. I'm not sure I have one.'

'Everyone has one.'

'Well, if you must know, I can juggle babies.'

'That's random.'

'I signed up for circus training a few years back, in Brisbane. My friend, Annie, thought it would be good for me, for stress release. I went every Saturday for eight weeks and they taught us to juggle. I happen to be able to juggle three babies at once.' She demonstrated, miming juggling three infants above her head.

'I don't know whether to believe you or not.'

'It's true . . . the circus training part, anyway. I can also do a complete backward bend.'

Haruka's eyes lifted as if to an imaginary screen; he was clearly picturing her bending over backwards.

'I don't actually juggle babies. They're far too likely to vomit and I really despise washing.'

Of course, she couldn't entirely ignore the tug of pain in her womb at the mention of babies. But it was a tug she was learning to live with. She wasn't able to ignore it, or push it down or make it go away. It was part of her. And she was learning that it might always be. Somewhere in the past couple of months she'd learned that she could go on living and go on experiencing

and—shock, horror—go on *enjoying* life and it could all happen at the same time as the pain and loss. It didn't have to be
one or the other.

'I'm afraid I'm going to need some proof,' Haruka said sternly.

'Of the juggling?'

'No. The backward bend.'

'Well, let's see how dinner goes first.'

Dinner, as it turned out, went fantastically well. So well that
now Elizabeth was heart-struck to realise that a big moment had
arrived. The moment when another man, someone very much
not her husband, was going to kiss her.

Her breath caught in her throat so she couldn't even begin
to utter any words of refusal. Because there he was, standing
before her, illuminated by moonlight, the shifting shadows of the
leaves of a willow tree above them caressing his face. A quiver
ran through each intake of her breath. He was going to kiss her
alright, no doubt about it. Right here on the footpath.

He was so close now she could smell the rum of his mojito
mixed with the sugary syrup and she leaned towards him, wanting to taste it on his smooth lips.

Somehow, Haruka wanted her when her own husband had
found her deficient and unworthy.

He lay his long fingers along her collarbone, smoothing over
her skin to her shoulder. She erupted in goose bumps.

His gaze rested on her lips. His brow creased in serious
concentration.

This was it. The moment was here. Part of her wanted to pull
away. She was a married woman. But her feet held fast.

He reached up his other hand so that both cupped her gently
on either side of her neck, a firm but gentle pressure drawing her

in. His face came closer and she closed her eyes in anticipation as their lips met for the first time.

She supposed, somewhere in the distant edges of her mind, that this must surely mean she'd now moved on from John.

My husband.

She shooed the voice away and melted even more deeply into Haruka's embrace. There would be plenty of time in daylight to analyse this moment. Right now, she just wanted him to keep kissing her.

17

Fullerton Frat House report: Keats decides to share new talent of flipping the bird with younger brother in back seat of car. James picks 130 kg bikie to practise on. Bikie rolls up beside window at lights. Dad practically wets himself. Kids cower in back. But bikie only wants to offer master class in the one-fingered salute. Laughs heartily. Kids squeal with delight. He waves goodbye and bares missing teeth. Kids fine. Dad's seen better days. Please come home soon and take control of your children. xx

Kate and Leila booked into a bed-and-breakfast in a small village of charming stone cottages with shingle roofs. Mighty willow trees hung over a river crossed by arched stone bridges; wooden coach wheels lay against the buildings; leafy green vines wound their way up walls; and window boxes overflowed with bright flowers. It was like walking through the set of an English country drama.

Kate was overwhelmed by the beauty and wished for the hundredth time that Mark and the boys were here too so they could share this adventure. She hadn't had an inkling of where her new job would take her after that first meeting with Simone at the Emporium.

Mark and Keats had been lying on the couch watching *Finding Nemo* when Kate returned from the Emporium. It was Keats's nap time and he lay sprawled over Mark's chest, sleepy but fighting to stay awake. She leaned over the back of the couch to kiss her baby. The sound of his tiny breathing was like the ocean, regular, soothing and hypnotic. She stroked his blond hair away from his forehead, which was damp with the summer heat, and was flooded with awe at how utterly adorable he was.

Mark reached out and touched her arm. 'How'd you go?'

Her eyes filled with tears. She nodded.

'You want it?'

'I really do.' Her throat clenched. Mark peeled himself off the couch and hugged her tightly. He smelled of oranges and play dough and she remembered thinking that this was surely what heaven smelled like.

'That's great,' he said quietly. 'Go, Katie.'

She pulled him into their bedroom. 'But what about Keats?' She winced with the pain of saying it out loud and sat down on the edge of the bed. It was not made, the sheets in tangled bunches. Above her, the rusted ceiling fan was clicking as it turned slowly around.

Her mother was out of the question. Age had slowed her right down till it was difficult for her to manage many simple tasks. Keats would be too much of a handful for her. Her father was in Cairns—and barely even knew his grandchild—and so was her sister. And Mark's family was in Melbourne, so that counted them out.

'We'll have to find childcare,' Mark said.

'No. I don't want strangers raising our child.'

'Agreed.'

They sat in silence for a few moments.

'What's the job like, anyway?'

Kate smiled for the first time since walking in the door, as she described Simone and the Emporium and the job, her excitement rising again.

'Imagine what we could do with the money,' she concluded. 'Leave this.' She gestured around the room. 'Buy our own place. Do it right. Go on holidays. Buy Keats a guitar or a pony. Build your business into an empire.' She stopped, the smile shrinking on her face. 'It's true what they say, you know. Money really does buy freedom.'

Mark's brow folded in on itself. 'Freedom buys freedom, Kate.'

'Of course, I know.' She waved him away impatiently.

'Never take a job for money. Only for passion.'

'I just mean it gives us more options, more opportunities. But yes, absolutely that is just the icing. It would be a creative dream come true.'

'The working from home option is great. You can be here half the time, and on the days you go to work I'll stay home and look after Keats. I'll just tell my clients I'm not available those days. It's easy.'

For a second, Kate's world brightened. Of course—Mark's mobile acupuncture practice was as flexible as he wanted it to be. He could work whatever hours he liked. But then the light faded. Sadly, she shook her head.

'Think about it,' she said. 'On the days I'm home I'll actually have to be working. Looking after Keats is a full-time job.

I can't work while he's running around and stealing my paper and drawing funny faces on it. If I'm going to do this job then I have to commit to it fully.'

Mark took a deep breath and leaned his head back against the wardrobe.

'And what about the new baby?' she said. 'It's the perfect job at completely the wrong time.'

'You really want this? Really, really want it?'

'Really, really,' she nodded miserably.

'Then we'll make it happen. I'll look after Keats and the baby. I'll change my business hours to nights and weekends only.'

'You can't do that,' she said. 'You're just getting momentum. It would be disastrous to stop now.'

He shook his head. His eyes were firm. 'Tsunamis, bushfires, earthquakes—those things are disasters.'

She recognised that look. It was one she couldn't argue with. 'But you love what you do.'

'And I'm not giving up. All I'm doing is changing my hours. I'll still be at the markets each week.' He smiled and reached for her hand. 'If it's important to you, then it's important to me.'

Outside in the lounge, Kate could hear *Nemo* coming to an end.

'But I'll never get to see you,' she said, her heart aching already. She and Mark spent so much time together. They didn't just live together; they shared their lives.

'We'll make it work,' he said. 'Lots of couples do it. And it's not forever. If it doesn't suit us, we'll change it. We'll re-evaluate as we go along. Besides, you might not even like the job. You might want to chuck it in after a week.'

The music for the credits was rolling and Keats appeared in the doorway, his eyes heavy, sucking his pinkie finger.

'Come here, pumpkin.' Kate opened her arms and he wandered in silently and leaned into her. She kissed his head and held him close, rubbing her cheek against his soft hair.

'So it's decided.' Mark clapped his hands together once. 'We'll do it our way. I will have my job. You will have your job. Keats and baby number two will have the best of everything. You and I will meet up for clandestine lunchtime rendezvous. It will be perfect.'

'Baby,' Keats said, pointing to Kate's belly with his wet hand.

'Yes, that's right,' she said. 'It's your baby brother or sister in there.' Then he kissed her belly in a gesture that made her want to hug him till he popped.

'So we're agreed?'

'Agreed,' she said.

'Problem solved?'

'All but one,' she said, rubbing her hands in circles on Keats's back as he lay across her lap. 'I'm going to miss my pumpkin.'

Kate and Leila were having dinner at the local pub—chicken curry on chips—when Kate's phone chirped. There was a message from Susan in Brisbane, just passing on how cold it was when she opened the store that morning to start the annual stocktake, and one from Bryony, asking whether she should put in an application for The Tea Chest to have a marketing tent at an upcoming Sydney food and wine festival. Kate sent commiserations to Susan, along with a weather report from the glorious Cotswolds, and an affirmative text to Bryony. Those stalls cost a lot, but they paid for themselves many times over in exposure. Or so Simone had always said.

There was also one from Mark.

Fullerton Frat House report: Have abandoned washing experiment.
Buying new clothes instead.

Her phone chirped again and the next message was a picture of Keats's open mouth with another tooth missing from the bottom row.

'Oh . . .' Kate was capsized by maternal angst. With each new tooth gone, she was hurtled back through time to those long nights holding her boys as their bodies burned with fever and their roars protested the pain of each eruption. So many hours soothing and singing and kissing away tears to have their hard-won prizes fall out such a short time later.

And James couldn't be far behind. Any day now he'd begin to lose teeth too.

Keats had taken to keeping his teeth in jars of water, lined up on the windowsill of the bedroom, a habit Mark found disturbing, but Kate found reassuring. Perhaps Keats wanted to hold on to his childhood just as she did. It was kind of nice to have the teeth around, these little buds she'd worked so hard to help bring into the world.

Leila's phone vibrated and she tapped it to read the message before blushing and snickering.

Kate raised an eyebrow at her. 'An admirer? Lucas?'

Leila's face flickered. 'No. Someone else.' She reached for her pint of cider.

'Have you heard from him lately?'

'Lucas? Mmm-hmm.'

Kate took a mouthful of curry. She'd wanted to ask Leila more about Lucas for a long time. 'Go on.'

Leila groaned and dropped her head into her hand. 'I'm stuck,' she said.

'Stuck?'

'As in a rock and a hard place. I really like Lucas. Always have. And I think we could be really great. And up until now, I would have jumped at the chance to have a go.'

'So, have you two, you know . . . ?'

'No. But it's not for lack of wanting to.'

'Then what's the problem?'

A backslapping round of laughter and good-natured ribbing burst forth from a dim corner of the pub where three Scotsmen clanged their pint glasses together. Kate took a moment to soak up their thick accents and ruddy faces and file them away in her memories.

A noise that was half whimper and half groan made its way from Leila's throat and brought Kate's attention back.

'It's a long story.'

'I'm not going anywhere.' Kate smiled, settling herself into the chair.

'Well, there's a roadblock of sorts to us getting together and I'm both the cause of it and the solution.'

'Okay, I'm intrigued,' Kate said. She couldn't remember the last time she'd had a truly juicy piece of gossip to mull over.

Leila went on to tell her about Achara and the email and Kate couldn't help but gasp with shock as Leila described deleting it.

'Oh, Leila.'

'I know, I know,' Leila said mournfully. 'I didn't have time to think properly. I just reacted and now I've trapped myself because I hold the piece of information that could set Lucas free from this cage of duty he's built for himself, but I shouldn't have the knowledge in the first place and he might never forgive me. And now he's booked a flight to Thailand. What should I do?'

'Gosh, I don't have the foggiest idea where to start with that tangled web.' Kate pushed herself back from the table and leaned against the tall wooden bench seat behind her.

'But you're a parent,' Leila said. 'Would you want to know or not?'

Kate chewed her bottom lip. 'Well, I couldn't imagine how painful it would be to have my child say she didn't want anything to do with me. It would be devastating. But, then again, Keats will probably be screaming he hates me in a few years time anyway. How old did you say the daughter is? Eleven? Well, there you go. Maybe it's just her age and nothing more serious than petulant rebellion. I presume they have that in Thailand too.'

'True,' Leila said, her eyes brightening with hope.

'Then again, maybe she won't change her mind at all and Lucas will arrive and she'll refuse to see him. It's a terrible risk.'

Leila's expression deflated. 'Yes.'

'No easy answer there, I'm afraid.'

'No.'

'What a mess,' Kate breathed, thinking how lucky she was not to have those sorts of romantic problems anymore. Then again, she and Mark had their own set of complications right now.

'What are you going to do?'

'I've got no idea.'

Leila's phone vibrated again.

Kate raised an eyebrow. 'So what's going on there, then?' she said, waving a finger in a circular motion around Leila's phone.

Leila reddened and it wasn't from the warm glow of alcohol. Kate slapped her gently on the hand.

'Come on. Spill.'

Leila held the phone to her chest and studied Kate, as if wondering whether or not she should share her news. 'Okay,' she said finally. 'I'll tell you. But I want you to know that I would never do anything to jeopardise The Tea Chest.'

Kate's heart knocked against her chest. 'Wait. What?'

Leila's eyes were bright. 'It's Quentin,' she whispered.

Kate shook her head, confused. 'Quentin? Angel investor Quentin?'

Leila nodded. 'Please don't be mad, Kate. I'm not mixing business with pleasure. It all happened after the deal was made.' Leila's eyes implored Kate to believe her.

'Oh.' Kate was struck dumb. A hundred thoughts raced through her mind. Was that okay if it all happened after the deal and did it really matter anyway? Leila had good business skills and she clearly loved this position, so surely she would want to make this work. Then again, it wasn't her life on the line here. Maybe this was all just a big holiday to her. An English summer fantasy.

She'd felt something at The Tea Chest that day Quentin had visited and now she wished she'd confronted Leila about it then.

Had she done the wrong thing in hiring Leila? Could there be some sort of sexual harassment issue between Leila and Quentin if it all went wrong? Had Leila been out wining and dining on The Tea Chest's budget while the rest of them were slogging it out in plaster and paint in the lead-up to the opening?

'And what about Lucas?' she said.

'Kate, please understand I didn't go looking for this. But Quentin and I, we just click. It all works. He's so smart and funny and kind and we get on so well. I know it's all terribly new and sudden but I feel I need to take this chance and see where it leads. Everything with Lucas is so up in the air and might never come to anything, regardless of what I do from here. Maybe I'm not meant to be with him. Maybe Quentin is my chance for happiness. I'm sure you can understand that.'

Kate looked at her employee's face. Surely if Leila had anything to hide then she wouldn't be sharing this news with her now. She took a deep breath and told herself she was just being silly. Leila was a young woman being wooed by a rich and successful man. She might be a little starry-eyed, but she wasn't malicious. Business was business and pleasure was pleasure. As long as the two stayed separate there was nothing to worry about. Kate had gone through the contract too and it all looked fine.

'I wish you'd told me sooner,' was all she could manage with any sincerity.

'I'm sorry. Everything's been so hectic—I just didn't want to add anything else to the mix.'

That made sense. It all made sense. Everything Leila was saying was perfectly reasonable. So why did she feel so uneasy?

They were booked into a room on the top floor of the cottage, their heads under the sloping roof and a window overlooking a rustic garden exploding with flowers. Kate had tried to phone Mark but had got the answering machine. He was normally home on a Tuesday. Where could he could be? Instead, she texted him from under the crisp white duvet in her single bed.

Great day in fields. Great suppliers of herbs & lavender. Thinking of u lots and how grateful I am to have you. Wish you were here. Love you xx

She was almost asleep when he replied.

Judy being difficult. I know it's late there so call me tomorrow. And I gotta run now. Love u too xx

Kate lay frozen on her side, reading and rereading the text.

Judy was always being difficult; that was nothing new. But for Mark to say it and ask her to call him about it must mean she was involving him directly now, trying to get to Kate through him. She was upping the pressure, that was for sure. And where was Mark running to?

She'd have to call him as soon as she could tomorrow.

She reached for a snippet of lavender she'd put next to her pillow and brought it to her nose to breathe in its gentle soothing tones. It would be okay, she told herself over and over. It would be okay. She just had to stay strong.

Hi Mum, things are going well with The Tea Chest and I've started seeing someone new. He's an investor in the company, American and rather lovely. Maybe you CAN have a career and a man at the same time. xx

The next day, Leila was leaving Kate to head to the lavender farm while she went to meet Quentin in a nearby café.

'He's on his way up north to meet up with another business lead,' Leila said, passing Kate her handbag. 'So he's dropping in to pick up the contract and the cheque on his way through and to give us the advertising proofs. Then he'll be back in London in a few days time to help us push things along.'

Kate flicked through the contract once more.

'Clive assured me it was all in good order,' Leila said.

'I know. It's just such a huge moment.'

'Here.' Leila took out her phone. 'Hold up the cheque and I'll take a picture. It *is* a big moment. But one to celebrate.'

Kate resisted at first but Leila egged her on until she held it next to her cheek and smiled.

'I'll send it to you so you can forward it to Mark.' Leila picked up her own satchel. 'I'll drop you at the lavender farm and meet you back there as soon as we're done.'

Leila, do you think it's a good idea to get involved with someone from work? Career first, men second, remember. Mum x

Quentin looked good in a fine pinstripe shirt and pressed trousers. His hair was a bit messier than usual, sticking up a bit at the front, but it suited him.

He kissed her hello, as was their way now, and she let her head fall back as his mouth covered hers.

'Well, good morning to you too,' she said, grinning.

'Would you like some coffee?'

'No, I've met my caffeine needs for now.'

'Can we walk instead?'

'Sure.'

They moseyed down a narrow street with greenery escaping between the rocks of the walls on either side, patted a couple of friendly sheep who could barely see out of the dreadlocks covering their eyes, and found a bench to sit on by a waterway, the early morning sun only just warm enough.

'Let's do the business bit,' Leila said, reaching into her bag for the contract and cheque. 'Here you are. All signed and ready to go.'

'Oh, thanks,' he said, with a cursory glance at the signatures. He rolled them up.

'Have you got the ads?' she said.

He leaned back on the bench. 'No, I'm so sorry. I forgot to put them in the car. But I've rung through and had the hotel courier them over to your house so they'll be there when you get back.'

'Oh.' She was disappointed, eager to see the proofs and offer feedback. She dug deep for a smile. 'I suppose I can wait another day.'

He reached out and took her hand.

'So serious today,' she said, leaning against his shoulder.

'Sorry. I've got a lot on my mind. New business ahead and all.'

There was so much she wanted to say then, but feared ruining this thing they had going. Feared exposing too much of herself. She wanted to ask him where this was going. How they could make it work when she went back to Australia and he to California, or wherever his next venture took him. Maybe he was feeling it too and that was why he was quiet.

She felt . . . what? Love?

But it couldn't be love because she already loved Lucas.

Suddenly, Quentin reached into his pocket and pulled out a small box wrapped in silver paper and ribbon. He held it tightly in one hand and ran the other through his hair as if searching there for the right words.

'I got you this.'

He handed it to her and shuffled his feet.

She took it, wondering what it could be. Adrenaline spiked. Was it jewellery? Had they jumped to the jewellery stage?

'Thanks,' she said. 'You didn't have to do that.'

'It won't bite,' he said, and she was relieved to see some of the stiffness had left him and his disarming smile had returned.

She relaxed and began to tug at the ribbon, noticing as she did that the gift rattled in her palm. Beneath the paper was a clear box filled with a hundred paperclips, all in different colours and shapes. Some were in the shape of hearts, others were ducks, flowers and cats.

'I love them,' she said.

'I know how much you like stationery and I wanted to get you something and then I saw these. They seemed perfect for you.'

'They're fantastic. Thank you.' She flung her arms around him and kissed him hard.

Eighteen years earlier

Judy stomped across the enclosed pedestrian bridge between the multi-storey car park and the Royal Brisbane Hospital, her eyes fixed straight ahead rather than taking in the sights of the Ferris wheel, pirate ship, chairlift and thousands of people enjoying the Ekka below. Although she and Graham avoided the show each year, she usually took pleasure in seeing the Ferris wheel fill the skyline and felt stirrings of nostalgia as the lights came on at dusk.

But not today. Today she was furious. And relieved.

She found Simone's ward and deliberately eased her pace as she entered the six-bed room, avoiding the eyes of other patients. Her sister's bed was near the window overlooking the traffic on the street below and, beyond that, wild rides flinging screaming patrons around.

Judy stopped at the foot of the bed.

'You didn't have to come,' Simone said, turning her head to the window to stare at the view outside. Her hair was wet. They'd obviously given her a shower.

'What was I supposed to do?' Judy hissed, trying to maintain a reasonable volume in the echoing room. 'They phoned me.

Again.' She gritted her teeth. 'I'm practically on a first-name basis with most of the nurses here.'

Simone rolled her eyes in an infuriatingly juvenile gesture.

Judy felt herself shake with rage. She'd spent the past three days searching for Simone. She'd even phoned the police, thinking she'd been kidnapped, or worse. And all the while she'd been out on a bender somewhere, completely oblivious of how much worry she'd caused when she hadn't bothered to show for their business meeting on Tuesday.

'Was he really worth all this?' Judy said.

Simone's hazel eyes flashed as she spun her head to face her stepsister.

Marco had been Simone's longest relationship. Two years. Relationships weren't normally Simone's thing, though whether it was entirely by choice Judy wasn't sure. The more the pieces fell into place about Simone's drinking, the more it was clear she was simply incapable of maintaining a healthy relationship.

It was a shame. Marco had been good for Simone for so long.

Judy took a deep breath and moved to the side of the bed and pulled a plastic chair towards the metal rails. She considered placing her hand on top of Simone's but it was both an unnatural gesture and one blocked by the IV needle and drip taped to her.

'What did the lender say?' Simone's voice quivered.

'I think it's safe to say he lost interest after your no-show.'

Simone nodded.

Judy had offered to help Simone find financial support from other sources, rather than relying solely on herself. She'd enjoyed her time in business with Simone, mostly. But she wanted her to be independent. And she knew it meant a lot to Simone to feel she'd made it on her own, without the help of her stepmother's money channelled her way through Judy. Judy had felt confident that Simone was capable of going it alone. But now, seeing how exhausted and fragile Simone looked, she wasn't so sure.

'I'm glad you're okay,' she said finally.

Simone shrugged.

They sat in silence for some time and Judy tried to think about how she could best help her sister. She'd offered to go to counselling with her, AA meetings, to see the doctor. She'd tried tough love. She'd tried to be supportive. She'd tried to be a friend. She'd tried to be a sister. But nothing worked. Simone didn't want to feel vulnerable. Didn't want to admit defeat.

Judy didn't know what the answer was, but she knew she could never live with herself if she didn't keep trying, no matter how frustrating Simone's behaviour was. At the end of the day, she was still the seventeen-year-old responsible for her younger stepsister.

She had no family of her own left. Simone was it.

18

'Where have you been?' Kate said. She'd just waved goodbye to the lavender farmers, a calico bag of cuttings swinging beside her, and was crunching her way across the gravel car park when Leila pulled up in the red Volkswagen.

'I'm so sorry,' Leila said. 'I just totally lost track of time.'

Kate looked cross and Leila felt unprofessional but also a bit harshly judged too. Kate had been a bit cool since she'd told her about Quentin and Leila had the impression she was watching her through a new lens, probably thinking she was slacking off. Her mother's text message didn't help. Everyone seemed to be down on her new romance. Why couldn't they just be happy for her?

'Did you get the proofs?' Kate said.

'He forgot to put them in the car but he's couriered them to our house so they'll be there when we get home.'

Kate studied her and Leila squirmed. She changed the topic quickly. 'So how did everything go?' she said with steely brightness.

Kate's face relaxed. 'Good. Everything's great. That's two from two. We just need the berry farm now.'

It was almost five hours from the Cotswolds to Newcastle upon Tyne, and they stretched it out longer than necessary by stopping to take photos of flower fields and stone ruins dating from centuries before. It was a bright, crisp day, perfect for photos. They stopped for hot chocolate and hamburgers, eating in the car, taking it in turns to drive.

On reaching their destination, they checked into a beautiful Georgian mansion for the night. Kate said things had been going so well that she'd decided to treat each of them to their own room so they could indulge in a four-poster bed, but Leila suspected she really wanted some time alone. Away from her.

It was probably a good thing. Ever since Quentin had given her those paperclips, a huge weight had settled on her shoulders. What did it mean for her and Quentin and what did it mean for her and Lucas?

What she needed was a good walk around the grounds to clear her head. She ambled in the woodland area with the sounds of trickling water and the occasional frog her only music. She surprised a rabbit as well as a pheasant that had been well hidden in the long grass.

In the time she'd been dating Quentin she'd of course thought about moving forward with him. And today, after his gift, she should have been feeling a lovely warm flush of new beginnings. But she wasn't feeling that. Instead, she was missing Lucas.

She missed their daily coffee, which he invariably bought for her despite her feeble protestations. She missed his witty observations about life. She missed the smell of his aftershave and peppermint gum.

But Quentin was here; Lucas was not.

It was ridiculous to go on wanting someone who'd made it clear they had no future together.

Suddenly, the fresh air had done its job and it was all very obvious. The only way she was going to be able to move on with Quentin was to force Lucas's hand once and for all.

When she returned to her room, she sent Lucas a text message with the number of the hotel and her room number and asked him to call. Strahan Engineering was an international company and people in Lucas's position made overseas calls all the time. It wouldn't be a problem. She sat down on her white and gold bedspread and waited for the phone to ring, which it did, twenty minutes later.

Lucas's voice smiled down the phone. 'How're you going?'

'Great,' she lied. 'And you?'

'Crazy as usual. But you don't need to hear about that. I want to know what you've been doing.'

She told him about the opening of the shop, the farm visits and the deal she'd brokered with Quentin, though she carefully edited out any hint of the romance between them.

Lucas whistled. 'Yee-ha. Sounds like you're making your mark on the world. You sound like you're having too much fun, though. Are you sure you'll be coming back?' The tone of his voice was joking.

'Well, actually, that's what I wanted to talk to you about. I'm thinking of staying here for a bit and travelling. Picking up work here and there.'

'Really?'

'My mother will probably keel over but now that I've seen this whole other world I realise the possibilities are just endless. I'm still young. I could be doing anything.'

They were silent for a moment. 'Lucas? What do you think?'

'I don't know, Lay. I can see why you'd be attracted to that right now. Europe's a seductive temptress.' He made a few throaty noises, like trying to decide what gear a car should be in. 'Have you thought about what you might be leaving behind?'

Hope bloomed. 'Like?'

'Well—' more gear changing '—your family.'

She barked out laughter. 'You've met my mother, right?'

He laughed too. 'Good point.'

'So what is it?' she urged.

Say it, Lucas. Just say it.

'I want to be a good friend here so I want to tell you to do whatever makes you happy.'

'But what do you really want to say?'

He clicked his tongue in thought and she could imagine him leaning back in his executive chair. 'You should do whatever makes you happy.'

Leila thanked him for his advice and hung up the phone.

Damn him. Why couldn't he ever just say what he was really thinking? She slumped down on the bed and thumped her fist into the mattress a few times to release some stress.

Why couldn't *she* just say what she was thinking?

But it wasn't that simple. Achara and the Great Secret lay between them. If the content of that email could change Lucas's mind about relationships then he had to know the truth. She might as well lay all her cards on the table. She might lose him but, hey, she didn't have him anyway. Not the way she wanted.

She texted him again and waited an agonising eleven minutes before he called her back.

'Hello?' He sounded guarded this time.

'I need to tell you something,' she said, forcing her voice to steady.

Come on, she urged herself. *It's just like ripping off a bandaid.*

'You still there?' Lucas said.

Leila's mouth was dry.

Kate might have been right. Perhaps Achara would change her mind and Lucas would never need to know or feel the pain of rejection. But if Achara didn't change her mind and rejected Lucas when he visited then he was going to need Leila to be a friend.

She opened her mouth to confess, then was hit by the responsibility she held. If she really loved Lucas then she would do anything she could to spare him the pain of that email. She might save herself by giving him a reason to be with her, but it wasn't about her.

She decided right then that she would never tell him.

'Leila? You were going to tell me something?' Lucas was beginning to sound distracted.

'I love you,' she said, resigned to speaking what she knew to be true and right.

Silence.

'Lucas? Are you still there?'

Just then, she heard muffled voices in the background and what sounded like Lucas placing his hand over the receiver and talking to someone. It went on for several moments, the conversation batting back and forth. She waited, mute.

At last she heard the hand scrape away from the phone.

'Leila? I'm so sorry but I've got to run. I'm late for a meeting. I'll call you later. Promise.'

'But . . .' she began to protest, but the call ended, the phone beeping at her with an awful finality until, in anguish, she clicked it off.

e

'We've got two days.' Mark's voice was tight. Kate's body contracted in response. 'Two days and then Judy will sue.'

'But what for?'

'She's contesting the will based on Simone's alcoholism. She claims Simone wasn't in a fit state of mind to write the will and that she'd had to assist Simone more and more over the years, and she was totally incompetent by the time she had the accident. She says the fact she crashed her car and killed herself while three times over the limit is a perfect example of her inability to look after herself let alone a global company. She says her lawyer's assured her she'll win.'

Kate's head spun. So The Tea Chest wasn't really hers. Or it was but it could be taken away. They could lose everything and this would have been for nothing.

No wonder Mark sounded stressed.

She closed her eyes and mentally willed herself to be calm and in control, the way a businesswoman of her standing should be.

'This doesn't make sense,' she said, sounding much calmer than she felt. 'Judy wanted out altogether. Why would she want to sue us when that would mean she was responsible for one hundred per cent of the company? That's even more responsibility than she has now.'

'But as the sole owner she can go ahead and dissolve the company immediately.'

'What about all the work I've done? The London shop is up and running. Thriving, in fact. And it's *beautiful*, Mark. Bigger and better than I'd imagined. I'm so proud of it. I wish you were here and could see it in person.'

Mark spoke carefully. 'Unfortunately, Judy's got a good case, Katie. And if she sues us we're in for a world of hurt.'

His last sentence stung. She'd had the chance to get out. Letting Mark down just wasn't an option, not after how he'd supported her, despite his secret valuation of the house. But she needed him to find some nerve now too. She couldn't do this alone.

'I think she's bluffing,' Kate said. 'She doesn't want to drag this out through the courts. It'll take too long.'

'But she knows it'll cost us a lot personally. She's banking on us backing down.'

She wondered whether Mark had taken Judy's side, whether he'd stuck up for her at all.

'Did you explain to her that if she could just be a little patient the London store will be flying and she won't have any trouble finding a buyer for her share?'

'I did.'

'Then she's bluffing. She has to be.'

Mark inhaled. 'Two days, Kate. What do you want to do?'

She closed her eyes, took a deep breath, and rested her head on the wall behind her four-post luxury.

'I can't just pull out now. You understand that, don't you?'

'I understand,' he said. 'Look, I've got to go. I've got a meeting to get to.'

A meeting. Mark had things going on these days she knew nothing about. She was about to ask him what sort of meeting when he said goodbye and hung up.

She shook herself, literally, standing on her feet and shaking her arms and legs, trying to rid herself of Judy's intimidation. If Mark had lost faith in her then she'd just have to step up and have faith enough for both of them. And if Judy thought she could push her around and scare her into submission she had another think coming. Kate knew she could succeed. Hell, she *was* succeeding.

She'd proven them all wrong. The glowing reviews for the London store kept coming thick and fast. She was handling it. She was doing it. Spreadsheets no longer terrified her. Business language no longer baffled her. She had a lavish advertising campaign in the works. She'd proven she had the nous, the determination, the creativity and the vision.

'Bring it on, Judy,' she shouted to the room, and air-boxed the posts of the bed for a while, dancing around and humming the fight-scene song from *The Karate Kid*, the original.

She *was* the best around.

Pow. She was Daniel. *Bam.* And Judy was Johnny. *Pow, pow, bam.* And she was going to kick Judy's arse. She threw an air kick just to finish off her fight and then stood with her hands on her hips, her blood rushing and breathing hard.

'Come and get me, Judy. You're going down.'

She hit the ground running the next morning, bouncing into the breakfast room and greeting Leila with a huge grin.

'Ooh, rough night?' she said. Leila's face was pale and her eyes heavy.

'You could say that,' she grumbled, biting into her toast and pulling a face. 'Wish there was Vegemite.'

Kate grabbed the jug of orange juice and began pouring. 'What happened?'

'Lucas,' she growled. Leila told her about their phone calls. 'You see. Nothing good comes of these conversations. I should never have said anything.'

Kate pursed her lips. 'I don't really know what to say. I'm sorry it's worked out this way.'

Leila growled again. 'Forget it. Let's bury ourselves in work.'

They finished their food quickly, checked out, wheeled their bags to the car and hit the road, whizzing through farmlands until they reached the Blake Berry Fields.

They were ushered into the kitchen of the farmhouse, shook hands with Seymour Blake, a man who looked as ancient and grey as the building he stood in, along with his three sons and several grandchildren. One of the sons—who went by the name Ringer, for unknown reasons—took them on a trip around the fields in his rusted-out truck.

Kate was relieved to find that the fields were far more well-maintained and fertile than either the Blake buildings or Seymour Blake appeared to be.

She couldn't but help feel joyful as they bumped their way over the fields, viewing acres and acres of rows of green leaves and bushes, all bursting with colour.

'We're right at the beginning of the season,' Ringer said. He had a slow, considered way of speaking, with an accent that had just the slightest Irish lilt.

'Raspberries are just coming in now. The blueberries were out last month. The blackberries should've been but were a bit late this year for some reason, but they're here now. We've also got gooseberries till the end of this month. And down that hill are the tayberries—they're a cross between blackberries and raspberries,' he explained in response to Kate's quizzical shake of the head.

'I'm really keen to get to know those tayberries and gooseberries. They're so foreign to most Australians.'

They finished their tour with Kate slopping through some muddy furrows to pick some berries. She pulled out her little cotton drawstring bag to fill with pickings for making tea.

Ringer took them back to the farmhouse, where they sealed their forthcoming deal with a handshake and bacon sandwiches, made in the greasy kitchen, along with black nondescript tea in pint-sized mugs.

Kate was having a rollicking good time. She'd managed to hold on to the determination and euphoria of the night before, and anytime she felt her confidence wavering, she just began humming the song from *The Karate Kid*.

Eventually, when they were back in the car and heading towards London, Leila began humming it too, drumming on the steering wheel as she drove, and then stopped herself with annoyance.

'I can't get this song out of my head,' she said.

'Which song?'

'"You're the Best", from *The Karate Kid*. I don't know why it's stuck there.'

Kate burst out laughing. 'That's because I've been singing it all day. It's my theme song right now. I need it.' She sang a bit more and air-punched in the car.

'Why?' Leila said. 'What's going on?'

'Judy's thrown us another curve ball, I'm afraid.' She told her about the threat to sue.

'Oh, Kate. That's awful. That's not what we need.'

'No,' Kate agreed. 'It's not. But you know what? As awful as it is, or could be, it's actually roused my fighting spirit. I've worked too hard—we've all worked too hard—to have her take it away now. She's out of line and I refuse to let her get the better of me. Not after all these years. Not when I've taken this huge risk. No, it's my time to shine.'

She clapped her hands together. 'We can do it,' she said, pumping the air.

Leila laughed. 'Of course we can.'

'I can't wait to see the ad campaign.'

Leila beamed. 'Me too. I think it's going to make a huge impact and it can only make us that much more successful.'

Kate put both her hands on top of her head. 'I can't believe I wrote a cheque that size.' She felt butterflies the size of cats begin to jump around in her abdomen.

'It's just a number,' Leila said, with the blasé attitude of someone who wasn't actually responsible for the money.

Kate took a deep breath. 'I suppose so. Have you been to the advertising office? Checked them out? Looked up their website or something?'

'No. Quentin's using a firm in the US that's actually a subgroup of his parent company. He says they're far better and cheaper than any he could find in England. He reckons they're the best. Just like your song.'

'That's convenient,' Kate said. 'You don't think he's come up with this idea of an expensive campaign just to line his own pockets, channelling it through his advertising business?'

'I did consider that,' Leila admitted. 'But at the end of the day, it wouldn't matter which advertising company we used. The ad campaign was part of the deal for him to help us open more stores. We need to make the London shop so attractive and so necessary to consumers that Quentin is willing to risk putting his money into more stores. It's sensible on his part. And the bonus of using his own company is that they *have* to do a good job.'

'I suppose,' Kate said, chewing her lower lip. She forcefully quelled her nerves. All the deals had been done. Now they just needed to get the ads produced and blitz London with their brand. If Judy went through with her threat to sue, that would be another matter to deal with. Until then, she had to proceed as if everything was okay. And it had to be.

19

Elizabeth waved frantically at the smoke billowing out of the griller and whacked the burning cheese on toast with a tea towel to smother the flames. Then she threw open the shutters, encouraging the smoke to head that way, though it seemed determined to waft to the lounge room instead.

Her father came into the room and she threw another tea towel at him, expecting him to help. But he just squeezed it together in his wrinkled hands. His eyes bugged out of his head.

'What's the matter?' she said, irritated he wasn't helping her. She dumped the blackened bread into the bin on top of some of Victoria's handwritten notes about chai. Elizabeth was tempted to peek at them, her competitiveness flaring, but resisted.

'Do you think Tennessee Blundell is involved?' her father said, breathless. 'I was just about to buy his new book. I'd hate it to be his last.'

Elizabeth supressed the urge to shake him and instead took a shallow breath through the smoke and tried to connect the dots. Tennessee Blundell was her father's favourite crime author. Tennessee Blundell lived in London.

Dot . . . dot . . . dot. Nope. She had nothing.

She stretched back a little further in her mind to the moments before the toast exploded. Her imagination had been a long way off, back at Haruka's flat, in fact.

After their kiss under the streetlight, she'd gone back to his place for coffee and they'd talked for hours. She'd been savouring every word of their conversations. Every sly flirty smile and spontaneous moment of shared humour. The way he never once tried to touch her, other than when their fingertips met as he handed her a coffee mug. The way he never once expected or even suggested they move to the bedroom. The way his dark eyes burned into hers until heat flushed her face and she had to look away, knowing he was still watching her. The way she instantly felt at home in his place. The excited way he talked about his art as he showed her his ceramic pieces, some half-painted, some drying, clay still splattered on the floor of his studio.

Her father's voice brought her back to the smoky room with a jolt.

'The writers have torched a double-decker bus and a police car and a row of shops.'

She tried to focus.

'Huh?'

'They've taken over London.' Bill twisted the tea towel into a knot.

Now, Elizabeth had to see for herself. She went to the lounge room, where Sky News was on the telly. Indeed, scenes of chaos, raging fires, looting and conflict with police flashed across the screen. She read the words running across the bottom and groaned.

'Rioters,' she said to her father, quite loudly. 'Not writers. *Ri-o-ters.*' She pointed to the text.

Her father put his hand over his heart and slumped into his chair with relief. Elizabeth rested on the arm next to him for a bit as they watched in silence. A peaceful protest over global economics had unexpectedly erupted into violence when the police began forcibly moving protestors on.

Elizabeth decided to embrace the moment of stillness with her father. She'd been so busy with the shop that she'd had next to no time to check up on him since Margaret had moved out. Although, she had to admit, he seemed to have moved on from depression to enthusiastic denial. She reached for the remote control and turned down the sound.

'Dad, have you spoken to Mum lately?'

'Yes, I'm sure I have,' he said vaguely.

'What does that mean? When did you speak to her?'

'Oh, I'm certain it was only a few days ago.'

From the cheerful way her father said this, Elizabeth wondered if he had cracked. She was just about to prod him some more when he turned the tables on her.

'Have you seen her lately?' he said, innocently enough.

No. She hadn't seen her since that awful day in the kitchen when she'd thought her own mother had hacked up her father and crammed him into a carpet bag. She hadn't spoken to her either. She'd picked up the phone once or twice but just couldn't bring herself to dial. What would she say?

Besides, she told herself petulantly, her mother hadn't contacted her either.

'Perhaps we should go see her together,' she suggested now.

Bill's facial features drooped like those of a bloodhound and Elizabeth's heart lurched.

'I think our time's passed, kitten,' he said.

'What do you mean? For visiting? Or do you mean as a family?'

'Your mother loves you, you know?'

Elizabeth raised an eyebrow at him.

'In her own way,' he conceded. 'But whatever's happening between Margaret and me is separate to how we feel about you. You need to know that.'

Tears sprang to Elizabeth's eyes and she shook her head. She couldn't believe she was having this conversation with her parent at this stage of her life. She wasn't a kid anymore and she of all people should have known that nothing lasts forever.

'What happened between you?' she said, as gently as she could.

He puffed out his cheeks, thinking. 'Time, I guess. We're not what we used to be.'

'How do you feel about her . . . um . . . shacking up with the preacher guy?'

'He's not a preacher,' Bill said. 'He is a minister of some sort, though.'

'You seem to know a lot about him,' she said uneasily.

'When you've been married as long as us, there are no secrets.'

'You knew about him?'

'Of course. We discussed it for a long time. Years, actually.'

'Huh.' Elizabeth was speechless. What a concept: no secrets. If only John had bothered to take some pointers from her parents. What whoppers he'd been hiding. But how would she have dealt with it if he'd told her the truth? Would they have talked about it calmly over a cup of tea? Not bloody likely. The end result would have been the same, she was sure of that. Except for the incident on the bridge in her negligee, perhaps. She could have done without that.

Maybe he'd actually spared her years of pain as they tried to work things out. *Cut to the chase. Bam. It's over.* Possibly not such a bad way to go after all.

She reached out and took her father's hand. 'I think you're brave.'

'No, not really. Just pragmatic. Probably too much so. Lost my sense of romance a long time ago. If I hadn't, she might still be here.'

Elizabeth rubbed his shoulder soothingly. 'Thank you, Dad.'

'What for?'

'For bringing me back to London. I don't know what I would have done without you.'

He reached up to take her hand from his shoulder. 'That's what parents are for, kitten.'

After a successful cheese-and-pickles-on-toast affair for them both, Elizabeth decided to leave her mother alone, partly to give her some time to settle into her new life, partly to give herself time to adjust to her mother's choices, and partly (okay, mostly) because she wanted to make the most of the first day off she'd had in a long time and that meant spending time with Haruka.

She'd checked in on Victoria, who was alone in the shop, and all seemed fine. Then she'd donned a pretty sunshine-yellow frock and chiffon scarf and shouted herself a taxi to meet Haruka at the Peter Pan statue in Kensington Gardens for a picnic.

He was there with a wicker basket, a green blanket rolled up under his arm, staring up at the bronze Peter Pan. Elizabeth felt a smile spread across her face. He cast a striking figure, his long legs and lean body so graceful.

He heard her coming and turned around. His eyes met hers and she giggled.

'Hi,' she said, a little breathless from her walk.

'Hello.' He grinned.

'Finding inspiration for your work?'

She was still a little awestruck from seeing his pieces at his flat the other night.

'I'm a terrible sculptor,' he said, shaking his head.

'Well, from what I've seen, you're putting your talents to good use.'

They wandered in amicable silence towards a shady patch of grass, where they unfolded the blanket and spread out Haruka's treats. Handmade wasabi chocolates, profiteroles, an array of sushi bites, strawberries and champagne.

'This looks amazing,' she said, taking a piece of salmon sushi between a pair of chopsticks.

'East meets west,' Haruka replied, raising his champagne flute in a toast to her.

Elizabeth nibbled carefully. If everything kept going well, she could be enjoying sex with this man. The prospect of lovemaking that was just for pleasure, rather than timed for procreation, was incredibly liberating.

'So,' Haruka said, gazing at her intently, 'how's your day off going so far?'

'Okay, I guess,' she said, momentarily feeling sad about her parents. Suddenly, she found herself talking to Haruka about them. He was a good listener, nodding in sympathy and asking an occasional question, but never trying to solve the problem or tell her what to do.

He was the complete opposite of John. Whenever she'd vented frustration to him, or shared her confusion or sadness, John had cut over the top of her with a 'Why don't you do this . . .' or a 'So go and do that . . .' It ate away at her, making her feel he didn't trust her to come up with her own solutions.

'I'm sorry,' she said, waving a profiterole in the air. 'I'm sure this is the last thing you want to hear.'

'Not at all.'

'For what it's worth, you're a great listener.'

She saw him suppress a smile of pleasure. He reclined on his side on the blanket, his right hand supporting his head.

'What are you thinking?' she said, before mentally slapping herself. What a line.

Haruka looked up at her. She shivered slightly as clouds passed across the sun and the temperature dropped several degrees in a moment. 'I was just thinking about you,' he said.

'You were?'

'I was thinking how this thing with your parents might be extra hard right now.' He spoke quietly. 'Given what's going on with your husband.'

Her smile dissolved. She reached for the chiffon at her neck, unravelling it and wrapping it lightly around her bare shoulders.

'Now I'm sorry,' Haruka said, putting his hand to his chest. 'Forgive me. I didn't mean to bring up bad memories. I was truly just moved, I guess, by your situation.'

'I suppose we had to talk about it sometime.'

They were silent for a while as she gathered her thoughts and feelings, wondering what to share, how much he knew already, and how much Victoria had told him.

Worse still, how much had she told him on the flight?

She didn't want to scare Haruka away. This thing with him was unexpected and it was sudden, and it had only been a few days, but she liked him. That was something she'd thought she might never feel for another man again. And he was here, listening to her like she was the most important person in the world.

Yes, it was fast. But she'd spent years with John and it turned out she hadn't known him at all. Maybe it was time for a different approach.

But that discussion with Haruka could wait. Why spoil the moment?

Instead, she tentatively stretched out her hand towards his. Their fingers connected and a small gasp escaped her throat before she could stop it. Instantly embarrassed. Her face flushing hot. She was twelve years old again.

Haruka smiled and intertwined her hand with his and held on tightly.

She laughed. It felt so good to laugh again.

He pulled her towards him. Their lips met and locked together perfectly. He tasted like chocolate from the profiter-oles. Her palm found the back of his neck and she traced light circles there.

His chest was aligned with hers. The sounds of other park visitors' laughter and chatter receded into the distance under his breathing as he kissed her.

Oh mercy.

She may have actually murmured it out loud because she felt his lips smile over the top of hers.

And then a splash. A big, heavy, cold splash plummeted from above and landed in her eye. She shrank into his body, shielding her face from the rain. More fat drops followed.

Haruka's eyes locked onto hers. 'Let's go.'

He shoved food into the basket and then they were on their feet, pulling at the rug and laughing and running hand in hand across the grass, heading for a taxi that would take them north to his flat in Hampstead.

They moved through the front door as one, limbs entangled. Her eyes were closed, their lips still tasting each other's. She couldn't see where he was taking her but she could smell the faint aroma of citrus-scented cleaner and some kind of paint fumes in the distance.

She was going to have sex! It was romantic; it was epic; it was a fairy tale.

It was a miracle.

Another door opened behind her and they entered his bedroom, dim thanks to the blinds he'd forgotten to open that morning. A neutral scent of washing powder. The bed was made. Nothing horrible lying around.

He was clean. This was good. In a moment she would be having sex with a clean man who washed his sheets.

Of course, John washed sheets. He loved nothing more than to take his clothes off and climb in between a thousand thread count.

Stop thinking about John.

They fell onto the bed and inched towards the headboard, shedding their clothes. She was enjoying taking off his clothes. John always liked to take off his own clothes.

Stop thinking about John.

Her whole body shuddered with anticipation as their naked flesh connected and brushed and bumped together.

He lowered his hand and . . .

'Wait!'

Haruka froze.

She couldn't believe the word had escaped her mouth and she clamped a hand across it to stop anything else following.

He gently removed her hand from her lips so she could speak.

'I can't do this.'

They lay on the sheet. Elizabeth covered her eyes. He was too far from her, his heat gone, cooling air already moving between them.

Stupid, stupid thoughts of John.

'I'm so sorry,' she mumbled. 'I didn't mean to lead you on. I wanted to. I just . . .'

Just what? She didn't even really know why she'd stopped, except that it likely had something to do with a sliver of loyalty to her scumbag, cheating, testicle-altering husband.

But that fear moved aside for a much larger one. Fear she'd completely ruined this opportunity to make a new start with a sexy, lovely, gentle Englishman.

She peeked from between her fingers and turned to her left to see what he was doing.

He was lying on his side, watching her. And he didn't look angry. He didn't look pleased either, admittedly. But he didn't look like he was about to yell, or throw her out of the flat, or give a big speech.

'Say something,' she said.

'Would you like a cup of tea?'

Haruka poured a hot green brew from an earthen teapot and handed her the cup to nurse between her hands.

She sat on his iris-blue couch, wrapped in his white robe. He wore a towel around his waist and she drank in the sight of him, just in case it was her last look.

'Thanks.'

'You can stay here for as long as you like,' he said, sipping on his tea. Outside the window, the sun shower had developed into persistent drizzling rain and even looking at the greyness made Elizabeth feel cold inside, despite the perfect temperature in the flat.

'I've really messed up,' she said.

He shook his head. 'Not possible.'

She considered him for a moment, his seeming devotion to her when he'd known her for such a short time. His graciousness about her bedroom blunder. His kindness.

'You're something else, you know that?' she said.

'Nah.' He waved her away and looked at the floorboards beneath his bare feet.

She sipped some more, the warmth of the tea soothing her. Her back arched and she reached around to find a ball of lime-coloured wool wedged between the cushions.

'This yours?' she asked, handing it to him.

'Oh, I think it's my mother's. She was here recently.' He took it and dropped it into a magenta ceramic bowl on the coffee table.

'So, I've been meaning to ask,' she said, eyeing him. 'I can't remember much about the flight from Brisbane. I'm almost afraid to ask, but was I horrible? I didn't vomit on you or anything?'

Haruka laughed. 'You drooled a little on my shoulder, but no vomit.'

'That's a relief. Did I keep you awake with my crying and ranting?'

'Only when you began to demonstrate all the different *efforts* you went to trying to get pregnant.'

Elizabeth froze. 'Oh, the shame.'

'It's okay,' he said. 'I learned quite a lot.'

She put her tea down on a section of the coffee table not covered with ceramics and buried her face in her hands. 'So do you know everything then? About my *husband*?' The word was stale in her mouth.

'That he cheated. That he had a vasectomy and didn't tell you. That he has another family in Japan. Yes.'

'And what about the bridge? And the nightly news?'

Haruka frowned, trying to remember. 'I don't think so.'

'Well, that's something. Oh, Haruka, you must think I'm such a nut job.' For a moment she'd thought she could start with a clean slate. But her dirty laundry was out there for all to see, thanks to John. 'I won't be offended if you never want to see me again.'

He shook his head. 'No way.'

'What do you mean?'

He stood, suddenly. 'Wait here. I have something for you.' He left the room and began to rustle around in a cupboard in the kitchen. He brought back a brown paper bag and sat beside her on the couch.

'Sorry for the lack of wrapping. I bought it months ago and put it away for you but I didn't want to get my hopes up.' He rubbed the back of his ear in a tender, self-conscious way.

'What do you mean you bought it months ago?'

'After the plane. If you open it, I'll explain.'

Elizabeth reached for the bag. It wasn't heavy, but there was something solid in there. Her hands touched bubble wrap and she pulled out a ball of it, stuck together with tape. She opened it. Inside was an exquisite peacock-blue ceramic figurine of a mother duck, a baby duck tucked under her wing. It was the size of Elizabeth's palm.

'Oh, it's beautiful. I love ducks.'

'I know. That's when I fell in love with you on the plane.'

'You *what*?'

'I think it was around the time of your sixth vodka. You told me you'd wanted to be a mother since you were twelve years old, the day you saw a mother duck risk her life to run out in front of cars and save her ducklings from oncoming traffic. She saved the ducklings but was run over herself. You said a love that fierce had to be worth dying for and you would spend the rest of your life making it happen. A friend of mine, another artist, someone who can actually create figures, made that piece and as soon as I saw it I remembered your story. So I put it away for you.' He shrugged. 'Just in case.'

Tears pricked Elizabeth's eyes and before she could stop it a fat droplet ran down her cheek.

Haruka knelt in front of her and reached up to cup her face, smoothing the tear away with his thumb.

'I knew right then you were a woman worth fighting for too.'

Elizabeth gently placed her beautiful duck on the coffee table, then reached for Haruka and kissed him. And this time, she didn't let go.

Ten years earlier

Local businesswoman Simone Taylor has been sentenced to three months imprisonment after a drink-driving incident that left a young woman with a broken leg. Ms Taylor recorded a blood-alcohol reading more than three times the legal limit. The victim was hit on a pedestrian crossing in the middle of the day while pushing her baby in a pram. The baby was unharmed.

The rosy glow of new love followed Elizabeth home and only threatened to wane when several police cars, sirens wailing, rushed past and she recalled the riots on the news. She momentarily wondered if she should be nervous, but she was tucked up warmly in a black cab, gazing at the lights gliding by.

It was late. Her father would probably be in bed and she would have to sneak into the house like she had when she was at school. She giggled. Life had come full circle and her other life in Australia—her job, her friends and, of course, her marriage—seemed like a dream. *This* was real, being back in her home city, working for someone who admired and needed her.

All around her there were signs of life. A new life for her mother, as strange as it was. Kate was succeeding against the odds. Her sister was thriving in the retail world and Elizabeth had a new appreciation of her skills and the way she'd matured. Leila had a blossoming new relationship with Quentin, according to her last text. And Elizabeth was building a new life and falling in love.

Her heart skipped a beat. Was that what she was doing? Falling in love? It seemed such a strange thing to be doing but she couldn't deny how wonderful it felt.

The cab pulled up outside her house with a squeal of brakes and she handed the fare over the seat to the driver and wished him a good night.

At her front door, she paused for a moment with her key in her hand and took in a deep breath of the chill night air. She'd made it through the worst. Satisfaction washed through her. There was hope yet.

And that hope lay in her plans to meet up with Haruka tomorrow afternoon, back at his apartment. She smiled again; it was becoming second nature these days.

20

The shop smelled even more divine than Kate remembered. Gentle wafts of rose and jasmine greeted her and she breathed in, revelling in the way it made her feel. Alive. Successful. Proud. The plants had grown. The water in the water feature sparkled under the morning light streaming down through the skylights. She charged up the laptop hidden behind the counter, clicked on the iTunes icon and began the day's playlist, a mixture of old-school jazz and tracks from *The Magic Flute*.

She turned her attention to opening the mail. She'd passed the postman on her way in. His satchel and wagon looked particularly heavy today, as did his demeanour. He was rushing, frowning, and barely acknowledged Kate's wave.

Leila opened the door, her mobile jammed to her ear. 'Give me a call when you can. Bye.' She put her phone back in her handbag and slid it behind the counter. Kate wished she felt half as good as Leila looked. She was bright and fresh, with an easy smile. Kate was happy to be back in the shop, though she couldn't deny the effects of Judy's threat hanging over her head.

'Cup of tea?' she asked Leila.

'Mmm, thanks.'

Kate boiled the kettle and began setting out the many glass jugs they would need for the day, to offer tastings to the customers.

'So,' Leila said. 'Judy's deadline approaches.'

Kate shook her hands, flicking off nerves. 'It does.' She still hoped Judy was bluffing, and she'd put on her most confident attitude this morning when she'd rolled out of her single bed in Elizabeth's parents' house. But she'd cautiously braced a small part of herself for bad news.

Leila was fussing around the store now, straightening stock on shelves and nipping off dead or dying leaves from the greenery with a small pair of sharp scissors. Kate ran water into a metal watering-can that had been painted white with yellow daisies. She was looking forward to a day of work, doing what she did best—serving customers, dreaming, creating, styling. It was her touchstone, the place she could return to when she needed to remember why she'd taken on this huge brain-taxing business challenge.

The front door opened; the bell jangled. And it was something in the sound of the bell and the forceful puff of air that made Kate's skin prickle, even though her back was to it. She turned to see a policeman standing squarely just inside the shop, his face set, and his hand hovering near his weapon.

In a single moment, Kate's mind jumped to various wild scenarios. There was a bomb threat in the street—they seemed to have a lot of those in London. Her husband was dead. Her children had been in an accident.

'Ma'am,' the officer said, directing his gaze at Kate and glancing briefly at Leila at the back of the store. 'I'm here to advise you to consider leaving your shop today.'

Kate's brain clunked. 'Why?'

The officer glanced back over his shoulder. 'The rioters are spreading quickly through the streets, breaking into stores, looting and setting fire to buildings. It might not be safe for you.'

She struggled to process this. Back at home last night after their trip away, they'd talked about the riots of course, but in a theoretical, 'Oh, isn't that terrible . . . now, what's for dinner?' kind of way. They hadn't considered for a moment the violence might reach them too. They'd moved straight on to moaning that the courier company hadn't got the ads to them on the day they said they would. Everyone was so hyped to see them. Leila left a message with Quentin asking him to send through the courier's tracking details straight away so she could sort it first thing in the morning.

Now Leila weighed into the conversation, striding to the front of the store. 'Shouldn't you be stopping them?'

A flicker of annoyance crossed the officer's face but his voice remained steady. 'We're doing our best, ma'am. But we're outnumbered at present. It's best to let these things burn themselves out.' And with that, he turned and left, moving next door to Angelique in Elegance.

Kate and Leila gawped at each other and then simultaneously made for the door, peering outside. Directly across from them, Lady Heavensfield was doing the same, her fingers clutching the string of pearls at her throat. She caught Kate's eye and Kate offered a weak smile, the type she might give one of her children when they were about to have an injection.

Lady Heavensfield turned away, making a hurry-up motion to her two waitstaff in black and white uniforms.

A ferocious smash of what sounded like glass and wood made Kate and Leila jump. Yells came from a distance and a car alarm went off. Kate's blood ran cold.

'I think we should go,' Leila said, rushing back to flick off power switches and turn off the laptop. She grabbed their handbags and took Kate by the elbow and marched her to the door.

Outside, the day was cold, with blasts of wind hurtling down the street, carrying with them an array of unpleasant industrial smells, like burning oil or chemicals, that made her mouth and eyes water. There were mob chants and yells, and the voices of the authorities booming over loudspeakers. They weren't coming from Kings Road, but they were close.

Manu burst from Roulette, tugging at his bow tie, striding towards Kate. Randolph scurried behind him.

'Come back inside now,' Randolph scolded.

Manu gripped Kate's hands in his fleshy ones. 'You've heard?'

She nodded.

'What will you do?' he said.

'Leave, I guess. I didn't really think we had much choice.'

Manu straightened and rubbed his bald head in circles. 'We're staying,' he said, his expression resolute. His words made her fret. If Manu and Randolph were brave enough to stay then maybe she should too.

'No we're not,' Randolph countered, his hands on his hips, glaring at Manu. 'Don't be childish, Manu. We're not exactly the baseball-bat-wielding types. It's not worth risking our safety.'

'Go if you want to,' Manu said petulantly, waving him away. 'But I'm staying to look after our shop and our livelihood.' And with that, he turned on his heel and went back inside.

Randolph gave a small whimper and turned to Kate, beads of sweat on his brow. 'You'd best get going,' he said, just as an explosion of some sort made them all jump. The noise was piercing. In fact, it sounded like a gunshot. Kate's ambivalence vanished. It was time to go.

'Are you going to stay too?' she asked.

He shrugged. 'It seems so. I can't leave him here alone.'

She nodded. 'I suppose not.' She rushed forward and kissed him on the cheek. 'Good luck then.'

'Thanks,' he said, his face paling as yet another siren began a high-pitched wail. 'We'll do our best,' he said, gesturing to The Tea Chest. 'You know, to help you too.'

'Thank you.'

Kate and Leila hurried towards Sloane Square tube station, close together, their eyes scanning ahead for trouble.

'I can't believe this,' Kate gasped. 'What the hell's going on?'

Leila shook her head in shock.

'Last night they were on the south side. How did they get here?'

'Walk now, talk later,' Leila ordered as they made a beeline for the station entrance, passing the newspaper seller who called out the headlines. People grabbed at the papers, wanting to make sense of what was happening to the city.

Kate made a move to take one too but Leila pulled her past the melee and through the turnstiles towards the edge of the platform just as the train arrived. They pushed their way on and stood amid a mass of visibly nervous people. A couple of youths down one end of the carriage shouted and jeered and Kate hunched her shoulders and looked at the floor, wishing for the ride to be over, and wishing she wasn't wearing high heels but rather something easier to run in.

They changed tubes at Victoria and again at Stockwell to head south-west to Clapham North station, a trip Kate could do in her sleep now, but that seemed to take an age this morning.

They burst in through the front door at Hemberton Road, puffing, a sharp stitch in Kate's left ribs.

Elizabeth was dressed in a powder-blue vintage dress she'd been planning to wear to work, but now paced the floor anxiously.

'Thank goodness you're back,' she said, wringing her hands. 'They're asking people to stay indoors. I was just about to call you.'

In the background, Bill and Victoria were in lounge chairs, their eyes fixed on the television. Utter chaos filled the screen: arson, angry men with face coverings and hoods, looters smashing shop windows with planks of wood and ripping flat-screen televisions from the walls, home invasions, riot police on horses chasing rebels, who threw marbles at the animals to bring them down, a mother clutching crying children to her side as she hurried along a street full of debris, burning cars, a burning double-decker bus, a burning police car.

It was a war zone.

'I've got to call Quentin,' Leila said, and left the room.

A map of England came up on the screen and icons of fires dotted around the country showed where the riots were. There seemed to be more fire than spare land.

'Blimey,' Victoria breathed, still wrapped in a pink dressing gown, a mug of coffee in one hand. She was tucked into the corner of the three-seater lounge.

'Why aren't you smoking?' Elizabeth said. 'Isn't that what smokers do in times of crisis?'

'I've given up.'

'When?'

'A while back. I just realised I didn't enjoy it that much.'

'Well, that's great,' Elizabeth said, rubbing her forehead in a classic gesture of overload.

Kate felt an unlikely mixture of numbness, fascination and distress. She thought of Mark and the kids at home; of her precious shop, beautifully crafted to every last detail; and of the flowers she'd planted in the window boxes at street level one day when she'd felt she'd taken on the world and probably shouldn't have. That simple act of pouring earth and potting the gerberas had lifted her spirits and calmed her. And now they were out there, exposed. The shop, a unique wonderland she'd so lovingly brought to life, now sat alone, vulnerable to attack. Then there was the money they would lose not only in today's sales but in the event of damage to the shop and loss of productivity time during repairs. And she was so far from home.

Leila returned to the room, her heels muffled in the carpet. 'I can't get hold of him,' she said, strain in her voice. 'I hope he's okay.'

'Mum,' Victoria said suddenly. 'Has anyone spoken to Mum?'

Bill, Elizabeth and Victoria all looked at each other and Bill shook his head.

Victoria jumped to her feet to fetch the phone.

Elizabeth clapped her hand to her mouth. 'Haruka,' she whispered.

Kate squinted, searching her mind for a reference to Haruka. She'd only been away a few days.

She turned to Elizabeth at the same time as Leila and they both said, 'Who?'

Elizabeth blushed. 'He's . . . a long story.' And she too left the room, presumably looking for her phone.

Kate's phone chirped. It was a text from Mark.

Have just seen news. You ok? The shop?

'Oh, it's made the news in Australia,' Kate said. She quickly sent a message back confirming she was okay but they were in lockdown inside the house. She asked him whether he'd heard from Judy.

Not yet.

Kate wasn't sure whether to be pleased Judy hadn't thrown any rocks into the pool yet or irritated that Mark so clearly believed it would happen.

Victoria returned. 'Mum's not answering her phone.'

'I'm sure she's fine,' Kate said. 'She's probably distracted by the news.' Then she remembered Quentin's ads. 'Damn, the couriers will be held up now, too.'

They settled in to watch more of the coverage, as reports of injuries began, including footage of people with head wounds and the injured being carried away on stretchers.

Kate got up to put the kettle on. While it boiled, she ferreted around in the cupboards for food. They might be in the house for a while and some primitive instinct (or maybe just a mothering instinct) had kicked in, driving her to check supplies and feed and water the flock.

Elizabeth came into the kitchen, now changed out of her beautiful dress and into more practical jeans and a shirt, just as Kate was opening a packet of pasta. 'Here, let me help you,' she said, taking out a pot.

'Is your friend okay?' Kate said.

Elizabeth smiled and Kate could see immediately the relief she felt was huge.

'Yes, he's fine. He was so wrapped up in his work he didn't even know what was going on. He's on the tenth floor of an apartment block. He'll be fine. We were going to meet up today, but we've rescheduled for tomorrow. This should all be sorted by then, surely.'

'Are you going to tell me about him?' Kate teased, reaching past Elizabeth for the cheese grater.

So together they made macaroni cheese, and Elizabeth talked about Haruka and their dates and how they'd ended up in bed and how great he made her feel.

'Sounds amazing,' Kate said. 'I wouldn't worry about how quickly it's been moving. When it's right, it's right. Why wait?'

Haruka might well be a rebound guy. But maybe not. Maybe it was fate they'd sat next to each other on the plane. And even if he was a rebound guy, it didn't mean it was anything other than wonderful.

'What was he doing in Brisbane to have you both end up on the same flight?'

'He'd been in Sydney, actually, for a huge ceramics show and he just happened to catch a connecting flight through Brisbane.'

They'd just started roasting some vegetables when Victoria padded into the kitchen in her slippers. 'I still can't get hold of Mum,' she said, her brow creased. 'What should we do?'

Wordlessly, as only sisters could do, she and Elizabeth moved to the window together to look down the street, like cats peering from a kitchen sill.

'It's pretty empty out there,' Victoria said. 'Eerie.'

'Maybe she and Angus have taken cover somewhere and she's forgotten to take her phone,' Kate suggested.

They continued cooking in silence, Victoria now pulling out tins and packets from the pantry, searching for cake mix. Leila moved into the kitchen as well, clutching her phone to her chest.

'Any word?' Kate said.

Leila shook her head.

'Oh. How about some music?' Kate suggested brightly, and sent Victoria off to organise something that would lift their spirits. She chose an ABBA collection, and Frida and Agnetha's voices snapped everyone to attention. Kate smiled, the disco beats relaxing her a fraction, helping to take her mind off things.

They were about to sit down for some lunch when Bill came into the room, wearing a brown coat and a cap.

'Dad, where are you going?' Elizabeth said.

'I'm going to look for your mother.' He fished his car keys out of the fruit bowl.

'You can't be serious,' Victoria said.

'Dad, you can't,' Elizabeth echoed.

'Don't bother,' he said, holding up his hand. 'You can't change my mind. I'll be fine. But we need to know she's alright.'

'But where will you go?' Elizabeth protested.

'To her flat—Angus's flat,' he corrected. 'No one's going to hurt an old man out for a wander. They won't even notice me.'

'Dad, you can't go alone.' Elizabeth rose to her feet. 'I'm coming with you.'

'Listen, kitten,' he said sternly. 'I'm the father and it's my job to protect you.'

'Dad, I'm thirty-one!'

'And you're still my daughter. What good is it to rescue my wife if I just go and put my daughter in danger?'

Leila replaced her fork quietly on the table beside her plate. Elizabeth looked stricken. Bill straightened.

'Rightio. I'm off,' he said, moving into the hallway.

'Dad!' Elizabeth leaped up to go after him and the others followed her until they were all wedged in the narrow entranceway. 'Please don't go.'

Bill began yet another protest but halted at the sound of a scratching at the keyhole in the front door. They all froze.

He found his voice first. 'Who's there?'

21

The front door opened to reveal Margaret Plimsworth, key in hand, her hair freshly curled, and her boyfriend Angus hovering behind her.

'Mum!' Victoria was clearly relieved.

There was a stiff pause as everyone else assessed the situation and Margaret hesitated in the doorway. Bill and Margaret locked eyes and she crossed her arms around her body. Bill looked from her to Angus and back again.

'For Pete's sake, get inside and close the door,' he said, and then turned and strode down the hallway.

Margaret and Angus hurried inside.

'Dad was just about to go looking for you,' Elizabeth said.

'Really?'

'Yes.' She took her mother's bag. 'Hi, Angus,' she said, seeming to recover from the shock of her mother and her mother's lover turning up at her father's house. 'I'm Elizabeth.' She held out her hand. 'Can we get you a cuppa?'

'Thanks,' he said, tucking his hands into his pockets. He had ginger whiskers and greying ginger hair and a wiry, lean body, and he was a fraction shorter than Margaret.

'What are you doing here?' Elizabeth said, leading the way to the kitchen. 'We were worried about you. We couldn't get hold of you.'

'I dropped my phone in a gutter,' she said. 'We ran. Literally. The riots were coming closer to Angus's flat. It's on the ground floor, which you'd know if you'd bothered to visit. And we couldn't find anything strong enough to bar the door or windows.' Margaret's voice wobbled and she tugged at her red and black tartan scarf, the colours strong against her pale face.

Beside her, Angus sat stiffly on the edge of the chair. His face was grim, but Kate wasn't sure if that was normal for him or if it was something new.

Elizabeth put her arm around her mother.

Margaret plucked a tissue from her bag. 'I hope it's okay, us being here. I don't want to upset your father. We just didn't know where else to go.'

'Ssh.' Elizabeth patted her hand and Kate made ginger tea from fresh gratings. 'Everything will be fine. He was really worried about you. The important thing is you're safe.'

Kate delivered the pot and teacups and excused herself to let them talk in peace. Back in the lounge room, Bill hovered, as though unsure whether to sit back down in his chair or head to the kitchen to join them for tea, or perhaps disappear to his room.

She gave him a smile. 'That was very brave of you.'

'Piffle.'

'I just made a fresh pot of tea.'

'No thanks, love.' He finally decided on standing with his arms crossed, facing the television.

'I'm going to phone the hotel,' Leila said from the corner of the room where she'd been standing with her mobile phone, fingers whizzing around the keypad. 'Hello, could you put me through to Quentin Ripp, please? Room 401.' She waited, tapping her foot. 'What do you mean he checked out? Well, do you know where he went? Where would he go with these riots going on?' There was another long pause during which Kate's fists clenched into involuntary balls. 'The *airport*?' Leila turned her huge eyes to Kate's, her mouth ajar, and then ended the call without saying goodbye.

It was at this moment that Kate felt the last wisps of self-belief vaporise like the acrid smoke billowing up from the streets outside.

'Tell me it's not true,' she whispered.

Leila sank onto the arm of the nearest chair and began pulling on her hair, clutching it in fists near her scalp.

'Tell me it's not true,' Kate repeated. Her exhausted mind was telling her to lie down and sleep, while her body was doing the complete opposite, thundering with adrenaline. 'Tell me what I'm thinking is crazy. That the couriers haven't been held up by the riots because there are no couriers because there are no ads. That he hasn't run off with the money. That we haven't been scammed.' She strode towards Leila.

Leila looked woozy. 'I—I don't know,' she said at last.

Kate grabbed Leila's shoulders, aware that her fingers were digging in but knowing it was the only thing keeping her upright.

Her phone chirped. She released Leila and pulled it from her pocket. There was an email alert. Apparently, Judy was up early and keen to share her decision.

Kate reached for a chair.

'What is it?' Leila said, recovering her wits.

'Judy,' Kate managed to whisper. 'She's going to sue.'

Just then, the doorbell rang. The whole house went silent for the second time in less than half an hour.

The bell rang again.

'I'll get it,' Victoria said finally, moving down the hall, pulling her robe around herself even more tightly.

Kate held her breath, her fingers still around the mobile phone.

There was a creak as the front door opened, but there was no other sound for several moments. Then footsteps. And the reverse creak of the door closing again. More footsteps. Then a tall man dressed in a lightweight jacket appeared and walked into the kitchen.

Ten years earlier

There was so much to do.

Judy cast her eye down the list again. Simone had signed a five-year lease on a shop space in Racecourse Road just prior to her sentencing, not believing for a second she would end up in jail, despite her barrister's warnings. And she'd signed a personal guarantee to cover the rent. *Fool.* So now it was up to Judy to sort out the mess and get this latest project started. There was still the insurance to organise, the business name registration, the signage, the fitout. She checked her emotions, controlling the anger that seemed to froth non-stop these days, both at Simone and at herself for being dragged into yet another of Simone's problems.

And right now, she'd rather be at home, relaxing, taking care of Graham. His recent cancer scare had really taken its toll and now he had a clean bill of health they wanted to go on a cruise and celebrate somewhere tropical. They should be heading towards retirement, not starting risky ventures.

'You could just say no,' Graham had suggested the night before, passing her a glass of wine.

Judy groaned. 'And watch her go bankrupt? I don't think I can handle any more stress from Simone. The only thing that ever seems to keep her functioning is when she's got a new business and it's going well. If she lost everything now . . .' She shook her head, tapping the wine glass. 'Well, I don't think *I* could cope.'

So now she was filling out paperwork for the registration of the name The Tea Chest. Paying the bills herself for the phone and electricity connection, the insurance and the contractors. Keeping all bills carefully documented. This wasn't going to be a free ride. If she had to sink money into this venture she'd better bloody well get her cut at the other end, if by some miracle it succeeded.

Of all Simone's business ideas this one had to be the worst. People bought tea in supermarkets, not expensive riverside boutique stores. As much as she knew Simone needed this to succeed, she wasn't so convinced it would. But if she could just get her through this phase, perhaps something good would come of it somewhere down the track. Though she couldn't imagine what.

The anger dissipated for a moment as she thought of Simone in a cold jail cell, behind bars.

At least there'd be something for her to come home to when she was released, even if it didn't last long.

Elizabeth jumped up and backed into the corner of the kitchen, her hands flying to her face in shock. She barely registered Kate and Leila coming into the room, or her father's voice calling, 'What's going on?'

Then her mother leaped to her feet and embraced Elizabeth's husband in a move that was so inappropriate it made Elizabeth want to slap her.

'What are you doing? Don't hug him!'

'He's still family, Elizabeth. And what can I say? I've become more understanding of problems in a marriage and they're not always straightforward.'

An awkward pause. Looks shot between Margaret, Angus and Bill, whose face was purple-red.

Elizabeth turned to John. 'What the hell are you doing here?' she demanded.

John tried to smile, the kind of sheepish smile he reserved for days when he'd spent money on joining a wine club or signing up for Foxtel without discussing it with her first. It was generally accompanied by a lot of *babe*s and *sweetheart*s, as well as shoulder massaging.

'I came to see you,' he said.

Elizabeth glared at him, feeling a torrent of emotions rushing like white water through her middle.

'Do you realise there are riots going on?' Victoria said.

'I do now. They stole my suitcase as I walked down the street.' He rubbed a hand through his curly hair in an unsettled gesture.

A flicker of leftover marital concern caused Elizabeth to say, 'Have you come straight here? From the airport?'

'Yes,' he said, his voice lacking strength. 'Twenty-four-hour trip. You know how it is.'

Angus rose to his feet and pushed his chair towards John. 'Please, have a seat.'

'No.' Elizabeth intervened, striding to the chair and taking it from John and tucking it under the table. 'He's not staying.'

It was unbelievable. She hadn't seen or spoken to her husband in almost three months and then he showed up unannounced, right when she'd started to move forward with her life.

He didn't move. No one moved. She wanted to grab him by the arm and lead him to the front door but the thought of touching him, an arm so familiar it was almost one of her own, was overwhelming and she faltered.

'Well?' She scowled. 'Go on. Get moving.'

John lowered his head and cleared his throat. 'Right.' He made a move to go.

'Wait a minute,' Margaret said, placing an arm out between John and Elizabeth. 'You can't send him out there. There are riots, Elizabeth. Be reasonable.'

'Reasonable? *Reasonable*? How reasonable was it for him to have another family in another country and lie to me for years?' Her blood pressure soared and she sensed Angus retreating a little. 'How reasonable was it for him to pretend to try for a baby when he'd had the snip? How reasonable was it for him to expect me to *forgive* him?' She was screaming now, thrusting her finger towards him. 'How dare you come here?' She kicked him hard in the shins.

He puffed in pain and crumpled, grabbing at his leg. There was a collective gasp from the others but, she was pleased to see, no one actually rushed to help him. She was especially pleased to see her father smother a smirk.

Her chest heaved with the effort of breathing and, to her horror, tears threatened. She stamped her foot instead.

John straightened, wincing, looking more than a little galled. But he raised his chin and said, 'Please, Elizabeth. I'd just really like the chance to talk to you.'

All eyes volleyed back to her.

Just then, a siren started close to the house, its piercing wail making the walls vibrate and Elizabeth knew no matter how angry, betrayed and hurt she was she couldn't send him back outside into that. It looked like the bastard had won again.

'Fine.' She left the kitchen and headed back to her old bedroom, John trailing behind.

Leila excused herself and went to the bathroom and shut the door. She sat on the edge of the peach-coloured bathtub and called Quentin's phone again, a vice-like pressure in her chest.

'Quentin, it's me. I called the hotel and they told me you'd gone to the airport. I'm really confused and I'm really worried and I don't know what to think and ... please, please tell me everything's okay with the deal. Call me. Urgently. As soon as you can.'

She snapped the phone shut and listened to the tap dripping, recounting the thirty-eight 'pros' she'd listed about Quentin the other day in her notebook. She'd marked the page with a cat-shaped paperclip.

But suddenly, words like *charming*, *stylish*, and *witty* didn't seem as important as words like *honest*, *decent* and *trustworthy*, which she hadn't even considered.

Elizabeth faced her husband across the bedroom. She leaned against the small white desk and crossed her arms.

'Nice room,' he joked, gesturing around. 'It's very *you*.'

'Cut the crap. You don't know me at all.'

His face twitched and he backed up to the wall.

She shook her head slowly, taking him in, her gaze roaming over the bloodshot eyes and the lines around them that seemed to have deepened since that day in their bedroom when he'd burned her world to the ground with just a few sentences.

I have another family in Japan. We won't be having a baby. I should have told you sooner.

And what was that beneath the buttons of his shirt? It looked like his breastbone, more prominent now than before.

'Have you lost weight?' she blurted, though she reminded herself that she didn't really care.

'A little. Look, Liz, I wanted to see you. I had to see you.'

He pushed himself off the wall and took a step towards her, then stopped short as she recoiled. His weary face fell. He reached into the pocket of his pants, pulled out a handkerchief and wiped at his brow, which was shiny with small beads of perspiration.

'Why?' she demanded, her voice edgier than she'd intended it to be. 'So you could humiliate me some more? Show me photos of your boys?' She halted, struck by images of two young boys, pale-faced with dark hair, sitting on John's knee. Cuddling in his lap. John reading them a bedtime story. Teaching them to tie their shoes.

'Does she know about me?' Her bottom lip trembled.

John took a deep breath and shucked off his jacket, revealing large pit stains of sweat on his maroon shirt. He went to the edge of the bed and sat on the pink duvet.

'Yes.'

It was amazing how a single word could be so shocking.

So many questions demanded answers. Had she thrown him out? Did he still see the boys? Would he be moving to Japan? Would *they* be moving to Australia? Did she forgive him? Had she known all along? How long had she known? And the question she was still somehow thrown by: was he here to ask for a divorce?

And if he was here to ask for a divorce, was that what she wanted too?

It was absurd. There was no turning back from this. This was not a situation where you just forgave and moved on. This was a deal breaker. No question. Yet, the word *divorce* made her feel like she was living someone else's life. Who was this person?

'It's hot in here,' John murmured.

'Oh. Is it?' She rubbed her arms, assessing the temperature.

'Would you mind getting me a glass of water?'

Elizabeth opened her mouth to unleash another round of abuse—how dare he ask her to fetch him water?—but the sight of him sweaty and crumpled on the edge of the bed made her stop. Clearly, the guy felt fantastically guilty. That gave her an edge of satisfaction and the motivation to take the high road and go downstairs to get him his damn water.

ce

Kate trembled. She was almost paralysed with fear.

Quentin was a fraud.

Quentin was a fraud.

Quentin was a fraud?

She tried to prioritise the issues facing her. Right now, she couldn't do anything about Judy's decision to sue. Quentin was a much bigger problem.

Perhaps he'd simply had to travel overseas suddenly. He did have investments all over the world. It was easily possible something had come up.

And Leila had checked him out. Hadn't she?

Kate paced the small bedroom and stared at Leila's bed and possessions as though searching for clues.

Leila was on her side—wasn't she?

She shook herself. She wasn't making sense. The whole world was spinning, there were riots going on all over the city, and it was hard to see straight.

Think, Kate, think.

She took a deep breath and tried to break the problem down into smaller pieces. Number one was the cheque.

She stopped pacing. The cheque! She could cancel it.

She rushed to the laptop on Leila's bed and flipped it open. She just needed to see if the cheque had been presented. If it hadn't, she could cancel it. She went to the bank's website, forgot all her log-on details and had to fish through her huge handbag to find the little card with the numbers in the side pocket, entered them, moved through the welcome screens and went to the transaction site.

She held her breath, waiting for it to load. It seemed to take an age for the transactions to appear on the screen. She gripped the laptop in her hands.

'Come on, come on,' she urged.

Then the numbers were there on the screen.

Her heart jolted painfully. It was too late. The cheque had been cashed and the money had been taken from The Tea Chest's account.

It was all over.

Elizabeth trudged up the grey shagpile-carpeted stairs, her husband's glass of water in hand.

Her husband. Was he her husband? She pondered all the nuances of the word. If he didn't behave like her husband, then surely he wasn't a husband. But the law said he was. But perhaps Annie, a staunch I-will-never-get-married type who argued marriage was an archaic institution and it was 'only a piece of paper' had been right all along. It hadn't protected her heart against anything.

She sighed as she reached the last step.

'Here,' she said, as she approached her bedroom door. She tried to sound as ungracious as possible. She certainly felt it.

But inside the room, sprawled out on the bedroom floor, apparently unconscious, was her husband. The man she had married, for better or worse, richer or poorer, in sickness and in health. He was there on the floor at her feet.

22

It was morning again and London residents remained behind locked doors. The sombre crew of Hemberton Road hunched around the television, watching Sky News.

Leila really didn't know why she was still in the lounge room. No one was speaking. Kate was avoiding her. Bill avoided any space or conversation that involved Margaret or Angus, especially the mattresses and bedding that had been left for them to sleep on overnight. Angus seemed excruciatingly uncomfortable in the home of his girlfriend's husband. The tension between Bill and Margaret was obvious. And Victoria had long since given up trying to bridge the uncomfortable silence with pleasantries and had settled down with a glossy magazine and a nail file, having finally got out of her robe and slippers.

Leila padded down the carpet towards the room she shared with Kate. She desperately wanted to leave the house, go to a café or bar, and breathe some smog-filled London air. She considered having a shower to wake up and give herself some energy. Instead, she sank into her narrow bed. Her mobile phone was clutched in her hand, where it had been for almost twenty-four hours. There was still nothing from Quentin. She scrolled through her contact list, hoping to find someone she could call for comfort. Her mother had sent several texts, worried by the images on the news at home, wondering if she was okay, as had her brother. Andrea from Zumba had texted too. And Gemma from Strahan Engineering, wondering the same.

But nothing from Lucas. Still nothing. Nothing since their phone call, when he'd abruptly hung up without responding to her revelation. Nothing since he'd promised to call her back and talk.

Kate's angry words bounced around her head.

'You've ruined my one chance to get this right,' she'd hissed at her in the kitchen, trying to keep her voice low in the small, over-populated house. 'I trusted you, Leila.' Her face had been twisted with pain and betrayal as she delivered her blow. 'There's no place for you at The Tea Chest anymore.'

The words were bullets through Leila's heart.

She'd been fired. Again.

And so she drifted in numb, ashamed silence except for one desperate call to Clive Evans to ask about the contract.

'You only asked me to view the contractual agreement,' he'd protested. 'It wasn't my responsibility to be a private investigator on each party to the contract. The contract terms were sound. Whether or not the other party upholds them is a different matter.'

Now, her finger hovered over her mother's name in her address book. But Leila's abject disgrace made it impossible.

Her mother would simply repeat the lectures she'd delivered the first time Leila was fired, only it would be much worse this time because of Quentin.

There was really only one person in her life who'd understand.

Lucas might not forgive her for kissing someone else. Then again, he might not even care. But he would know what to do. She was sure of it.

She brushed away any fears of what he had to say about her personally or about their pseudo relationship. This wasn't the time to be protecting her pride. She needed practical business help. Now.

She dialled his mobile number, knowing it was late in Australia but that he was a night owl and was probably still up. He answered on the second ring, his voice a mixture of surprise and wariness.

'Hi,' he said. 'Aren't you in riots?'

'Yes. I'm holed up in a bunker with an interesting combination of people. I've got cabin fever already.'

There was a moment's silence. She could hear the echo of her voice down the line—a split-second delay between her and Lucas that made her feel fragile, as though she might be lost at any moment.

'Glad to hear you're okay,' he said softly. 'I've been thinking about you.'

Her spirits lifted.

'I'm sorry I haven't called back after our last conversation. I just haven't had a chance, you know? The time difference and all.'

She nodded at the other end of the phone, bracing herself for what he might say.

'Thanks for saying what you did. It's about time we talked.'

Suddenly, she didn't want to know what he had to say. Any sentence that began with 'thanks' carried an air of polite professionalism about it, like a rejection letter following a job application. *Thanks for your interest in the position, but we won't be needing you at this time.* Or the answer to your party invitation. *Thanks, but I am unable to make it.* Any sentence that began with 'thanks' in response to a question or proposal inevitably led to 'but'.

'Look, let's not talk about that now. I've actually got bigger problems I need your help with,' she said.

There was a creaking noise from his end, as though he'd just stretched out against a wooden chair. 'Are you sure? I wasn't avoiding you. I really do want to talk.'

'No, I don't have time. Please, can you help me? It's about business.'

'Sure.' His voice became firmer as he settled into safer territory. Business was his thing. Business was something they talked about often. Business was business.

'Just promise me one thing,' she said, gathering her courage.

'Anything,' he said, and the enthusiasm in his voice made her ache to see his smile.

'Just forget it's me talking. Pretend this is a case study or something. Something you need to look at objectively. Hard facts. Solutions. Okay?'

'Done.'

Leila took a long, steadying breath, reminding herself that now was not the time to be precious about her feelings.

Lucas cleared his throat, prompting her to begin.

She told him her story carefully, honestly, and with supreme control of her emotions, something that an hour earlier she wouldn't have imagined she'd be capable of. Perhaps it was the way

Lucas allowed her to talk, not interrupting, murmuring at the right moments and encouraging her to go on when she began to waver. She pushed aside the fear that her story would ruin his impression of her and make him think long and hard about what sort of person she was. Then again, it probably didn't matter anyway.

Finally, she reached the end.

'What should I do?' she said, her voice small.

She could hear him tapping a pen on a table top, something he did when thinking, and she realised he must have been taking notes as she'd spoken. She felt warm gratitude for his commitment to her. He wouldn't blow her off. He might lose respect for her, but he wouldn't abandon her. She squeezed back tears.

'Alright,' he said after a contemplative pause. 'If I had to summarise your situation, I'd say you had three main issues.'

'Go on.'

'First is this Quentin guy,' he said, his voice grating over his name. Leila felt herself flush and put a cool hand to her neck to ease the heat. 'Email me everything you know about the guy, his name, if he mentioned where he was from in the US, the name of the company he works for, anything at all. I'm going to see what I can find out at this end.'

'Okay,' Leila said, buoyed by the opportunity for direct action and the slim hope that someone else could help her out of the mess. She reached for her laptop while Lucas kept talking.

'Second, you've been fired. I'm sorry to say there's not a lot you can do about that right now. The best way to fix that situation is for us to track down Quentin and solve the problem for Kate.'

Leila's heart quickened at the way he'd said *us*.

'She might not forgive you or give you your job back, but she might at least let go of her anger. And it will make you feel better and you won't have this guilt hanging over you for the rest of your life, or a—' he paused '—tainted record, so to speak.'

He was right. Something like this could follow her for the rest of her professional career, like a prison record.

'And third, you're stuck inside a house in the middle of riots with a crowd of people who are all barely keeping their issues with each other under control and you have to share a room with Kate, who pretty much hates you right now, and you can't leave the house because of the mass of looters and crims outside your door.'

'Pretty much.' She was impressed with Lucas's ability to see not only the business problems but the personal ones and take them seriously. No wonder he was so highly paid. He could get to the crux of a situation on all levels.

'I wish I could come and get you,' he said.

Leila let the sentence float in the air. If only he would repeat it just so she could hear that concern in his voice again. But he moved on quickly.

'Tell Kate you've got some people working on the problem and you hope to have some answers by the end of the day.'

'Seriously?' She couldn't see how that was possible but she was willing to jump at anything.

'Then say you don't want to make matters worse so you'll be sleeping on the couch to give her some space. And as soon as the coast is clear, book yourself into a hotel and get out of the house. Then look at changing your flight home.'

Leila thought about that long flight home, like a morning walk of shame, but fifty times longer and more humiliating, coupled with the knowledge she'd ruined someone's life and business.

'But don't make any changes to your flight until you hear from me, just in case you need to do some sleuthing in London.'

He said goodbye with energy and enthusiasm and she ended the call almost believing that everything would be okay.

TV news presenter: Now to more news on our city in crisis.

Rioting made the job of emergency services more difficult yesterday, when crowds of weapon-wielding rioters blocked the path of an ambulance taking a man who'd suffered a heart attack to hospital. The man's wife, Elizabeth Clancy, said the experience was terrifying.

Mrs Clancy: They blocked the road and grabbed the van and rocked it from side to side and banged on the sides. I thought the windows would break and my husband was going to die.

Presenter: Police services later escorted the ambulance to Lambeth Hospital, where Mr Clancy was treated for a mild heart attack. Mr Clancy is visiting here from Australia and earlier in the day had his suitcase stolen by thugs.

Not a good day in London.

John opened his brown eyes and gazed at Elizabeth with a mixture of surprise and familiarity.

'You're still here,' he said.

Elizabeth eased herself up in the chair, her body stiff from the sitting and the lack of sleep.

'Tell me this, John Douglas Clancy. Why is it that every time I see you of late I end up on the bloody television news?'

He gave a small, sad smile. 'Just lucky, I guess.'

She took a lungful of air and blew it out with controlled force. Above John's bed, on the small television hanging from the ceiling, was the footage of her on the news again, her hair in messy wisps and shadows under her eyes, the twenty-four-hour coverage of the riots necessitating story repeats.

She grabbed the remote from the trolley and switched it off. 'Just once I'd like to end up on the news for something happy, like winning the lottery, dressed in an evening gown with my hair done, not in a negligee or after a sleepless, stressful night in hospital.'

'You look beautiful to me. Like an angel.'

She shook her head with impatience. 'Your charm doesn't work on me anymore.'

His face fell and he levered himself up in bed and adjusted the oxygen tube under his nose.

'We need to talk,' he said.

'Actually, I think you need to talk,' she corrected. 'Explain yourself. You show up here unannounced, have a heart attack on my bedroom floor, force me to head out into riots, with my unconscious philandering husband in an ambulance, then fill in forms in a hospital as your next of kin. Do you know how awkward that was? I had to check the box that said *spouse*, wondering what that word meant anymore, and wondering if I would have to make some horrendous legal decision about your life and your future should you not wake up. And then, if you actually died, I would have to go and find *her* and tell her and *your* children.'

The monitor beside the bed was making bleeping sounds, presumably signalling an increase in John's heart rate.

'Explain yourself,' she said again. 'What are you doing here? What do you want from me?'

To his credit, John's eyes darkened with pain, and she was fairly sure it wasn't from his heart—at least, not his physical one. He rubbed at his face with the palm of his hand, searching for words.

'I wanted to tell you how sorry I am.' He spoke slowly and deliberately.

She scoffed.

'I did love you,' he said next and, despite herself, she felt her heart pull on the word *did*.

'I never meant to fall in love with Eiko.'

Elizabeth stilled. There it was. Her name. Eiko. She was no longer some mythical monstrous *other*. She was real. She had a name.

Infuriatingly, her eyes filled with tears as she felt a profound sense of loss; random, unwanted sympathy for her husband as he lay in bed in a white gown attached to tubes; and sweeping finality.

It was over.

John hung his head. 'I was a coward, Liz. I should have told you. I should have ended things with you years ago.'

Just as quickly as the tears had arrived she was overcome with sudden rage.

End it with *her*? How about ending it with Eiko? How about never *starting* it with her in the first place? She ground her teeth and narrowed her eyes.

John's eyebrow flickered as he registered her dangerous look. He spoke quickly. 'I'm sorry. I know it's not what you want to hear. I'm not lying. I did truly love you.'

'But?'

'But I loved her more.'

She felt the blow of his words, but for the first time since that last morning in bed together, she knew for certain she wouldn't crumble.

'I've contacted a solicitor,' he said. 'I've set everything in motion. You can have everything in Australia. I don't want it. I'm moving to Japan to be with Eiko and the boys. I'm so sorry.'

'No,' she said, moving closer to him and lowering herself closer to his face, conscious that the ward had gone silent as other patients and visitors stopped conversations in favour of this live melodrama. 'You don't get the last word. I do.' She took a long look into his eyes, forming her final words in her mind.

'I loved you. I was a good and faithful wife. And I deserved more.' She swallowed hard. 'I will go on. I will get my happy-ever-after. I will get my babies. You have nothing to offer me anymore. You are my past. My future is waiting for me here in London.'

She was just about to tell him to sell everything in Australia, that she didn't want it, but she stopped herself in time. Why shouldn't she get something out of this? She'd spent more than a decade with this man in another country, and her wages had helped pay the mortgage too. She deserved some sort of compensation, not because she was bitter and wanted to hurt him, simply because it was fair.

Straightening, she adjusted her clothes to make them neat. John fidgeted with the corner of the bed sheet. He looked small and boyish and like a totally different person from the one she remembered. And as she experienced this distancing, like nothing she'd ever felt before, the rage slid away and an unexpected calm descended. She was done.

'Goodbye,' she said.

He opened his mouth to speak, then closed it, and nodded. He held out his hand to her and she took it, reluctantly at first, then relaxing into their final embrace. She didn't hate him. But she didn't love him anymore either. And she was pretty sure that somewhere in the future she would even forgive him. She could feel him and all their shared memories and experiences moving to a different corner of her heart, one reserved for important and significant people who had shared her life's journey. And this opened a whole other space for the great love of her life to inhabit.

He smiled at her. There were a million more things to say and yet there was nothing more to say.

It just *was*.

She took back her hand, knowing it was the last time she would touch him, picked up her bag and left the room.

23

By the second night of lockdown, the violence had migrated to other parts of the country, leaving debris and burning buildings in its wake.

An unknown phone number appeared on Kate's screen.

'Have you any news?' Lady Heavensfield's clipped English tones asked without preamble; obviously she assumed Kate would know who she was. Kate was about to pretend she didn't but the seriousness of the situation made her put pettiness aside.

'No,' she said from where she stood on the top step of the entrance to the Plimsworths' house. She'd bravely unlocked the front door and taken a step into the cool and drizzly air, pausing just outside the entranceway. Colourful sweet peas reached up from where they grew in pots and waved at her legs. She didn't actually plan on going anywhere. The street was deserted, quiet, but there were deep shadows that could be harbouring unseen menaces. It was enough for now just to take back the couple of square feet of space outside the door—a symbolic gesture of freedom.

Lady Heavensfield took in a short, impatient breath. 'Nor do I.'

'I could contact my rental agent,' Kate suggested, kicking herself for not thinking of it sooner. 'Let me call you back.'

'Fine. Do that,' Lady Heavensfield said.

Clive Evans answered his phone on the fifth ring.

'Where are you?' Kate said, hearing the sound of bird calls of some sort in the background, though she didn't recognise them.

'Oh, it's my meeting night,' he said, evasive.

Kate waited, blinked a couple of times, and listened to a raucous clatter of short, barking bird calls.

'Are you in a jungle?'

'It's my ornithological evening,' he said. 'It's our exotic bird gala.'

Now that she listened more closely, she could hear the gentle tinkle of glassware and murmurs of conversation, a spontaneous eruption of gentle laughter and a polite round of applause.

'Can I help you?' he prompted.

'Oh. Yes.' She tried to pull herself back to the task at hand, but she was absolutely fascinated by the prospect of something going on outside of this house. Anything would be better than the frigid, tedious and depressing mood that pervaded the air at Hemberton Road. 'So you're not in London?'

'No. Cardiff.'

'Wales?'

'Yes.'

'And you have exotic birds flown in from around the world?'

A resigned sigh followed. 'Nooo. We have bird calls on MP3 files and we're currently competing to identify them and match them with the colour pictures around the room. Once a year all the ornithological societies in the UK come together for a black-tie gala.' His voice was warmer now, buoyed by passion for his topic. 'We raise quite a lot of money for conservation research. The theme for this year was "Out of Africa" and we're studying East African birds.'

There came the sound of short, high-pitched, rapid-fire cheeping, not unlike that of a baby chicken, Kate thought.

'Madagascar Flufftail!' Clive shouted suddenly and a cheer broke out, along with some hardy roars of appreciation and good-natured ribbing.

'That's the Madagascar Flufftail,' he repeated to her, his voice brimming with excitement.

'So I heard.'

He sighed again, a happy winner's sigh. 'So, what can I do for you?'

'Er, you know about the riots, don't you?'

'Of course. But there's nothing I can do about it so I decided to fulfil my duty as treasurer of our club.'

'Okay, well, I'm just wondering if you've heard anything about our shop—or other shops in our road?' Her voice pinched think-ing about Manu and Randolph. 'We've been locked away for two days now so we really have no idea if our shops have been burned to the ground, or looted, or what.'

'I've heard nothing,' he said. 'But no news is good news.'

'I guess. Not that it probably matters much now anyway,' she muttered, still coming to terms with Quentin's betrayal and what that meant for her and Mark. 'I'm sorry to have bothered you. I hope you have a wonderful night.'

She called Lady Heavensfield to report she knew nothing at all and they both agreed that, providing the rioting didn't resurge in their area, it would be in their best interests to go to their shops in the morning to see what, if anything, had happened. Until then, there wasn't anything more they could do.

Kings Road the next morning was a far cry from its usual genteel self. Metal bins smoked. Glass crunched under Kate's boots. Shocked faces of those venturing out for the first time, like her, stared around at the scene before them. It had rained overnight and there was a thin, tacky film of mud and ash covering the ground and footpath. A few voyeurs were there too, either actual tourists or hometown tourists, out with their cameras, chattering like excited monkeys.

Kate led the way, flanked by Elizabeth and Victoria, with Margaret and Angus bringing up the rear. Bill had seized the opportunity to get some space from Margaret and Angus, but had hugged Kate tightly before she left and promised to be there if she needed him.

They moved as one unit, mostly silent bar the occasional gasp and tut-tutting as they pointed to bent street signs or the blackened shell of a burnt-out car. Her heart was wedged firmly sideways in her throat.

She'd messaged Mark about Quentin and the money, but he still hadn't replied.

They were nearly there. The road curved, obscuring The Tea Chest up ahead. They passed Lush, completely untouched, and her hopes soared. But then there was Ye Olde Lolly Shoppe, whose front window gaped open and whose contents spilled onto the footpath as though the shop had been shot and the wound had bled unchecked.

Margaret's hands flew to her face. 'Poor Mr Rathdowney. I was there just last week to get a toffee. He's near retirement age now. Been there for decades. This is the last thing he needs.'

On the other side of the road, Bartlett's Chocolate and Coffee looked intact, save for a wonky metal shop sign by the front door.

As they passed Roulette, Manu dashed out to greet them and flung his arms around Kate. 'Our shop's okay,' he said, rocking her from side to side. 'Everything. We were so lucky.'

Randolph was there too, eyes shining.

'That's wonderful,' Kate said. 'Did you stay through the whole thing?'

Manu released her and stepped away, looking sheepish. 'Ah, not exactly,' he said, tugging at his bow tie.

Randolph elbowed him playfully. 'He bolted at the first sound of biceps bulging through a khaki shirt.'

'I didn't bolt,' Manu protested.

Kate nodded but she couldn't really concentrate. She spun around to see her own shop.

Manu and Randolph fell silent.

'Sorry, princess,' Manu said.

Elizabeth, Victoria, Margaret and Angus all stood staring at The Tea Chest.

The huge front window was shattered. The window boxes containing her precious gerberas had been smashed and dying flowers were scattered on the ground. Pain stabbed her chest as she picked up a limp stem. It was a horrible symbol of the failure of the entire enterprise.

'Kate,' Elizabeth said, clasping a hand around her arm. 'Your flowers.'

Margaret clucked in sympathy.

'We'll leave you to it,' Randolph said gently. 'But please let us know if there's anything we can do.'

Kate nodded silently.

Aside from the window and the flower boxes, there was a streak of random green spray paint in an arc across the solid wooden door, like a scar across its red face.

'Not too bad then,' said Angus. 'We'll get it cleaned up in no time.' He gave Kate a determined smile, for which she was grateful.

'Thanks.'

'Such senseless rubbish,' Margaret scolded. 'Wicked, wicked people. No right . . .'

Kate tuned Margaret's voice out while she fished in her bag for the store keys.

'Oh,' Victoria said suddenly, grabbing her other arm. 'Look.'

She turned to see. Across the road, Heavensfield House stood dishevelled and forlorn. The whole window frontage was shattered and glass had sprayed across the footpath. Through the broken windows, she could see tables and chairs overturned, and plates and glassware in tatters, cake trodden into the ground with the ugly prints of boots. Towards the rear of the shop stood the small figure of Lady Heavensfield as she talked with a police officer, her hand at her throat as she gestured around the room.

'Come on,' Kate said. 'This can wait. We need to help her.'

She led the way, sidestepping an abandoned bicycle, and entered Lady Heavensfield's store. She halted just inside the doorway, not wishing to intrude. The policeman cleared his throat, handed over his card and put his notebook in his pocket.

'We'll be in touch,' he said, and tipped his hat first to her and then to the group in the doorway as he left.

'Lady Heavensfield, I'm so sorry,' Kate said across the space between them.

Lady Heavensfield raised her chin. 'Mindless peasant thuggery,' she said. 'No place for it in a civilised country such as this.'

'No,' Kate agreed.

'I was just saying the same thing,' Margaret said, adding some well-practised *tsk-tsking*.

There was a moment's silence as the crowd took in the surrounds.

'We'd like to help,' Kate said.

Lady Heavensfield shifted on the spot and put her hands on her hips. 'What about your own shop?'

Kate shrugged. 'It can wait. It's just cosmetic.'

'Well, I have staff members coming later but if you can spare the time . . .'

'Tell us what we can do.'

Three hours later, the team had swept, hoovered, mopped, dumped rubbish, rearranged furniture, cleaned benches and table tops, made a list of broken pieces and those to be replaced by the insurer, contacted a glass contractor to fix the store windows in both their premises, and organised a locksmith to replace the broken locks on the door.

Kate had even been over to The Tea Chest and picked some of the living white daisies to help brighten Lady Heavensfield's shop. She'd also made a pot of warming chai, picked fresh rose petals and added them, along with a drop of rose oil for a deeper aroma and healing balm to soothe and lift their spirits.

Lady Heavensfield, in turn, loudly declared that it was an abomination to ruin fine English tea with 'oriental spice' and 'garden pickings', but she went on to drink two cups anyway, with several cubes of brown sugar thrown in for good measure.

They consumed toasted marshmallows, the smell of the roasted coconut far more pleasant than that of the lingering smoke outside, then followed them up with macarons. They washed the dishes before Kate collected her flock to go.

'Let us know if there's anything else we can do,' she said brightly. 'You know where we are.'

Lady Heavensfield looked over Kate's shoulder to The Tea Chest and nodded gently, as though finally resigned to the permanence of the shop, right when Kate had lost it all.

'Thank you,' Lady Heavensfield said, with gratitude that seemed as though it might just be authentic. 'I am most appreciative of your efforts.'

Back in The Tea Chest, the group decided on how best to approach the spray paint and the window boxes.

'I can fix the boxes, no trouble,' Angus said.

'Really?' Margaret looked surprised and impressed by her man's secret talent.

Angus seemed to grow under her eager gaze. 'I did an apprenticeship as a cabinet maker when I was young.'

'I didn't know that,' Margaret said.

'I've many talents you haven't seen yet,' he said with a wink.

'Oh my.' Margaret blushed.

'Stop it,' Victoria groaned.

'What?' Margaret protested. 'It's okay for the young to have a love life but not the old, is that right?'

'Not if you're our mother,' Victoria said.

Elizabeth wrinkled up her nose as an unwanted image clearly passed through her mind. Then she shook herself. 'Speaking of which, I haven't been able to get hold of Haruka. I need to talk to him.'

'Who's Haruka?' Margaret said, stumbling over his name.

'He's my friend,' Elizabeth said. She exchanged a look with Kate.

'What sort of name is Haruka? Is he foreign?' Margaret said.

'No, Mum. He's English,' she said, omitting the part about his Japanese father.

Margaret scratched at her arm as if thinking about something. She frowned. 'Haruka. Haruka. That name sounds familiar.' She turned to Angus as if he might know the answer.

'Don't look at me,' he shrugged.

'He was the chap that sat next to Elizabeth on the plane,' Victoria explained. 'I told you about him when I brought Elizabeth home.'

'That's right.' Her eyes shot open. 'Now I remember. He phoned yesterday.'

'What?' Elizabeth gasped.

'When you were at the hospital. He called the home phone because he couldn't get through to you on your mobile. You'd left it at home, of course, when you rushed out in the ambulance. He'd seen you on telly.'

Elizabeth slapped her forehead. 'I was supposed to meet him yesterday. I completely forgot in all the drama. What else did he say?' Her voice was rising. 'What did *you* say?'

'I told him you were with your husband and I didn't know when you'd be back,' Margaret said innocently.

Victoria groaned.

'And what did he say?' Elizabeth said carefully.

'I asked him if he wanted to leave a message but he said no. He said he understood and hung up. He was rather evasive.'

Elizabeth turned to Kate. 'I've got to go. I'm sorry, I've got to run.'

'Of course.'

Elizabeth turned to leave.

'Wait,' Victoria shouted at Elizabeth's retreating back. 'I'm coming with you.' And with that, the sisters were gone.

The phone number of the pizza shop where Leila had first met Quentin rang out. Leila hung up. Presumably they were shut due to the riots. But even if they were open, there was no guarantee they'd know where Quentin was.

She turned her attention to Facebook instead. Leila had often searched for a name—perhaps someone she'd just met or a new work colleague or a potential new date. All of a sudden, that cute guy in logistics was a guy with a family (possibly even kids), friends (possibly even a girlfriend), a dog, and favourite movies, music and hobbies.

You could get more information about someone in a few minutes of Facebook sleuthing through photos and status updates than you could in hours of conversation.

Leila wished now, as she clicked and scrolled and googled yet again, that she'd done more sleuthing on Quentin long ago. It just hadn't seemed necessary. Now, she'd spent hours trying to hunt him down in all the usual places—Facebook, Myspace, LinkedIn, blogs, websites and through Google and Bing searches. But there was nothing interesting other than a news article about Quentin Tarantino letting rip about his iced water, which was apparently not iced enough.

She drained her third instant coffee for the morning. Each one had tasted worse than the last. The white mug clinked against other empties as she slid it along the desk. She should get out of her pyjamas. Have a shower. Get dressed as though she still had a job to do. Eat something besides Coco Pops. Be sociable with Bill, who looked like he could use some cheering up after spending time with Margaret and Angus.

In short, be the person she used to think she was. The person who was efficient and reliable and capable. Not the one who made monumentally bad choices, made decisions without consulting the people who mattered most, and let her personal feelings affect her judgement—and all because she was desperate to prove to her mother, to Kate, to Lucas and to herself that she could and would succeed on her own terms, with or without the man she loved, with or without job security.

But she'd blown it—with everyone.

She remained seated in the shadowy room on the western side of the house, the laptop glowing uselessly. Her emotions rolled slowly between depression and anxiety. Visions of her failed future played out in her mind like movies: of having to take temporary admin work here and there, just like her mother predicted; of waiting tables in cafés because no one would ever trust her with an important job; of having to buy her clothes from Target rather than boutiques in the Valley; and of eating tinned spaghetti on toast for dinner.

Alone.

She jumped. Her phone was ringing. Lucas's name was on the screen.

'Hello?'

'I've got news,' he said, and she could hear a note of excitement in his tone, mixed with trepidation. 'Quentin's not his real name.'

She dropped her head into her hand. She'd considered that possibility briefly, but she hadn't seriously allowed herself to believe it could be true.

'Go on,' she managed.

'It's Daniel Jackson.'

'Daniel Jackson? Dan Jack? Like the reverse of Jack Daniel's whiskey? What sort of stupid name is that?' She coughed out mirthless laughter.

'He's an actor,' Lucas continued.

That was a slap in the face.

'Rubbish.'

'Well, he's a wannabe actor. He's with Tower and Hart Agency in Los Angeles.'

Leila's brain clunked and groaned its way through the information. 'How do you know this?' she said, more as a way of giving herself time to process the information than actually caring how he knew.

'Remember Oscar Martin who was over here last year?'

Leila searched her memory.

'Up on the top floor,' Lucas prompted. 'On the three-month exchange?'

'Oh yeah, the American.'

'Well, we kept in touch. He emailed me recently and was saying how the company had sent him on an acting course as professional development.'

'Are you serious? What a complete rort.'

'Well, you could look at it that way,' he said. 'But he's in business development. His whole job is to pitch to prospective clients and build relationships, so it could be seen as legitimate skill-building.'

'Keep going.'

'So I sent him an email saying I was trying to track down a guy called Quentin Ripp, not because I thought he was an actor at that stage, but just because he was American, and Quentin was American, or so we think, and, you know, if I was going to play the Six Degrees of Separation game, then I figured I should start with someone in the same country. Right?'

'I guess so.'

'So, Oscar's sitting in a restaurant with a mate when the email pops up on his phone. His mate happens to be a PI.'

'Of course he is,' she said. 'Only in America.'

'Well, the PI friend says he can send out a blast on his phone to a social network he's part of that he uses to help track down people, asking if anyone knows Quentin Ripp. He does that, then someone jumps online and says they did an acting course with a guy called Daniel Jackson who used to assume the name of Quentin Ripp in character sketches. The PI tells Oscar, and Oscar contacts his acting school and says he's looking to track down an actor in LA and asks the school for agency contacts and then sends them to me. Then I sit on the phone and go through the list until I find one that represents Daniel Jackson. Presto.'

'Okay, that's pretty impressive. But how do we know it's right? How do we know it's the same guy?'

'I told the agency I was casting for a tourism commercial in Australia, featuring American tourists, and asked her to send me head shots and specifically requested Daniel Jackson's as I'd heard good things. I've just emailed you his photo to check.'

Leila stiffened. She reached for the mouse and navigated to her email. There it was—an email from Lucas with the paperclip attachment symbol. Her heart flip-flopped. She clicked it open and there he was: Quentin Ripp. Daniel Jackson.

She took in a sharp breath.

It was a black-and-white headshot and his face was tilted to the side, his eyes boring through the camera lens to meet hers.

'Leila?' Lucas prompted. 'Is it him?'

She blinked a few times, staring at his face, outraged to find she still wanted to take it in her hands and kiss it.

'Yes.'

He waited a moment, giving her a chance to get her thoughts together.

'I'm sorry,' he said.

She nodded, still fixated on the photo in front of her.

'But, Leila, there's more.'

More? She couldn't possibly take any more. What else could there be?

'The agency told me that Daniel—Quentin—is currently on a job. A private job, which is due to end soon.'

Leila clicked the photo shut. 'So?'

'So it seems he's not actually the brains behind this fraud at all. Leila, someone hired him to do this to you.'

24

The black cab hissed to a halt in the wet guttering. Elizabeth lurched from within, her plimsolls landing in the wet street, leaving Victoria behind to take care of the fare. It had started raining as soon as they'd left The Tea Chest, slowing down traffic as drivers adjusted to the conditions. Almost as suddenly as it had started, it had stopped again and now muddy rivulets ran across the bitumen, and the smell of fresh rain rose from the road. She pulled her coat tightly around her.

The cab door shut and Victoria arrived at her side.

'Nice place,' she said, nodding at the modern glass entryway to the block of flats.

Elizabeth didn't answer her. She was stuck. Stunned. Staring at the doors. She had no idea what Haruka thought was going on between her and John.

'Come on,' Victoria said, taking her elbow and leading her forward. 'Make love while the sun shines.'

At the intercom, Elizabeth hesitated again, her finger hovering over his number.

'Well, go on,' Victoria urged, sounding like an exasperated parent.

'But what will I say?'

'Um, der. *Hi? It's me? Can I come up?*' And with that, Victoria thrust her polished nail at number 24 and it lit up.

Silence was all that came from the intercom.

Elizabeth hopped from foot to foot. Behind them, residents swiped key tags and the glass doors clicked open and swooshed shut.

'Let's go,' Victoria said at the next opportunity and pulled her through the doors behind a man in a business suit.

Elizabeth held her breath as they entered, half expecting someone to catch them out and ask them to leave. But no one did. They crossed the echoing black and white tiles to the elevator and pressed the call button.

'I can't believe how hard my heart is pounding,' Elizabeth said. She might have been catastrophising, but she truly felt as though the world would end if she couldn't find Haruka and clear up any misapprehension that she might have reunited with her husband. Any thoughts of John and what she'd said goodbye to back in that hospital room vanished. Haruka was all she wanted now.

Victoria gave her a sympathetic look and squeezed her hand just as the elevator binged and the smooth chrome doors slid soundlessly open. 'Here we go,' she said, leading the way.

On the tenth floor, they stepped into a warm, brightly lit hallway and Elizabeth hesitated, staring at all the closed doors. Waves of doubt unsteadied her. She placed a cool palm to her forehead.

'What's wrong now?' Victoria said.

'What am I doing? Maybe I got this all wrong. Haruka and I haven't known each other for long. I could have misinterpreted everything. This is crazy. So what if he thinks badly of me? What does it matter?'

But even as she said it her heart ached. It mattered. It mattered a lot.

'Elizabeth Catherine Clancy nee Plimsworth, soon to be just Plimsworth again, I don't want to hear another word. You've waited a long time to be happy. Here's your chance. Don't waste it. Now get over there and get your man.'

With that, she smacked Elizabeth across the rump and shoved her towards door twenty-four.

Kate was running. Running away from her shop and the well-meaning, good-hearted friends who were working to fix it. Running from the weight of impending doom she knew would swallow her if she stopped for just a moment. She was jogging down slippery footpaths, dodging puddles and weaving through pedestrians who had hunched shoulders and weary faces under their dripping umbrellas.

It had been decades since she'd run like this. It felt good to be sweating, to feel her heart pounding in her chest and her breath raking over her throat, inhaling diesel fumes and cigarette smoke.

She'd lost track of where she was. She'd passed an off-licence, clothing stores, a jewellery maker and countless cafés and coffee stations. Tube stations, too, had flown past without her registering much more than the red circle sign. She'd turned corners and run down alleys, passed neon signs and guitar-playing buskers, and avoided riot debris. She'd been in London for three months but she could still lose her way if she wasn't paying attention.

Her chest burned and her right knee began to ache; a new development, she noted. She slowed to a brisk walk, pushing past people who stared at the woman dressed in jeans and a long-sleeved shirt and sandshoes. Clearly, she wasn't a real jogger. She was touched to see concern on one woman's face. There was a momentary pause and her mouth opened a fraction as though she was about to ask if there was something wrong. But she closed it again, gave Kate a tight smile and looked away.

There was something wrong, alright. Everything, in fact. And she was suffocating under the inevitability of her spectacular failure and how she was ever going to reconcile her husband to it.

She turned another corner, this time into a quiet, narrow laneway, and found herself at a second-hand bookstore. She pushed open the heavy oak door and was greeted by a petite, stylish young woman, who looked somewhat at odds with the mustiness of the store. Bookshelves towered over her.

'Good morning,' she beamed, her red lipstick bright against her translucent skin.

'Hi,' Kate said, still gasping to regain her breath.

'Would you like a cup of tea?' the woman asked. She gestured to a warmly lit corner of the shop where a huge maroon couch sat.

'Don't suppose you've got any whiskey?'

The young woman raised one eyebrow, checked her watch, and nodded. 'An Irish coffee it is.'

'Perfect.'

Kate curled up on the couch, pulling her knees to her body and hugging a cushion to her chest. Her phone vibrated in her pocket. She rushed to retrieve it, hoping it was Mark. She'd sent repeated texts and a voicemail begging him to call her. She needed him. And she needed to know what he was thinking and feeling, how he was reacting to the news about Quentin.

But it wasn't Mark; it was Leila.

She considered letting the call go through to voicemail. She really didn't feel strong enough to speak to her former assistant right now without saying things she might regret later. But at the last minute, she took the call.

'Kate, where are you?'

'Out,' she said curtly. Leila had no right anymore to know where she was.

'I'm at the shop but the others didn't know where you'd gone. You left your bag behind so they didn't think you'd be gone long but they say it's been ages.'

'Oh.' Kate stiffened, realising she'd left her purse behind and had no way to pay for the enormous mug of coffee the assistant had just placed in front of her.

Thank you, she mouthed at her.

'I'm at a bookshop,' she said to Leila.

'A bookshop? Where?'

'I don't know, actually.' She stared blankly at her surroundings, looking for clues. 'Hold on.' She dropped the phone to her lap and waved at the assistant, who was unwrapping books from a postal satchel.

'Excuse me. I'm sorry, but where am I?'

The assistant smiled sympathetically and patiently explained where she was, and Kate relayed it to Leila.

'Okay,' Leila said. 'Stay right where you are. I'm coming to you. There's something I've got to tell you right now.'

'Wait,' Kate said, before she could hang up. 'Could you please bring my bag with you?'

Kate watched Leila enter the bookshop, speak to the woman at the front, then weave her way through the books to stand in front of the couch.

'Hi,' she said, a wary smile on her lips. She extended the handbag to her.

Kate took it and dropped it at her feet.

'Would it be okay if I sat down?' Leila said. 'I really have to tell you something.'

'You can sit,' Kate said, pointing at a chair to her right. 'But I have a few things to say to you first. I have a bone to pick with you. A whole carcass, actually.'

Leila sat stiffly on the edge of the chair. 'Okay.'

'You deceived me. Right from the start. You used Lucas as a professional reference when really he was your best friend and love interest. He was always going to say whatever he needed me to hear for you to get this job.'

'Lucas is a professional. I'm sure he would have spoken the truth,' Leila said evenly.

'Why did you leave your last job?'

Leila bit her lip and held her knees with her hands. 'I was fired.'

Kate rolled her eyes and shook her head slowly. 'Perfect.'

'I kind of lost it one day and I shoved a co-worker and threw a paperweight at his head,' Leila said.

For a moment, Kate forgot how angry she was with Leila and stared at her in shock. 'You're kidding.'

'I wish I was.'

Kate laughed, a bit hysterically, then pulled herself together. 'What else haven't you told me since we've been in London? Leila, how did this all go so wrong?'

Leila took a big breath and leaned back in the chair, looking tired. 'I decided early on, when I did the risk assessment, that there were four areas of risk that needed to be managed.'

'Four? We only talked about three—schedule, budget and brand recognition.'

'They were the three I showed you. The other area of weakness, I felt, was you.'

Kate felt as though she'd been kicked in the chest. 'Me?'

'You were nervous and lacking confidence. You almost fell apart when you saw the state of the shop.'

Kate folded her arms tightly across her chest. That was true.

'But that didn't last. I got better.'

'You did. But the schedule was so tight right at the start, and I really wanted The Tea Chest to succeed, and I guess I felt you needed a bit of managing. If I could shield you from some of the stress, then I should do that and let you get on with what you're so good at.'

'Just like you did when you deleted Lucas's email.'

'Yes, I suppose that's true. But in this case, I wanted to prove that I could handle more responsibility. Being fired from a job was a pretty big blow to my ego and I needed to prove to myself that I wasn't a bad person and I could turn it all around.'

Kate was still stinging from the notion she needed managing.

'You said you'd get back to me about meeting Quentin, but you didn't. But—' Leila said, holding up her hand to forestall Kate's protest '—I should have reminded you. I should have just made the appointment and had him turn up at the store. Instead, I decided to keep quiet until after the grand opening, and that was wrong.'

'Because you liked Quentin.'

'At that stage, I thought he was nice but we hadn't spent a lot of time together. It was more because I just wanted to believe we could pull it all off without a hitch. I underestimated you and I'm sorry for that. If you had met him before the launch, maybe you would have read him differently. Maybe you would have seen something I didn't.'

Kate got to her feet and paced, absorbing all Leila was saying. She caught the attendant's eye and signalled for two more Irish coffees. If she was ever going to take up drinking, this day seemed as good as any other.

In all likelihood, even if she had met Quentin before the launch, it wouldn't have changed anything. They hadn't been flooded with offers and they needed to make hard decisions, fast. Leila was right in that the intense time pressure had created a situation that made them vulnerable no matter what they'd done. And even when she met Quentin at The Tea Chest and sensed a vibe between him and Leila, she'd ignored it.

Leila went on. 'I should have investigated who he was right at the start. And I absolutely shouldn't have handed over the cheque to him the day he was supposed to deliver the ads. I should have realised something was wrong. It was the time pressure.' She grimaced. 'No. Actually, on that particular day, I was distracted by my feelings for him. I stuffed up big time. Huge. I trusted him, like an idiot.'

Kate flopped back into the chair as the coffees arrived and the attendant handed them a plate of ginger biscuits, the spicy nutmeg scent catching Kate's attention. Hearing Leila say it out loud was agony. That moment had been their last chance to get it right.

But she couldn't turn back time. What was done was done.

'It's not your fault,' Kate said, nibbling on the edge of a biscuit. 'At the end of the day, the buck stops with me. I accept that. I was the captain and I dropped the ball.'

'There were a lot of balls in the air to be dropped.'

'That's true. Maybe it was just such a monumental task that we were never going to succeed.'

'Maybe it's not over yet,' Leila said doubtfully.

Kate dunked her biscuit into her coffee. She'd like to have believed that. She'd also like to have believed she hadn't irreparably damaged her marriage, but the longer Mark's silence went on the more likely it seemed that she had.

'Have you spoken to Quentin?'

Leila shook her head. 'I've left so many messages, but he's ignoring me.'

Kate grunted, thinking of her own unanswered messages to Mark. She didn't blame him for being mad. They'd had the perfect opportunity to cash in and be living a comfortable, stress-free life right now.

'Kate, I still need to tell you my news.'

'There's more?'

'I'm afraid so.' Leila filled Kate in with the research Lucas had done, finishing with the fact that someone had hired Quentin to pull off this charade.

'Unbelievable,' Kate repeated, over and over again. 'Unbelievable.'

'Kate, I hope you know how deeply sorry I am,' Leila said, her voice strained with unshed tears. 'I honestly believed Quentin was the real deal. I've loved this job since the moment I started—it's been a dream come true. Well, it *was* until it turned into this nightmare. I've made horrible mistakes but I would never intentionally have done anything to jeopardise your business. I know what this company means to you. It was your passion for it that showed me how wonderful business could be.'

Perhaps it was the whiskey, but Leila's words began to soften Kate's heart. She knew what that was like, to find a position in a company so filled with passion and creativity. It was magic. A chance in a million.

Simone had plucked Kate from a market stall and given her a whole new world. Kate had almost done the same for Leila. For Kate, it had been Judy who'd tried to sabotage her career. But she'd been lucky to have Simone to fight for her at every turn. Leila had been sabotaged by Quentin, and Kate had to accept that she'd let Leila down because she was a leader now, like Simone, but she hadn't fought hard enough for Leila. She'd let her fall.

Suddenly, she sat bolt upright on the edge of the seat.

'What?' Leila said, putting her coffee down.

'Leila, I know who did this.'

'Who?'

'The same person who's been sabotaging me from the beginning. But this time Simone wasn't there to protect me and I've let her get the better of me.'

Leila's eyes narrowed, then suddenly opened. 'Judy?'

'Yep. Judy. And now it's time for me to grow up and defend myself.'

Beside her, Victoria raised her hand to knock but Elizabeth slapped it away.

'Wait.'

'What's wrong?'

'You've never told me why you don't have anyone serious— any men—in your life,' Elizabeth said.

Victoria raised a shoulder and dropped it. 'And?'

'I want to know. Will you tell me?'

Her sister dropped her eyes to the floor. 'I just always feel like a bit of a Gumby,' she said. 'All clumsy and dopey and boring.'

'But you're not,' Elizabeth said firmly. 'You have a lovely heart. And you're fun to be with. Everyone loves you. That's why your sales record at the shop is so good. No one can resist that smile.'

Victoria's face lit up with pride.

'It's just confidence,' Elizabeth said. 'You'll find it when you're ready.'

'And what about you?' Victoria said, tilting her head to the door. 'Feeling confident?'

'Not in the slightest.' She raised her hand to knock and then dropped it again.

'What is it this time?'

'I just wanted to say thank you. You've been such a rock for me since that day in the hotel when you first called. You got me here, you picked me up, you brought me hair dye and cups of coffee and kept me from going mad.

'And thank you for setting me up with Haruka, however it turns out with him now. I was so angry at you to start with but I should have said before now how right you were. You said in the shop that you were waiting for me to be in a better place before you got us together. That was insightful and sensitive. After Haruka and I went out; well, I've been so wrapped up in the joy of it all that I completely forgot I had you to thank for it.'

'You're welcome.'

Elizabeth hugged her.

Then Victoria reached up again to knock. Three short raps. 'Come on, Queen Lizzy, it's not over yet. It's time for you to get your happy ending.'

From behind the door came muffled music and low voices. Then there were footsteps. And the clatter of plates and glasses.

Elizabeth turned to Victoria. 'He's got company. Quick.' She grabbed her sister's arm and turned to leave. But the door had opened behind her. She spun around, plastering a smile on her face, just as Haruka stuck his head out into the corridor.

'Haruka, hi,' she said.

Haruka's mouth twitched into a small smile, but his eyes were unsettled, moving from her to Victoria. He stepped into the corridor, pulling the door most of the way closed behind him.

Oh crap, oh crap, oh crap. He's probably having an orgy in there. Playing naked Twister.

Elizabeth wished the universe would split open and suck her through time and space to anywhere that wasn't here. Her eyes flicked past him, trying to see what he was hiding, though she wasn't sure she really wanted to know. Naked Twister could be most disturbing.

He moved his body to block her view.

'Um, what're you doing here?' he said, and then must have realised his tone was accusatory because he tried to soften it with a strained smile. 'It's great to see you,' he added.

But clearly it wasn't.

She scrambled for something to say.

'We were in the neighbourhood,' she said, knowing full well he would see through the lie. 'Er, this is my sister, Victoria.'

He cocked his head to the side. 'Yes. We've met before.'

'Oh. Right.'

An awkward silence followed while Haruka guarded the door.

'For the love of chocolate,' Victoria said. 'Haruka, what's going on in there? You got company? A woman? Or two? What?'

'No,' he emphasised. 'Nothing like that.'

Just then, there was a burst of loud, unmistakable, *male* laughter.

Elizabeth and Victoria looked at each other, then looked back to Haruka with raised eyebrows.

'So you've got men in there?' Victoria pressed.

'No.' Haruka looked horrified. 'I mean, yes, but it's not what you're thinking.'

'Can we come in then?' Elizabeth said, finding her voice and her courage. No one was going to make a fool of her again. She had to know why he was being so secretive. Better now than later, when she'd fallen in love and invested years in the wrong person only to find out the truth when it was too late.

Actually, it was already too late.

He reached up a hand to rub his forehead and looked at the floor.

'Haruka,' Elizabeth said. 'What's going on?'

He sighed, then stepped back and opened the door wide. 'Come in.'

They walked down the short hallway and entered the open-plan living space. Five men sat on the couches and chairs, plates of pastries and a pot of coffee and white mugs on the coffee table. They looked up when the trio arrived; their hands, which a moment ago had been busy with wool, suddenly paused mid-activity.

Victoria scratched her head like a cartoon character trying to figure out what was going on.

Elizabeth turned to Haruka, her face screwed up in puzzlement.

'Hi,' one of the men said, jumping in to break the silence. He was in his late twenties and immaculately dressed. He was holding a crochet hook in one hand. In his other hand, he clutched some kind of pink project—a work in progress that looked as though it might one day be a beret. The other men slowly began to resume their work: blanket squares, baby booties, doilies, even a tea cosy.

Crochet work. All of it.

Somewhere through her shock, Elizabeth wondered if maybe Kate would be interested in retro tea cosies for the shop. But she shook herself back to reality. This wasn't *normal*.

Haruka crossed his arms over his chest and Elizabeth could see the outline of his pecs through his shirt. A crazy giggle began to tickle her chest.

'These are my friends,' he began, gesturing to the crowd. 'We have a sort of club, I guess. Like a book club. But it's, you know . . .' His voice trailed off.

'A knitting club?' Victoria prompted.

'A crochet club,' corrected the young man.

'Yes,' Elizabeth said, as if that explained it.

'Cool,' Victoria said, and put down her handbag and went to the couch to squish herself between a burly man cradling a tiny pair of booties and a white-haired man working slowly on squares. 'Can you teach me too?'

'Sure. Grab that ball of wool over there.'

'So what's this all about?' Elizabeth said. She was trying to sound supportive, but she had dozens of questions and the uneasiness had found its way into her voice. And most of all, there was part of her thinking, *See, I didn't know him at all*.

Haruka tilted his head and indicated for her to follow him into the kitchen. He leaned against the black marble bench top, took a deep breath, and then laughed.

'This is not how I wanted you to find out about this,' he said. 'This is at least a ninth-date conversation.'

'Ninth date?'

'Maybe tenth.'

She relaxed. She began to tingle again, just being in his presence.

He put his hand on his heart. 'Hi, my name's Haruka and I'm addicted to crochet,' he confessed.

'Well, at least it's not scrapbooking,' she said.

His face straightened. 'Oh. I was saving that for the twelfth date.' He reached out and took her hand.

Electricity shot up her arm and she raced to keep up with the charge to her heart.

'It's an artist thing,' he said. 'Very good for fine motor skills and the right brain, and I often find ways to incorporate it into my designs.'

'It's like art therapy for artists,' she suggested.

'Exactly.' His face had relaxed so much she found it difficult not to reach out and take it in her hands and kiss his lips and his nose and his eyelashes. And maybe back to his lips. Maybe to his ears. And down to his chest. And maybe lower . . .

'Elizabeth?'

'Huh? Oh. What?'

'I'm really happy to see you,' he said, still holding her hand in his and rubbing his thumb over her wrist. 'I thought when you didn't show up yesterday . . . And then your mum said . . .'

Elizabeth groaned. 'My *husband*. Yes.' She gazed into his eyes. 'He showed up unexpectedly and then had the audacity to have a heart attack on my floor. I had to take him to hospital.' She paused. 'I'm sure I could have been charged with some sort of offence if I hadn't. He's fine now. And I want you to know I made it clear I want nothing more to do with him. It's over.'

'So you're free to see other people.'

'Not exactly,' she said.

'Oh.' His dark brows drew together.

'I only have eyes for one person.' She twisted her foot on the ground in a coquettish manner, inching it towards his leg.

'Is it me?' he said, a glint in his eye.

'What do you think?' She began to nudge his toe. 'I tried calling you on the way over,' she said. 'I was worried you'd given up on me.'

'My phone's been off. Part of the crochet club rules.' He reached out his toes, covered only by a grey woollen sock, and flexed them against the arch of her foot.

She tugged on his hand, drawing him towards her. 'So, we're okay then?'

'Definitely,' he said. Then he kissed her.

'Should we give this thing a go then?' he said.

'Crochet?'

'Us.'

Elizabeth soared out of her body and travelled to the place of princesses, princes, fairies and rainbows. It was a nice, warm, joyous place. She looked around at her sparkly new life, at her castle and her handsome prince, and knew she couldn't be happier.

She opened her eyes and came back to Haruka in his kitchen.

'Definitely.'

25

Kate and Leila were now sitting in the back corner of a dark Irish pub in Kensington, a large pint in front of Leila and strong coffee in front of Kate.

She had her mobile phone in her hand and was stabbing at the keys. It was around ten o'clock in the evening in Australia. She dialled Judy's mobile number, but it rang out twice to voicemail. She phoned again and this time it went straight to voicemail, as though Judy had switched it off.

'You're not getting away from me.' Kate took a large sip of the sweet, creamy coffee then dialled again, this time the home number. Her chest heaved with furious deep breaths. To her shock, the phone picked up on the fourth ring. She opened her mouth to spit venomous words, but caught herself just in time when she realised it was Judy's husband, Graham, who'd answered. He sounded breathless, as though she'd woken him, and she felt a stab of guilt for a second.

'Oh, Graham, it's Kate. Sorry if I woke you but I need to speak to Judy.'

'Kate,' he said warmly, as though he had no clue of the war that raged between her and his wife. 'How lovely to hear from you. I'll just get Judes.'

There were some muffled noises and shuffling, then the unmistakable sound of Judy's jewellery-encrusted fingers wrapping around the phone. Kate's heart hammered in her chest. She could hear Judy mumble something like, 'Go back to sleep,' to her husband, close the bedroom door gently and walk down the long hallway. She heard the glass door open and close and Judy step out into the night air, cicadas shrilling in the background.

'Kate, what is it? It's late.'

Kate was thrown. Surely Judy knew why she was calling? A wave of doubt rushed over her. Maybe she had nothing to do with this at all.

'Er, hi.' She was about to apologise for calling so late and obviously waking Graham. But beside her, Leila set her face and made encouraging 'go on' motions with her hands.

'Judy, we need to talk.'

'Well, make it snappy.'

Kate braced herself. 'I know what you did.'

Now it was Judy's turn to pause. And before she could get another word in, Kate went on, shooting out her words before her nerves got the better of her.

'I know you hired Quentin Ripp to act as a fake investor. You must know that he's taken our money. It was a vicious and cruel act of corporate espionage.'

Espionage? Was that what it was? She wasn't sure of the legal term but, at any rate, it sounded good.

'What you've done is illegal,' she declared.

Wasn't it?

'And I will sue you, Judy, I will sue you for every last dollar you have for ruining The Tea Chest's reputation, business viability, employee security and my own family's livelihood. It's completely unacceptable and I won't let you bully me anymore.

'I get why you would do it to me.' She paused. 'Actually, no I don't get it. I never did anything to you but you never gave me a chance. Not from the start. Were you jealous of me? Did you hate me because Simone liked me more than you?'

Beside her, Leila was nodding along and murmuring in chorus like the congregation at a Baptist service.

'So, okay, you hate me. So you wanted to hurt me. But I can't for the life of me fathom why on earth you would do it. Why on earth would you sabotage your own company? Why now, right when you want out and need a buyer? Why would you take the money out and create such instability, something we might not be able to come back from? That's the last thing any buyer would want to see. You might have wanted to get back at me for some imaginary injury I've caused you, but I also know you've got a good business head on you, so why would you destroy something so valuable?'

Judy *tch*ed as though she really would rather not be having this conversation.

'Explain yourself, Judy. You owe me that at least.'

Kate was shaking now with adrenaline and caffeine. She'd prepared herself for a fight. For a screaming match. She was prepared to swear and threaten and even beg if she had to. But she wasn't prepared for the weariness that emanated from Judy in her next sentence.

'Graham's dying,' she said simply. Her words hung in the space between their continents for a moment while Kate's brain raced to catch up.

'What?' Kate's mind reeled. It was like she'd been having one conversation but had somehow stumbled accidentally into someone else's.

'Cancer. We don't have much time. That's why I was so desperate to sell. We want to spend our last months together free of any ties or complications. We want to travel, where we can. The last thing I want to think about is this business. I'm tired, Kate. I don't want to fight anymore. With anyone. I just want to focus on my husband and then on . . . on the time afterwards. On getting through it. Where to go from there.'

Her voice drifted off.

Kate's throat tightened. She immediately thought of Mark and her chest lurched somewhere towards the other side of the world where the love of her life was waiting for her, she hoped. Losing Mark was something she allowed herself to contemplate occasionally, but it filled her with such fear and despair that she would push the thoughts away quickly and make sure she greeted him with a smile and a kiss the next time she saw him.

She turned to Leila, who shook her head quizzically and spread her hands, questioning what had suddenly changed in the conversation and brought about such a shift in Kate's posture.

Judy sniffed, then pulled herself together.

'I needed out and you weren't playing the game. I panicked. I wanted to force your hand.'

'Why didn't you just tell me?' Kate said quietly.

'I don't need your sympathy,' Judy bristled.

'No, of course.' The tone of the conversation slid back to a familiar footing. 'But why Quentin? Judy, where is the money? The Tea Chest can't survive this.'

'The money is in my bank account. That was part of the deal. I just needed to scare you into action.'

Kate was glad she was sitting down. 'So, wait—the money is still here? It's still in The Tea Chest?' She clutched her heart.

Beside her, Leila bounced up and down and squeezed Kate's arm.

'I just need to transfer it back,' Judy said matter-of-factly, as though it had been as simple as ordering a latte and returning it to the waiter. 'Despite what you think of me, Kate, I do honour Simone's legacy.'

She paused. Somewhere in the background of Brisbane, a frog began to croak. It must have been raining, Kate realised.

'You remind me a lot of her, you know,' Judy said, her voice the softest Kate had ever heard. 'You've got that same creative drive and uncanny vision. Something I never had,' she admitted. 'I guess that's why she liked you so much.'

Kate sat silent, unable to think of a single thing to say.

'Huh.' Judy sighed as though pulling herself back from long-held memories.

Kate waited a moment, then cleared her throat.

'Judy, are you saying everything is okay, The Tea Chest is fine and everything is back to normal?'

'Not quite,' Judy said, and Kate's heart plummeted to the floor. 'There has been a change.'

Kate braced herself.

'I've sold my share in the company,' Judy said.

Kate almost catapulted off her seat. 'To who? How?'

'I can't go into details,' Judy said. 'But the new owner intends to contact you soon to introduce herself and make plans for the future of the business with you.'

A new owner? Someone she didn't know was coming into the company and had the same number of shares as she did. Someone with new ideas and plans. What if she wanted to change everything about the company? What if they didn't get along and it was even worse than it had been with Judy?

Leila watched, squeezing her hands together so tightly her fingers were white.

'So, congratulations,' Judy said. 'You won.'

Maybe. She wouldn't know that for sure until she met the new owner.

'Well, I guess you did too,' she replied, before remembering Graham and wishing she could take it back. Life could be so painful. 'Good luck, Judy,' she said. 'I hope you both find some peace together. I'll be thinking of you.'

And with that, Judy was gone.

Leila sniffed bouquets on the footpath of the flower shop. It was a gorgeous warm day, with a blue sky and puffs of clouds. It was as though all her worries had vanished as she'd walked past the leafy, iron-fenced terrace house, just a stone's throw from Kensington Gardens. In these surrounds, anything seemed possible and everything seemed easy.

She brought a basket of Peruvian lilies to her nose and inhaled. The gift was an apology to Kate and encouragement for the new path ahead.

She was just about to enter the shop when her phone vibrated in the pocket of her slim jeans. It was Quentin. Her hand froze in indecision. He was calling her. From America. She stepped back from the doorway and put the lilies down.

'Hello?'

'Thanks for answering. I wasn't sure you would.' At the sound of his voice, her hand began to shake. Part of her, the part that had cried so many tears and was sure she'd never hear from him again, wanted to speak to him. The other part wanted to throw her mobile phone as far away as she could.

'Please, just listen,' he said. That suited her. She wasn't sure what she would say to him anyway.

'I need to apologise.'

'I should think so,' she said, suddenly finding her voice.

'Leila, none of this is what you think.'

'Really? You're not an actor whose name is actually Daniel Jackson? You weren't hired by Judy Masters to pull off this horrible deception and nearly ruin so many people's lives?'

Quentin whistled air in through his teeth. 'How do you know that?'

'I guess I'm smarter than you think,' she said, working as much smugness into her voice as she could.

'Then you know none of it is true. The money is safe. I'm not an investor and I never did anything illegal.'

'I think that's debatable.'

'But, Leila, the reason I wanted to call you is to tell you how sorry I am. I'm sorry you—no, *we*—got caught up in this mad scheme. I can't tell you how many times I wanted to pull out or tell you the truth.'

'Then why didn't you?'

He was silent for a moment. 'I needed the job, the money, I guess.'

At least he had the decency to be honest.

'Once I was in it I just couldn't work out how to get out of it. But I really like you,' he said. 'Now that this is over I want us to start again. I really think we could be something good, you and me.'

'But you're in America,' she said, momentarily floored by the possibility.

'You could come here,' he said. 'See California.' She could hear the smile in his voice. 'We could see how we are when there are no strings being pulled by someone else.'

'A few weeks ago, that would have been a tempting offer,' she said wistfully. 'But the problem is, you're just too good an actor.'

'Just what every actor wants to hear.'

'I don't know what's real anymore.'

'All those times we went out and I didn't want to talk business—those were real.'

She remembered the kiss under the bridge, punting down the river.

'And the paperclips too.'

'What about the pizza shop?'

'Ah, okay. The shop's obviously not one of my investments. I just worked there, making pizzas when I first got to London. You know, the typical out-of-work actor scenario. I became friends with the owners and they agreed to let me use the restaurant as a stage. But I can really make dough. You saw that for yourself.'

'So why'd you do it? Why make me jump through imaginary hoops? What was the point?'

'I liked the sound of your voice when we first spoke. I wanted to get to know you better so I invited you to the restaurant. You've no idea how psyched I was when you turned up. You were even prettier than you'd sounded on the phone. And I knew I could spin a good pizza base. It was my chance to impress you by just being me. The real me.'

Her frosty resolve softened remembering that night. They'd laughed so easily.

And now he was telling her that was the real him. Maybe there was something between them after all.

She raised her eyes to the afternoon sky and considered what he was offering. A whole new adventure. The possibility of love. Here was someone she had genuine chemistry with (well, okay, *genuine* was debatable, but she had to acknowledge there was genuine *potential*) and he was asking her to be with him. And it wasn't like she had any other offers on the table as far as love went.

'I don't know yet where I'll be working,' she said.

'We'll find you a job here.'

'But I love my job with The Tea Chest. I'd like to try to convince Kate to take me back. She fired me, you know. Because of you.'

'I'm sorry.'

'You should be. But I'm hoping it still might all work out.'

'Maybe it will,' he said. 'It's the choice between the known and the unknown. I get that.'

She'd forgotten to put decent, honest and reliable on her list of pros and cons about Quentin and that had come back to bite her. She wouldn't make that same mistake again.

'The point is, though, I *do* know you will put your own agenda above doing what's right. You deceived me. You hurt me. And there's no coming back from that.'

She said goodbye and finished buying Kate's flowers.

Elizabeth sat in silence. To her right was Haruka, valiantly attempting conversation. To her left was her mother, then Angus, with her father completing the circle around the kitchen table.

From the looks of the benches—teapots, spilled black tea leaves, kitchen spices—Victoria had been working on her design of a chai blend earlier today before she left for the shop.

This afternoon's tea session had been her mother's idea for them all to get to know Haruka, though Elizabeth was still uncertain how they'd all ended up back at her parents' house.

She mentally corrected herself. No, it wasn't her parents' house anymore. It was just her father's.

'More tea?' Margaret offered generally, gesturing to the green teapot on the table as if this were still her kitchen. Clearly, it wasn't just Elizabeth who was having difficulty making the adjustment.

All declined. Margaret eased back into her chair and crossed her arms.

'It's so nice of you all to make the effort to meet me,' Haruka said, making eye contact with each of them.

There was some polite murmuring and then silence, filled by the ticking of the kitchen clock.

Silly clock. Nobody had clocks that ticked these days.

'So,' her father began. 'Would we have seen your work anywhere?'

The absurdity of the meeting suddenly struck Elizabeth as being so hilarious that she began to laugh, quietly at first, and then her body heaved with great silent racks of laughter and tears streamed from her eyes.

'Elizabeth, what on earth has got into you?' her mother asked.

Still unable to speak, Elizabeth gestured around the table. 'This,' she managed at last. She took several deep breaths, then blew her nose and heaved a final large sigh. It had been a huge, satisfying release of all vestiges of the emotions she'd been carrying around.

'What are we doing here?'

'Some of us are being polite,' Margaret said.

Elizabeth shook her head. 'One day, we might all be ready for this. But that day isn't now,' she said, a note of sadness creeping into her voice. Her parents looked quickly at each other and then down at the table. Angus remained sitting straight in his chair, his eyes fixed somewhere on the middle of the table.

'I love you both dearly for trying to make this work,' Elizabeth said. 'I even love you a little bit for it, Angus.'

Angus gave her a grateful smile.

'But I think maybe we should do this again, at a different place and with only one of my parents in the room. I'm sorry this has happened to you. I really am. I wish it could be different. But it's not. My wish is for both of you to find true love and happiness for the rest of your life. But if it's not with each other, then so be it.'

Here she passed the tissue box to her mother, who snatched one and dabbed at her eyes.

Elizabeth rose and went first to her father and then her mother, wrapping her arms around them and kissing them on the cheek. She squeezed Angus's shoulder.

'We're all going to have to take some time,' she said, realising that her parents needed her to be an adult here and maybe even to help them through this awkward phase of their lives. She looked at her father's lined face and realised she was glad she had come home to London for several reasons. This was where she was needed. For now.

'We'll all get through this,' she said firmly. 'And we'll be better for it on the other side.'

She beamed at Haruka and he winked at her in return. A powerful current ran through her at even the hope of all that was to come with him. Maybe marriage. Hopefully, children. But she would make sure it was right and she'd know when it was. She was after forever this time and would settle for nothing less. It was daunting to put her heart out there again after having it broken so badly. But Haruka was worth taking the chance. She was sure of it.

e

Leila was walking down Gloucester Road, heading to the tube station, when her phone vibrated again. She stopped, placing the flowers on the footpath at her feet.

Lucas.

'Hello?' She puffed lightly from the weight of the flower basket.

'Hi.'

'Where are you?' she said, checking her watch. 'It's two in the morning.'

'Couldn't sleep. I'm at home. I needed to talk to you.'

She looked around for somewhere to sit, but she was at a particularly broad section of the road, with imposing white buildings and pillars flanking marble steps and no benches in sight. She moved to the edge of the footpath and leaned against a short iron fence, pushing her basket of flowers to the side with her foot.

'Go on.'

'I've been thinking a lot about what you said.'

She remained silent, her heart racing. A brown sparrow flitted to her feet and hopped from side to side as though expecting her to drop some crumbs.

'You told me you love me.'

'Yes.' She kept her eyes on the sparrow, watching it skip and wag its tail in the search for something to eat on the spotless footpath.

'I think I've made a mistake,' he said.

Yep, here it comes. This was where he told her he'd been wrong to accidentally lead her on when there really wasn't anything between them. He was right, of course. He shouldn't be investing so much time in her when it clearly wasn't going anywhere.

The sparrow flitted away and she closed her eyes, waiting for the axe to fall.

'I think I've been unfair to you,' he said.

'Mmm.'

'In fact, when I think about it, I think I've been unfair to a lot of people. Including myself. And Achara.'

She opened her eyes. 'What do you mean?'

'Men really are stupid sometimes,' he said. 'I can't believe I get paid as much as I do. I'm a complete moron.'

'You're far from a moron.'

'Okay, maybe not a moron. But a git. Definitely a git.'

Leila laughed. 'What are you going on about?'

'I've been people-watching.'

'People-watching?'

'Yep, and I've learned something about myself I hadn't seen before.'

'That you're a git?'

'Apart from that. I was at Southbank the other day for a business lunch, schmoozing a couple of fellow gits from Norway. It should've been a cushy afternoon. It was one of those great, hot August days at the end of winter.

'I should have been kicking back with a few beers on the company's tab, but all I could do was stare at the fake beach with its mechanical wave pool and watch the parents with their kids. And I kept thinking, *That could be me.*'

'With Achara?'

'Yes. Except there were clearly two types of dads there—the ones with their mobile phones jammed to their ears shouting about takeovers and contracts, and the ones in the water with their kids on their shoulders, pretending to be sea monsters. It was plain as day.'

'Er, what was, exactly?'

'I'm not proud of this. But I realised that I have a sense of *duty* to Achara, and maybe even a bit of guilt. But I don't *love* her. Not yet.' His sadness wafted over her.

'You're doing the best you can,' she said.

'Maybe. But maybe I'm doing the wrong things. She's eleven years old. She doesn't care what I do for a living or how much money I have. When I meet her in person, she'll only care about how I relate to her. I've been copping out. It's easy to play the role of provider, not so much to play the role of dad.'

Leila's skin went hot, thinking of the moment when Lucas met his daughter, fearful it would be a sour experience, wondering yet again if she should tell him about the email. But she forced the thought away. At this point, she'd be telling him more for her own absolution than to protect him. His journey with his daughter had just taken a dramatic turn and he was on the right path to building something beautiful with her.

'It's not too late,' she said. 'You've got plenty of time to get things right. This love thing doesn't always spring up instantly. It can be a process. Maybe for a while, love for you will be a verb rather than a noun.'

'Huh. You can be very wise, Lay. And you're right. I do have time. With her. But . . .' He seemed to be searching for words. 'But what about with you?'

'Me?'

'You.'

She remained silent, not daring to breathe, or speak, her heart ramming against her chest so hard she could see her breastbone lifting with every beat.

'Are you still there?' he said.

'Yes,' she said softly. 'I'm here.'

'I don't want to make the same mistake with you, closing off my heart and burying myself in work.'

Leila pressed her lips together for fear of speaking.

'So I guess that's what I wanted to say. That I, you know, love you too.' She could hear the cheeky grin in his tone. 'And I don't want to be without you anymore because I've been a git long enough. And if you come back to Brisbane things will be different.'

'Sounds tempting.'

'Besides, that Quentin guy really *is* a total git.'

She breathed in a lungful of air that was gently scented with blooming jasmine growing on someone's balcony and allowed herself to feel the joy.

'I'm sure even *I* can do a better job than that guy,' Lucas said, protective jealousy lending a throaty growl to his voice.

'It wouldn't be hard.'

'So, I have this voucher for a hot-air balloon ride,' he said. 'Don't suppose you'd want to come with me?'

'I'll be on the first plane home tomorrow.'

'I'll be waiting for you.'

Judy scoured the unidentifiable sludge on the kitchen window. She'd spent years trying to get rid of it. It appeared one day from nowhere and refused to go. Just like the cancer.

She rubbed at the glass with steel wool, scratching the smooth surface. She didn't care. There was a deadline now. Things needed to be tidied up before . . .

Before.

Her knees buckled and she slid to the floor, her back against the fridge door, its strange warmth and quiet hum behind her like a soothing voice. She sobbed into her hands. It was too cruel.

Her fists at her face, she rocked back and forth and wailed silently.

Please, God, please, just make it stop. Make it stop.

But it didn't stop and it wouldn't stop until it was over.

At last she was left only with numbness. Her eyes roamed the lounge room.

There was their wedding photo in black and white, confetti falling like snow, Graham's sideburns and her cat's-eye glasses the height of fashion at the time.

Graham's collection of LP records were shoved at the bottom of the television cabinet, always collecting dust, never played but never discarded because her husband was a romantic fool at heart and believed they should be saved. What would she do with them after?

After.

There was her cross-stitch hanging over the wooden rail, a threaded needle held there, waiting. It was a forest scene in Austria, somewhere they'd always wanted to visit. Somewhere they'd never go now. She should throw it away.

She stood shakily and pulled the cross-stitch from the rail and shoved it into the bin. Anything that was sad had to go. They couldn't have these reminders lying around, taunting them.

A friend's early Christmas invite was stuck to the fridge— a weekend away at the Sunshine Coast with gourmet cooking classes. Graham probably wouldn't make it.

Into the bin.

A life insurance renewal bill. A high school reunion. A reminder to lodge his tax return.

Bin.

In the dining room cabinet, she found this year's goals and resolutions they'd set in January. *Learn French* and *go to Kakadu* would never happen now. She slammed the notebook shut with disgust and was just turning to take it to the bin when something else caught her eye. It was a flash of something shiny, wedged behind a row of coloured bottles.

That most definitely had to go, right now.

26

Kate was alone at the The Tea Chest. It was early in the morning. She'd just drifted off for an hour when she woke up in a panic and decided to cut her losses and head to the shop.

Her anxious night had begun with thoughts of Mark and hadn't stopped through the many hours of tossing, turning, nose blowing, visits to the loo, drinks of water, cups of herbal tea, sniffing of geranium essential oil (for balance), massaging of acupressure points, deep breathing and positive visualisation.

The many times she checked her phone also didn't lessen her anxiety. Still nothing substantial from Mark. Just a short message to say that he had lots to tell her and would call her.

Her temporary victory at discovering The Tea Chest was still financially viable had been wrecked first by Judy's announcement that a sale had been made to an unknown woman and second by Mark's avoidance of her. And there was still the issue of where to go from here now that the angel investor and his money were out of the picture.

Yet she still tried to hold on to her sense of accomplishment because she *had* accomplished a lot here. This store was beautiful and it was popular. She'd grown as a businesswoman and she'd opened a new store in another country in record time and the positive press reports kept coming. She'd managed to honour Simone's legacy and set up a future for her employees and for the ongoing growth and expansion of The Tea Chest. She'd created a new role and adventure for herself, one that was immensely tough and satisfying at the same time. And most importantly, if things kept moving forward the way they were, then the future looked promising for her family and one day she would have a legacy to leave them. She'd have to look at the figures carefully, but it was just possible they would succeed without an infusion of money from an investor to prop them up after all.

The only fly in the ointment was the woman who was now her partner. She was a totally unknown entity. Kate was both anxious to hear from her and terrified of what she might bring to the company.

Now, she soothed her ragged nerves by cutting ribbon into lengths for gift wrapping, enjoying the sound of the dressmaker's scissors as they so assuredly cut through fancy pinks and lime greens. There was something so solid and reliable about dressmaker's scissors. Something from a simpler time.

She laid the ribbons out into straight lines, gathering them in accordance with their colour and their varying lengths, and tied them with a pretty bow.

It was while she was bent under the counter that the bell rang above the door.

She didn't wish to be grumpy about it, but her lack of sleep meant she was weary and not in the mood for early-morning hagglers. Anyone who got up at this time was a haggler, someone used to hunting bargains at flea markets at dawn, armed with torches.

She straightened up to face the customer and tell them to come back later.

But it wasn't a customer. It was Mark. And her two boys. All standing on the other side of the counter with goofy smiles and sleepy eyes.

They were a vision. They had to be. Both the boys were wearing board shorts, which seemed strikingly out of place in London.

She couldn't think what to say or do. It was so bewildering. So sudden. So *wrong*. They should be on the other side of the world.

'Mummy,' the boys cried, impatient for her reaction. They ran behind the counter and threw themselves at her, wrapping their arms around her waist, their collective weight throwing her off balance so she had to grab the bench top. She could smell some kind of gravy on them.

'What are you doing here?' she said, kissing them.

'Surprise,' Mark said. His face was still Mark's. There was no reason it shouldn't be, but he looked both exactly the same and also different. He had a small shaving cut on his chin. The lovely laugh lines around his eyes were deep and his expression radiated . . . something. Fatigue, certainly, but there was more than that. The distance had made her look at him anew.

And she liked what she saw.

Yet she stilled the arms that ached to fly around him to hold him tight. She tried to read him for potential pitfalls. Anger, disloyalty and hidden truths. Emotional ties that might once have been tight but now were uncertain.

She was different. She'd taken on an enormous challenge, had faced her fears and defeated them all. She wouldn't be the same ever again.

And if that was true for her, it would be true for her beloved husband as well, living a different life in a different place.

It was possible they didn't fit together the same way anymore.

All of this became clear to her in deep, transformative knowing in the blink of an eye. She was just lifting her arm to reach for him when a body popped up between them and broke their eye contact.

'Look,' Keats demanded. He held up a small Boeing model plane. 'They gave it to me to keep. And these as well.' He pointed to plastic golden wings pinned to his chest.

'Me too,' said James, not wanting to be left out.

'You look like little pilots,' Kate said, cupping both of their adorable chins in her hand and squeezing their soft cheeks just a bit too tightly. It had been far, far too long since she'd had her boys in her arms.

'How did this happen? Why are you here?' she said.

'We went to the house first and dropped off our bags. We thought we'd be early enough to surprise you but Elizabeth said she heard you leave at the crack of dawn to come here.'

Finally, he touched her. He reached out and stroked her hair, a look of wonder on his face as though he couldn't quite believe she was in front of him and she closed her eyes, melting under his hand.

'Your hair's longer,' he said, running his fingers through it, sending shivers down her spine.

'I haven't had the time to get it cut.'

James shot a small toy car towards her and it smacked into her foot.

'I've got so much to tell you,' she said to Mark, rolling the car back to James with her toe.

'I'm so sorry,' she said first. 'I should never have taken such a huge gamble with our family. It hasn't been fair to you at all. I want you to know that you—all of you—are the most important thing in my life. Everything else is just window dressing.'

'I know that.'

'And it's all okay.' She reached out and took his hand. 'I don't know if you got my messages, but the money hasn't disappeared at all. It was Judy.'

Mark smiled. 'I know.'

'How?'

'I'm the buyer.'

'Buyer of what, exactly?'

Mark roared with laughter, his Adam's apple bobbing, joy spilling from him in a way she hadn't seen for so long. 'Of Judy's share.'

'But Judy said it was a woman.'

'Did she? Well, I did ask her to keep it a secret so I could surprise you. I guess she decided to help me.' He shook his head in amazement. 'Good old Jude, surprising us till the very end.'

'Wait—I don't understand.'

'I know I should have discussed it with you,' he said, looking contrite. 'But I wanted to show you how much I believe in you, one hundred per cent. I sold my practice.'

'What do you mean?'

Keats looked up in alarm at the sound of her voice.

'I've had a buyer sniffing around for a while. He wants to create an alternative health superstore, of sorts. He finally made me a good offer at the right time and I accepted.'

'But that wouldn't have been enough,' she said, shaking her head.

Mark nodded. 'The rest is a business bank loan, secured against the house,' he said.

'But you love your business,' she said, trying to make sense of it all. 'You built it from nothing.'

'I love you and us more,' he said. 'And I love The Tea Chest too. I know it hasn't been my baby like it has yours, but I think I've been a pretty good uncle.'

'The best.'

'When I thought about it, it was actually quite simple. I'm sorry if I've been a bit hard to contact or a bit vague about what I've been doing,' he said. 'Turns out buying a company takes a lot of work and I was worried if I spoke to you too much I'd give the secret away and I didn't want you to try to talk me out of it. And I didn't want to get your hopes up in case it didn't come through. You had enough going on.'

Kate put her hand to her forehead. 'I thought you'd lost faith and were planning to sell the house to bail us out of trouble.'

'No. Why would you think that?'

'You accidentally answered a call from me when your phone was in your pocket and you were getting the house valued. I only listened for a few moments and hung up. I didn't want to spy. I've been waiting for you to tell me about it but you didn't so I thought you must have been trying to protect my feelings because you thought the end was coming.'

He reached for her and wrapped her in his arms.

'Never, Katie. Never. I have total faith and trust in you, now, forever and a day longer than that.'

'I'm sorry,' she said. 'It was just the stress and the distance and not being able to talk to you in person and feeling alone, I guess. It all went a bit crazy in my head there.'

He took both her hands in his.

'I'm sorry too. I know it was wrong to do this without speaking to you first. But I wanted to show you, once and for all, that we're on the same side here. No more ships in the night. No more separate lives. You and me together, captaining this ship to ever increasing greatness.' He studied her blank face. 'Are you *very* mad?'

She looked at him. Looked at her two beautiful boys. Looked around at her inspired country garden tea shop. Considered the financial risk they were taking. Considered Mark's actions, having done all that without involving her—a near unforgivable thing to do in a marriage.

But all she felt was gratitude and love.

'No,' she said. 'I'm not. I think it's the most romantic thing you've ever done.'

He reached into his pocket and pulled out a sticky orange Burger Ring.

She gave him a look that said, *You've been giving the boys Burger Rings?*

'You try keeping two boys amused for twenty-four hours. I'm lucky to be here alive.'

'Fair enough.' Imagining him with the boys on that journey, all by himself, made her love him that much more for being so determined to get to her.

'It's come all the way from Singapore airport,' he said, slipping it onto her finger. 'Kate Fullerton, will you be my business partner for the rest of our lives?'

She bit into the stale barbeque-flavoured ring.

'Yes,' she laughed. 'But only if you'll be mine.'

London, forty-one years earlier

I know I'm not supposed to take my hands away from my eyes but I can't help it. I let my finger drift towards my ear and a slither of light breaks through.

'I saw that, Simone. Cover your eyes.'

Mumma is guiding me down the hall to the lounge room. It makes me nervous walking with my eyes closed, though I suppose it's not much different to walking in the middle of the night.

'Alright, stop there,' Mumma says. Her fingers leave me and I hear her move in front of me. 'Now open them.'

I drop my hands and squeal.

'Happy birthday,' she says, and her smile shows her lovely straight teeth. I smile too and poke my tongue through the hole in the bottom where I lost a tooth last week. Mum looks beautiful. She's wearing her church best, with her waistcoat and stockings and shiny shoes and gloves.

'We're having a tea party,' she says, and ushers me onto the chair nearest to where I'm standing. I sit down, careful to keep my back straight and my knees together, smooth my dress over my thighs and make sure I fold my hands in my lap, just like she's been teaching me. She's given me the good chair, the one with the soft green cover on the seat. She sits opposite me and picks up her folded napkin and shakes it out to put on her lap below the level of the lace tablecloth. I copy her.

It's cold in this room but I don't say anything. I know we're not allowed to have the heaters on before nightfall because it is too expensive. Instead, I concentrate on the treats laid out on the table.

'Would you like tea, madam?' Mumma says in a funny voice that makes me giggle. I put my hand over my mouth so I'm not showing my missing tooth. Father hates it when he can see it. He says it's rude and I especially shouldn't show it at the table.

'Yes please,' I say in my polite voice. Then I remember to add, 'Thank you kindly.'

The steaming tea comes out of the aluminium teapot and swishes into the fine bone china cup that was Grandma's. The tea is dark brown against the white of the china. I am nervous. Mumma's never trusted me with the good cups before. I hope I don't spill anything. Or break the cup.

'It's Lyons tea,' she says. 'A special treat for my little girl who's so grown up on her tenth birthday.'

'What a fine spread,' I say, remembering the words my mother speaks when we're invited to tea. 'You must have gone to such trouble.'

Mumma looks as though she's trying not to giggle. 'Why thank you, Miss Taylor.' She passes me a pretty floral plate with scones and I take one. It's still warm, despite the cold, and must have just come out of the oven. I break it open carefully, then use my knife to spread blackberry jam and whipped cream. It tastes so good I think I could eat ten of them.

I sip my hot tea to help wash down a mouthful that was a little too big, and my pinkie finger reaches for the sky.

'For your sixteenth birthday, I plan to take you to The Ritz in Piccadilly for high tea. There they have waiters in tuxedos, and waitresses with frilly white aprons, and many types of tea. They have three tiers of plates with tiny sandwiches and cakes.' Her eyes are bright as she talks about *this high tea and her cheeks are rosy. 'They play music. And there's even champagne.'*

I look at the mended curtain and the patched armchair by the window and I can't imagine anything more beautiful than what Mumma is describing. A waiter in a tuxedo. Like our very own butler, the way rich people have.

She passes me a tiny butterfly cake, with whipped cream and icing sugar dusted on the wings.

'Do movie stars go there?' I ask, wondering if I would see Cliff Richard or Sean Connery. Mamma always says Sean Connery is dishy.

'Sometimes.' Then her face drops. 'People like us don't normally go to high tea there. My mother wanted to take me for my sixteenth birthday, but . . .' She sighs. 'But we will get there,' she says, tapping the table. 'We deserve to enjoy the fine things in life too. I know sometimes it might not look like it,' she said, her eyes roaming the room, 'but we're just as good on the inside, Simone. Don't ever forget that.'

I swallow my cake. I don't always feel as good as the people who wear nice clothes or who have a car or who go on holidays to France.

Mumma smiles again and claps her hands. 'You must always be looking forward to something new, some new way to improve yourself and your lot in life. As long as I'm your mother, I will make sure you get every chance in life you deserve. And we will have that high tea on your sixteenth birthday. And maybe we'll invite Cliff Richard to join us. I know you like him.' She winks.

'Could we?'

She raises her cup of tea and saucer and sips daintily. 'You never know, my darling girl. You just never know what will happen if you believe in yourself. No matter what your clothes say or how much money is in the bread tin. Your time to shine will come. Happy birthday.'

And she blows me a kiss a across the table and I pretend to catch it like I do sometimes when we walk out in the park after school.

This is the best birthday I've ever had.

Tonight, I will dream of high tea at The Ritz.

Kate had been busy with personal consultations for individual tea blends. She had three weddings and a fiftieth surprise birthday party to design for and her mind was happily occupied sketching, blending and writing tasting notes. She was also thrilled with the three blends the girls had come up with for the chai challenge.

Elizabeth had gone for a peppermint-chocolate chai. She'd even found a mint-green and chocolate-brown vintage dress, which she said had been her inspiration and she was wearing now while stocking shelves.

Leila had decided on vanilla and marshmallow chai, with wee pieces of white marshmallow included. It was an interesting blend and had real promise. Leila presented her notes and even a couple of sketches to Kate as she'd said her goodbyes, luggage in hand, on her way to the airport.

'I have to get going,' she said, hugging Kate. 'Don't want to miss my plane. Lucas is picking me up. And I need to have a good long talk to my mother. She's been researching the ancient art of arranged marriages and has teed up several suitors for next week. She says that since my career is obviously not my strong point I should concentrate on finding a good man instead.'

Kate hugged her once more. 'Good luck with that one. We'll keep in touch.'

Then Kate had declared Victoria the winner for her creation of honeycomb and lavender chai, with real pieces of honeycomb and lavender flowers. It really pushed the idea of chai to a new level and she loved that.

Victoria, currently humming while she polished silverware in a vintage fifties apron, had turned out to be such an asset to The Tea Chest, given her easy banter with customers and her enthusiasm for tea quality, which grew with each passing day. She'd declared she was getting out of the nail business and wanted to work at The Tea Chest full time, forever, and that suited Kate perfectly.

She looked up from her notes to see Mark showing a new customer—a university student, or perhaps artist, judging by the ink on her fingers and multiple earrings—how to use the *pot-pour-tea* garden to make her own blend. Keats was watering plants with a metal watering-can and James was stacking and unstacking boxes of tea into pyramid shapes. *Pyramid* was his latest word. Every time he completed one, he yelled out, 'I made a pyramid,' and obliging customers would clap in congratulations. It was only awkward on one occasion, when he yelled out, 'I made a period,' instead.

'Ah, bless them,' Mark had smiled at the silent customers and their puzzled faces. 'Kids are fun, aren't they?'

Kate was mentally combining black tea with caramel flavouring and a hint of truffle oil, and wondering what would happen, when the postman came through the door, the bell tinkling with his entrance and bringing a waft of diesel fume from the traffic outside.

'Hi, Burton,' Kate smiled. He was so much friendlier, with his ready smile, tuneless whistle and bushy eyebrows, than the meaty, sweaty postman of Ascot in Brisbane.

'Mornin', young lady,' he said. She was relieved to see he was back to his old cheery self after the stress of the riots. 'Parcel for ya today.' He dropped a yellow padded postbag with a large airmail sticker onto the counter, along with a pile of envelopes.

'Thanks.'

As the bell chimed on his exit, Kate flipped the bag over to see it was from Judy. She groaned. That couldn't be good. What final curve ball had she sent her now? Probably a wad of unpaid bills.

She sensed Mark watching her from behind the cabinet of teacups and saucers. He raised his eyebrows at her in the silent question *Everything okay?* She gave him a nod and ripped open the bag.

Inside was a solid item, wrapped in newspaper, then wound heavily in bubble wrap, all held together with many applications of thick brown packing tape. It was about the size of a football.

She reached for the dressmaker's scissors under the counter and cut away the packaging. The bubble wrap crinkled and popped. Inside, stuck to the newspaper, was a small yellow envelope with her name on it.

She opened it.

Kate,

> *I enclose Simone's ashes. I'm sure you'll know what to do with them better than I.*

> *Judy*

With trembling hands, Kate tore off the newspaper.

Inside was a silver tea chest. It had a curved lid, locked closed with a tiny padlock that resembled something you might find on a charm bracelet. The chest had filigree decorations and lion's-claw feet. A tiny key was sticky-taped to the chest's lid and Kate gently pulled it off and squeezed it tightly in her hand.

She ran the tip of her finger along the lid of the tea chest.

'Hi,' she said to the ashes inside.

She didn't need to think for more than a few seconds. On the wall behind the counter was a shelf, about head height, where precious items were displayed. Antiques that were too special to sell: tea chests and artworks from China; silver spoons from France; and an English bone china teacup and saucer from 1860, with scalloped petal edges and hand-gilded details.

Kate rearranged them gently, creating a space in the centre for the new silver tea chest that would take pride of place, watching over the shop for as long as it continued.

Simone had finally come home.

27

Four months later

It was snowing.

'Well, that kind of wrecks dinner plans, then,' Elizabeth said, staring out of Haruka's flat window.

He stood behind her, his arms wrapped around her waist, and they watched the scene below. Women tottering along the slippery footpaths in inappropriate shoes. Cars covered in thick white powder, their wipers constantly brushing away more ice as they moved slowly down streets thick with slush. Flakes falling from the sky, spinning and twisting through the air, the streetlights giving them a yellow glow.

'But it's terribly romantic,' Haruka said, nuzzling her ear.

'Yes.'

'Sadly, you won't be able to go home tonight.'

'It's lucky Dad has Douglas now. You know he lets him sleep in his bed?'

'All love's good love,' Haruka said. 'I think it's great your dad has found love again after your mum.'

Elizabeth shook her head. 'Victoria thinks he's cracked. She's even talking about moving home again to keep an eye on him. Can you imagine? That dog takes up more room in the house each day. I'm sure one night I'll find Dad out sleeping on the couch while Douglas is tucked up under the duvet with the electric blanket on.'

'I'm sure Douglas would let your father sleep at the foot of the bed.'

She turned in his arms and kissed him, his lips covering hers and his hands moving up under her shirt.

'Maybe you should stay here,' he said.

'Well, yes, that's what we were just talking about, weren't we?' she muttered back, her fingers working to undo the buttons on his shirt.

'No, I meant permanently,' he said, his hands moving down to pull at the zip on the side of her shirt.

She stopped, her fingers still hooked around his buttons. 'Permanently?'

He began to kiss her neck. 'It is traditional for husbands and wives to live together.'

'Husbands and . . . ?' She took a step backwards.

He grinned and went to his coat, which was slung across the back of a dining room chair. He fiddled in a pocket and Elizabeth's palms began to sweat.

He turned back to face her, his hand clenched tightly into a first. 'I was going to ask you tonight,' he said. 'With wine and carbonara and a serenading violinist.'

She remained silent. And still. Her mind reeling.

'And this,' he said, opening his palm to reveal a white-gold ring with three diamonds that sparkled like stars. It was breathtakingly beautiful.

She gasped excitedly and reached for it, but just as her fingers were about to touch the ring, Haruka closed his fist around it again.

She pulled her hand back, confused.

'There's just one more thing,' he said, his eyes serious.

'What?' The word almost stuck in her throat.

'I'd like to have babies with you. Lots and lots of babies. Babies from the floor to the ceiling. We'll pack them into every nook and cranny we can find. The cupboards. The attic . . .'

'You don't have an attic.'

'We'll put them under the couch, in the bottom drawer of the kitchen and on top of the fridge, but we won't stop until we've filled every inch of this flat with fat, crying, singing, pooping, eating, grizzling, charming, wobbling babies that smell of talcum powder and make every parent in the world jealous of our amazing offspring and your incredible baby-juggling circus act.'

Elizabeth's eyes prickled.

'Oh, but before we begin,' he said, holding out the ring again, 'would you do me the honour of marrying me?'

She covered the ring in Haruka's hand with her own and squeezed it tight between them. 'Yes, I will marry you.'

'Phew.' He grinned.

'And yes, we can start making babies to fill the flat as soon as you want.'

He tipped his head and his eyes began to roam down her body. His hands cupped her shoulders, fingers caressing her back. Shivers ran through her and she moved towards him.

'How about we start right now?' he said, laying tiny kisses on her throat.

'No arguments here.'

And that was when they created their first little duckling.

Ko Pha Ngan, Thailand

It was hot. But not so hot it made them miserable. In the week they'd been in Thailand, Leila's skin had turned a flawless golden brown and she'd begun to wear sarongs and cotton singlets every day. She revelled in their softness, the bright colours and the way they moved around her body. She'd never realised how much clothes could change her mood. She moved more freely, breathed more deeply.

She sat on the corner of the king-sized bed, the rattan fan clicking gently above her head. Lucas paced the wooden floor, his hands behind his back. He paused for the hundredth time and gazed out through the sliding wooden doors to the dazzling white sand that nudged the footings of their own private deck.

Leila had long given up trying to console him. His nerves were making him tetchy and a little snappish and so she concentrated on trying to calm herself. This was the moment she'd been both fearing and longing for since the moment she'd hit delete on that email.

'Perhaps we should go wait on the beach,' she suggested. 'Get out of this room.'

He stopped his pacing. His brows crossed and he looked as though he was about to argue but instead he took a deep breath. 'Okay.'

They sat on the sand under the shade of a tall palm tree and watched the rhythmic rolling of the azure water and Leila felt her heart rate slow. Thailand was a sensory feast of spices, deep blue skies, crystal-clear waters, green-clad islands, brown skin, white sands, red and purple clothes, gentle breezes and cooling rains. She could feel herself uncoiling.

She reached over and took Lucas's hand in hers and squeezed it.

He turned to look at her and she gave him a smile. 'I think it's going to be okay.'

He squeezed her hand back. 'Yeah.'

She was just about to speak again when she saw them. Nootsara was slender, shorter than Leila, in a printed sleeveless dress, her hair pulled back in a ponytail. And beside her was a young girl in a white T-shirt and a pink skirt. Achara was skipping, her jaw-length hair swishing around as she leaped. She was holding her mother's hand and their hands swung back and forth. The girl was chattering. A lot. And Leila could see her huge smile even from a distance.

They were about a hundred metres away and were moving towards them, their bare feet splashing through the shallows. The woman held two pairs of shoes in her free hand as they walked.

'Look,' Leila said.

Lucas swung his head in their direction.

'Are you alright?'

He nodded. Then shook his head. 'She's here.' He rose to his feet, white sand plastered on the back of his shorts and Leila stood beside him, looping her arm through his.

Nootsara looked up, stared at them for a few seconds, then raised her hand with the shoes in it and offered a wave. Lucas raised his hand in return. Nootsara stopped walking and turned to face her daughter. She bent down and spoke to her and pointed to where they stood.

Achara, her body still now, looked over at them. The sunlight reflected off her dark hair. She moved a little closer to her mother and they resumed walking.

Lucas and Leila made their way slowly down the beach.

Nootsara and Achara stopped a couple of metres from them. They were near the water's edge and the froth from a wave washed over Leila's feet.

'Hi,' Lucas said, his voice gravelly.

'Hello, Lookis,' Nootsara said.

She smiled and then dropped her eyes to the ground, her long lashes brushing the perfect skin of her face as she dipped her head slightly. She put her arm around Achara's shoulders.

'Achara, this is Lookis,' she said. 'And his Laylar.'

'Hi,' Lucas said.

'Hello,' Leila said, smiling in what she hoped was a universal assurance of friendliness.

Lucas held out his hand towards his daughter. 'It's nice to meet you.'

Achara considered his hand then turned her huge brown eyes up to her mother's face. Nootsara spoke a few rapid words to her, nodding and gesturing towards Lucas.

Leila waited, holding her breath, willing Achara to respond.

Achara took a moment, looking from Lucas to Leila and back to her mother.

Then she stepped across the sand and reached out her small hand to place it inside Lucas's large one. 'Meet you,' she said, and an enchanting smile lit up her whole face, followed by a tinkling giggle.

It was storming. A summer thunder and lightning show that darkened the sky and promised to bring relief from the intense heat of the day.

Inside The Tea Chest, the air conditioning had been an appealing choice for the Christmas shoppers, who hung around a little longer than they needed to, inhaling aromas of seasonal spices and touching the boxes tied with red ribbons and, ultimately, ringing up inspiring quantities of purchases.

Kate and Mark sat alone now, at the small distressed wooden table and chairs near the street window, next to the living Christmas tree from which hung small boxes of tea for decorations. Susan had just left for the day, off to meet up with another new man in her endless search for love. And Bryony was leading the Sydney store through to a midnight Christmas shopping event.

Heavy spatters of rain percussed the road outside.

Kate plonked down the purple folder that contained her research on their secret project, the one no one else knew about yet.

'I love this time of day,' she said. It was their once-a-week Fullerton Futures meeting, where they got to bring all their ideas to the table for The Tea Chest's growth and development. It was at this table that she'd come up with the Wisdom Tea concept, a range of blends that included a card with an inspirational message in the box. It had taken off like a jet plane.

Now that Elizabeth was firmly established as the manager in the London store and Leila was due to move to Sydney next month and begin as assistant manager down there (time would tell if she and Lucas would survive a long-distance relationship), Kate and Mark had their eyes and hearts set on a new adventure.

A year out of Australia. Learning a different language. Immersed in a different culture. The boys in a foreign school.

Both she and Mark had been researching cities they thought could offer a great business opportunity and a great opportunity for Keats and James.

'So,' Kate said, 'I've made up my mind.'

'Me too,' said Mark, pumping the air with his fist. He dropped his own folder of research onto the table. It was even thicker than Kate's.

'Impressive,' she said, raising an eyebrow.

'I try.' He leaned back in his chair nonchalantly.

'You can go first,' she said, catching a whiff of nutmeg as it wafted across her face on the current from the air conditioner.

'No, no. Ladies first.'

'I insist,' she said.

They faced each other like friendly gunslingers. 'Together then,' he said.

'Fine. On the count of three.' She held up her fist and unfurled first her thumb, then her forefinger, and when the middle finger joined them for the count of three they both spoke at once.

'Hong Kong!'

Kate squealed and clapped her hands.

'Great minds,' Mark said.

'Are we really going to do this?' she said, clutching her hands together at the thought of packing up to spend a year in an Asian city.

'We must be nuts thinking we can sell tea to the Chinese,' Mark said, rubbing his head.

Kate shrugged. 'We're selling tea to the English.'

'It's a big chance to take,' he said, his voice serious now.

'Yep. It is.'

Outside, there was a burst of shouting and laughter from a group of people dressed in business suits dashing through the rain with umbrellas, probably on their way to a Christmas function. Kate watched them for a moment, thinking how ordinary and safe a thing to do that was.

'Doubts?' Mark said.

She took a deep breath and let it out slowly. 'Lots.'

Later that night, Kate wandered barefoot down the hallway of the upper floor of their house in the Paddington hills, enjoying the feel of the new cream woollen carpet under her feet. It really wasn't a practical choice for a home with two young boys, but it was one of her celebratory purchases, one that made her feel successful and nurtured.

A pang of homesickness struck her at the thought of being in another country, so far from this beautiful house they'd worked so hard for.

But it's not for long. Not really.

She poked her head into the boys' room, standing in the shadowy doorway and watching them sleep, listening to them breathe. It was her nightly ritual, one she took her time to enjoy. Because this was what it was all about. All the hard work and the fatigue and risk-taking. It was all to make a better life for herself, her marriage and her boys. And it was working.

A satisfied smile crept across her face as she continued on to the master bedroom, pausing to listen to Mark's breathing too as she slid across the smooth cotton sheets and tucked herself up against his back, enjoying the few moments of serenity she had each night as she ended another creative, successful day alongside the love of her life, before sleep came.

Trust yourself, Simone had said.

And that's exactly what she would keep on doing.

Acknowledgements

Heartfelt thanks to the lovely Monica McInerney for pluck-ing my manuscript from obscurity and placing it in front of her agent, Fiona Inglis of Curtis Brown, who then became my agent too. Thank you both for being willing to take a chance on me.

Thank you to the entire Allen & Unwin and Allen & Unwin UK teams for making me feel so very welcome in your house and throwing your belief, energy and expertise into the book. Very special thanks to Annette Barlow for being so sensitive and insightful and giv-ing me the gift of brilliant editorial counsel. Thank you also to Kathryn Knight, Ali Lavau and Sarina Rowell for taking great care of my words as they made their way to the pages, and to Patty Di Biase-Dyson and Marie Slocombe for your publicity and market-ing skills and enthusiasm, which are so important in bringing an unknown writer out into the world. And to Lisa White for the mouth-watering cover design. Thank you to Sam Redman and Clare Drysdale, my UK publishers, for your generous enthusiasm and commitment to bringing my book to readers on the other side of the world.

Kate Smibert, whose exceptional foresight, critical analysis and targeted feedback helped to direct early drafts of this manuscript to the place it is today, and for telling me right from the start that this book absolutely would get published. You are a fellow writer's angel and a treasured friend. Thank you also for the description of the man with more facial piercings than face.

Kathleen Lamarque, who patiently read my manuscript, assisted with London specifics, caught errors and answered endless questions, loaned me jewellery, took author and publicity photos, and was an all-round champion of my journey.

My sister, Amanda Wooding, for being unreasonably enthusiastic about this book (and every manuscript before this that hasn't made it to the shelves), reading an early draft, helping all my characters find homes in London, and, most importantly, drinking cocktails and sharing high teas with me on the pretence of vital research.

Michele Cashmore, for reading and advising on early drafts, drinking loads of coffee, and supplying tissues and pep talks over the years for every rejection and disappointment along the way.

Geraldine Schoenwald, Brian Schoenwald and Pamela Schoenwald have all been important in this book's journey, from allowing me to live rent-free while I wrote my first novel, to pep talks and enthusiasm, through to airport runs and much-needed childcare and grassroots promotion. I am so incredibly grateful.

My son, Flynn, for being an endless source of joy and wonder and making every day a diamond day. I see the world anew through your eyes.

And most important of all, my husband, Alwyn Blayse, for brainstorming scenes and plot twists with me in the middle of the night, for making me laugh every day, for painting the house while I went away for weekends to work, who did more midnight feedings with the baby than was fair, and for always having the right things to say at the right times. And for simply being the best support and cheer squad a girl could ever want. I love you forever and a day longer than that.

Dear Readers

I do hope you've enjoyed the world of *The Tea Chest*. It's a sensual, joyful place and I'd love to think you could take a piece of that into your home, right now. Whether you've got some precious alone time or want to get a handful of friends together, why not experience your very own tea tasting?

You can enjoy a tasting with different types of tea (e.g. one person has chai, another green, another rooibos, and so on) or with different brands of the same type of tea (e.g. everyone has chamomile).

In the following pages, you'll find notes on how to hold your own tea tasting experience. But there are no real rules here; the main thing you need is a sense of fun and adventure.

Go forth and brew!

Love Jo x

TEA TASTING NOTES

MAKING THE PERFECT BREW...

Before you do anything else, inspect your dry tea, paying particular attention to the shape, colour and texture. If the colours are mixed then it is likely to be a blend.

Always use the same weight of tea – generally, a heaped teaspoon (around 3 grams) will do – and use the water you normally drink, always freshly boiled.

A glass teapot will help you see the colour of the tea as it brews, and glass or plain white crockery is the best so you can really see the appearance and colour of the tea (or 'liquor').

The ideal brew time is 3-4 minutes to enable all of the goodness of the tea to properly emerge. But if you're using tea bags, don't overly squeeze the bag as this will release more tannins, making your tea taste bitter.

TASTING YOUR TEA

We mainly taste through our sense of smell so the first thing to do is consider the aroma of your tea. Hold your brew as close to your nose as possible and take a big deep breath. What flavours do you pick up on?

Next, you get to actually taste the tea! (And remember to take notes as you go.)

Take a spoonful of tea and slurp the liquid up from the surface of the spoon. The louder you slurp, the better, as slurping the tea mixes the liquor with oxygen and gives you the maximum flavour.

When tasting tea, not all aromas and flavours come through at the same time; tastes have many complex layers. With the first slurp, you'll get the main flavour, and then by sucking air through the tea whilst in your mouth, you'll experience the secondary and more delicate flavours. Does the tea make a strong impression? Assess whether it has a, full, medium, light or round body. Is it smooth? Does the flavour leave a lasting and memorable finish or dissipate after swallowing?

The final element of the tea tasting comes down to mouth feel – put simply, the way the tea feels in your mouth. Is it thin/rich, oily/creamy and after you have drunk the tea, does your mouth feel dry, moist or coated? This is the connection between taste and smell; it's what makes us want to taste the tea again.

READING THE LABEL

As a last point of interest, look at the box and label of your tea, read the ingredients, and see if you find anything interesting. What are the ingredients? Which ingredients are listed first? Are there flavours added? Do you know the country/region/origin of production? How much did the tea cost? Does anything surprise you? Does any of that matter to you or to the taste?

Now get the kettle on and start tasting!

TEA AND ME

When I was very young, I had a severe cow's milk intolerance. With my parents despairing about how to feed me, my maternal grandmother took the opportunity to acquire some dairy goats to supply me with goat's milk, straight from the goat. This meant we frequently made trips to Nana's house to collect the milk, and play with the goats and the horses, and we'd stay for tea. The 'good cups' would come out of the glass cabinet and the knitted tea cosy hugged the pot, steeping black tea, and a piece of dry, boiled fruit cake sat on the side. These are my earliest memories of tea, as well as sipping sweet, milky tea out of a child's Peter Rabbit mug (which I still have) in my pyjamas at the kitchen table.

I am not a tea expert but I do hold an intense love of tea, teacups, tea ceremony and the rituals that go along with tea – the connections between tea and life events, family and loved ones.

Somewhere in the early nineties, I moved on from black tea to green tea. I have always been interested in natural medicine and so I began to drink herbal teas more than anything else. Then when I began to formally study traditional medicine and, especially, aromatherapy at college, my interest in the medicinal power of herbs and oils began. I have a deep belief and appreciation of food as a physical and emotional healing tool in our life – everything starts with food.

While writing *The Tea Chest*, I spent a lot of time out in our garden, picking herbs and flowers and making fresh teas to see what would happen. It will always remain a very joyous and special time in my life. Tea is very much a part of me and I look forward to making new tea memories with my son as he grows up.